DAUGHTERS
of the
RIVER HUONG

UYEN NICOLE DUONG

DAUGHTERS
—— of the ——
RIVER HUONG

Stories of a Vietnamese Royal Concubine
and Her Descendants

PUBLISHED BY

Published by AmazonEncore
P.O. Box 400818
Las Vegas, NV 89140

ISBN-13: 9781935597315
ISBN-10: 1935597310

To my family and the Vietnam I left behind

ACKNOWLEDGMENT

My thanks go to Terry Goodman, who discovered my works; David Downing, Emily Avent, and Wendy Jo Dymond, who diligently read my manuscript, raised questions, and refined even the smallest of details; Sarah Tomashek, who helped bring this book to readers; Raymond Tanloc, who helped conform this book to his home, Paris; and last but not least, the late maternal grandfather of my niece and nephew, Uncle (Bac) Hoi of the Nguyen Phuoc royal family, whose knowledge of his ancestors and Vietnam's royal past has helped inspire this novel. The creation of the character Madame Cinnamon is a gift to my niece and his granddaughter, who is the namesake.

CONTENTS

MAIN CHARACTERS' NAMES AND CONTEXT

First Generation

Huyen Phi (1880–1930)—the Paddle Girl from Hue's Perfume River who became the Mystique Concubine to the king of Annam, 1895–1910

Thuan Thanh (1870–1945)—king of Annam, formerly Buu Linh, the Crowned Prince, who reigned as king, 1884–1910

Son La (1840–1935)—eunuch, servant to Huyen Phi, the Mystique Concubine

Mai (1890–1968)—chambermaid to the Mystique Concubine, nanny to Dew, later a rebel, revolutionary, spiritual medium, and fortune teller

Sylvain Foucault (1865–1950)—*Résident Supérieur*, State of Annam, French Indochina

Second Generation

The children of the king of Annam and the Mystique Concubine:

Que Huong (1906–1976)—Princess Cinnamon, Grandma
Que to Simone
Sam Huong (1906–1949)—Princess Ginseng, daughter of
the Revolution
Que Lam (1911–?)—Prince Forest

Third Generation
Mi Suong (1934–)—Dew, daughter of Princess Cinnamon, wife
of Hope, mother of Simone
Tran Giang-Son (1934–)—nicknamed Hope, professor, husband
of Dew, father of Simone
André Foucault (1935–1990)—lawyer, teacher, writer, grandson
of Sylvain Foucault
Dominique Clemenceau (1940–)—wife of André Foucault

Fourth Generation
Simone Mi Uyen (1955–)—firstborn daughter of Dew and
Hope, singer, refugee, New York lawyer
Christopher Sanders (1930–1985)—American reporter in
Saigon, who married Simone
O-Lan—housekeeper for Princess Cinnamon, Hue noodle seller,
illegitimate daughter of Mai
Mimi Mi Chau (1959–)—second daughter of Dew and Hope,
younger sister of Simone, in America, taking on the legal
name of Mimi Suong Giang (pronounced Sean Young)[1]
Pierre (Pi) Phi Long (1965–)—son of Dew and Hope, younger
brother of Simone and Mimi.

---

1   Mimi is the protagonist in *Mimi and Her Mirror*, by the same author, published by
AmazonEncore.

THE FAMILY TREE

Huyen Phi (1880–1930)   +   Prince Buu Linh (1870–1945)
(The Mystique Concubine)   (His Royal Highness Thuan
Thanh, King of Annam)
/reign: 1884–1910/

/MARRIAGE/

DESCENDANTS OF HUYEN PHI
AND THE KING OF ANNAM

Princess Que Huong
(Madame Cinnamon, or Grandma Que)

Princess Sam Huong (Aunt Ginseng)
Prince Que Lam (Uncle Forest)

DESCENDANTS OF MADAME CINNAMON

Mi Suong   +   Tran Giang Son
(Dew)   (Hope)
Born 1934   Born 1934

/MARRIAGE/

CHILDREN OF MI SUONG AND TRAN GIANG-SON

"Simone" (Mi Uyen) (born 1955)
"Mimi" (Mi Chau) (born 1959)
"Pierre" (Phi Long or "Pi") (born 1965)

PRELUDE

Petals of a Black Rose

Les plus rares fleurs,
Mêlant leurs odeurs,
Aux vagues senteurs de l'ambre,
Les riches plafonds,
Les miroirs profonds,
La splendure orientale,
Tout y parlerait
A l'âme en secret,
Sa douce langue natale.
Là tout n'est qu'ordre et beauté,
Luxe, calme et volupté.

> *The rarest flowers,*
> *Mixing their fragrance,*
> *In the vague scents of the amber.*
> *The rich ceilings,*
> *The deep mirrors,*
> *Magnificence of the Orient,*

Everything would speak there,
In the soul in secret,
Its sweet mother tongue.
There, everything is only order,
Luxury, peace, and sensual delight.

Et tout, même la couleur noire,
Semblait fourbi, clair, irisé,
Le liquide enchassait sa gloire,
Dans le rayon cristallisé.

And everything, even the black color,
Seemed to polish up, clear, made iridescent,
The liquid set its glory
In the crystallized beam.

Voici venir le temps où vibrant sur sa tige,
Chaque fleur s'évapore ainsi qu'un encensoir,
Les sons et les parfums tournent dans l'air du soir,
Valses mélancoliques et langoureux vertiges.

Here comes the time when vibrating on its stalk,
Every flower evaporates like fragrance from a censer,
Sounds and perfumes turn in the evening air,
Melancholic waltzes and languishing dizziness.

Le soleil moribond s'endormir sous une arche,
Et comme un long linceul traînant à l'orient,
Entends, ma chère, entends la douce nuit qui marche.

The dying sun falls asleep under an arc,
And as a long shroud trailing toward the east,
Listen, my dear, listen to the soft night that walks.

Excerpts from *Les Fleurs du Mal*
Charles Baudelaire (1821–1867)

PART ONE:

REMINISCENCE FROM NEW YORK CITY

1. THE MARRIAGE AND CHRISTOPHER

(New York City, 1985)

I turned the key and opened the door to the apartment that was my home.

Christopher must have sent Lucinda home for the weekend. The lacquered clock chimed six thirty as I closed the apartment door behind me, my heels clicking and pivoting on the hardwood. I knew that, down the hall from where I stood motionless in the vestibule, he could have heard my turning and hushing the key out of the lock. Through his library window, the sun must have been paling to rose, the last trace lingering along the glass that separated him from Manhattan's skyline. I know he'd been sitting there, waiting for the world to darken completely, his broad back humped in front of the long row of bookshelves.

A long time ago, he began his habit of shutting himself into the library when I formed my own morning routine. Ever since

I arrived in New York City to live with him, at the beginning of the day I often woke up before he did. In the bleary early morning, I would turn away from him in bed to face a reproduction of Renoir's couple dancing arm in arm. Morning after morning I scrutinized the dancers hanging on the wall: the man's haggard face nestling against the woman's plump, rosy cheeks, his uncombed raven hair against her swirling mass of chestnut brown strands. At some point in the formation of my routine, my husband caught on. He began sighing when I turned toward the wall. When that did nothing, he would rest his palm awkwardly on my shoulder, waiting for some kind of response. We would lie in silence waiting for the sun to rise, as if there were a chance it might not. Finally, he would get up, jab his arms into his robe, and head toward the dark library. I used to wait for his square-tipped fingers to start striking the computer keyboard.

On this day, Lucinda must have put out a fresh arrangement of irises and stargazer lilies on the hallway table to welcome me home. Christopher must have heard me walk past the mirror, past the slim table legs, past the patina-framed black-and-white photos of his grandparents, great-grandparents, uncles, aunts, and cousins—the Sanders family I never knew. Soon, I would be pushing on the library door, and then I would be facing him for the first time in months.

———

Ten years had gone by since the fall of Saigon, and the young girl from Vietnam that had clung to him was a creature of the past.

The last fight between us, which happened about three months ago, was over nothing, despite all the drama. However, in its aftermath, there was a major merger and acquisition closing in my firm. Work on the merger could last for months, so I announced that I needed to stay in the Hyatt Regency adjacent to the office rather than riding the subway back every night to our condominium.

But then, just yesterday, Christopher had called and asked me to come home, although he must have known I was only two days from the closing that could determine my career. As a general rule, he never interfered with my work schedule, no matter what the demand was. He never objected when I had to stay away from home during my three years of law school to participate in study groups, or during my first year of law practice, when I had to pull all-nighters to meet the partners' demands. He'd always behaved like the perfect supportive husband of a modern career woman.

On the phone, when he mentioned the jade phoenix and the two ivory plaques, I decided to cancel the rest of my hotel reservation. The phoenix and the plaque had once belonged to my family's altar and had been locked in a safe-deposit box at Chase Manhattan for almost ten years. The only other previous mention he had ever made of them was to let me know that these heirlooms were there, at the bank.

On the phone he had said in his calm and casual way that it was about time these items be turned over to me.

Why the return? I had to find out. So at the end of my workday, after his phone call, I went home for the first time in three months. Since my workday didn't end until ten o'clock at night, I knew I'd find the door to our bedroom closed, and I'd be spending the night in the guest bedroom.

In the morning, I found a note he had written for me, reminding me of my follow-up appointment with my psychologist. Her office had called our home as a reminder, and he was simply relaying the message. When he didn't show up for breakfast, Lucinda said that he had had an accident and had not been feeling well.

An accident? Lucinda had nothing more to say.

I left for the subway in a state of uncertainty, not knowing what had happened in the three months we'd been apart. That morning, the yellow and red leaves of New York City blazed. I hadn't seen them like that since I began law school at Columbia and the frenetic pace of studying had numbed everything. I had been glad for the intense work schedule then, since I didn't have to think about my family, who had settled down in Houston, or about my husband pretending that the past he shared with my father in Vietnam did not exist. There had been a time in my former Saigon when Christopher knew my father as Hope, the journalistic stringer who helped newsmen of the Associated Press interpret South Vietnam's culture and politics, and passed on news tips that helped the reporters grasp the complexity of the war. In addition to his teaching position at the University of Saigon, my father did the stringer's job for Christopher without pay, believing that the West's accurate coverage of the war would ultimately help the public understand the South Vietnamese's cause against the Communists. This was the goal he shared with Christopher, my father once thought.

Instead of working, I spent the entire morning in Dr. Cookie D'Amico's office, discussing with her again my recurring dream. I tried to describe the lush green rainforests turning swiftly into the low charcoal sky of the highlands, the sky brightened only by the wildflowers blooming beside the red dirt road. In my dream, topless Montagnard women with dark brown torsos climbed the winding slopes on bare feet. I could feel the sprinkling rain of the highlands and the ache in my knees when I tried to run uphill after the women. I ran until the foliage, and the cliffs telescoped into blackness and were replaced by the lithe bodies of the royal dancers of central Vietnam. They held buds of lotuses in their hands, and their legs bent into a diamond shape while their lovely heads tilted beneath gold and jade headpieces. Then a fog swept through the dancers and cleared to reveal a procession of coffins floating on a silent river. In the dream, I could feel intense heat rising off the coffins as they passed, heat that drowned my lungs and nostrils until I woke up choking.

All of this was déjà vu.

It was this disturbing dream that caused me to move out of the apartment. We had been together almost ten years when I decided to reveal the dream to Christopher. A few days after hearing about the dream, my husband gave me Dr. Cookie D'Amico's office number. Dr. D'Amico is Southeast Asian like me, and he thought she would be of help. I began seeing her, and after a few months, Dr. D'Amico the psychologist gradually became Ms. Cookie my friend, although initially I was a little suspicious of the psychologist's pep talks. I told her what I knew from my heart: that the dancers were the women of the extinct culture of Champa. She did some research and formed a theory about the connection between my central Vietnamese ancestry and the story of the Chams, an extinct race.

I was too strong-willed to believe entirely in Western psychotherapy, although in Ms. Cookie I eventually confided all of my fears. Since the fall of Saigon, I had dreaded any kind of separation—the anxiety of leaving a place knowing perhaps I will never see it again. Cookie said the anxiety naturally must have come from my traumatic departure from Vietnam. The whole circle of my husband's friends in New York City must have heard of my airlift escape from Saigon in 1975 atop the U.S. Embassy, during the last hours before the Russian tanks rolled toward Saigon's Presidential Palace. I'd heard enough comments made behind my back at cocktail receptions and Christmas parties. The story went that I was my husband's underaged mail-order bride straight from a refugee camp. I'd never bothered to correct the record: technically I was not a mail-order bride because we actually met in Saigon days before the change of guards.

Initially, I had gone to see Cookie only to please my husband because, after all, he was paying her enough money to feed a whole Vietnamese village. Having a shrink was part of my becoming American, something considered trendy in my Manhattan life, like the fox coat he had bought me as a birthday present to protect my fragile frame from New York's harsh winters. So, when I first heard Cookie's interpretation of my dream, I had the urge to tell him. The check he sent to Cookie monthly had to bear its fruit. I mentioned this to him at dinner one night.

"You've heard of the Chams from central Vietnam?" I asked.

"Of course," Christopher answered. "I reported on the place."

"According to Cookie, I'm a descendant of the Chams, and that's part of my problem."

"Huh. Actually, I could see the connection between you and the Chams." He leaned back in his chair. "The bridge of your nose is higher than the average Vietnamese nose, and you're much taller than the average Vietnamese. If it weren't for your fair skin, I would say you look partly East Indian. You're also not exactly the typical unexpressive Vietnamese woman."

I went on excitedly like a passionate lecturer before a class of wide-eyed students.

"My mother and maternal grandmother are from central Vietnam. Before the fifteenth century, central Vietnam used to be the Kingdom of Champa. Back then, the Chams fought the

Vietnamese quite often, until the King of Vietnam married off his sister, some beautiful duchess, to a Cham king in exchange for land. So, the duchess was sold off into a loveless marriage for the good of the nation. Later, she might have been burned to death in accordance with Cham custom when her older husband, the Cham king, passed away. It must be my cultural subconscious mind that created those dreams and all my nostalgia."

"Are you truly nostalgic, or just resentful?" Christopher asked casually.

"According to Cookie, I bear in me the collective subconscious of an extinct culture, with all its tragedy, which could trace back thousands of years, and that's why I am never truly happy, although I have all the reasons in the world to be happy. You see, I'm so lucky..."

I had been speaking more to myself than to him, until he made a sound with his glass of water, causing me to stop. He had put the glass down on the table perhaps too forcefully. When I looked, he had finished dinner, and his glass was empty with the linen napkin thrown over it. He got up from the dining table, apparently heading toward the library.

"Really?" he said. "That's interesting, but the theory sounds awfully complicated and far-fetched. I have a better explanation for your unhappiness, although I'm no psychologist."

He stopped to turn around to meet my eyes. "You've already hinted to me several times about the Vietnamese duchess who was sold off in exchange for the Chams' land. You're obsessed with the story. What's her name?"

"Huyen Tran. It was also the name of the street where my ancestral house was in Hue. The street was named after the princess."

"But this isn't about the name of a street, is it, Simone? For years you kept singing a folk song about this self-sacrificing duchess in the shower."

"Did I?" I stopped eating. "I must have, but I didn't think you noticed."

"Oh yes, I did. I notice everything. In fact, I know the folk song. You forgot too quickly that I lived in your former home for years. It was your father who taught it to me: '*Pity her, a lily-white rice grain, bathed in the disgrace of shameful stain, washed out in muddy water, burned in straw flame…*'"

He took his eyes off me and turned toward the door to the hallway, while continuing talking:

"I think you sang it deliberately for me to hear, Simone. If you could, you would sing it, too, in the middle of our lovemaking."

He stopped momentarily at the door and turned toward me again. I lowered my eyes to avoid his gaze.

"I married you, Simone, but I'm not the man you wanted to marry had it not been for the fall of Saigon. I'm not stupid. The simple truth is you're always unhappy because you are here with me, and I can't do anything about it but to send you to law school, and then to Cookie. But what was the alternative? Should I have left you in Vietnam with the Communists?"

I dropped my napkin and leaned over to pick it up from the floor.

When I looked up, he was gone.

———

That night, as he was reading in bed, I opened the closet to find the gift box that contained the sequin dress he had given me for Valentine's Day. The dress had never been worn.

I knew what I wanted to do. I had been his faithful girl, but despite our years together, I could not bring myself to tell him I loved him, knowing that the words were what he longed for to fortify our peace. The nature of our marriage was supposedly understood between us. It was not to be spoken. I thought we both accepted that code of conduct. Yet, this night, he had broken that code by speaking the truth, which had become an accusation of how I had wronged him.

There remained the other truth, never once spoken—his friendship with my father in Vietnam. He married me but, as a son-in-law, had never made an effort to speak to my father. Of course, it was awkward. So, he just conveniently chose to ignore this other truth.

So, I held the dress up and asked him to get me a pair of scissors.

He was sitting on the bed, doing what I disliked most: smoking his cigar. I stood for a long time holding the black, clingy material in my hands. I could put the dress back in the closet, go over, and stretch myself out next to him so that the tension between us would quickly evaporate. Yet I stood still. Cigar smoke lingered on my skin, on every strand of my hair. From the bed, he got up casually, too casually, in order to put on some jazz music. He returned to the bed and put on his reading glasses.

I repeated that I would like a pair of scissors.

When he didn't move, I became overwhelmed with a titanic anger that made my hands shake. I tore at the sequin dress, scratching my knuckles. He remained nonchalant, watching me the same way he watched a late-night TV show. Then he slid open the nightstand drawer, took out a pair of scissors, and yanked the dress from me. He began cutting, and sequins fell around us like confetti. I slumped down on the carpeted floor, terrified to see the sharp and swift blades shred the sparkling fabric. I began crying. He grimaced as he threw the scissors against the dresser mirror, crashing the glass into threaded shards. There, I found our distorted faces. My tears must have moved him, and he leaned over and gathered me into his arms. I might have fought him, but he was twice my size. He put me down on the bed and collapsed next to me, as though the whole episode had the unbearable weight of a building falling in an earthquake. We lay there, perhaps both feeling sorry for what we had done to each other, yet knowing not what to do or say. I wanted badly to climb over him and kiss his chest to seal the gap between us. Perhaps he would raise his chin and catch my lips, and we would make up. But I remained stiff.

For a long time, I listened to him breathe sadly next to me. Finally, with the constructed effort of a defeated soldier, I curled up in the fetal position. Slowly he moved to face me, entangling my limbs. I wanted to pull him to me so that the weight of his dense body would shield me from the cold that had begun to creep up in my chest.

Another déjà vu. It was the same sweeping cold that chilled me that day in April 1975 when I first met him. Room 210 in the historic Continental Hotel downtown Saigon. Then, his rhythm, no matter how ruthless and relentless, was, after all, the only thing I knew how to use to rid me of the cold that had seeped from the marble floor of the Continental Hotel into my skin and limbs, the icy spread of a city's death. I knew, then, that in any passion he had for me, I would feel nothing but death spelling itself out, in coffins floating on the river of childhood.

I had not even told Cookie about the coffins during those couch sessions in her office. I had wanted a sacred place for them, a secret burial ground. The secret became my last bond to my childhood, and to the woman who had raised me. Her name was Cinnamon, and she lived and died in Hue.

Madame Cinnamon was the one who first saw all those floating coffins. On what I called the River of Cinnamon.

Those were the Coffins of Cinnamon.

The flashback was gone when my husband began to move. He got up from the bed to gather the pieces of sequins from what was left of the dress. He even picked up the scissors and placed them back in the drawer of the nightstand.

"Oh, Simone," Christopher said, "whom did you love so much that you're still crying for him? Did he even exist, or has he become all of Vietnam in your pretty head? I can always beat up a man, but how can I beat up a place that's already been beaten down in a war we lost?"

———

The following morning, I packed a few things and moved to the Hyatt uptown under the pretense of having to work. He helped me pack and even drove me there. There was no ultimatum, no discussion, as though we each had reached an implicit understanding of the future. I had a marketable degree, a career, and could survive without him. I had grown used to the fast pace of New York City. At thirty, I still had my radiant youth, the beginning of a promising career with a prestigious Manhattan law firm, and a hefty starting salary.

I could have given up my key to our apartment, but he insisted that I keep it. He was so calm about it that I wondered whether he suffered at all from my decision, whether he had ever loved me, still loved me, or had stopped loving me.

—

I took my eyes off Lucinda's flower arrangement and continued walking down the hardwood hallway with careful footsteps. Behind the library door he must have been listening with equal care, as though counting the rhythm of my heels to decipher my emotions. I reached the library door, and the silence made me quiver. I drew another deep breath and pushed the door open.

The chair behind the mahogany desk was empty. The library was not well lit. I heard a quiet cough and then the sound of the lighter. I spotted him near the bay window, lighting a cigar. His face was haggard, as though he hadn't slept in days. It had been months since I had last seen him, and somehow his face had changed. He nodded at me. As he tried to move away from the window, I saw he was in a wheelchair.

"What's wrong with you?" I panicked.

He blew out a writhing stream of smoke.

"Right after you left, I fell and broke my knee; I couldn't get my balance anymore. They discovered bad cells in my bone marrow. After all the tests, they told me it had gotten to my brain. I decided not to have the surgery at first, but I'm going in tomorrow for the operation. That's why I called you."

"Why didn't you tell me sooner?" I said, anguished.

"Why? I've had symptoms for months and you didn't even notice."

I knelt next to his wheelchair, and he turned the wheel away to avoid me. I tried to reach him with one hand, and he let out a small cry of pain, which took me aback. In what was left of the afternoon sun from the bay window, his face looked thin and pale, but his jaw line was set with a stamp of resolution.

"Don't touch the knee. It hurts," he said.

14

Quietly, he stroked my hair and raised my chin to look into my tearful eyes. "You should make it a goal in life to remarry, this time to someone you love."

It felt as though some thick, unseen curtain divided us in the surrounding silence. Above us, the Swiss cuckoo clock struck its notes. Seven of them. Clear, factual, and precise, like the polished furniture in his library. He leaned over to pull me to him, but the wheelchair got in the way. He sighed but managed to hold my shoulders nonetheless. He unbuttoned my silk blouse and caressed the curve of my flesh, but his touch was so slight, and I felt almost nothing except for the dry skin of his fingertips.

He let go of me, wheeled himself away from me, back toward the window.

"You don't understand, do you," he said, "that every man, bright or mediocre, rich or poor, cruel or kind, ugly or handsome, has his own fantasy: that he is loved unequivocally by some beautiful stranger who just happens to throw herself at him out of no reason. All these years since you arrived, I've kept on hoping that someday you would beam at me, tell me the fall of Saigon was a blessing in disguise, and that the day we met in the Continental Hotel was the day you accidentally found your Prince Charming who made your life right."

"You did make my life right. More than that, you kept your promise."

"That was all, wasn't it?"

I stood still. He was a proud man. A proud man does not reveal his vulnerability unless he is certain he is encountering death.

"You've always been too honest to lie," he said. "You kept telling me you were a refugee. All a refugee wants is a refuge."

I thought of the mutated cells inside his bone. Fighting me had to be his way to fight them. He had paused to take a drag, and a wry grin appeared on his exhausted face.

"I thought a lot about how you would finally leave me," he said. "Some man from Columbia Law School, down Madison Avenue, in Central Park, or at that goddamned law firm of yours, would come along to take you away, and there wouldn't be a thing I could do about it."

He signaled for me to move away, enough to create space between us. He put his hand inside the robe's pocket and took out a key.

"It goes to the safe-deposit box, where I keep your family's heirlooms. In there, you'll also find an old tape. Remember when you came in to my hotel room, the tape recorder was on, and I was dictating? It's all there, what happened."

I moved back next to the wheelchair and placed my head on his hand.

He raised my chin and looked into my eyes. "Those eyes. I fell in love with them. Yet I don't think I even know you. How could that be true? For almost ten years I've watched you, and I still can't see underneath."

I blinked, and a tear fell onto his wrist, like a crystal through which I could see part of my childhood. I began to talk. It was the first time I spoke to him about the little girl. More tears flowed down, falling like rain onto the little girl's lotus ponds, all in an ancient city that existed no more. The image blurred amid my tears, like in autumn rain and spreading mist.

The year was 1965. The ancient city of Hue, central Vietnam. That year, the little girl had just turned ten.

2. LOTUS PONDS

(Hue, the Republic of Vietnam, 1965)

Mauve lotuses and their mossy green leaves covered one side of the road on my way to meet the Spirit of the Perfume River.

On that day, I was wearing a dress with prints that told the story of "Snow White and the Seven Dwarfs." In bright sunshine, Snow White and her blue dwarfs whirled against a pinkish sky along the hemline of my dress. When I walked, they all walked with me. The dress had spaghetti straps hidden under a short-sleeved bolero jacket. I had just turned ten, and the dress had been a birthday gift from Grandma Que.

We were going inside the Citadel to see Mey Mai, who would tell my fortune for the first time. We lived outside the Citadel that once separated commoners from the royal Violet City, situated in the center of the ancient capital, Hue. The Citadel, Thanh Noi, represented the king of Annam's abode and Hue's past glory.

Mai was the fortuneteller's given name. *Mei* meaning "the old wise" in Vietnamese, was a courtesy title reserved for old women. As a young girl, Mai had been a royal chambermaid in the Violet City, serving my great-grandmother, Huyen Phi, the Mystique Concubine of the king of Annam. When the king abdicated, Huyen Phi and Mai left the Violet City for a new life in the village. My Grandma Que, the daughter of the Mystique Concubine, was only five years old then, and Mai, the royal maid, became Grandma Que's nanny. Together, Huyen Phi and Mai learned how to raise silkworms. They supplied fine silk to all of Annam and beyond, even to French and Indian merchants off the coast.

I knew before I learned to write my own name that we were descendants of the legendary Mystique Concubine. An ink-on-silk portrait of Huyen Phi hung behind the family altar. I stood for hours looking at her, scrutinizing her features. Her eyebrows were two swordlike, slanting ink strokes, the nose another vertical stroke, and her mouth two dots forming a little cherry. Huyen Phi did not look like a real person, let alone any of us.

Nor was there any picture of Mai. I was told that during the Japanese occupation, the country was starving and Grandma Que had to let Mai go. Mai cried and cried and refused to leave. Grandma Que had to shove Mai onto the streets. No one in my family knew what happened to Mai immediately after that, but after the Japanese occupation and the end of the last Vietnamese monarch, Mai reemerged as a new woman. She rented a little house inside the Citadel and set up an altar to worship the female deities and goddesses of Vietnam. Before long, news spread past the small circle of the Citadel out to the green bamboo hamlets: the former royal chambermaid had developed a psychic ability to communicate with the dead, review the past, and foretell the future. Mai never married.

Every other month, Grandma Que went to see Mey Mai to get a reading from the psychic. Grandma Que had taken over the family's silk business and added to it the trading of cinnamon from Quang Ngai, the jungle province of central Vietnam. After all, her given name, Que, meant cinnamon. Her twin sister, Ms. Ginseng, had joined the Revolution, been captured and tortured, and then released by the French. She returned to the ancestral house in Hue to die. There was no picture of Ms. Ginseng in the house, either, although she was said to have been a mirror image of Grandma Que. At Ms. Ginseng's death, all the secondary schools in Hue flew a mourning flag, and the young schoolgirls wept for one of the first daughters of the Revolution. Grandma Que believed her twin sister's spirit had blessed the family's trading business, which required her to purchase the best of cinnamon and ginseng found deep in the jungles.

The war between the Republic and the Vietcong was underway. By then, the Vietcong's night ambushes were regular occurrences, and Mey Mai's fortunetelling helped Grandma Que pick safe routes for the transport of her merchandise along Highway One.

"Don't travel that route on that day," her fortune said, and sure enough, when that day came, dynamite would blow up a bus. Grandma Que would light an incense stick on the ancestral altar and reward the psychic with a handsome sum of money, jewelry, furniture, or medicine. No one knew what the psychic did with the money and gifts she had gathered from the inhabitants of Hue. Her fame grew.

In those days, Grandma Que frequently spoke to me of the mossy palaces and royal tombs of Hue. Our ancestors, the nine lords and thirteen Nguyen kings of Vietnam, reigned consecutively for almost two centuries, made Hue their capital city, and built their tombs while they were still alive. The most ostentatious royal tomb was built after French colonists had arrived in Vietnam, with their romanticism as well as their firing cannons and the best of seagoing ships. So on the outskirts of Hue, on a hill overlooking the greens of the ancient city and a miniature Versailles look-alike garden bordered with lotus ponds at the bottom of the hill, the bronze statue of a pro-French Nguyen king sat among somber walls studded with blue porcelain pieces and gold enameled bird and flower motifs.

The River Huong flowed through the heart of Hue. *Huong* means perfume or scent, so the inhabitants of Hue call their city's heart vein the "River of Fragrance." The international tourist agencies call it the "Perfume River." Hue had a violet horizon, so the kings' palaces were called the Violet City, Tu Cam Tranh, where my great-grandmother, Huyen Phi, once resided.

Hue was not just a city of kings and queens, but also of lovers and poets, dreaming always about a fragrance and a violet horizon that symbolized their romantic spirit. So, the river had to be called Perfume, sparkling green beneath violet clouds at sunset. Hue was not just a city, but The City. Their City—those beautiful women speaking with the musical Hue accent, hiding their demure smiles beneath the cone hats that shaded their lacquered stream of long hair, moving their lithe bodies in their black silk trousers and white *ao dai*—the silky, body-fitting tunics that split on both sides into fluttering wings.

That was how I should remember Hue, Grandma Que said.

Not how it was in the bloody eighteen hundreds, when the mandarin's army—men who went barefoot and had no guns—started an uprising against French colonists, and thousands of Hue inhabitants died during a few days of fighting. The young king, Ham Nghi, was behind the short-lived coup, so he and what was left of his army had to abandon the Violet City and escape to the jungles of central Vietnam, where he disguised himself as a Montagnard. The French captured his teacher and took the old man with them to the jungle in search of the young king. French troops went hunting, using the old Confucian teacher as bait. The French recognized as the king of Annam the first Montagnard who immediately knelt upon seeing the old man.

It was a clever trick, but in Grandma Que's opinion, French colonists were not astute enough to know that the king's parents and teacher were the only people before whom the king would automatically kneel. The trick had to be the work of those Vietnamese traitors—the Viet Gian—who, for materialistic rewards, would broker their culture, sell their own roots, and betray their king.

I thought it was dumb of the young king to kneel like that. If it had been me, I would have escaped deep into the jungle. Maybe I would have disguised myself as a rabbit—better still, as a bird. I would grow wings and fly away from those Frenchmen with guns.

The French spared the young king's life and exiled him. For a Vietnamese king, exile, according to the Grandma Que, was the equivalent of death. At times, Grandma Que said, death was better than life because death ennobled and immortalized. I thought of those dragonflies hovering over blooms of honeysuckles and birds of paradise in the ancestral house's backyard; days later, I would find them lying on the front porch, flying no more. I would pick one up and stare at its corpse. Grandma Que said too much summer heat and flower fragrance had killed the dragonflies.

I did not see anything ennobling in their death.

Exile. Exile. Exile. I remembered the Vietnamese word Grandma Que had used that day when she told me of Ham Nghi, her great-grandfather, the young king. The word sounded mysterious. I liked the way it was spoken. Starting with the high ascending pitch, the *accent aigu*, and ending with no pitch. *Kiep tha-huong. Kiep vien-phuong.* The destiny of those who had to live away from their homeland.

Every little girl of Hue roots was destined to have a poetic soul, Grandma Que said. If my younger sister, Mi Chau, and I ever had to live away from Hue, I should always find ways to grow a big, tall tree—for example, the classic, popular *longan* tree of Hue—in order to create a shade under which I could recite poetry and nurture my poetic soul. She told me to wait patiently, even if it should take years for the tree to grow, bear fruit, and provide a shade large enough to cover a swinging hammock. I watched her as she described the tree to me. Her soulful eyes shone on me, those black pupils reminding me of lacquered, perfectly round *longan* nuts.

"Wait patiently," she said.

"I will," I murmured to myself, and to a pair of moving *longan* nuts that could see my soul.

———

On that memorable day in 1965, Grandma Que and I boarded a cyclo. We sat in the sedan chair at the front of the vehicle, and the driver biked behind us. I loved riding the cyclo, enjoying the wind that caressed my face and blew my hair backward. When the cyclo came to a slope, the driver would get off his bike and push us up the slope; I'd turn around to find his sweaty face hidden beneath the old, frayed cone hat. I understood the hardship of a cyclo driver's life. Grandma Que always gave him a big tip and told me to address him as "Uncle Cyclo."

Lotus ponds appeared along one side of the road as we approached the Citadel. Grayish-green and mossy, the ancient wall blocked the other side of the bumpy road. We moved along the Citadel, bumping up and down in the sedan chair as Uncle Cyclo pedaled and breathed heavily behind us. Approaching the main gate of the Citadel, with its carved dragons and curved roof, I saw a row of rusty cannons lined up in a vestibule pointing away from the Citadel. Grandma Que called them the bodyguards of the king, now useless, but once representing a golden era respected by China and admired by Siam.

The cyclo moved slowly through the front gate to the other side of the mossy Citadel, and my eyes were filled once again with lotus ponds. Lotuses floated over wide leaves covering the surface of the water like a peaceful, soothing plate of mauve, lavender, and dull green. When the Snow White dress got old, I would ask Grandma Que to make me a lotus pond dress. The hemline would have drawings of mauve lotuses among beds of jade leaves floating on the dark, mossy water. When I walked, my lotus ponds would go with me, dancing around my knees against the clear white background of floating clouds. The wind would blow freely on my shoulders down to my lotus ponds.

3. MEY MAI'S SÉANCE

"Good morning, Princess," Mey Mai said to Grandma Que as we entered her place of worship.

Those days, Mey Mai always called Grandma Que "Princess." The term often brought a smile to Grandma Que's solemn face and brightened her dark, inscrutable eyes. An energetic and plump woman, Mey Mai stood in stark contrast to Grandma Que. Energy and warmth emanated from the old woman's animated, birdlike eyes and rosy, round face, almost wiping away signs of sagging muscles associated with her more than seventy years of life. She stood with her back straight: too tall, too imposing, and too exuberant for an old Vietnamese woman. There she stood to greet us, the cheerful Mey Mai, her satin-clad body almost filling up the narrow entrance. When she hugged me, I smelled cedar incense on her satin sleeves.

The main room was already filled with so many other visitors whom I did not know. They sat solemnly on colorful, dyed straw mats that surrounded the altar, from which rose a fog of burned incense. Grandma Que took her place at the farthest side of the room right across from the altar, and I nestled next to her. Behind the altar was the painting of a woman with sharp, slanting eyes and leaflike eyebrows, whom Grandma Que explained was the Goddess Lieu Hanh, deity of Vietnamese womanhood. Mey Mai sat on the center mat. She had put on a loose, seven-color satin smock over her *ao dai*. The horizontal blocks of colors and the fabric's sheen made her body appear even stockier. She placed her palms together in the middle of her chest, closing her eyes in concentration, and her lips pulled into a broad, euphoric smile.

A group of women dressed in green satin gathered in front of the altar and started chanting. I could not figure out their words. One of them stepped forward to place a piece of red silk cloth over Mey Mai's head, covering up her grayish bun of hair.

Mey Mai began to shake her head, gently and slowly at first and then faster and faster, picking up the rhythm of the drumbeat. Sitting directly behind her, the drummer wore a purple turban and a loose *ao dai* designed for a man, worn over purple trousers that matched his turban.

Mey Mai stood up and swayed. She raised one leg and turned around on the supporting leg, her body tilting and rising as she tried to balance herself. She swayed to the hypnotic, eerie chorale. And then she spun. Her head shook and swirled underneath the red silk cloth, straining and quivering like a shapeless animal yearning to escape its cage.

I held my breath and stared.

The thickened incense smoke made me cough. The coughing tore at my itchy and burned throat, and I could not stop. Grandma Que placed her hand over my mouth, smoothing my chest with her other hand. Under the red silk cloth I caught a glimpse of

Mey Mai's white eyes, looking my way, as though she had slightly raised the cloth for the sole purpose of looking at me. Her black eyes had almost disappeared behind her swollen, wrinkled eyelids. For a moment, I thought my lips had frozen. Just at the point when my ears were starting to go numb, the drumbeats stopped and Mey Mai convulsed and fell backward. The red silk cloth fell off her head as two woman chanters leaped forward to catch her before she hit the floor.

A thick silence followed as Mey Mai lowered herself to the floor, her legs crossed in Buddhist meditation, her face grimacing in pain. Someone had opened the door, and a cold draught swept over my limbs. I hung onto the flap of Grandma Que's *ao dai*.

When Mey Mai began to speak, the voice that came out of her lips was someone else's voice, no longer deep and solemn like that of an old woman. The tone was now light and clear. The words came in garbled strands, with complicated nouns and verbs of the adults' world. I recognized only one word—that mysterious and melodious word I had heard from Grandma Que. *Exile. Exile. Exile.*

Grandma Que shifted slightly in order to pull me closer toward her. I pulled my limbs together so that I could rest all of me against her chest until I could feel the warmth of her breath at the top of my head. Even then, I still nervously pulled the flap of her *ao dai* to keep myself calm. Squeezing my hand, she bent over and whispered into my ears.

"There is nothing to fear. This place is full of ancestors."

I looked around. No one in that smoke-filled room looked like the set of black-and-white photographs that lined up on the altar at the house. Nor did anyone resemble the translucent Huyen Phi in her silk-and-black-ink portrait. No one looked anything like Grandma Que. In sum, I saw no relatives in that crowd. My feet were trembling against my will. I grabbed them and tugged them under the hem of my Snow White dress.

One of the chanting women had struck a bell, which gave a sharp, jingling sound, and Mey Mai bent down as though struck with pain. She started hissing. She leaped forward, and her two hands came together in a worshiping gesture, as she broke out crying. My cough had returned, although I tried desperately to suppress it. I could hear Mey Mai's sobs in unison with my cough and the racing of my heart. All that time, people around us were bowing their heads all the way down, their foreheads touching the straw mat.

When Mey Mai's sobbing and convulsions stopped, my coughing abruptly ceased, too. She turned her head up to the ceiling, but her eyes dashed around the room. Again, she spoke. This time I understood her words.

"Soon," she said, "during a Lunar New Year celebration, after almost a hundred years, this City will undergo another massacre. Hell on earth will be waiting."

The crowd immediately reacted with rising whispers. The steady beats of the drummer were eventually lost in the audience's murmuring. Oblivious to her audience's reaction, Mey Mai was parading, and my eyes followed her footsteps. She stopped in the middle of the red and ivory straw mat that dented under her naked heels, tugging her fingers inside her sleeves. She closed her arms into a circle and then swung them rhythmically forward at the space, murmuring strings of sounds, which at times were swallowed into her heavy breathing. Mey Mai made a couple of rounds in front of the altar before she again fell backward as though pulled by a powerful force, her neck swollen, her eyes rolled up, and the whiteness of her eyes expanding.

She was strangling herself, rolling on the straw mat, and the audience stirred in chaos. The chanting women stepped forward and gathered around her, pulling the hair around her temples.

Someone announced across the room that a spirit had entered the room and had got into Mey Mai.

I swallowed with difficulty and my stomach began to hurt as though the unknown force that tortured Mey Mai had also gone over to me. I squeezed Grandma Que's hand for assurance, hearing her prayer to the Compassionate Buddha: "*Nam mo a di da Phat...*" I concentrated on her prayer to calm myself, closing my eyes to avoid the irritating incense smoke.

"Little one, open your eyes!"

I opened my eyes and saw Mey Mai's euphoric face. She was speaking in a young woman's melodious voice—a stranger's voice.

"You, my dear, will escape the massacre."

I turned away from her and squeezed the corner of the flap of Grandma Que's *ao dai*, wet and wrinkled from my unconscious nibbling on it.

"I will always protect you," Mey Mai said, in the voice of the stranger. She reached out for my hands, but I avoided her touch. The incense smoke confused my eyes. I rubbed them with my knuckles.

"Hush, hush, calm down," she half sang. "Your fate, my dear little one, will be in faraway places. Exile. Exile. Exile."

I turned to Grandma Que. "Is she talking to me?" I asked.

Grandma Que said nothing, and the stranger's voice continued to emerge from Mey Mai's lips.

"Yes, I am speaking to you, and don't be afraid, my child."

4. SPIRIT OF
THE PERFUME RIVER

I felt lightened and exposed, as though a thousand beams of light were traveling through me, and in this streak of focused brightness I began to see things. I no longer smelled burning incense. Instead, the fragrance of blossoming lotuses filled my nostrils.

I saw shapes of stone, brick pyramids and towers, their reds and grays mingling with the dull green of moss. The pyramids dwindled into cone shapes situated solemnly on the coifed heads of silent women moving among the ruins of old temples. The women held flickering candles burning over lotus buds growing from the middle of their palms. Their bare feet quickened over moss and brick, then floated over an expanse of lotus ponds. I heard the tiny splash of frogs jumping around the banks mixed with the click of the dancers' copper anklets. The women danced in smooth, slow, and deliberate movements, their curved fingers closing and opening to the chanting human voices coming from so far away—a thin echo that cut through the stuffy air. The sounds rose and the dance formed. The women joined hands. With their bodies and fingers they formed shapes and circles, pyramids and half-moon fans. They moved stoically, surrounding me, at times hovering over my head. I blinked. The women were lining up in front of me with candles burning in their hands. Slowly, their palms opened and the wax from their candles turned into blood dripping onto their wrists, the thick redness permeating through the yellow, mauve, and pastel green of blooming lotuses underneath their naked feet.

Someone must have lifted me, and I felt the sensation of flying through that stuffy air. I was being laid down on floating lotuses, then moved to the top of a gigantic tower. Grave, ebony eyes looked down upon me. The dancers' candles were spilling into me, and I felt the heat of burning wood. The horizon had turned reddish, and I felt the presence of some being, powerful and engulfing, suspended in the air, bearing down on the women's limbs as they were slowly transformed into a display of frozen silhouettes. I alone was flying high in the heat of a flaring fire.

Then the tantalizing presence merged into me, and I felt free.

I flickered my eyelids and the dancing women disappeared, replaced by Mey Mai's jovial face. I held my spinning head, curled up in Grandma Que's lap, and wanted badly to cry. Strings of whispers kept emerging from Mey Mai's wrinkled lips.

The voice asked me to look up and meet the Spirit of the Perfume River.

I looked up and saw only Mey Mai.

As the sugary voice poured words into my ears in the fog of incense smoke, I saw on Mey Mai's face Grandma Que's black *longan* eyes. The eyes grew larger and larger until they filled up the horizon of my mind, looking out at me through Mey Mai's wrinkled eyelids. And then they dwindled into two small dots, as Mey Mai's face was replaced with the face of a woman I had never seen before, her silhouette edged against the translucent horizon that met a sparkling river. All turned dark except for a moving spot of light.

In the spot, I saw the woman. Her dark hair was tugged behind her ears beneath a gold turban, and her black lashes moved like flickering shadows under the long, slanting, painted brows of a queen. The lashes cast shadows of small, pointed arrows onto her fine and translucent cheekbones. Her earrings sparkled into a thousand stars. Her thick, curvy lips moved slightly as she mimed the words I read from her mouth.

"My child," the stranger said, "wait patiently."

She was repeating Grandma Que's favorite phrase.

That was how the Spirit of the Perfume first spoke to me in 1965: through Mey Mai's wrinkled mouth and eyes, and in the clear voice of a young woman. The spirit told me that she resided in the Perfume River and would always wait for me there, as the matriarch of my maternal family, my guardian, my protector.

She went on to tell me her life story as the Mystique Concubine of the Violet City.

PART TWO:
TALES FROM THE VIOLET CITY

HUYEN PHI, THE MYSTIQUE CONCUBINE

1. THE WAIT OF A ROYAL CONCUBINE

(Hue, the capital of Annam, French Indochina, 1910)

"*Wait patiently!*"

I once heard that phrase in a popular drum song. It was about the time when the king sent out his messengers to announce the royal decree across the land, calling for the people to defend the country. Noblemen responded and left their home to traverse jungles, climb mountains, and assemble under the king's torch. Flags were flown, horses galloped, the royal sword was passed on to the commander general. Noblemen wore their gun smoke–saturated cloaks into battle. They tore out pieces of their cloaks, wrote the message of victory on them, and let singing birds carry it home, to the villages.

In the villages their wives held small babies, waiting for the return of their husbands, for that glorious day when victory over invaders would be declared and the national territory restored under one Heaven-chosen king. Daily the women cooked their rice, casting their sorrowful eyes upon the smoke that came out of their rice pots. The silver smoke traveled past the treetops and through layers of clouds. The women waited for the singing birds that carried messages of victory from far-off battles. The wait seemed to last forever.

Or the singing bird might just carry home the news of death. Dead noblemen turned into gods through the flow of their blood— gods that protected the royal sword as it made its way home to the king's throne. Heaven mourned their deaths, and their widows wilted away in loneliness, still waiting for warrior husbands who never returned. The singing birds all turned sentimental. Their sad songs echoed over oceans and forests.

One young wife refused to believe her husband would not return. She kept hearing songs of victory, seeing flags flying home, longing for the galloping sounds of her husband's horse. Leaves in the forest budded and fell, and seasons changed, and she kept waiting. One day, carrying her baby, she climbed to the top of a cliff overlooking the ocean so she could see her warrior husband ride his horse home, when the singing bird would sing the joyful song of reunion.

She stood there day after day, night after night, forgetting time.

"Wait patiently," she kept murmuring to the harsh wind, and the singing bird repeated her call. She was alone on top of the cliff. Her baby had fallen asleep.

And the legend goes, the woman eventually turned to a limestone statue, holding her baby, waiting for her warrior husband. The wait was eternity.

For hundreds of years, the limestone statue has watched over the South China Sea, guarding the coast of Vietnam. The waiting wife has become the sorrow of the Vietnamese woman in wartime. She has become the culture itself.

2. THE FACE OF BRUTALITY

I have heard the legend and know what it feels like to wait for my husband, although he is not at war.

I lean on the half-moon window frame carved into coiling dragon shapes, looking out at the night. The lanterns in the courtyard flicker against the silver threads of an elusive moon.

I see it. The face.

Its contours merge with the night, so the face no longer has shape. Yet I know it snarls at me, since the beam from the pair of beastly eyes follows my movements. I see the red eyes moving in the dark.

For years I have stood here looking at the night, sensing the presence and seeing the face. I call it the Face of Brutality. It mocks me every night, telling me to stop waiting. But I wait and wait. One night passes. Another night comes.

Tonight my senses are sharper than usual. This is my last night in the Violet City.

I go back inside to look after my daughters, Cinnamon and Ginseng. The twin girls are holding hands in their sleep, their tiny, rosy fingers intertwining, the tips fragile and pinkish like young roots. The girls' joined hands rest in the hollow between their bodies, their black, fuzzy heads leaning against each other. The twins seek comfort from each other's warmth. Occasionally they stir gently, their hands separating and rejoining as they breathe steadily.

I sit by the edge of the lacquer divan where they sleep, running my fingers over the mother-of-pearl inlays and shining black paint. We will be taking the lacquer divan with us tomorrow. The entourage will consist of my chambermaid, Mai; my eunuch, Son La; my twin daughters; and myself. We will depart in the morning to a village approximately two hundred kilometers away from the Violet City, on the outskirts of Hue, on the way to the Port of Thuan An. By this same time tomorrow night, the half-moon window will be closed behind me, and my life in the Violet City will be in the past.

But I know the Face of Brutality will still be out there. It goes where I go.

———

The lacquer divan was a special gift from my husband before the girls were born. The wood came from the forests near the foothills of the Truong Son, the Elongated Mountains, in the province of Thanh Hoa, known for its cinnamon and cedar wood. He had the divan made and delivered to me during my seventh month of pregnancy, in anticipation of the arrival of a son.

I, too, had expected a baby boy. The day the court's physician confirmed my pregnancy, I ran to my window and stared triumphantly at the Face of Brutality, right into the eyes of that secret animal that had been watching me and haunting my life. I sneered at it. My son could become the future king of Annam. Heaven had answered my prayers.

It was my maid, Mai, who first discovered my pregnancy. The round-faced and dove-eyed Mai is the only daughter of an herb doctor and is more talented, versatile, and resourceful than the average maid. She claims knowledge of astrology and astronomy, as well as principles of herbal medicine, passed to her by her learned father. She also boasts to me about her sixth sense and psychic ability.

I remember so well the night when, in helping me change for bed, Mai began examining my eyebrows. The eyebrows of a pregnant woman, in the early stage of her pregnancy, stand up a certain way. Mai nodded quietly as she brushed my brows backward with her thumbs. She then left my boudoir to fetch her medicine box. When she returned, she removed from the box a small piece of dark green jade. She tied a red silk thread to my left wrist and connected it to the piece of jade, then pressed her thumb against the soft skin on the inside of my elbow. She bent her head over my wrist, and listened attentively to my pulse.

"My lady, you are very, very pregnant," she announced.

She asked to examine my belly. I took off my tunic without a word. I had noticed the change in my body for weeks, so Mai's excitement didn't surprise me. She told me to lie on my side and examined my lower abdomen from that side view. "I hear a very strong heartbeat," she said, "as though there are two of them. Strong kicks, strong turns. I have no doubt it will be a boy, my lady."

She helped me up and took both of my hands in hers. "Your life will be different. You will be the mother of a prince. No more waiting."

Before I could react, she placed a finger on my lips. "There is so much jealousy among the royal concubines, so you must keep this a secret, until the baby is stronger and more mature. That way, no one can harm you and the baby. Only then will we summon the court physician."

It was a difficult pregnancy. I was sick quite often, and by my seventh month of pregnancy, I had become so big that at times I could barely move. When I looked down, I could no longer see the hemline of my smock or the green phoenix wings at the tip of my velvet slippers.

Even the court physician expected a healthy, huge baby boy.

I felt a sharp pain in my chest and womb when I saw my husband, standing behind the red and gold brocade curtain, turn and walk away after the midwife announced the birth of two princesses. My husband left as the maids put the crying infants into my arms, one on each side of me. So I kissed my daughters and named them Cinnamon and Ginseng, in memory of the forests of central Vietnam, where my ancestors came from.

3. THAT PADDLE GIRL

I remember it was a cool night like this when he first met me on the Perfume River—a meeting that ended my life as a poor orphan, a Champa girl making a living by paddling passengers across the river.

We, the Chams, are the disappearing Hindu minority of central Vietnam. The Kingdom of Champa was officially annexed into Vietnam during the fifteenth century, and by the start of the sixteenth century, most Chams had taken on Vietnamese last names.

My family, too, took on Vietnamese last names. Only in our minds do we hold on to what is left of those ancient, abandoned mossy temples, of those stone towers, wood and rock carvings, and the sad candle dances of our Hindu heritage.

We are the Chams: the conquered, the extinct.

My extended family made their living by chopping wood and searching for ginseng and cinnamon in the forests until the French came, imposed high taxes, and controlled the trade. My family then moved away from the foothills of the Truong Son Mountains and concentrated instead alongside the various rivers of central Vietnam. We needed to learn a new trade. We began making a living by paddling passengers across these rivers, as though paddling away our pain, resentment, and nostalgia for our lost kingdom. My folks settled in Kim Long, an area around the main boat dock of Hue. Typhoid fever decimated my family, just as malaria had claimed the lives of generations of Cham cinnamon and ginseng traders. Only my parents and I, their only child, survived.

The surviving Chams of the defeated, extinct kingdom of Champa had always rotated their trade between the jungles and the water. Paddling along rivers to us was a sacred art. It was told to Cham children that after the last battle, the Viets captured the queen of Champa and transported her by boat back to the north. The exodus began in the rivers of our kingdom. Under a full moon, the captured queen, crying for the defeated, jumped into the river and drowned herself. The surviving Chams called out after her, *"Mee-ey, mee-ey,"* meaning "that noble woman." The sound *mee-ey* entered history and was mistaken as the name of the Champa queen.

After centuries, the mourning sound of *mee-ey* worked its way into the folk tunes of central Vietnam, or what's left of the Champa Kingdom. I know these tunes very well, from the "Nam Ai" ("Mourning for the Southern Land"), to the "Nam Binh" ("Peace for the South"), and the "Mai Day" ("Mourning of the Paddle"). The wailing sounds of the pentatonic scale were heartbreakingly sad. The Chams believed Mee-Ey's soul never left the water, so when we paddled along our rivers, we hoped to catch her spirit. It was believed that the spirit came alive particularly in moonlit nights.

By my generation, the Chams' resentment toward the Viets had dwindled. I grew up knowing I was Cham, the ethnic minority of central Vietnam, and part of the heritage of Mee-Ey. I accepted, too, that I was also part of the State of Annam, under the Vietnamese king, as I was told, regardless of who once claimed ownership to the land.

My father died when I was five. From my mother, I learned to paddle our boat, carrying on the family trade. We stayed in Kim Long, upstream from the Perfume River that ran through the City of Hue. After my father's death, my mother took me farther down to the banks of the Perfume River in the heart of the city. We moved there to attract a more exclusive clientele and to avoid the fierce competition in commercial Kim Long. I grew up on our boat, learning the art of paddling against the wind, in heat as well as in cold. I also learned the art of cooking a clay pot of rice on burned logs in the middle of the river, amid whirling wind and sparkling waves.

When I turned twelve, my mother died, leaving me to paddle alone on the Perfume River. I did not think of her as being dead. Her spirit had soared high to join the star-filled sky of Hue and reunite with the spirit of Mee-Ey. My mother reappeared each night, shining above me and watching over me, keeping me company as I paddled. I got the strength to carry on my existence that way. None of my passengers knew where I came from. No one asked. To the inhabitants of Hue, I became the sound and sight of the Perfume River itself. To disperse the loneliness, I sang into the sky. Singing kept me going, even in the coldest night. I also learned poetry from mandarin scholars who crossed the river. I could recognize those learned men immediately: white trousers, black tunics and turbans, and in their arms, cloth bags stuffed with Chinese books, chest games, and baked clay teapots.

They spoke in poems and conversed in verses. These poems, they told me, depicted the sufferings of the people of Annam under French rule. They wanted the king of Annam inside the Citadel to hear them. The French, I was told, suppressed the mandarin scholars and the people, but could not extinguish their poetry.

Sing on, they told me, sing for the king of Annam and the whole city of Hue.

So I sang. To the rhythm of my paddles, I sang.

I grew up without noting the passage of time. One day, in the radiant sunshine, I leaned over the edge of my boat, which was also my only home. My skin was dark, my brows bushy, my legs long and muscular. These characteristics of my Cham blood had become more distinctive from the long days and nights of paddling, which helped accent my small waist against my full hips. With my paddles and strong arms, I learned to guard against the roving eyes and hands of male passengers. But the mandarins, who told me that they were students of Confucian thoughts, were always respectful. In their poems I found my solace, even if I did not understand the words. I pushed my chest forward, filled my lungs with air, and words burst from my mouth, my paddle cutting through the surface of that dense water. I felt full singing their words. I felt alive.

I kept on paddling and singing until I met him. I had turned fifteen that year.

4. THE KING OF ANNAM

On the night of our meeting, as a fifteen-year-old paddle girl who had never encountered an aristocrat, I did not see in him the image of the king of Annam. Rather, I saw a lean young man, extraordinarily handsome in his turban and black organza tunic. His style of dress—that combination of black and white—identified him as a mandarin.

But this young mandarin was different. It was the proud way he carried himself, looking at no one. He also carried no cloth bag, had no books or chest game or clay teapot with him. He looked not more than twenty-five years old, perhaps a little too slender and frail despite the healthy shine of his dark skin. His frailty contrasted vividly with the fierceness of his face—he had the serious, sullen, and cocky countenance of a lion. I had seen the painting of a lion's face in a banner carried by an opera troop that once boarded my boat. If I were to transform that holy animal on the poster into the image of a man, it would be this mandarin.

He boarded the boat along with the other passengers. I paddled across, but when the others disembarked, he stayed on. He crossed the river again, back to the other side and, again, stayed on with the boat while the others disembarked. His heated eyes shone; my body felt heavy under his dark, probing gaze. I sang to calm myself, and he listened attentively, his eyes never leaving my belly and waist. By the fourth time we crossed the river, he had paid all the other customers a silver coin each for them to stay onshore. As we took off, he told me he wanted to take over the paddling, and that was how we crossed the Perfume River, bathed in the soothing breeze of the wind and the illuminating glow of the moon, intoxicated by each other's presence. Then he gave me a gold coin. Far too much. He was touching my hands and looking into my eyes. Embarrassed, I tried to remove my hands. And then he asked me, "How would you like being married to a king?"

I giggled and said I would love to marry a king, but no king ever took a boat across this river in the middle of the night.

He told me his given name. "Buu Linh," he said. It meant a holy animal, a royal one, he explained.

"A lion, perhaps?" I giggled.

He did not reply. He gazed, instead, deep into my eyes. Before he left my boat, he said he would send somebody to fetch me soon, and then I would be with my husband king.

Of course, I did not believe him.

—

Before she passed away, my mother told me it would be better for me to marry a Cham man, someone robust enough to help me with the paddling trade. My mother hinted that I should stay away from Vietnamese men, who would never accept a Cham girl like me and hence would treat me like a second-class citizen.

I never thought much of my mother's advice until my unexpected wedding day, chosen and planned for me by people I had never met.

My mother hadn't warned me of the magic of the Perfume River and its moonlight, which could turn life into dreams—even if they were sad dreams that would ultimately imprison a woman with muscular arms and legs and with eyes accustomed to searching the blackened sky for a star to guide the lonely boat she paddled. I discovered the meaning of dreams on the day the royal guards appeared all along the riverbank to take me away. Those guards paraded in yellow and red uniforms, their slanting eyes hidden under cone hats embroidered with gleaming gold threads. They lined up along with the royal musicians dressed in blue satin and violet raw silk.

That was how a royal bride was taken to her husband: by royal guards and royal musicians. I was told this later, after five women got on the boat and started to dress me. For the first time in my life I wore a silk *ao dai* and felt its softness caressing my skin. The women put a red brocade smock over the golden silk *ao dai*, topped my head with a green turban, and hung heavy gold earrings from my earlobes. Those earrings, together with bracelets, pendants, and anklets, felt like shackles on both sides of my face and all of my limbs. The women gave me a perfumed fan to hold and told me I was being costumed to become the chosen royal bride.

I was in a daze. All I can remember is the sight of the main road leading to the Citadel circling around the royal palaces. As I peeped from behind the red curtains of my rickshaw, I saw the amazing sight of lotus ponds: thousands of lotuses bloomed under sharp sunlight. I looked behind me at the progression of women dressed in green satin and carrying golden boxes, followed by the fleet of musicians and guards. I tried to imagine my new life, but I could envision nothing. I closed my eyes and felt in my palm the shape of the gold coin given to me by a young man whose face reminded me of a lion. I had kept the coin with me all this time for good luck.

When the rickshaw stopped bouncing, its curtains were raised and my eyes were blinded with blazing lights. In my bewilderment and confusion, I could not tell whether they were sunlight or lanterns. The women who had dressed me quickly gathered around my rickshaw. Two of them raised my arms and literally lifted me off the carriage. From there on, they carried me along and I was placed on a red satin mat in the middle of a grand hall. A hand gently pushed my head down, and someone whispered to me that I should not look up. I kept my head bowed but discreetly rolled my eyes upward and saw the lower body of a tall, trim man. I focused my attention on his gold boots, the golden hemline of his shimmering *ao dai*, and the sharp, pointed end of a gold-carved scabbard dangling on his right side.

I had never seen a man carrying a gold sword before.

He took three steps forward toward me, and I trembled. The women pressed my head down so low that my forehead and all that oiled, coifed hair beneath the green turban almost touched the satin mat. I could not see his face. His boots and sword made a swift turn, and he walked slowly away from me. I saw the boots climbing up a stage, on steps that were bordered with carved gold dragons. The man sat down, his boots resting on the last step of the pedestal above my head, and the same whispering voice told me to keep kneeling and bowing.

I heard the salute shouted by men: "*Le nap phi!*" the offering ceremony for a royal concubine to enter the palace.

The shouting continued. "Long live Heaven's son! A thousand years of life and happiness!"

The music began. The whispering voice told me to kowtow and bring my head to the floor numerous times. I was supposed to worship my husband-to-be, formerly Prince Buu Linh, now the king of Annam presiding under his dynastic name, Thuan Thanh.

So this was the man, I thought, to whom I should sing the mandarins' songs depicting the sufferings of the people of Annam. But I was not singing any song. I was bowing endlessly to a pair of golden boots.

This whispering voice and dozens of female hands guided me along, telling me I was already in the grand West Palace inside the Violet City. Through all the rituals I was to keep my head low, my forehead to the floor, and my eyes lowered. So I moved along as though sleepwalking, thinking of the lion face on display in an opera troop and wondering where that royal husband of mine had gone and how in the world I could recognize him in this crowd. I kept looking for the familiar pair of gold boots and the pointed tip of the gold-carved scabbard. After a while, gold boots and scabbards seemed to be everywhere.

I caught glimpses of carved dragons, phoenixes, and lions. I lifted my eyes once and saw the solemn faces of men, so many men, together with the rosy cheeks and curious, surreptitious glances of women all dressed alike—their heads were bowed like mine, yet their eyes met mine. They, too, were peeping, looking at me, the royal bride. It was my wedding, a joyous occasion, yet no one was smiling. I kept moving in a trance, unable to decipher whether I was happy or sad.

When the fanfare died out, I found myself in a perfumed tub. The heavy clothes and jewelry had been removed, piece by piece, by unknown hands. The bath was elaborate, and numerous fingers ran through every muscle group, every fold in my body. When the bath was over, they draped me in loose pantaloons and a camisole, topped with colorful outer garments. I was moved along a narrow corridor where several men lined up on both sides, their heads bowed. I jerked back reflexively at the sight of these men, conscious of my naked flesh underneath the loose layers of sheer silk. I reached out for the familiar feel of my paddle, but my hand hung empty in the air.

Someone pressed upon my back for me to march on. The whispering person told me not to be afraid, as those solemn-faced men were all eunuchs. Eunuchs were men who were no longer men, the person explained. The women kept moving me along the corridors, a walking puppet covered in layers of silk.

A symphony of stringed instruments and jingling bells started, paused, and restarted. When the music died out, I found myself sitting alone on a lacquer bed between shiny wood pillars circled by carved dragons. The sudden silence intimidated me, so I wiggled my hanging feet, and the velvet slippers dropped to the floor. Cold air brushed my naked heels.

5. THE EUNUCH SON LA

It was then that I heard a crisp knock at the door. The curtains were raised, and in the smoky red lantern light, a diminutive old man entered the room, followed by two women carrying a porcelain sink. The man approached the bed, knelt down before me, and introduced himself as my servant, the eunuch Son La. The two young women knelt docilely with him, their faces expressionless and their eyelids lowered.

A moment passed and the women took hold of my dangling feet. I jerked them away, and the old man looked up with kindness in his eyes. "My lady, please relax. We are here to wait on you."

I looked down at the man kowtowing before me and found the attentive and wrinkled face of an old man with the grin and gaze of an earnest child. The women dipped both my feet into the hot water, and the eunuch firmly grabbed my heels.

I shuddered and struggled to escape, but he murmured, "My lady, do not fear me. I am not a man, and I am here to serve."

I looked again at the old man, puzzled by his statement that he was not a man. With his soft, skilled palms, he pressed upon my skin, and his fingers adroitly made their way through the cracks between my nervous toes. When he felt the calluses of my paddling life, he sighed sympathetically. He rubbed and lotioned my feet, again and again, with the attentiveness of an artisan. "Pay no attention to me, my dear lady," he said. "I aman old eunuch. A eunuch is a man, but he is not a man. Take notice only of what I can do for you, my lady."

I drifted in and out of senseless, indecipherable dreams, and my skin burned. The eunuch was drying my feet and rubbing them against some soft, fuzzy fabric; but just at the point when I thought the massage was over, I felt the coolness of lotion upon my skin again, and the rubbing recommenced.

Finally, the two women raised my feet and gently pushed me back against the pile of pillows. I lay on my back with my eyes closed, the wild beating of my heart loud in my ears. I felt the gentle touch of probing fingers on my body again; the women were slowly peeling off my camisole and pantaloons. Startled, I opened my eyes and found the two young women undressing me, handling each piece of garment expertly. The eunuch remained kneeling on the floor, his head bowing, on the other side of the curtains that separated us.

All of my modesty vanished when I observed the waxen, emotionless faces of the women, their chins pressed down into the hollows of their necks as they went mechanically about their business. To them, this was apparently a routine job. They were just preparing me as though I were a statue ready to be displayed. They oiled and powdered my body with soft cotton balls and silky brushes, and then they wrapped me again in layers of soft white silk. All this time I had managed to clutch on to my gold coin, but finally one of two women undid my fist and removed that good luck charm. I uttered a feeble sound of protest.

"This is a necessity, my lady," the old man said to me from the other side of the curtains. "You are being presented to Heaven's son, wrapped in perfumed silk. That way, no weapon can ever be carried by a royal concubine."

The eunuch Son La got up and, with a quick, almost imperceptible hand gesture, signaled to the pair of women, and they backed away toward the door, carrying the porcelain sink and bowing their head, as usual. I thought he would leave, too, but he knelt down by the bed and spoke softly. "Those maids, my lady, they may or may not be your friends, but I am. You see, I have one-fourth Cham blood in me."

I stirred in the bed and caught sight of his dark face and fierce brows on the other side of the curtains. Those were the typical genetic features of a Cham face. All of a sudden I felt less lonely.

"You have been part of an unusual occurrence, my lady, a historic event. Never before has a woman like you been admitted to the palace this way. You were brought here in a formal wedding, the same way daughters of cabinet ministers—the *thuong thu*—were married to Heaven's son. You have already been given a place in the West Palace, among the highest honors accorded a royal concubine. Normally, commoners are admitted as dressers or maids, never in a formal wedding."

He kept his head bowed to the floor, and I had to lean forward to hear him more clearly.

"His Highness must have been smitten by you. He has broken all traditions, making you into an object of envy and curiosity.

But this is a very difficult time for Annam, and we will all be affected. Things are changing, and you must be prepared for your fate."

I heard footsteps outside and saw shades of flickering lanterns passing by the half-moon window. The old man immediately changed his manner of speaking. He was wishing me a thousand years of happiness and a hundred children.

A hundred children? I did not want a hundred children.

"Close your eyes and pray," he continued. "In fact, all you need is one child: a son. His Royal Highness might leave you. So keep him with you as long as you can, and Heaven will grant you a son."

6. CONJUGAL BLISS

Behind brocade drapes and muslin curtains, I leaned against the satin pillows and listened to my own pounding heart and the shuffling of fabric as I shifted within the bundle of silk. I wondered whether the moon had ascended yet. I missed my boat and my river. An immense loneliness had just come over me when, again, I heard footsteps.

The double doors swung wide open, and there entered the entourage, headed by that wealthy passenger who, in that fated night on the Perfume River, had insisted on paddling my boat. His steps were forceful and his gaze direct. I recognized the familiar pair of golden boots but no longer saw the golden sword. He was approaching me steadily, and when I lifted my eyes, I saw the face of a lion.

"Buu Linh," I whispered to myself. That holy animal.

I no longer had the gold coin he had given me to hold on to, so I clenched my fists to calm myself. My heart sank when I saw a dozen women following him in pairs. Dressed in blue and white satin, they gathered around him and began helping him undress. A sense of both modesty and excitement took over me. My face and body felt feverish.

First, his turban was removed. Then one by one the buttons of his gold *ao dai* were undone by the women's adroit hands, traveling across his costumed body like little birds wavering over a landscape. His eyes were fixed upon me when each garment was peeled off. He became a silhouette in a dream, a blurry figure who moved his limbs deliberately and slowly to facilitate the women's undressing of him as though he were performing a dance. All the golden and multicolored garments were eventually gone, and he displayed a brown torso over a pair of white silk slacks. The dream dance came to a stop.

He raised the curtains, and we looked at each other face-to-face. I quietly registered in my mind the facial features that had become curiously familiar to me, since I had memorized them and envisioned them every night since our encounter on the Perfume River. Yet the face remained a stranger's face.

He sat on the edge of the bed and leaned toward me. His breath was heavy and hot on my cheek, and I felt the same magnetism I had felt when he had touched my palm and given me the gold coin on the boat. Self-conscious, I glanced toward the women, who had all lined up and knelt down around the bed. My eyes rose to meet his with an unspoken question.

"They are trained to surround us," he whispered into my hair, and then he nibbled my earlobe. My embarrassment lingered on, and I stiffened when his hands reached underneath my armpit to undo the silk wrapping. As I slightly resisted his touch, he understood and withdrew his hand.

He left the bed and stood in the middle of the room, the light from the red lanterns flickering onto his naked back. The women rose, acknowledged his hand gesture, and left the room quietly like ghosts. "He came back to the bed, and this time, he slipped one hand underneath my wrapping silk while pulling on the string of his silk pantaloons with his other hand." He was skilled at unwrapping me, suggesting to me he had done this many times. I shuddered as his fingers traveled underneath the silk. My cheeks felt hot as my eyes followed the wave of the soft fabric that rolled down and gathered around his thighs. My skin was burning when he kissed me one, twice, and then too many times to count. His musky body smell reminded me of the night he had crossed and re-crossed the river with me, and it seemed as though we were paddling against the waves there behind the curtains, the boat rocking and rocking.

Instinctively my muscular arms and legs wrapped around my dream, and I became my Perfume River, liquid and flowing, heated and cooling at the same time. I let go of the security associated with the familiar feel of the damp, wooden paddles that smelled of moss. I let go of all those hidden tears blended into those Hue rivers upon which my ancestors paddled away the sorrow of the defeated Cham race, forever longing to recapture the spirit of Mee-Ey mourning her lost kingdom, towers, temples, and tombs. I let go, too, of my mother's monotonous words uttered before her death, advising me not to fall in love with a Vietnamese man.

I had become a river that merged with the flesh of a Vietnamese man.

I let go of myself. I bit down on his shoulders when I felt him piercing me. Like an arrow he traveled until he reached the shooting star once presiding over the Perfume River and guiding me in my paddling pattern. The arrow he had become cut a silky path on which I arched my back to touch my new rainbow and find that excruciating pain and tantalizing delight of knowledge.

I turned sixteen that year. The Annamese believed that sixteen was the age of a ripened moon.

—

The morning after my wedding, he must have left while I was still sleeping. The royal decree came and was read to me when I was still dreamily resting in the mess of wrapping silk. The decree said that the king had waived all royal protocols when it came to me. For example, I was allowed to rest during the procedure that followed: the announcement of my title.

The privilege did not exactly please me. I had wanted to see and feel his face next to me when the sun hit those muslin and brocade curtains, yet I was greeted only with his official words, read to me by eunuchs.

Words of a king, not a lover.

The decree said that the king had given me my permanent quarters in the West Palace. He also gave me my official royal title. I was to be called Huyen Phi, "the Mystique Concubine."

He was back the following night, enraptured, his eyes locked on mine, while a dozen women took off his royal clothes before my eyes. I became my Perfume River and he became my shooting star, again and again, traveling up where a cooling river met sun and sun melted into cooling river and I created my own universe. Every time he came to me, he was the tender and passionate lover who cherished and adored and who caressed not only my body but also my soul. He touched not only my skin but also my heart, with his loving fingers as well as his sensitive eyes. There was something else, too—something very real yet surreal, because I did not quite understand it. Nor could I give it a name—some sort of a deep emotion that sent waves of vibrating sensations from the sight and closeness of him right into my heart. Something so sacred it touched me so deeply, so privately, bestowing me with a sense of permeating, overwhelming happiness that made me want to cry.

It had to be the strong and special feeling described by the human race as love.

He did not talk much, just enough to explain to me the meaning of my royal title. He considered our encounter on the Perfume River mystical, and my royal title was to memorialize that mystique. No Nguyen king had ever picked his bride the way he did, my lover said. I would enter history as the myth of Hue, as the woman who brought the tunes of the common people to the heart of the king of Annam. But, as the Nguyen kings honored their founding father's tradition of not crowning a queen, every consort could only be titled as a royal concubine. Only one would be chosen as queen and so crowned if her son became the crowned prince. The fact I was given a royal title immediately and allowed to take my place in the West Palace was a testament to his adoration.

I did not know then that adoration, by its nature, was short-lived.

Once again, he was gone before dawn. There was no telling when he would come back, if he would come back.

My new situation had intimidated me, but in that situation, there was he, who had excited me beyond all expectations. Yet his disappearance every morning while I was still sleeping also brought me a terrifying sense of insecurity and discomfort.

So against my wishes, I began the emotional ritual of waiting. Each night, my entire being was focused on the sounds I anticipated to hear at the door, signaling his arrival. The warnings given by the eunuch Son La—that I was born into a time of changes—came back nightly to haunt me:

"Things are changing, and you must be prepared for your fate..."

What was my fate?

"His Royal Highness might leave you. So keep him with you as long as you can, and Heaven will grant you a son."

How could I obtain and secure the birth of a son?

So, every time I got up alone, finding him gone, I faced my panic and isolation, sensing the terrible feeling that this nervous waiting game could be my fate.

Later on, I gave that terrible sixth sense a name. When my fate was played out, in ways that I could not have predicted, I began calling that sense of calamity the Face of Brutality.

7. THE LUXURY OF WORDS

After a month or so of intense passion, the routines of my conjugal life with the king of Annam began to form. It was a relationship in which body movements substituted for the luxury of words. During the day, I patrolled the courtyard nervously, missing the sparkling waves of the Perfume River and the silver moon to which I used to sing the folk tunes of central Vietnam and the poems of my mandarin passengers.

At night, his hunger for me shut off all opportunities for songs, poems, or conversations, and I responded to him as a lioness who moaned and screamed but did not speak. I knew all about his body and nothing about his mind. I became acquainted intimately with every cell of his skin and the raising and calming of his flesh and hair roots, but nothing of his thoughts.

In the peak of my delight, discovery, and curiosity, I was already haunted by the fear of abandonment and tragedy. Lying in his arms, I could not help remembering the words of Son La, and those warnings of his about my terrible fate became the prison torturing my mind. I hung on to my king, hoping I would bear a son, as the old eunuch had advised me to do. I tore off the silk wrapping at the clicking of my king's golden boots outside the double doors. My fierceness and passion became our bondage. The more I despaired at the thought of him leaving me the next day, the more fiercely I loved him, like a wounded, starved lioness.

Yet the inevitable could not be avoided. Like all concubines, I was doomed to a wait.

He was with me night after night for a while, joining and meeting my fierceness with his own, and then he would disappear for days, or at times, months. He would return as a surprise, but only for a while, and then he would again depart. Between his visits, I waited and waited, concocting all the words I would like to speak to him when he returned. When he did return, the hunger took over and I had no occasion to deliver my words.

And then the waiting began again as his visits became even more sporadic. One day, Son La told me that it was about time for me to wait, not just for the return of the king of Annam, but eventually also for a pregnancy that could result from any such encounter. Only the right pregnancy could solidify my place in the Violet City. Under Son La's encouragement, I began to learn the patience of counting days and nights.

"Wait and wait patiently..."

——

I didn't need the protection of my wooden paddles against roving eyes and hands of men, as there were no men. My world consisted of chambermaids and my eunuch Son La. I could no longer sing, as there was neither sky nor river to sing to. The isolation caused me to lose my mind.

Sometime during the process of waiting, I started screaming at night, but my heart-wrenching screams were swallowed by the four walls of my boudoir, muffled by the thickness of those brocade drapes and curtains. When my throat got hoarse, I stopped screaming and listened to the stillness of the night. The only person who knew of my hysteria was my Son La. The old man often looked at me with bewilderment, murmuring to himself that in his more than forty years of servicing the Royal Palace, he had never heard a concubine express herself this way. I would mourn and call out my lover's name, "Buu Linh, Buu Linh," and Son La would try frantically to silence me, cautioning me I was not supposed to call the king of Annam by his given name. I should be addressing my husband by his dynasty name, the Royal Highness Thuan Thanh. In response to the stern warning, I would disdainfully pout my lips, beat on my chest, and utter vicious words. Son La would be kneeling by my bed, confused and in despair, fearful that the guards would hear my blasphemous curses and whining.

"What can you expect, Son La?" I sobbed. "I'm a common paddle girl!"

Every time I passed a night without Buu Linh, I cursed against both Heaven and Earth. I even ripped a down pillow into pieces, having wetted it first with my tears. When my king did not appear for months, I hated him and wanted him dead. I shut my eyes and imagined him loving a dozen women whose fingers traveled across his brown skin when they undressed him. I pulled on my hair until the hairline around my forehead became red and raw and developed into blisters.

In my moments of rage, Son La would massage my feet and kiss my toes to calm me down.

"Hush, hush. You cannot say those bad words about Heaven's son! It's the most hideous crime. You can be sentenced to death, and all members of your extended family can be beheaded as well."

"But I have no family," I sobbed. "I am an orphan. They can kill me, but I have no relatives for them to behead. In any event, it is better to die than to love a man who leaves me like this. I am imprisoned here. I can't go anywhere."

"But he loves you," Son La said quickly.

I stopped sobbing, looking at Son La with disbelief. "How do you know?"

"He must love you. He has not been with anyone as much as you. He has some fifty wives, mostly daughters of the ministers, who show no zest for life. You're different. Look at you, you are full of life. After all, he found you by the Perfume River." The old man rubbed my toe.

"Perhaps this will make you feel better," he said, raising my toe to his mouth and closing his lips over it.

I did calm down. I looked at the old man's face and felt tremendous affection for him. But he was not Buu Linh, and I was alone.

———

I tumbled into the courtyard one day and found Son La moving slowly in the courtyard, his limbs shifting like branches in a slight wind.

"What are you doing, Son La?"

"Tai Chi. An ancient art to balance your body, soul, and spirit." Son La stopped midway and bowed respectfully. "Move with me, my lady; it will help you," he urged.

I mimicked his watery circles in air. "It's like a dance," I said.

"It is the freeing of the soul from the body. Breathe, my lady, breathe."

———

"Tell me more about freeing the soul," I told Son La one night.

"Good, my lady, I will teach you Himalayan Buddhist meditation. Again, it will help you."

He sat down on a rug in my boudoir, and I sat with him, imitating his posture. The exercise went on, and I lost track of time. I was surprised by the old man's dexterity and suppleness.

"How did you learn all of this?" I asked him.

"I am a eunuch, my lady." He was pressing his palms together over his head. "We have only our minds to develop. It is my greatest resource; otherwise, I would have wasted away, living inside the palace."

Day after day, I learned to press my palms together while pressing my heels into the ground, with Son La as my coach. As I pushed myself farther and farther into the center of the earth, my spirit began to roar, and a strong wind of energy flew up from the core of my body. Soon, Son La no longer had to suck my toes to keep me from screaming. I had learned the art of gathering my energy and dispersing it at the same time.

My husband's conjugal visits had become more and more infrequent. His absence, rather than his presence, became my way of life. I accepted my circumstances while waiting for the unknown.

When my screaming at night fully stopped, I concluded that God had sent Son La to me to compensate for my misery inside the palace.

8. CONFIDANTES: A LEARNED EUNUCH AND THE SHREWD CHAMBERMAID

Son La was the oldest son of a low-level mandarin and his concubine, an opera actress. His mother, the illegitimate child of a Vietnamese man and a Cham woman, gave Son La his one-fourth Cham blood. Son La was the oldest of ten children. When the French occupied Annam, Son La's father joined the mandarins' army and was killed during the king's uprising against the French in Hue.

Opera performers and artists were classless citizens, forbidden from sitting for the mandarins' exam, and occupied the bottom of society. As such, they were free from Confucian protocols, although they frequently portrayed characters that epitomized Confucian ethics. Off her stage, Son La's mother was an outcast from society, a woman of Cham descent, concubine and widow of a poor man, a washed-out actress who had prematurely aged because of poverty and childbirth. After his father was murdered, Son La's mother no longer had the health and good looks to carry on the life of a performer. She became a curtain drawer for small opera troops performing in faraway villages, and her ten children were dragged around with her to do odd jobs. During rice harvests, they learned to pick up scattered rice dropped onto the dirt road from farmers' baskets for their dinner. Son La passed his early childhood in hunger and yearning for a decent meal with plenty of rice and meat. As a child, he had already devised his own method to conquer hunger. He let his mind drift to the sky and immersed himself in thoughts that he imagined filling the cavern of his belly.

When Son La turned twelve, he was castrated so he could begin a career with the royal court. Manhood went in exchange for better subsistence and a means to feed the many mouths of an extended family, all sharing the last name of a poor mandarin. Son La insisted on telling me that becoming a eunuch was his personal choice, for he knew he could gain Confucian knowledge living among the aristocracy. On the day of his castration, his family gathered at the ceremony, where a specialist summoned for the occasion numbed Son La's flesh with herbs. After the procedure two men carried him and ran around in a circle fifty times to help stop the bleeding and ease the pain. The ceremony was considered an ennobling act.

The plan went well and Son La's goals were achieved. Son La soon became the sole supporter of the extended family, feeding not only his nine siblings and aging mother but also his father's first and second wives and their children. When he was assigned to me, Son La was already fifty-five years old, an eager, attentive old man with the innocent grin of a young boy. As a eunuch, he was wise, careful, and loyal. A genuinely noble quality existed in him that was lacking among the petty personnel inside the royal court. I did not fully recognize this quality until much later, after my chambermaid, Mai, had joined me in the West Palace and together my pair of servants introduced me to the wonders of learning.

It was Son La who brought Mai into royal life.

"Let me present to you, my lady, this very smart young girl," Son La said to me one day, pointing to the dove-eyed girl who had followed him into my boudoir. She was a chubby girl, quite tall and large-boned for a Vietnamese woman, yet surprisingly swift and animated. Dressed as a royal maid, she smiled at me and immediately lowered her head, as they had all been taught to do. Her smile remained on her full lips, and I began to see it as a smirk. I frowned with displeasure.

"She is not your ordinary maid, my lady." Son La read my mood and immediately came to the young girl's defense. "She is the only daughter of an herb doctor and teacher in my village. The scholar failed the Confucian exam only because he rebelled against the examiners' rules. This fourteen-year-old girl knows how to read and compose poetry better than a mandarin."

"Poetry?" I asked, arching my eyebrows, although secretly my heart lifted as I remembered my favorite mandarin passengers on the Perfume River.

"Yes, my lady, poetry," the girl said. And then she began to speak in verses.

"Did you learn those words from the mandarins who travel the Perfume River?" I asked, unable to conceal my excitement.

"No, my lady. I learned them from my father's books."

"Books?"

I did not know a woman could learn from books.

"You, too, my lady, could learn to read." She raised her eyes to meet mine and was no longer bowing her head.

For the rest of my life, I would always remember Mai as I first saw her that day in my boudoir. I could never forget the surreptitious glance and mischievous smile of the young girl who did not always bow her head as she was taught to do and who introduced me to my first Confucius book. Son La had brought Mai into my secluded life, another blessing. Together they uncovered my thirst for learning, and took turns teaching me how to read "chu Han," Vietnamese characters adopted from Chinese. It was a slow, elaborate, and frustrating process, but I eventually succeeded, having dedicated to ancient characters and calligraphy the same passion I had dedicated to paddling.

9. THE PREGNANCY

Inside the Citadel it was the head eunuch who announced nightly where His Royal Highness had decided to spend the night. The head eunuch was a very old man, as old as the walls of the concubines' courtyards. He walked slowly, his back bent almost into an arch, his eyes to the ground. He talked to us, the women of the Violet City, without looking at us. Slow and thrifty with words, he never said more than what he needed to say. When the sun went to sleep behind the elongated shape of the Truong Son Range that separated Hue from Laos, we, the lonely women of the Violet City, leaned against the carved pillars under our curved roofs, looking out to our respective courtyards. We waited for the lantern that signaled the arrival of the head eunuch, who always took time with his announcement, as though to tease us. Yet he delivered his words with a stern face, and there was no teasing in the pair of eyes so dry and dull they reminded me of cracked earth.

It was an autumn night, and the lotuses must have blossomed fully all around the Violet City when the head eunuch announced the arrival of the king of Annam in my courtyard. As in the old days, my royal husband entered my boudoir with his entourage, dismissed the woman dressers, and reached for me with the same hunger as during our first night as husband and wife. But it had been a long time, so I received him calmly, with control. I finally pulled away from him and retreated to the farthest end of the lacquer bed. There, I remained reclining placidly while he disrobed. I observed the same lover in a different light, as a different woman.

That night, the lioness in me cooled and transformed into hissing steam. I savored him in the steam of my soul, one that had known sorrow and the impermanent nature of things. In many ways, I had been reborn and reformed. The young teen lioness had matured into a calm, poised woman who, like all women of the Violet City, learned in her desolate life that she could love and belong to one man, yet share him with hundreds of other young, beautiful, and obedient women. Every night there was a happy, blossoming woman and many weeping ones. Some of us kept waiting and others gave up, as our youth and beauty faded away, along with our capacity for anguish.

I had long known that the women of the Violet City had taken an immediate dislike to me due to my Cham blood and common background and that they had cheered when the king of Annam stopped returning to my boudoir. My lack of sophistication had helped me survive the vicious comments of my peers. Quite often, I did not even understand their mockery. And I was lucky to have a protective eunuch and a clever chambermaid, who both helped shield me from misfortunes and the snares of royal protocols.

That night, when the head eunuch's announcement was heard over all concubines' courtyards—that His Royal Highness would soon arrive in my boudoir—I knew the surge of jealousy would be revived among my competitors in the Violet City. The comfort of his arms that night did not soothe away my knowledge of possible danger, even though the cells of my skin danced under his fingertips.

He had shuddered into a long-lasting rest with his perspiring face buried in the stream of my hair when I gathered all of my courage and spoke. I spoke casually of the sufferings of the warrior's wife who turned into a limestone statue because of her wait, and he raised his head to look at my face. Panic appeared in his eyes.

"What are you suggesting, woman?"

I instinctively covered my lips with my hand and began whispering, not knowing why the secretive manner was called for. I recited to him the poetry of the mandarins who had traveled my river, wanting me to convey to the king of Annam the sufferings of his people. With Son La and Mai's help, I had learned the meanings of those words. They described the responsibility of Heaven's son to stop the sufferings of his populace, including the wait of those longing individuals, which could harden human flesh into stone. I was thinking solely of myself, my own longing and despair. I wasn't sophisticated enough then to think of Annam.

But he must have construed the poetic words more profoundly, as the mandarins had intended. He sat up in bed and arranged the sheets around his waist. He said he was a powerless king, that it was just a matter of time before the monarchy would end, that to be a citizen of freedom was better than being a king in slavery and bondage. He lowered his head, and I might have seen tears in the corners of his eyes. Something broke inside me to see tears on a lion's face.

That night, I became pregnant.

10. MONSIEUR SYLVAIN FOUCAULT, THE FRENCH RÉSIDENT SUPÉRIEUR

Despite the good news of my pregnancy, I continued to be saddened by the knowledge that to me, the king of Annam had remained a total stranger although my womb bore his seed. I wanted to travel within his mind the same way he had traveled my body. I wanted to understand his fear.

I turned to Son La for help, as usual, telling him one day that perhaps I had seen the king's tears. The eunuch's wrinkled face immediately turned grave and somber. He pondered for a while, and then looked at me with profound sadness.

"A son, my lady, is important to you. To him, there is also the State of Annam."

"What about the State of Annam?"

"We are not free, my lady. What happened to the Chams a long time ago is now happening to the Viets. Annam is under French protectorate now. Our king is…just a king."

Son La finished his sentence with a touch of irony. I gave him a blank look. Sighing, he took out a small book and showed it to me. It was completely different from the Confucius books from which I had learned to read and write. For one thing, there were no characters.

Son La opened the book and pointed to the painting of a skinny, bearded man, scantily dressed, stretching his limbs on a cross, his head dropping to one side. "This man is called Jesus Christ. Many people, including the Vietnamese, believe he is the son of God. A different God, one worshipped by French priests."

"Why is he hanging there?"

"According to the French priests, he is a sacrifice for all mankind."

Son La went on to explain to me how Catholicism had brought the French to Vietnam and how our king, the son of Heaven, had become jealous and fearful of Jesus Christ, the son of a Western God. The result of the conflict was the colonization of Vietnam by the French. The emperor of Vietnam was reduced to the king of Annam, controlled by a French *résident supérieur*. This led to the king's uprising and the massacre of Hue, which had killed Son La's father. All of these occurred before my Buu Linh occupied the throne.

Son La concluded that no one could predict what would happen to the Annamese monarchy.

"The Can Vuong, the King's anti-French Loyalists' Movement, headed by the mandarins, is now gradually changing to the Cach Mang, the Revolution." Son La closed the book of Jesus Christ. His voice had gone tight and quick when he mentioned Cach Mang.

"What does that mean, Cach Mang?"

"It means changing Heaven's mandate. There are Confucian scholars who no longer believe in Heaven's son. They are seeking other ways to gain independence for Vietnam. One scholar advocates following the Japanese model. Another scholar advocates the demolition of the monarchy. The king, controlled by the French *résident supérieur*, is seen by them as a puppet."

A puppet? I thought of myself on my wedding day, being dragged through the bathing routines, then along the corridors that led to the conjugal bed where I was wrapped in silk.

"Who is this French *superieur*?" I asked.

"A Frenchman by the name of Sylvain Foucault. We call him Monsieur Foucault, and your royal husband resents him with all his heart."

———

Through Son La, I learned more about my husband and his conflicts with the Frenchman, as well as the intricate chaos of my time.

Several kings of Annam and their royal concubines had a passion for the opera, and various troops were allowed to perform inside the Citadel. My husband, in particular, was an opera enthusiast. Son La had been serving on the king's opera-viewing committee for years. He and other court personnel formed liaisons with the various opera troops to set up royal performances and to research the art. Occasionally, he was even allowed to leave the Violet City and tour Hue as part of this opera recruitment and research mission. The mission enabled Son La to reach out to old friends of his actress mother, who became the resourceful eunuch's network of spies. Son La loved the job, as it allowed him the opportunity to see and listen to the outside world. Without Son La and his opera network, I would have been just one of those longing concubines of the Violet City, shut off from the world, idle and unconcerned even if hurricanes had reached the Port of Thuan An and swept away half of the capital.

Son La became my eyes and ears for political events and underground news, and he helped me understand the chaos of my time.

From Son La, I learned that armed resistance and anti-French literary movements led by the mandarins had filled the nation with tension. Inside the Citadel, my royal husband and Monsieur Foucault carried on their silent and bitter cold war. In between the two of them, the royal cabinet, Co Mat Vien, administered the bureaucracy plagued with power struggles and petty politics, while the real power over the country rested with the French.

That was how the Annam court moved into the twentieth century.

——

To the world outside the Violet City, my marriage to the King had become a myth. Because of how uniquely I had been brought to the palace, I had become symbolic of the king's connection to commoners. My arrival in the West Palace also added to my husband's image as the unconventional, anti-French king, almost a cult figure searching for the deeper roots of Annam—its Cham heritage.

The anecdotes fed to me by Son La through his opera network described my husband as a stubborn teenager who had come to the throne at fourteen years of age and who, in his young adulthood, had turned into a serious scholar of Confucian philosophy and ancient literature. To keep up with his time, he cut his hair and also learned French.

From the beginning, my husband disappointed the French *résident supérieur*. After the young king's coronation, the *superieur* built a bridge inside the Citadel and honored the young king by naming the bridge after his dynasty. The fourteen-year-old king was not at all pleased. He felt it was an insult to bestow the dynasty name on a bridge frequently walked upon by French protectorates. During the ribbon-cutting ceremony, the *résident supérieur* jokingly told my husband, "If and when this bridge collapses, you will have your country all to yourself and the protectorates will respectfully withdraw."

My husband, according to Son La, said nothing in reply, but the young man remembered Foucault's boastful promise.

Foucault did more than just name a bridge after the king of Annam. During the coronation of the fourteen-year-old king, Foucault also had photographs taken of the teenager sitting awkwardly on the throne. The Foucault family owned several commercial enterprises in Vietnam, including a publishing house in Tonkin and a tourist agency. The Foucault family made the photograph of the young king into a postcard and marketed it in Europe and Africa to attract tourists to Indochina. The postcard also traveled among anti-French patriots who wrote the word *puppet* across the face of the photograph. The young king of Annam had become a commercial commodity for French colonists and an object of ridicule among Vietnamese dissident poets and freedom fighters.

It was not until my husband turned sixteen that he discovered he had appeared on a postcard for commercial gain. Humiliated, he issued a decree ordering the discontinuation and destruction of all such postcards. The unwritten norm of royal protocols in Annam allowed all royal decrees to be reviewed and vetoed by the French *résident supérieur*. It was alleged that when Foucault saw the decree, he laughed and threw it in the trash basket.

My husband heard the news. He did not touch his meals for two days, and then left for a hunting trip to the jungles of central Vietnam. He allegedly fired at trees and then broke out crying in the jungle.

During the same year, the bridge named after my husband was damaged during a monsoon hurricane. My husband went to see Foucault.

"Now that the bridge has collapsed, will Monsieur Résident Supérieur keep his promise and give independence to Vietnam?"

Foucault was stunned. "Your Royal Highness, if I ever made such a promise, it was made in jest."

"Just when did you learn to make statements in jest regarding the affairs of Vietnam?" the young king angrily retorted.

It was then that Foucault fully realized the crowning of the insolent teenager had been a mistake. The relationship between the colonist-bureaucrat and the young Vietnamese king was openly hostile thereafter.

A free spirit, my husband grew up into a young man with a passion for the opera. He played the drum with royal opera troops and frequently escaped the palace at night to travel outside the Citadel in civilian clothes. Rumors continued to spread about my husband's bizarre behavior, including the story of how he had found me and brought me to the palace. His way of picking and choosing a bride and his insatiable sexual appetite became the incessant gossip of the Violet City and among the citizens of Hue.

King Thuan Thanh was as infatuated with jungle hunting as he was with the opera. This dangerous hobby quite often put the lives of his domestic staff at risk, as he relentlessly pursued man-eaters like leopards and tigers. News traveled to the countryside that once the king had fired a pistol shot at the booted feet of one of his cabinet ministers to test how the mandarin would react. The king missed the minister, but the shot was shocking enough to send the poor old man leaping high into the air before he collapsed in tears.

His Royal Highness's exoduses outside the Citadel became more and more frequent, almost always ending up with beautiful women being brought to the palace. The rumors went on and on, portraying less his concern for state affairs and more his insane behavior, incessant demands, and bizarre habits. Foucault was reportedly quite concerned with the young king's lavish spending and the growing budget needed to support his entourage, including his women.

There was other news as well. Certain mandarin scholars believed Thuan Thanh faked insanity only to bypass French surveillance. Stories traveled about how the king frequently sent back to Foucault and the royal cabinet documents left unsigned or marked with changes. He questioned French authority by citing previously executed treaties in the margins of the documents that he was asked to sign, pointing out how the documents violated those treaties. Outside the Citadel, his citizens whispered tales about his secret trips to Tonkin to make contacts with anti-French resistance forces, and how the French *résident supérieur* likewise gave secret orders to isolate the king of Annam inside the Violet City as a form of house arrest.

In such a climate, I quietly prepared for the birth of, hopefully, my son.

11. HATRED AND INDEPENDENCE

I had no idea how Mai's prediction was broadcast, since Mai had sworn herself to secrecy, but by the fifth month of my pregnancy the speculation about the anticipated arrival of a son born to a Cham concubine had traveled like electricity around the Violet City. My husband already had several sons born to other concubines, but none had been made a crowned prince, and never before in the history of the Nguyen dynasty had a son been conceived by a concubine of Cham descent.

Those were the happy and hopeful days of my life in the Violet City, despite the fact that during my pregnancy, my husband stopped coming to my boudoir. He would soon return, when his son was born. I delighted at the thought.

It was a clear, moonlit night when I decided to dismiss all my chambermaids. I wanted an evening all to myself. Mai had asked to retire early, and I was left to walk the courtyard alone. I returned to my boudoir and decided to prepare my own bath.

The chambermaids had boiled water, perfumed it, and poured it into a large porcelain bowl. I started to pour water from the bowl into the tub. At the bottom of the porcelain sink, I saw numerous dots of brown and black dirt. The water was full of them. I paused, took another look and the dirt appeared to move. I looked again. The dirt spots were indeed moving. I rubbed my eyes and then stared without blinking. The dirt spots appeared larger, this time wiggling and swimming vigorously.

I dropped the porcelain sink and screamed.

Only Son La heard me, and he rushed in, finding me struggling in the mess of shattered porcelain and water, with dirt spots moving and swimming at my feet. He took me into his hands and began rubbing off the dirt spots. "Oh, Heaven," he blurted.

I saw his face turn green and then everything around it began to turn black.

—

When I opened my eyes, I saw Mai's and Son La's faces staring down at me.

"They were leeches, my lady," Son La said. I saw anger in his eyes.

"Leeches?" I cried.

Having grown up around water, I knew about those slimy, stubborn creatures. They sucked upon flesh and engorged themselves with human blood. They clung to the skin and did not let go. Farmers often got bitten by them, and only a heavy application of raw limestone liquid directly upon the parasite could disconnect their hungry mouth from human flesh. They traveled swiftly in water and could invade orifices of the human body. They were nearly impossible to kill. To incapacitate the creature, one had to nail it on a surface and dry it under direct sun until it became dehydrated and dysfunctional. But the moment it hit water, the creature could revitalize. Chop one in half, and each half would turn into a new leech.

I could have been sitting in a tub full of young leeches that would have invaded my body and destroyed the baby inside my womb. Who could have done such a thing inside the West Palace? It could have been anyone. Mai knelt down by my bed, kissed my feet, cried, and told me how sorry she was to have left me alone.

I told them I was once the paddle girl on a wild river and was not afraid of leeches.

Together, Son La and Mai cleaned up my washroom, talking among themselves as they performed the task. When they came out, they had a plan to deal with the situation. It needed my approval and cooperation, they said.

———

We did not report the incident, and in the following days, I participated in all rituals and protocols of the West Palace as though nothing had happened. Yet I could tell from the glancing eyes and the whispering lips that the royal community had heard of the terrible mischief. The whole Violet City was wondering how I could have survived the ordeal. I noticed eyes glancing up and down my tummy in blatant curiosity.

The rumor had begun—spread by Son La and Mai—that I was well protected by the spirit of Mee-Ey, the ancient queen of Champa who watched over her land and descendants. I was so strong and so well guarded by the spirit that when the leeches hit my skin, they immediately deteriorated and became dirt.

And, the rumor went on, my unborn son was also protected by Champa's queenly spirit, who was demanding her land back from the Vietnamese. My son would become Annam's greatest warrior. After such a rumor, Mai whispered into my ear one night, perhaps my unknown enemies in the Violet City—any of those jealous concubines and their loyal eunuchs who resented the forthcoming arrival of my son—would surely leave me alone. Who wanted to be cursed by the fierce and powerful spirit of Mee-Ey?

—

I was not harmed by the leeches, but fate played another trick on me. I gave birth not to a son, but to twin daughters.

After their birth, the king of Annam stopped coming to my boudoir altogether. I became the lonely Mystique Concubine who no longer carried her mystique.

Still, the women of the Nguyen Dynasty lived on. I did, too, carrying a placid death in my heart. We, the royal concubines of King Thuan Thanh, survived by turning our energies to mundane purposes such as preparing, in the special Hue way, the fifty or so royal dishes at every meal—shaping them into artful flowers and leaves, and arranging them expertly on tiny translucent blue-and-white porcelain plates. We also performed the myriad tasks routinely planned around the queen mother, a diminutive old woman whose fragile frame was buried under layers of cloth, whose eyes had lost focus, and who lived in perpetual fear of sunshine. In the ceremonial hall, when the eunuchs placed her on the pedestal for a court ceremony, she would clutch her shoulders, bringing her limbs together into a fetal position to escape the light. Perhaps at one time, before the arrival of French protectorates, the image of a queen mother was a figure of authority inside the Citadel. But those days were over, and in my time, my husband's mother lived like a ghost and a reminder of the bad time when the throne had changed hands. It was known all over the royal courtyards that her husband, the late king Dai Duc, the father-in-law I never met, was placed on the throne while the French were shooting at our port. Three days later he was poisoned, and his cousin succeeded the throne. After his death, his favorite concubine, the beautiful lady Tu Minh, escaped the palace with her baby son, Prince Buu Linh. Tu Minh and her son Buu Linh spent fourteen years living as commoners in the villages of central Vietnam. My husband had been raised in the countryside, and thus had acquired his taste for the commoners' life. On the day the French protectorates announced the selection of Prince Buu Linh as the new king of Annam, troops had to go to the countryside to fetch mother and son. The mother had tried to hide her son in a rice field. When they found him, she cried and lamented that Heaven had once more betrayed her. The royal troops had to drag her back to the palace, and she put up a fierce fight, murmuring all the way that the throne was the source of death.

At my husband's coronation, his mother was crowned Hoang Thai Hau Tu Minh (Tu Minh, the Mother Queen of Annam), the highest royal title accorded a woman of the Violet City. At the ceremony, the poor woman—once beautiful, cheerful, and kind—talked to the blank space in front of her, diminutive and terrified on the ostentatious throne with its carved images of flying phoenixes. Afterward, she turned mute. The fanciful clothes the ladies put on her and the salutes of the young women who bowed to her couldn't shake her silence. At official ceremonies, I watched the royal concubines moving around their mother-in-law, never understanding what she wanted. Nobody cared. The direction for our daily lives came from the head eunuch. But the royal rituals went on, and at every occasion the queen mother was treated like the ink painting of Confucius, which we worshipped and bowed to without thought. Yet her dull eyes, jerking limbs, and trembling lips all rubbed fear into our skin. We became afraid of our own tomorrows. We all knew kings and queens could be killed, or, if they survived, go insane.

Apart from fear, our lives became stagnant, surrounded by inanimate objects. We waited for the monthly cycles of our menses, and news, any kind of news. That was how I acquired the habit of standing by the window, looking out into the night, deeper and deeper until my eyes could perceive the moonlit Perfume River of my past. Since childhood, my eyes had been accustomed to piercing through darkness. For years I had made my way across the river at night that way. In the Violet City, I had to train and retrain my eyes to see through the night in order to regain a sense of control over my fate.

But then something happened in the process.

In my effort of regaining the sharpness of my vision, I began to see the Face of Brutality—a pair of beastly eyes with no sockets. Just the bright, red eyes staring at me, willing me to make a mistake so the Face could laugh.

—

I survived the difficult birth of my daughters and the disappointment of an abandoned wife, and began to concentrate, instead, on raising my twin girls.

When the twins were one month old, my husband issued a royal decree giving them their official titles. My older daughter, Cinnamon Fragrance, was ordained Nam Tran Cong Chua (the princess of the South Sea Pearl), and my younger daughter, Ginseng Fragrance, was given the title Nam Binh Cong Chua (the princess for the Peace of the South). I did not like the pompous titles. I called my little girls Cinnamon and Ginseng—symbolic of the jungles of central Vietnam where my ancestors had come from.

As Son La fed me gossip about the Revolution and the changing of Heaven's mandates, I began to think more about the State of Annam. In my boudoir, I asked Son La one day:

"The state affairs, the welfare and independence of Annam—aren't they the duties of everyone?"

Son La was preparing an ink plate for his calligraphy. Without looking up, he said, "Yes, my lady. It is the duty of everyone who inhabits this land, Cham and Viet alike."

"If that's the case, that everyone shares in this duty, then what happens to Heaven's daughters? Why should everything be centered around the king as Heaven's son, according to Confucius?"

Son La jumped up, almost dropping his ink plate. His worried eyes still failed to meet mine.

"Because," he said, "a daughter gets married, bears the name of her husband, and becomes property of the husband's family."

I became upset, as though months of practiced self-control had amounted to nothing. During those days, I had picked up knitting and embroidery to pass time, and on that particular day, after Son La had forewarned my possible fate, I caught myself repeatedly stabbing my forefinger with the needle. A tiny drip of blood stained the front of my silk gown, yet I was oblivious to the pain.

"Who said so—*Heaven*? Dictating that a daughter is the property of her husband?" I asked contemptuously.

Son La, seeing the drip of blood, was speechless.

My whole life rushed through my head, and I realized how the Violet City had turned me into a piece of property belonging to my husband inside his Citadel. And I wasn't even valued property, since even the people of Annam might have viewed their king as simply a puppet. Hence, even the king's love and the presence of my two daughters had not alleviated my sense of worthlessness. When I was still paddling my boat for a living, life was hard, but I belonged to no one. In so many ways, I was free and secure then.

"I haven't heard a word from Heaven. It sounds more like the saying of Confucius, a man," I added sarcastically.

I put the basket of yarn aside and began to recite. "The pious woman has as guidance the rule of the Three Obediences, according to which she is to obey three masters of her life: father, husband, and son. Her subjugation is due to her inferior nature: she is weak, ignorant, and prone to mistakes and thus must depend on men's wisdom to conduct herself. To reflect favorably on the honor of these men, she is most of all expected to uphold the ultimate value of chastity. Chastity in the unmarried girl means virginity. In the married woman, it refers to her unconditional faithfulness to her husband, alive or dead. To play her designated role, she is reminded to cultivate the Four Virtues according to their proper meaning: diligence in housework, attractiveness in person, reticence in speech, and modesty and politeness in behavior."

I paused to breathe and continued. "We Cham women do not take on the husband's name, do we?"

Son La was still eyeing me with concern. "No," he said, "Cham societies are matriarchal, my lady. The Cham woman takes control of her household." He paused and darted his eyes around the four walls of my boudoir. Casting them toward the floor, he covered his mouth with his sleeves and lowered his voice. "You don't have to stay here," he murmured. "You can escape. I can make it happen."

Neither of us was able to speak. My head began to spin. I had never once considered the option. Son La rushed out of the room, even forgetting to kowtow and bid farewell.

He had suggested the ultimate taboo.

That night I couldn't sleep, thinking of the future of Cinnamon and Ginseng. I thought, too, of the intimacy I shared with the king and the warmth of his flesh. I recalled the special feeling that overwhelmed my heart when I was in his presence. Somehow my heart continued telling me that perhaps the magnet between my husband and me only happened once in a lifetime and that our bond was more than just our physical closeness. It had to be the essence of what love meant, between a man and a woman.

But how could I know? I had never known any other man. I was doomed to the fate of a pious concubine. I rushed to the half-moon window and stared out at the night. The Face of Brutality was staring back at me.

I collapsed onto the muffling silk of the bed and wept. I could not give up waiting for him. I could not leave as long as I clung to the scintilla of hope that he would return to my boudoir. The longing for him that had been suppressed burned inside me again. I tossed and turned, and the deepest part of me longed for the warmth of his body—his alone, and no one else's. It must have been love that made a woman willingly monogamous.

In terror, I realized I had been imprisoned, not by the teaching of Confucius and his virtues, nor by the courtyards of the Citadel, but by my own heart.

12. THE EXODUS

That Face of Brutality took more vivid form when Son La passed along more details about the deteriorating relationship between my husband and Monsieur Foucault. According to Son La, the rumors were so widespread they had reached the countryside, circulated among the hamlets near the port of Thuan An, and traveled up and down the coast, north to Tonkin and south to Cochinchina.

The latest rumors related to my husband's all-female military troupe. The beautiful women he brought to the Violet City were ordered to practice combat skills, ride horses, and use weapons. These women, including his old and new lovers, dressers, and chambermaids, wore royal guard uniforms. His all-female troop grew to consist of some three hundred young women, consuming a sizable part of the court's budget. The rumors also portrayed him as a psychotic and sadistic king who abused the throne: he allegedly whipped or cut of the breasts of those women who refused to obey orders.

If there were such a female troupe, he had kept it away from his ordained royal concubines.

Gossip about the insane, uncontrolled king crossed the land, igniting the anti-French fume among subversive resistance movements and setting the stage for more and more piecemeal guerrilla uprisings. The royal concubines of the Violet City waited and waited for another night with His Royal Highness, who isolated himself all the more from his consorts.

I waited like the rest of his concubines, until one day when Son La rushed in, kowtowed, and whispered into my ears the most shocking news.

Foucault had received a telegraph, the official words of the minister of colonies, Monsieur Bernard Bronti. Due to overspending and budget mismanagement, neglect of the affairs of the State, and deteriorating mental health, the king of Annam, His Royal Highness Thuan Thanh, had been requested by the protectorate government to abdicate. His temporary new home would be Cap St. Jacques, a resort beach in Cochinchina, until final arrangements could be made for him to settle permanently on the island of Reunion, Africa—another French colony.

———

I was luckier than most royal concubines. The tragedy that befell my husband became my tragedy, but it also occasioned our last night together.

The abdicated king did return to my boudoir, for the last union, before the final change of guards. Almost ten years had passed since we first met on the river Huong, and I was about to turn twenty-five.

As the head eunuch announced His Royal Highness's arrival, I sadly realized that too much pain and waiting had killed off the palpitation of young love and infatuation in my heart. Once more, I calmly received him, with the same muscular tone of my belly, arms, and legs. I was the same robust paddle girl, and these past idle years had not substantially changed my physique.

Emotionally, however, I felt that I had aged a hundred years.

Son La had told me my husband would be taking two of his concubines with him. They were both in their teens. I was over twenty and, hence, was not chosen for the exodus to the island of Reunion. He did not want me to be his consort for the forthcoming life in exile and old age.

In the early morning, he left me in bed and went to my half-moon window. There he stood, for hours. Looking at his elegant back from the bed, I wondered if he, too, saw the beastly eyes of the Face of Brutality.

As the sun appeared and the first morning rays hit the courtyard, he began reciting a poem. I knew it wasn't dedicated to me; he was simply reading to himself. He must have viewed me as an uneducated woman, as in our time together, never once did he try to discuss anything literary, artistic, or political.

Son La's and Mai's teaching had paid off. I understood what the poem was about. As he spoke, I memorized every word:

Literary men, military men, all lining up before my velvet cloak
A lonely king, I bear my cross
Three times a royal toast, like the people's blood
My sorrow, my tears, or Heaven's flood?

I had not sung since my entrance to the palace. The loss of the Perfume River and the rhythm of my paddles had robbed me of my melodies. All of a sudden, inspired by his words, I felt the urge to sing my husband's poem in the wailing melodies of my Cham heritage. So I did just that. I sang. I repeated every word he had spoken in the stream of melodies dormant in my veins. Each word became some fifty notes of music, vibrating across the land to the depths of my Perfume River.

When I stopped, I found him staring at me in the same way he had focused upon my belly and waist the night we met on the Perfume River. But his gaze was devoid of lust. Instead, his eyes signaled some sort of emotional longing and appreciation. He no longer looked like a lion. He had the countenance of an exhausted prisoner folding up at the hour of persecution.

"I've always known you were special," he said.

For me, that was enough for a farewell moment. I was his Mystique Concubine. In the thin space between us, I felt two souls reach out for each other because they were the same. We looked at each other, a polygamous husband and a monogamous wife, for a long time.

Then he asked to see the twins.

He watched the identical girls for a while and attempted to embrace them, but they resisted, rubbing their eyes with their lotus-root fingers before settling down to sit on both sides of him, pulling on his robe. He stroked their hair, and they warmed up to him, little by little. Ginseng eventually climbed up and sat in his lap, while Cinnamon unsuccessfully competed for the same space. Cinnamon rushed over to me, her big, dark eyes looking back at him with curiosity. He signaled to her, and she carefully approached him, finally placing her face in his lap.

They were together, father and daughters.

He turned to me: "I'll go, but you must stay with Annam. It is your land."

I nodded. He kissed the forehead of the girls.

"You will tell them of the Perfume River."

I nodded.

"You will teach them to sing my poem."

I nodded.

And then he left.

I found on the pillow something he had left for me. It was a jade phoenix, intricately carved and imprinted against a plaque of gold, bearing the dragon and royal seal of the Nguyen Dynasty. The phoenix was a symbol reserved only for a Nguyen Dynasty queen, seen in public only at two occasions: at her coronation and upon her death.

He must have taken it away from his prematurely old and silent queen mother Tu Minh, and passed it on to me, his Mystique Concubine. My tears fell onto the cool stone. I lifted my tunic, wiped the tears from the radiant jade, and clutched the phoenix to my bare belly, feeling the cold texture of gem against the sensitive skin. I knew something was taking form inside my womb after our last night together. This time I knew with certainty it would be a boy.

I even knew what to name my son: Que Lam, meaning the Forest of Cinnamon.

13. THE ENCOUNTER

Things seemed hatefully normal the following week among the inhabitants of the Violet City, although the directions of Sylvain Foucault were hardly normal. According to Son La, my husband had left for Cap St. Jacques, Cochinchina, but his entourage from the Violet City, including the two chosen concubines, had not departed. Foucault had ordered that they be held up inside the Violet City until further instructions, leaving the entire royal court bewildered and wondering. An ambiance of tension filled the Violet City, but nobody reacted outwardly or made any inquiries. No one dared to gossip. The cabinet, as well as all female inhabitants of the Violet City, were holding their breath, waiting for Foucault's further instructions or telegraphs from his government in France. No one knew for sure what would come next, or what would happen to the concubines and children of King Thuan Thanh.

I waited, as usual, with the rest of the concubines.

It was a bright morning and I was watching Cinnamon and Ginseng play in the common courtyard of the West Palace when I heard ruffling fabric and jingling bells. The head eunuch and his entourage were rushing through, asking all of us to clear the way. Mai helped me pick up the twins and retreat.

I stopped a eunuch and asked him what the fuss was about.

"The *résident supérieur* is coming, my lady."

"What?" I could not believe the words. "The Frenchman is coming here?"

"There will be sessions for many of us to be photographed by a Westerner. The *résident supérieur* has so requested."

"Sessions?"

"Yes, my lady. Meaning posing and staging. We dare not be disrespectful, but please clear the way. It is an emergency request."

The eunuch turned and walked away, his mind obviously focused on carrying out the Frenchman's order. The eunuchs began to stage the courtyard like an opera stage. I went back to my boudoir and pondered. The taking of photographs! I had never seen such a thing. But I had heard of the postcard incident and how it had angered my husband. I called for Son La and Mai, and they arrived together a while later, a look of concern shadowing both faces.

"The Foucault Enterprise has organized tourist attractions for European subjects to come and visit Annam, my lady," Son La said. "The project has been going on for a while. They've been taking photographs of the lotus ponds, the dragon gate, the Thai Hoa cabinet meeting hall, the throne, the grand altars honoring the Nguyen Founding Lords, everything. Now they are moving inside the West Palace."

"It is highly inappropriate, my lady," Mai added, her eyes reddening. "It is good that His Royal Highness is gone. Otherwise, the humiliation! For almost two hundred years, no outsider has been able to have an audience with the royal concubines of Hue, my lady." Mai wiped her eyes with her sleeves.

I had been told the rules since my first day of residence in the Violet City. The West Palace was off-limits to men, except Court personnel—the eunuchs—and the king of Annam.

"Today, a number of royal concubines have been asked to pose for the photographers," Mai said. "Not even with the courtesy of a warning, my lady."

I thought of the Confucian rules of the Three Obediences—absolute submission to father, husband, and son. Under the French protectorate authority, it appeared to me that my husband's concubines had to obey an additional boss, that French *résident supérieur*, Monsieur Foucault. I sighed and told Son La and Mai I did not wish to see what was going on in the common courtyard.

"Close all curtains and shut the entrance," I instructed.

Much to my dismay both stood still with their head bowed.

"What are you waiting for?!"

Mai finally spoke. "I think the head eunuch will be coming here soon to speak to you,"

"About what?"

Mai burst into tears. When Son La began to speak, his voice was weak and remote. "The *résident supérieur* has asked to see you. I heard it is something about a special postcard."

———

The head eunuch arrived shortly thereafter. The stooped old man did most of the talking. I sat at my tea table while he stayed closer to the entrance, his eyes fixed to the floor but for his occasional glances up to the rosewood footstool—a barricade that adjoined the entrance connecting my boudoir to the courtyard.

The footstool had always been there. I had always just taken it for granted. To enter my boudoir from the courtyard, one had to lift the flap of one's long dress and step over it. The barricade kept people from rushing in. Only the king and his eunuchs had stepped over the stool to enter my boudoir. No other men could be permitted.

For the first time in my life inside the Violet City, I focused my attention on the barricade, as I listened to the head eunuch describing the wish of Sylvain Foucault.

No real man except King Thuan Thanh had set foot in my boudoir. The head eunuch and Son La, of course, were not real men. During my pregnancy, the court physician, who was sixty-five years old, had to be lifted by eunuchs over the stool to reach my bed. I lay behind brocade curtains, and the old man felt my silk-clad belly by extending one arm between the curtain folds, without ever laying eyes on me. To feel my pulse, he placed his ears and thumb over a silk thread that had been tied to my wrist. There was never any direct, skin-to-skin contact.

The head eunuch had finished his speech and was still kow-towing near the entrance when I left the tea table to walk around my boudoir. For the first time, I became keenly aware of every piece of furniture, every carving, every fold of the curtains sur-rounding the bed. I felt the shiny wood pillars that accented the room and divided it into quarters. I moved my palm along the edge of the lacquer divan and felt the smoothness of the mother-of-pearl.

I began to see the brown torso of my husband, the silky slacks that draped the columns of his thighs, and those long fingers of his that once molded my flesh. I saw traces of my husband everywhere on the impersonal and familiar furniture that made up my existence. The emotions overwhelmed me, and I had to place one hand over my heart, almost losing my balance. The head eunuch, who, all this time, had kept his head bowed and his eyes toward the floor, failed to notice my shift of emotion.

My king was not here, yet I could feel him. I turned to the head eunuch. "I will not comply with the monsieur's wish."

The head eunuch remained kneeling, his eyes glancing again and again toward the footstool barricade, obviously looking forward to the time when he could step over it to return to the common courtyard. For once, I had the urge to see the barricade grow higher and higher so no one would be able to step into my world.

Years ago, after my husband stopped coming to me, I had once harbored the desire to escape the West Palace so I could roam Hue at my whim. But the days kept passing by, and gradually I grew accustomed to my fate, losing all desire to escape the confines of my boudoir. To sink into the freedom of my Perfume River, I simply stood looking out my half-moon window. The sudden recognition of the gradual change made me want to weep.

The head eunuch had started a new speech. He told me of the time predating my birth, when French gunmen had first entered the Violet City. The late emperor Tu Duc passed on around the same time the Treaty of Patenôtre was signed, forming the basis for French colonial rule in Vietnam—France directly controlled Cochinchina, while Annam and Tonkin were protectorate states. One French officer, Lieutenant Mahee, dug up the tomb of the late emperor Tu Duc to search for treasure. Too bad for him, he could not find the late emperor's coffin. To this day, the French had never been able to discover where the emperor was actually buried.

"The Frenchman wanted to excavate the late emperor's tomb, and he did, my lady," the head eunuch droned.

"I am sure there were people who objected," I replied.

"The minister of protocols and culture, my lady. He spent the rest of his life objecting, yet the digging was done."

I moved toward the window and raised the curtain. I could see part of what was going on in the main courtyard. Never had the West Palace been so animated. I recognized the royal concubines who were preparing themselves for the photography session, among whom were the two young women, both sixteen years old, who had been chosen to accompany my husband in exile and were awaiting departure. Some of the children, the young princes and princesses of Annam, had also been dressed up in royal attire to have their pictures taken. The participants were shy, yet beaming in a festive atmosphere. The day must have been the highlight of their dull existence, ironically brought on by the departure of their husband and father. No one expressed sadness or anger. Beautiful furniture was being moved to stage the scene. The eunuchs ran around like bees. Among those little people, a black box towered on a three-legged stand, and I saw the silhouette of a tall man bending over it.

"Is that a camera?" I asked, pointing.

"Yes, my lady." The head eunuch had leaped to his feet and was standing behind me. "It has a lens, through which you can see yourself upside down."

"Upside down?"

"Yes, the size of a bee. The equipment makes a noise and your image is captured on paper. The West can do many a splendid thing."

"And the man who stands behind it?"

"The photographer, my lady. A Western man."

I had never seen a camera before. Nor had I seen a Western man, although I had studied the painting of Jesus Christ inside Son La's book. To me, the man on the cross, with his dark beard and long hair, represented the image of a Western male.

"I want to walk the common courtyard," I told the head eunuch.

We stepped over the footstool barricade, passed the double door entrance of my boudoir, and he followed me toward the gleaming central courtyard, full of sunshine.

—

I took my time scrutinizing the machine called the camera and the face of the tall Western man who bowed before me. The camera was exactly what the head eunuch had described. I even peeped inside the black box and saw the bee-sized, upside-down image of the posing concubines and their children. As to the Western man standing behind the machine, he could not take his eyes off me, and I had to remind him to bow his head. I could not tell his age. In many ways, he looked very old. His pores were extremely large, and his gold hair grew everywhere, on his uncombed head, around his lips, along his square jaw, even on his hands. His arms were awkwardly long. He reminded me of an old golden ape. On the other hand, he exuded all the characteristics of youth. His back was straight, like a bamboo tree; his movements, swift; and his cheeks, rosy, bumpy, and shiny, a sharp contrast to the smooth, olive complexion of my husband or the dry wrinkles of the old eunuchs. Most fascinating was the light blue of his eyes, as though the sky had reflected itself in the clear irises. I had never seen such blue eyes before, yet I could not stare at him very long for fear he would lose respect for me.

I suspected he must have dyed his irises with eye drops, perhaps to perform Western witchcraft or magic. There was nothing in his appearance of the grim darkness and melancholy of the sacrificing Jesus Christ.

My curiosity was satisfied.

According to the head eunuch, Sylvain Foucault did not want any picture of my daughters and me wearing royal attire and posing in the courtyard. Other concubines of the abdicated king Thuan Thanh could easily perform that task. Foucault desired a special scene for a special postcard. There could be no other convenient time to stage the scene than after the abdicated king had been dragged off his throne, leaving a bunch of dependents and descendants unattended and uncared for, disposable at the mercy of the protectorate authorities.

I could read Foucault's mind. He must have congratulated himself on the availability of the Mystique Concubine, the orphan paddle girl. I lifted my chin to the sky and thought of the mysterious Heaven that had set my life onto courses I could never have predicted. Once and for all, I wanted some control over my fate.

So I communicated to the head eunuch clearly what I wanted done.

I told the head eunuch I wanted a personal audience with the Frenchman who had sent my husband away. I wanted to move the lacquer divan to the open courtyard. A chair should be placed in front of the divan, far enough to create a noticeable distance, but close enough for conversation. I would be sitting on the divan, dressed in ceremonial attire. If Foucault wanted to change me into a postcard, he had to do it my way.

—

Dressed in the best of costumes, made of thick, heavy, crisp satin and brocade that completely hid my body shape, I sat on the divan in the middle of the courtyard from dawn until sunset to wait for Foucault. My burning rage intensified as the hours passed slowly and he was nowhere to be seen.

I had told Mai and Son La to come and get me when the sun died out, and if Foucault had not come by then, we would repeat the waiting game the following day.

I knew that from those half-moon windows overlooking the courtyard, the curious eyes of the concubines, their maids, and eunuchs were peeping out to watch me. Foucault's intention to use me in a postcard was known to Son La and Mai. It must also have been known to the petty gossipers of the Violet City, who were all dying to know my reaction.

Whether my exiled husband could be humiliated rested entirely in my hands.

When beams of sunlight turned yellow, signaling the end of the day, I cast my eyes across the tiled courtyard toward the half-moon window of my boudoir, where Mai would be raising the curtains and nodding her head. Just before I could adjust my posture to remove myself from the divan, I heard footsteps.

An imposing figure approached my lacquer divan from across the courtyard. Soon, I saw standing before me a tall, stout, thick-shouldered man dressed in a fitted gray outfit, a crisp white collar protruding from underneath, with an accenting red bow in the middle. The man wore high boots and a matching hat. Strands of brown hair protruded from the hat, and a pair of chestnut eyes. Like a cat's eyes.

The man resembled neither the golden-ape photographer nor the bearded Jesus Christ. He moved his stocky frame with the combined grace of a crawling python and a hungry leopard, and his fierce face, with its high-bridged, dominant nose and thick whiskers, exuded an intimidating, animalistic quality. Under the brocade gown, my shoulders felt weak. I moved my perfumed fan and averted my eyes to maintain my composure. I did not want him to think I was afraid.

I had expected to see an interpreter, but Foucault was alone.

"So this is the famous Mystique Concubine," he said in Vietnamese, his voice deep and throaty, with a perfect Tonkinese accent. He stopped by the chair I had set up for him, sat down, and crossed the muscular columns of his legs, his coarse and bulky hands resting on the chair's arms.

I had set up the chair, knowing that the Frenchman in charge of Annam would not kneel down to kowtow the way a eunuch would. I had also deliberately ordered for the chair to be situated at a distance from my lacquer divan, but still close enough for conversation.

The man shifted his gigantic body as though the chair were too small for him, unbuttoned his sleeves, and rolled them up. I noticed the fuzzy brown hair on his arms. Another ape. He was everything my husband was not.

"I expect you to say the proper greetings, now that I know you speak our language so well," I said.

"D'accord," he said as he stepped out of his chair and bowed. "Thua ba, my lady." As he sat back down, his eyes fixed on me as though they were grabbing my limbs. "What are you doing sitting on that silly divan, wearing those bulky clothes?"

"What makes you think I would allow a Western man inside my boudoir? Especially the man who has just helped exile my husband!" I asked contemptuously.

"Suppose my photographer and myself had come to your boat on the Perfume River?" He was crude and uncultured, and did not speak to me with the refined and humble manners like the mandarins or the eunuchs. I didn't know what to say or how to act.

"*Thua ba*, right now you look incredibly beautiful because you are offended," he continued. "But I wish you would get off that divan and move around. You must realize the Annamese protocols do not become you."

I snapped the fan shut, enraged.

"I saw you getting out of your bridal rickshaw when you first came. I said to myself, what a fine woman, built like a Westerner, with hips and height and dark skin like us swarthy Mediterraneans. What a waste to have you in Buu Linh's possession. Your husband is a fool." He sneered.

My fan flew in his direction and hit his face, then dropped to the floor. For a moment, I thought I heard *oohs* and *aahs* from my secret observers behind those half-moon windows overlooking and circling the common courtyard.

The whiskered ape bent to pick up my fan. I was trembling. I had shown my temper. Despite hours of thought and preparation, I had not done the right thing. Would he kill me, as he had my husband's father, the late king Dai Duc, or would he exile me elsewhere off the coast of Vietnam?

The whiskered ape did not seem in the least offended. In fact, the whiskers rose and his thick lips pulled into a smile. He stretched his body in the chair and eventually bent down to pick up my fan. He turned it back and forth to scrutinize it.

"Dainty little thing. Like all things that belong to poor Buu Linh and his dynasty. I wished he had not acted up so badly. The three of us—Buu Linh, yourself, and I—share one thing in common. We all have a bad temper."

"Stop talking that way about my husband," I said sternly, "and live up to the refinement of the French Empire." I was remembering how Son La had educated me about the empire of France and thinking of all those missionaries who had come to our land and befriended the earlier Nguyen Lords.

"The refinement of the empire is not my concern," he said. "My ancestors, like you paddle people, used to fish in the Mediterranean Sea and around the island of Corse before they moved to their castles in Loire."

He was mentioning places I did not know, and again, my sense of power collapsed.

"Don't turn down my photographer's lens too quickly. See first what photography can do for you." He stood up from the chair, reached inside his gray trouser pockets for some kind of object, and approached the lacquer divan. I folded my arms defensively, but he stopped at the edge of the divan, where the wings of the carved phoenix rested. I breathed out a sigh of relief.

He bent forward to hand me some glossy cardboard squares. I was curious enough to reach for them, as they might have an impact on the future of my children. Strangely, the beast did not withdraw his hand. He seemed to hold on to the squares for too long. Unexpectedly, the tips of our fingers touched slightly under my wide brocade sleeves. The contact seemed to linger on for a second as though he had deliberately caused it, and I frowned with irritation. This ape had no sense of propriety or respect for the royal court that had created my identity.

Again, I felt helpless. I was at the mercy of this man.

My curiosity took over, however, and I examined the squares. They were pictures and not drawings. These were things I had never seen before. From the scenes portrayed, I imagined an array of vast sapphire seas and pink or white castles—a manner of majestic grandeur completely different from my Perfume River and the West Palace

"You are an enticing belle, but I have no interest in Buu Linh's women. Twittering Annamese birds." His whiskers pulled up into an enigmatic smile. "I'm more than twice your age, more than old enough to be your father. I have a purely commercial interest in mind."

Again I was struck by his accent, which was that of a native Tonkinese speaking standard Vietnamese.

"A wealthy European acquaintance of mine has expressed an interest in making postcards of the royal concubines inside the palace," he said, waving his arm as if shooing away a fly. "He's fascinated with the Annamese camisole, *cai yem*, so different from the Victorian lace corset, but it's got to be worn by a genuine royal concubine. The caption will read 'Bath of a Royal Concubine.'" As he announced this, he wrote the words in sweeping gestures across the sky before him.

I remained silent.

He went on. "Some say perversion. Some say art. Some say a taste for the exotic. I say my patron will be paying lots of money to the Foucault gallery. A view of you in this royal setting would be perfect. As a former paddle girl, you're most likely not too prudish."

I was correct. He had picked me because of my past.

"Nothing complicated, nothing too out of line." He raised my fan to his nose, inhaled, and closed his eyes. He looked like a monster in repose. "Just a picture of your naked back, the profile of your face and hair next to a royal blue porcelain sink of steaming water, maybe among a gaggle of little maids or eunuchs.

Have your photograph taken in a second or so, and you will be well fed for the rest of your life."

He handed me my fan and I turned away. The fan dropped onto my divan. I would not touch what he had touched.

Thoughts rushed through my head while I pretended to smooth the corner of my costume. "Very well, then," I said, enunciating each word. "If the refinement of your French Empire is not your concern, neither is the State of Annam my concern. After all, I am Cham."

I paused to let this sink in.

"Above all, I want to live. Disobeying you, I suppose I can be killed. So here I am. In the open courtyard. If you want your postcard, take my picture this way. You know the whole Violet City is watching right now. Go get your photographer. Send your men and women and set up your scene. But I will sit here, dressed like this. It will be a struggle to get all this fabric off me. You will have to drag me around to get the kind of picture you want. Capture my image and you will see on paper the scene of a woman dragged against her will. This is the only way you can have my picture taken."

In the clear brown of his eyes I could see the flame I had ignited. I saw also the reflection of the bright redness of my gown. I threw his pictures back at him. "If you had come to me on the Perfume River," I told him, "I would have knocked you off my boat with my paddle."

His eyes seized mine in rage. I did not move.

I continued, sharply and proudly. "Your predecessors came in here and dug up the late emperor's tomb for treasure. Now you come in here and want a wife to undress and smear the honor of her husband. These are acts of spoiled children, barbarians who carry weapons. I was just a paddle girl, but I can tell you when an act is barbaric."

His brown eyes had turned glacial, and they were affixed on mine still, his whiskers vibrating furiously over his tightened lips. I watched the Western man rise and walk away as the last ray of the afternoon sun died out on his gray suit. I shivered.

His face had become the Face of Brutality.

14. CONQUERING THE FACE OF BRUTALITY

The following month, the head eunuch made a special announcement. The eight-year-old Prince Vinh Quang, son of Bang Phi, the Concubine of Egality, would soon be crowned the new king of Annam. The selection of Vinh Quang had already been endorsed by the French Protectorate Government. Prince Vinh Quang was the youngest of my husband's twenty-eight sons, believed to be the most docile. For the coronation, the troop had to fetch him. He was crawling under a table.

The French *résident supérieur* had also made the decision to cut the royal budget. Because Thuan Thanh had abdicated, certain of his concubines and children would have to leave the Violet City. My name was at the top of the list.

The head eunuch had a meeting with me to deliver a short and impersonal message. I could keep all of my jewelry. I could take the lacquer divan as a token from my husband. Acting on Mai's advice, I had hidden the jade phoenix beneath my camisole.

No allowance would be coming from the court or the protectorate government. I would have to find a means to support myself, my daughters, and my two servants. In preparation for my departure, the head eunuch had asked me to choose a new place of residence. He showed me a map of the outskirts of Hue.

In those few seconds, I envisioned the life I wanted for my daughters. The Perfume River was my origin, but my daughters would not paddle passengers across rivers.

I looked at the map, and the name Quynh Anh caught my attention. I had heard the name of the small hamlet from Son La's opera network. A quite famous opera troupe had started there. Since I had learned to read, I knew Quynh Anh as a literary name with its roots in ancient Chinese, meaning the crystallized essence or glistening spark of a dewy flower that blossomed at night and opened its petals into the early morning hours. I thought of my encounter with my husband under a full moon on the Perfume River and of how I had stood at the window, night after night, hoping to find the same moon hovering over the Violet City. I asked the head eunuch about the village of Quynh Anh. He said the villagers raised silkworms and produced silk of the finest kind in central Vietnam. Quynh Anh was also the birthplace of several scholars and officers of the court, among whom are a mandarin of the first rank, Hong Lo Tu Khanh, who had served as my husband's astronomer, and Nguyen Tung, the admiral of the Vietnamese Royal Fleet, which guarded the Port of Thuan An before the arrival of French colonists.

I asked the head eunuch for details about the duties of these two officials. Despite the French presence, the Nguyen kings continued their tradition of Te Nam Giao, an annual ceremony that took place in the outskirts of Hue, in which the king would pray to Heaven for the good of his people. The king's astronomer was responsible for organizing the ceremony in accordance with the configuration of stars. The Vietnamese Royal Fleet existed in name only, although Admiral Nguyen Tung was still in command. The French, with their cannons, gunpowder, seagoing vessels, and navy force, controlled the port.

These two court officials had a reputation for their integrity and loyalty to the monarchy. They made their birthplace, the village of Quynh Anh, famous. I envisioned them as the future teachers and father figures for my two daughters. And my son. I could build a life for my children in the village of Quynh Anh if I learned to profess the silk trade. What's more, from Quynh Anh, I could always count on Son La's opera network to help keep me informed on the fate of Annam. After all, my son—the son of the only royal concubine to whom King Thuan Thanh had entrusted the dynastic jade phoenix—would certainly be the crowned prince of Annam.

So I told the head eunuch I would like to move to Quynh Anh, and I would trade my jewelry for gold taels, enough to buy myself a small silk farm.

———

It is my last night in the Violet City.

I stand by my half-moon window to take one last look.

I cannot forget the whiskered face of Sylvain Foucault, his chestnut eyes, and the threatening anger they hold.

I know outside, the Face of Brutality is still waiting.

PART THREE:

WHAT HAPPENED TO THE FEMALE WARRIOR?

SIMONE

1. AFTER THE SÉANCE: THE MISSING AUNTIE GINSENG

(Hue, Vietnam, 1965)

"Wait, and wait patiently..."

The message from the Mystique Concubine, spirit of the Perfume River, spoken by Mey Mai, stayed on with me.

We were on the way back from Mey Mai's séance, and the cyclo passed by the lotus ponds again. I immersed myself into the mass of twinkling pastels and fell into a full, heavy sleep. Among the lotuses, I saw the edge of brilliant green jade in the shape of a phoenix, standing against the flying golden dragon. The phoenix sat on the chest of a woman who looked like Grandma Que. With her eyes closed, she floated on a mossy green river sparkling under silver lights. Her red brocade smock opened up and floated on the water like a parachute, and gradually turned into a slender boat. And then the boat changed into the shape of a coffin. A floating coffin.

"The Mystique Concubine, Her Royal Highness, please wake up and talk to me," I whispered with all my heart, imitating the voice of Mey Mai. I watched her dark lashes until they moved and her eyes flew open.

"Wait patiently," she intoned.

I woke up as the cyclo came to a sudden stop at the familiar white colonial villa under the shade of a tall magnolia tree. Grandma Que lifted me off the sedan and led me into the house, passing by the row of orchid baskets hanging in front of the French bay window.

"Home!" Grandma Que called. "Look how beautiful—and built by the Mystique Concubine herself!"

———

After dinner, Grandma Que retired to her quarters on the other side of the courtyard, and I knocked on my parents' bedroom door. The door swung open and I announced immediately that I had met the Spirit of the Perfume River. I repeated Mey Mai's words: there would be another massacre in Hue during a Lunar New Year celebration, and I would escape from it.

Dew, my mother, the only daughter of Grandma Que, was sitting on a sofa before a fruit bowl, peeling a guava. She dropped the knife.

My father, who had opened the door for me, frowned. "You'll be escaping all right, young lady—from all this nonsense started by your superstitious grandmother." Ignoring the hurt look on my face, he turned to my mother. "Your mother took the girl to a séance inside the Citadel."

He darted out and I stayed on with my mother. She had bent over to pick up the knife from the floor. Her fingers trembled upon the handle. She did not look at me, and her silence meant that she was deep in thought. I told her that I was sorry to have been the source of any trouble, and she assured me that it was not my fault.

"Was it Grandma's fault, *Maman*?" I began to cry.

"No, no, no. Of course not."

She told me that perhaps my attending Mey Mai's séance was something destined to happen, sooner or later, and she was trying to figure out a way to explain this destiny to my father, who would never understand.

Standing by my parents' bedroom window, I looked out to the interior courtyard and saw Grandma Que's quarters lit up. She met my father on the porch. I flung the bedroom window wide open and craned my neck out to listen better. It was obvious my father was not giving any deference to the Spirit of the Perfume River. He accused Grandma Que of spoiling my mind with super-stition, and she accused him of acting like a Western man who paid no respect to ancestors. After a while, they were both talking at the same time.

I rushed into my bedroom and shut the door. I went to bed, and within moments I was seeing small ripples on the surface of a river under the clear, bluish moonlight. I was walking along-side the river, inhaling the freshness of rainwater and the clean, natural scent of tree bark and red soil. I drew into my lungs the pungent scent of betel juice and dried *boket* nuts when their bean shells were broken. I gazed into the calming water. Its darkness became a velvet cloak stretching across to the other side of the river, where I saw the almond shape of a paddleboat moving slowly and silently in the hot air of a tropical night.

———

That summer, I spent most of my time wandering in the garden, chasing butterflies and reading folk stories underneath *longan* trees. I devoured plenty of *longan* fruits; my hair and shirt smelled like syrup, and my face and hands were perpetually sticky from *longan* juice. Between feasts, I thought of the woman lying in the red coffin, and I whispered alone under the patchwork shade of those trees.

"The royal Mystique Concubine, please let me see you again," I prayed.

Occasionally, she would appear in that open floating coffin and speak to me. A few times, she even stepped out of the coffin as it turned back into a boat. She took my hands and led me onboard. The boat carried bundles of sparkling silk threads. Two little girls sat among the bundles of silk. They were about my size and looked identical in their black silk trousers and pink blouses, with matching pink bows on their hair.

The Mystique Concubine smiled. "Meet my twin daughters, Ginseng and Cinnamon," she said.

But before I could say hello, one of them fell into the water and disappeared.

"It was Ginseng who fell. She was always the careless one," sighed the Mystique Concubine.

—

A few weeks later, my mother caught me crying one day under the *longan* tree and asked me why. I shook my head, and she took me inside the house and wiped my face with a steamed cloth. She told me not to be silly, and it was about time I should begin acting like a big sister to set an example for my younger siblings, Mi Chau and Pi. The steamed cloth sent heat through the pores of my face. I leaned my back against my mother's lap for her to wipe my neck.

"Cinnamon is Grandma Que, but where is Ginseng?" I asked. "I think she fell into the Perfume River and died."

"Who gave you that idea?" My mother sounded alarmed.

"What happened to her, then?" I asked in my tiny voice.

My mother frowned and said nothing. She began fiddling with the corners of the steamed cloth. A moment of silence passed before she took my hands. She led me to her bedroom and we both lay down. One of her arms became my pillow. With her other hand she waved a straw fan slowly over my swollen face as she talked.

"I was named Dew—Beautiful Dew, Mi Suong, the purest kind that clings to flowers at night and in the early morning before sunrise. Aunt Ginseng picked the name for me before I was born, before she was sent to Hoa Lo, the death row prison in the north for revolutionaries and patriots of Vietnam. I only saw her twice; the last time was right before she died."

That night, I learned from my mother how the soul of her only aunt, Princess Ginseng, had blessed the magnolia tree.

DEW

2. AUNT GINSENG, DAUGHTER OF THE REVOLUTION

(Hue, the Protectorate State of Annam, French Indochina, 1949)

The first beautiful woman I met in my life was my own mother. The villagers of Quynh Anh called her Princess Cinnamon. The silk merchants called her Madame Que. I called her Ma.

The silk traders and villagers of Quynh Anh who came to the house to take orders from Ma and to help her prepare festivities for ancestor worship ceremonies said the skin of her cheeks was smooth like porcelain, glazed with a healthy sheen of pink, like lotus petals. They said the stream of her black hair was shinier than polished lacquer, and they compared her slender frame to the loveliest of willow trees that bent graciously in the strong wind without breaking. They alleged that as a young girl, Ma once took a nap under a magnolia tree, her stream of black hair spreading around her head, emanating the fragrance of cinnamon oil, which she loved. A snake was enticed by the fragrance and crawled into the stream of her hair. Struck by the beauty of Ma's face, the snake became spellbound, frozen as though it had seen a goddess. When Ma woke up and moved her head, the snake silently crawled away. Even the meanest of creatures would be awed by Ma's beauty, they said.

I was the ugly daughter of a beauty. The silk traders and villagers said I was a cute and nice little girl, but no one described me in terms of porcelain, lotuses, lacquer, or willow trees. My nose was too flat, my mouth too full, my skin so pale it almost reflected a bluish shade. Only my eyes resembled Ma's, which the traders and villagers compared to *longan* nuts in autumn ponds.

Ours was a household full of women and no men. Ma had all kinds of domestic help, all coordinated by Nanny Mai; like a fortress of humans, they surrounded Ma, catered to her needs, and supposedly protected her. Yet, unknown to Ma, the servants gossiped, feeding me with information about certain things. For example, the servants disputed the traders' overblown ideas about Ma's beauty. Even Nanny Mai would join in and agree that Ma was not anywhere as pretty as the Mystique Concubine herself. Or Ma's twin sister, my aunt Ginseng.

Ma told me the Mystique Concubine had died at the height of her beauty, falling into a deep slumber from which she never emerged. Her soul just simply flew away, escorted by nightingales. Ma was twenty-four years old when the Mystique Concubine passed on. Aunt Ginseng had already left home, too busy fighting in the jungles of north Vietnam to return home for her mother's funeral. Like Lady Trieu of ancient Vietnam fighting the Wus from China, Auntie Ginseng wore her golden armor, pointing a sword to the sky, riding an elephant. Every little girl born in Vietnam (even a product of French elementary school like me) knew the legend of Lady Trieu, who pledged she would ride the wind to save her people from drowning in slavery. The enemies were looking for Aunt Ginseng all the time, so I had to keep the secret that I had an aunt who had followed the footsteps of Lady Trieu to fight a war that would liberate the people. I was never to mention Auntie Ginseng to anyone outside the household.

"I don't understand why your mother has to tell these tales," Nanny Mai said one day. "Your grandmother died in a fire in the middle of a war, and your auntie has been in a French jail up north for having spied for Ho Chi Minh troops. There's no such thing as a young woman riding elephants nowadays."

When I repeated Nanny Mai's words to Ma, she went after Nanny Mai and slapped the poor woman in the face. "How can you betray me so?" Ma uttered through clenched teeth.

Nanny Mai collapsed into tears and apologized over and over again. Seeing the red marks on Nanny Mai's cheeks, Ma knelt down on the floor and begged for the nanny's forgiveness, apologizing to the woman who had helped raise both her and me. Shocked to see Ma on the floor, Nanny Mai asked me to ignore the bad stories she told me earlier, saying she was very sorry to have confused me, confirming that indeed my aunt was a woman warrior riding elephants like Lady Trieu and that my grandmother died on her lacquer bed, in her sleep. I watched the two grown-ups with amazement and amusement. I knew, even then, that not only did Ma have beauty, but she also had a genuine, fierce flare for the dramatic.

———

Despite the number of female servants, Ma insisted on doing certain things herself. Like taking care of the altar room.

It was in the altar room that my father, an Annamese mandarin, presided together with his father, the Hong Lo Tu Khanh, a first-rank literary officer and astronomer of the Nguyen Court, next to Admiral Nguyen Tung, who had adopted Ma. They all "lived" in an array of black-and-white photographs framed in rosewood carvings, which Ma polished every day with fresh lemon juice to make the rosewood shine.

All photographs and silk paintings were placed lower than the photograph of my emperor grandfather, King Thuan Thanh of Annam, taken at his coronation. Later, I discovered the same picture had made its way into history books. My grandfather had become a legend in Vietnamese history as an exiled, anti-French king, admired by generations of Vietnamese patriots. But in the picture sitting in that smoky altar room, my emperor grandfather looked like a boy and did not seem much older than I. He didn't even seem all that handsome or smart, just a dazed boy dressed up in fancy clothes. At least he was a real person. His wife, the dead Mystique Concubine, on the other hand, was preserved in a silk portrait. There were no photographs of her anywhere. In the silk painting, she looked surreal, and I could not imagine her face.

Much later, there was a time when I turned sixteen and was about to leave home to study at the French *couvent* in the highlands. This was a costly and complex arrangement that Ma had taken great pains to accomplish, since the *couvent* wasn't for just any girl. Before I left, I asked Ma whether she loved my father. She looked at me as though the question was totally inappropriate, as if love were a concept meant to remain unspoken forever.

I couldn't remember exactly when Ma first took me to the altar and made me learn those names and faces of those dead men, including my father's. In early childhood when the children I played with asked me where my father was, I would say automatically that he was on the altar. Ma would burn incense every day and place plenty of fresh fruit there. The ancestors' spirits could only consume the fruit symbolically, so I got to eat it all, getting all the blessings of my ancestors by devouring their leftovers, each time Ma rearranged her tray. My mother discouraged me from eating all that fruit, which had become holy offerings to the dead. But I still devoured those offerings behind her back.

—

Three items on the altar received Ma's special attention. She polished them with cinnamon-scented oil and covered them with a satin red silk cloth. I often watched her handle them with utmost deference. Occasionally she let me touch them. Just a light touch. The bright green jade phoenix that shone under candlelight, and the two ivory plaques, each bearing carved red Chinese characters, spoke of Ma's royal and mandarin heritage. The jade, as well as the elephant tusks from which these plaques were made, must have been thousands of years old, Ma said. The older they were, the prettier they got. The phoenix, a gift from King Thuan Thanh to his Mystique Concubine, identified my grandmother as the uncrowned queen of Annam. The two ivory plaques were like ID cards, held by my two mandarin grandfathers, commemorating their lifetime career and loyalty to the Nguyen Court.

When I touched the items, the coldness of the jade and ivory sent chills up my spine. To reach them, I would have to stand on the lacquer divan, studded with mother-of-pearl inlay, imposingly situated in front of the altar table.

On the altar were two rosewood frames that remained empty. Ma reserved them for Aunt Ginseng and Uncle Forest. She polished the empty frames the same way she polished the dead men's photographs. She said her sister and brother had left home. Either they would return one day, or they would become spirits to join the ancestral altar.

"Why did they leave home?" I asked.

Ma pulled me into her lap and whispered the stories to me. There was an airplane circling the air over the village Quynh Anh once, and a young village girl, friend of Auntie Ginseng, had taken out a handheld mirror she always carried in her blouse pocket. French soldiers thought she was trying to send a signal to anti-French rebels so they could shoot down the plane, so the French soldiers shot the young village girl. Aunt Ginseng saw this. She became mad. So she left home to make sure no innocent young girls would ever get shot again.

Uncle Forest, on the other hand, left for an entirely different reason. He had been raised not only by his mother, the Mystique Concubine, but also by his adoptive father, Admiral Nguyen Tung. The old admiral died the same year Uncle Forest turned eight years old. Years later, after a devastating flood swept through the village of Quynh Anh, the family had to move the admiral's skeleton to a new burial ground. The admiral's remains were uncovered, and the young Forest got to hold the skull of his adoptive father in his hands. Something touched the core of his soul during the experience. He made his decision then. He left a note for both my grandmother and Ma bidding farewell, announcing that he'd be joining Auntie Ginseng somewhere in the north. He even wanted to go to Japan to study the Japanese experience of industrialization and decolonization. That was what both his biological father and adoptive father would have wanted him to do, he wrote in his note.

The year was 1925. My Uncle Forest was fourteen.

—

"What do Auntie Ginseng and Uncle Forest look like?" I asked Ma.

"Like Lady Trieu and Thai Hoc the Patriot."

It was easy for a young girl to get a notion of Lady Trieu, because even the maids who couldn't read a newspaper would talk about the gold-armored woman. It was not as easy to get acquainted with Thai Hoc the Patriot.

"Did he look anything like Napoleon?" I asked once.

"No, no, no, no!" Ma's voice was shrill. "Not at all! Napoleon was French!"

I was disappointed. Napoleon was the conqueror, the patriot, the greatest man of all men.

Something must have clicked in Ma's head after my question that day. She abruptly withdrew me from French Catholic school to enroll me at Lycée Dong Khanh. I had to sit through an examination first, and to the best of my recollection, I did very poorly. The maids in the house gossiped that when one was the daughter of the richest woman in Hue, one got admitted wherever one wanted to be! There, on the steps of the red brick schoolhouse called Lycée Dong Khanh, a group of older students showed me a leaflet with Thai Hoc the Patriot's face on it. I formed my first notion of Uncle Forest then. On the leaflet appeared a short-haired, square-faced man with a trim moustache and bushy brows, looking out grimly at me. He was no Napoleon, but he had his own appeal.

The students told me Thai Hoc the Patriot led a revolution and died at twenty-six years of age on a French guillotine before I was born. Before he died, he said something like, "If a man does not achieve success, at least he achieves a legend." That's what I remembered from the tales told by the older students. In my mind, Thai Hoc the Patriot died, so he became a legend. So, to me, legend must mean death. Death was what happened to a man who led a revolution and achieved no success. Only those who succeeded lived.

At least my matriculation to Lycée Dong Khanh helped me understand why Ma left those two frames blank. Auntie Ginseng and Uncle Forest left home to become legends. They could be dead at any time. Then, they would join the spirits that became my roots, my home. Meanwhile, I was to keep another secret. I wasn't supposed to mention Uncle Forest or his noble mission to anyone outside the household. I did not want Uncle Forest's enemies to capture and guillotine him like in the case of Thai Hoc the Patriot. I pledged to myself I would keep my lips sealed.

3. WHITE MAGNOLIA

Growing up with Ma in her ancestral house on the slope of Nam Giao also meant getting to know her magnolia tree in the front yard. It was Ma who had taken care of the tree day after day, making it grow so tall and spread its leaf-heavy branches over the roof, sprinkling white petals over the front yard. The tree became the benchmark of how far I could go back to my earliest memory of living with Ma.

Ma said white magnolias reminded her of Ginseng. As a young girl, Auntie Ginseng often picked a magnolia bloom and placed it next to her face. She would cock her head and pretend she was being photographed like a silver-screen star of the West. The translucent white petal shone onto her young skin. And then Auntie Ginseng would take the bloom and place it next to the Mystique Concubine's face to compare. Mother and daughter would laugh, and Ginseng would throw the bloom at Ma, asking Ma to do the same thing. Ma would refuse just to irk Ginseng.

Ma called Ginseng the magnolia thrower of the house. At times, Ma said, the magnolia thrower would lick off the fresh drops of dew on the white petals.

"Sweet, sweet, sweet," she would claim, licking her lips.

Ginseng said when she grew up, she would get married and have a baby girl, whom she would name Dew. Not just any Dew, but the best of Dew. Mi Suong. Beautiful Dew. Ma took Ginseng's idea for a girl's name and gave it to me, her own daughter. So that was the origin of my name.

Of course, as a grown woman, Ginseng had no time for a baby because she was busy wearing golden armor, even wooden shoes like Joan of Arc. My aunt pointed her sword at the sky and rode giant elephants in the misty jungles of North Vietnam.

—

I was grateful to the absentee Auntie Ginseng for having come up with such a beautiful name for me. Ma told me that before Auntie Ginseng left home to join the Revolution, she wanted Ma to get married some time and to have a daughter. Ma was to name her firstborn daughter Dew. My aunt knew that as the warrior, she would be giving up the dream of having a daughter of her own. That was the sacrifice she would have to make in order to pursue the cause for the people. My aunt wanted Ma to fulfill the dream Ginseng had to abandon. I was that dream.

I was equally fascinated with Auntie Ginseng's riding elephants. But occasionally, I questioned how she could throw those dainty magnolia blooms around like table tennis balls. At times, I sadly concluded that Ginseng must have had a mean streak in her to treat magnolia blooms that harshly.

The big blooms rested tender in my hand; those ivory petals were large enough to fill a porcelain winter melon soup bowl that could feed five adults. Ma would place the blue-and-white translucent bowl out on the mossy porch to collect rainwater. Every day, she would pick a fresh bloom, severing it from its long, grainy stem with a pair of scissors. She would float the cut bloom inside the bowl and place it on the rosewood altar table. The floral scent filled up the room, lingering upon the ivory lace curtains and the edges of the dark furniture that shone with lemon juice.

Much later, I fell in love and married a philosophy student at Sorbonne whose nom de plume was L'Espoir, the French word for his pen name "Hope." When he brought home to me my first bottle of Christian Dior perfume from Paris, I sat dumbstruck until I could recall what the scent reminded me of: the cut magnolia blooms that permeated Ma's altar room.

—

I imagined, too, the flowers would turn into a woman's face, smooth and white like magnolia, with painted brows like two slanting ink strokes, just like in the silk painting that hung in the altar room and supposedly captured my grandmother, the Mystique Concubine. The woman's face that I imagined as the metamorphosis of a magnolia bloom became my notion of my grandmother, the Mystique Concubine of the Violet City and the matriarch of my family, a household consisting of women and no living men. Through generations, Ma said, we, the women and young girls of the ancestral house, would be bound together by that absentee woman, in her silk portrait.

I imagined she would evaporate into a tiny stream of air, traveling so lightly from her silk portrait to the porcelain bowl. There she would then transform herself into the bloom of magnolia floating in the rainwater that smelled like the early morning dew on the perspiring glass window behind the curtains. And then, like smoke, she would curl herself out of the bowl, her long black hair floating behind her back. Like Ma, she wore white silk pajamas, the soft fabric reminding me of the rich, smooth texture of the white petals that covered the ground of our front yard.

In that dark altar room, I imagined my grandmother would float through the dark space, her naked feet suspended slightly above the tiled floor. At times, my three dead grandfathers would also come alive, walking out of the black-and-white pictures that held their images. The emperor boy would pull my sleeves, making me bow. The two old men—a paternal grandfather and an adoptive maternal one—would approach me, placing their dry hands on my forehead and dragging their long, curled fingernails across my temples like the touch of a dry bamboo branch.

And I would faint.

Of course, Ma knew nothing about my fantasy. She would think I was impious.

The fear and excitement combined made me regard the altar room with both love and awe. Most of the time, I avoided the altar room by spending my days in the front yard, drunk in the sweet smell of waxy blooms. They were mine and not just Auntie Ginseng's little table tennis balls.

But soon, I discovered that, just like Auntie Ginseng, I had my own mean streak.

When the white blooms fell like rain onto the damp ground, I picked them up and placed them in a bamboo basket. I had a little shovel and, one morning, tried to replant those blooms into a flower bed that followed the half-moon shape of my bedroom window, directly underneath it.

I wanted to create my own magnolia tree.

In the process, I never expected to see those pitiful earth-worms. At the sight of them, I threw the shovel and ran back to the house. The reddish-brown creatures were shaped like chopsticks, yet grotesquely soft and wriggling. They could crawl through the cracks between my fingers. My shovel had stabbed them in half, each half still corkscrewing through the dirt as though gasping for life.

Inside the house, I held my dirty hands together and stared at my palms. I had seen earthworms living and dying. A tear fell into the middle of my joined hands; in my palms, I saw a clear little pond in which I could still imagine shadows of the reddish creatures wiggling in despair. Even in death, they still moved. I cried into the pond of my palms because I knew I had killed them.

Yet I would do it again, trying to plant my tree. I had become obsessed with the idea even though I knew the planting of my dream tree had killed, and would continue to kill.

In the only two times I met Aunt Ginseng, I never got a chance to ask the thrower of magnolia blooms why she did such a thing. What was so compelling that she had to pull a petal apart, the same way I had to stab earthworms to get to my version of a dream?

———

The first time I met Aunt Ginseng, it was in the middle of an autumn night, yet the air outside was full of fog. It was the day of the "August Moon Festival" in the lunar calendar, which, under the Western calendar, occurred late in the month of September. We were supposed to get a clear, full moon.

I had eaten lots of greasy sesame cakes during the day and woke up in the chill of the night, my eyes catching the stream of that festive moon from the open window. I was busy listening to the rumbling noises in my stomach, concentrating all of my attention on my belly. In the stillness of the night, I realized that the window was wide open. It was the fog that had gotten inside and made me sick. It had got into my belly button and given me a stomachache. I turned over on my stomach and hid my face into the pillow. From the corners of my eyes, I raised my eyelids and glanced upward at the window frame.

Ma was standing outside the window, holding the lantern, staring back at me. Ma, standing still, behaving oddly and strangely dressed. She had on dark cotton pajamas and a funny-looking, unattractive, green hunter's hat. Her eyes were fixed on my face, intensely, like a stranger. Her hair was divided and tightly woven into two Chinese braids, hanging on both sides of her face, protruding from the hat rim. The lantern flickered in her hand.

I noticed she was not wearing the green jade bangle and the gold carved bracelet, which had been blessed with the holy water of the female Buddha Quan Yin at a temple. Something was not right. Ma wore that jewelry all the time, even in sleep.

The intensity of her glare was so haunting I could not continue looking at her. I had to close my eyes again.

And then the terror struck.

It was not Ma at all at the window frame. It was a stranger I had never met. She had Ma's face.

———

I must have fainted for a few minutes. When I regained consciousness, I remained frozen in fear. I opened my eyes again and the first thing I saw was the empty window frame. The woman was gone.

I heard voices coming out of the altar room, racing and competing. Ma was speaking to another woman. It must have been the stranger whom I had seen at my bedroom window.

"She betrayed all of us," the stranger said.

"Don't say that about your own mother," Ma was pleading. It was strange to hear her voice choked and weak.

"You and your bourgeois life, think of the sufferings of this country!"

"But I am your flesh and blood!"

I got out of bed and left my room. The voices became clear and clearer. I was approaching the altar room. I pushed lightly on the door, already ajar. I peeped in. The room was well lit. All lights had been turned on, and all lanterns and candles were burning.

There were two of Ma in the room. But no, there was only one Ma. My Ma in her ivory silk pajamas, her dark long hair falling to one side, the jade bangle and gold carved bracelet circling her wrists, the velvet slippers enclosing her feet. The other woman, a replica of Ma, was everything I did not want Ma to be. If Ma was a willow tree, the other woman was a bamboo shoot. In the black pajamas and rubber sandals, she looked and acted like a foul peasant—somehow too robust, too monstrous. And she was yelling at my Ma:

"Face up to reality! Your revered mother slept with the enemy for wealth and security…People are dying every day, and you are well fed! Why?"

Ma's hands covered her face.

"You know what the irony was, sister?" the replica continued. "It was Foucault who secured my release. Without him they would have executed me along with Nguyen Thi Minh Khai, the first Vietnamese woman to join the Party in Moscow!"

I pushed on the door and stepped in. "Stop yelling at my mother, you monster!" I screamed hate at her. "You scared me at the window!"

The two versions of Ma turned toward me simultaneously, both standing awkwardly in front of me, as though they had been caught stealing.

I burst out crying. The two versions of Ma stood there and watched.

"Dew, meet your Aunt Ginseng," Ma said softly, brushing her long fingers through my entangled hair.

I looked at the woman who was supposed to be Auntie Ginseng. There was no gold armor. No wooden sabots. No pointed sword. Just a dark-skinned version of Ma in coarse peasant's pajamas and an ugly hat.

"Come here, Dew," she said, extending her arms, her eyes softened and her voice soothing.

"No."

"Don't be sullen, Dew," Ma said. "Your aunt has come back home for a few minutes. Just a few minutes. She is fighting a war for the good of all of us, remember, like Lady Trieu."

The unwelcomed auntie was approaching me. I could smell her peasant smell, like dirt and rainwater and wild cuckoos and roosters. I turned away, but she got me just in time. I struggled against her embrace but finally yielded to her warm hand and amazingly soft touch.

"Hello, Dew. I saw you sleeping from the window," she said, her voice sturdy and friendly.

"Where's your gold armor?" I asked.

Aunt Ginseng chuckled. "In here," she said, pointing to the middle of her chest. "My gold armor is in here."

I looked at her face and acknowledged the resemblance. In close proximity, she was indeed my Ma. The exact same face, except the skin was coarser and darker—a shade between amber and brown sugar.

"I'll give you something to replace the gold armor," she said, reaching inside her blouse pocket and displaying in her palm a pebble. "I found it in a stream near the Chinese border. I saved it for you."

I stared at the tiny pebble, the size of a peanut. It was a very pretty pebble, multicolored and smooth.

"Look closely at it. It gives off golden light, see?" she said.

I looked, and she was right. I saw the golden spark. Maybe she was right. Maybe the pebble had Lady Trieu's gold armor in it. Maybe it was magic.

"I love you very much," she said. "I have to go before sunrise."

And then she let go of me.

———

So that was how I met my only aunt. Aunt Ginseng came and went like a ghost, a dream, a wind, between the midnight moon and dawn, in all that fog. I could not decide whether to love or dislike her. For one thing, she had made Ma plead. I knew, however, that the servants were right: Auntie Ginseng was very beautiful, even in those dirty looking, ill-smelling black pajamas and funny hat of hers. The amber-brown-sugar skin shone like the color of light from the lantern she held in her hand the moment she left us. Yet, she could not be as beautiful as my Ma. She was never graceful like a willow tree. Ma said wherever Ginseng went, in that long journey of hers, her fate was probably with the goddesses of Vietnam.

I kept Aunt Ginseng's pebble in a little satin bag that used to hold Ma's pearl strand, and from that day on, I thought of Aunt Ginseng in a different light. She was no longer the elephant rider but instead a lone traveler who chopped down bamboo logs and walked through muddy ponds, in humid whirling winds, across winding streams that held golden frogs and silver trout. There, she collected golden pebbles for me. Lady Trieu's golden armor had shattered into pieces that sank into the bottom of those streams and turned into smooth pebbles. The woman warrior with braided hair, clad in black pajamas, jumped from tall trees like a leopard and crawled through marshes like a crocodile.

4. A WAY HOMEWARD

In a way, I wished Aunt Ginseng had never come home the second time, so that I could continue dreaming about her as the black-clad tigress whose fate belonged to the Vietnamese goddesses.

But she did return home the second time. And the last.

The years passed and I reached my teens, eventually celebrating my fifteenth birthday in 1949. The news of Aunt Ginseng's return arrived in the summer of 1949 in a telegraph from Tonkin. Ma started crying after reading it, almost hysterically, and then the household was suddenly animated because Ma ordered the servants to make preparations. Weeks of preparation, anticipation, and celebration ensued. Ma announced to everyone in the house that although Aunt Ginseng had been captured again and imprisoned for years at Hoa Lo—that infamous prison in the north—the protectorate government had finally pardoned her. This was more understandable since, at the turn of the century, the progressive liberal socialist Albert Sarraut came into power as governor general of Indochina. He had implemented more humane and liberal policies in the colony, and had become the hope for many Vietnamese intellectuals.

So, my aunt Ginseng, the female warrior, would soon return home to rest.

And since my aunt would come home soon, Ma joyfully announced, perhaps we would soon be hearing from Uncle Forest. Ma's eyes sparkled, her voice rose an octave, and her words started running together with the excitement of an earnest child. The prospect of a reunion between the three children of the Mystique Concubine became the rejuvenating potion that made Ma a new woman.

Hopes were high and preparations, lavish. Ma hired teams of seamstresses to cut, sew, and embroider silk and linen for Aunt Ginseng. A new bed was built by the carpenters out of rosewood. New lace curtains were made. Dried birds' nests were stocked in anticipation of her homecoming, for the preparation of a special kind of nutritious soup to help improve her health.

I was still going to school daily. The students of Lycée Dong Khanh talked about my aunt's release, confirming to me my aunt was indeed famous. Every day after school I came home to Ma's joyful eyes and the house's bubbling, festive spirit. Her laughter rang in the air as she paraded around, supervising the teams of cooks and seamstresses. She wanted everything to be perfect. Weeks went by, and Ma's happiness was almost too full and her animation, too high.

I came home from school one day to an abnormal silence. No light had been lit, and the house was absolutely quiet, as though the heat of the desert had brushed through the air.

I went into the new quarters set up for Aunt Ginseng and found Ma sitting alone in the dark. All the servants had retreated to their own quarters. The door to the bedroom reserved for Aunt Ginseng was left ajar.

"Don't go in there, Dew. Your aunt has come home and needs to rest," Ma said quietly, as though she had no energy left.

I dashed my eyes around, knowing something had gone wrong. Very wrong.

I pushed the bedroom door open. The room, decorated with hanging silk scrolls, lace curtains and satin blankets, was empty. I stood in the middle of the room, bewildered and upset. And then I heard someone speaking, out in the interior courtyard, together with the sound of uneven footsteps.

I rushed to the courtyard and found her, the shadow of the woman who had come home. Ma had followed me, trying to catch up.

"Dew, your aunt is very ill."

The shadow turned around and I had to jerk back. I found not the young, vivacious woman in black pajamas who had yelled at Ma and had given me a pebble, but a stooping, limping old woman with dead eyes and a scarred face. Parts of her brows were missing. She stared at me without seeing me.

"Do you have a womb and a pair of breasts?" she asked.

I approached her and grabbed her hands. The wrists, too, were full of scars. One little finger was missing.

"Do you have a womb and a pair of breasts?" she repeated.

"Don't listen to her, Dew; she is not herself," Ma said.

I felt her face. No longer that amber-sugar-brown skin. The scar tissue rubbed against my fingers. She smiled. The mouth was crooked. I noticed, too, part of her upper lip was missing.

I let go of her and stood dazed while Ma tried to catch the disfigured woman and bring her inside. She faintly resisted but still managed to push Ma aside. Limping on her foot, the old woman ripped off her blouse. Under the dying twilight, I saw scar tissue on her breasts. The nipples were missing. I covered my eyes.

The topless woman was singing strings of senseless words.

"Do you have a womb and a pair of breasts?" she finally sang the question like a chorus.

———

Ma had forbidden the servants to come in. That night, I helped Ma feed Aunt Ginseng her bird's nest soup, and then we washed her together in the porcelain tub, rubbing a hot towel over her scarred and nipple-less breasts. I felt her rough scar tissue, thinking of the smoothness of white magnolias. My tears dropped onto her shoulders, and I could not make a sound. Ma was biting her lips all the time. She did not cry.

That night I sat by my bedroom window looking out at the magnolia tree. Aunt Ginseng was singing her question like an imbecile.

I saw Ma walking the front yard under all that moonlight. She circled the magnolia tree several times, bent to pick up blooms from the ground, and placed them next to her face. And then she threw them at the tall tree. She repeated the gesture several times, and I watched the white petals scattering around her.

I called out to her, and she turned toward the window where I sat. I could see her face under that moonlight. It was full of tears.

"I will not take this, Dew! I will not!" she yelled, competing with the sound of Aunt Ginseng's gibberish singing from inside the house.

"You and I, Dew, we will write Albert Sarraut!" she went on yelling. "We will write Sylvain Foucault in Paris!"

I saw Ma spring forward and then fall to the ground, among all those white petals. I climbed onto the window and grabbed the iron rods, my hand reaching out to her.

From the bed of white magnolias covering the damp ground, Ma looked up at me.

"They've butchered my beautiful sister. They've destroyed her mind."

——

In the following weeks and months, Ma prohibited most of the servants from entering my aunt's quarters. Caring for Aunt Ginseng became the exclusive task of Nanny Mai. Ma and I wrote letter after letter, and Ma started making trips to Saigon and Hanoi to present my aunt's case and press for the prosecution of her torturers. She contacted newspapers and hired translators to prepare papers to be sent to Paris. I had never seen Ma so feverish.

While Ma was away for her trips, I cut magnolia blooms and floated them in the porcelain bowl. I cleaned the rosewood frames with lemon juice and burned incense sticks. Aunt Ginseng would limp around the house singing her favorite line. She took off her shirt at least once a day, displaying her disfigured torso and smiling her crooked smile.

I no longer dreamed about Lady Trieu's golden armor or the black pajama tigress. My aunt had come home, but my perfect notion of an unbeatable female warrior was tarnished. As it turned out, the former governor general Albert Sarraut did not respond to Ma's plea for justice, and my uncle Forest never came home to join his sisters.

The return of my disfigured aunt in 1949 imprinted tragedy onto my otherwise peaceful, well-protected life. Understanding the tragedy became my entree to the turbulence of Vietnamese history. That summer, I learned that in 1945, while I celebrated my eleventh birthday, safe and secure in Ma's big house in Hue, the Vietminh occupied the Opera House in Tonkin up north and declared independence for the country. But France returned to Indochina shortly thereafter, and the Vietminh fought the French. My aunt Ginseng and my absentee uncle Forest became legends in that war. They were among the famous sons and daughters of the Vietnamese Revolution. But to me, my aunt Ginseng became my notion of tragedy, and my uncle Forest remained just a name. Their pictures never filled the empty frames in Ma's well-polished altar room.

After the summer of 1949, I lived through the Revolution and greeted my young adulthood in the false sense of protection offered by Ma's beautiful house and its beautiful garden. In my growing ambivalence about my sheltered existence, I watched the dying days of French colonialism. In 1954, the Vietminh won the war, at last. Defeated in the battle of Dien Bien Phu, France let go of Indochina, leaving space for the Americans, the Chinese, and the Russians.

And another war ensued, allegedly against the Americans, making Vietnam famous.

———

During the summer of 1949 when Aunt Ginseng stayed with us, no one in the house spoke very much. But in all that sadness, fate found a way to make me believe, again, in the mystical relationship between my aunt, me, and Ma's magnolia tree. It happened one night when Ma was away from home, somewhere in Cochinchina or Tonkin, searching in vain for justice and for a forum to prosecute the colonists' crimes committed against her twin sister.

I woke up in the middle of a summer night, feeling the heat coming from outside. I saw the window open, framing imbecile Ginseng's scared and crooked face. The moon was hanging behind her. Apparently she had wandered into the front yard and had pushed my window open. She was staring at me, with a lantern in her hand, just like the first time we met.

"Come inside, Auntie; you are letting in the heat," I said.

She did not respond, the lantern flickering in her hand.

I reached out for the satin bag underneath my pillow, where I had stored her pebble, and showed her the stone. "Remember this?"

She was still staring. I approached the window, holding the pebble against her lantern, the iron rods of the window frame separating us. "See this? The golden shine. It's a piece of your golden armor, Auntie."

She grabbed onto the iron rods to scrutinize the stone in my hand. "It's yours, Dew," she said.

Oh, Heaven, she had just called me Dew.

"I am Dew, you remember?"

I was overjoyed. My aunt was lucid. "You named me, remember?"

"Of course I remember. You are Dew, my niece. I am in Hoa Lo, behind bars, and you've come to visit me."

My aunt had regained at least part of her memory. I wished Ma were here to see for herself.

"You are no longer in prison, Auntie; you are home now," I said, and she nodded.

I rushed to the front yard and took her to her bedroom. She began taking off her shirt.

"Don't, Auntie!" I took her hands and led her to the mirror. "You are a lady. Don't take off your shirt."

I sat her down in front of the mirror and combed her coarse, prematurely gray hair. I divided her hair into halves and made two braids.

"Remember how you came home the first time? You had braided hair like this. You were very beautiful then."

She stared at herself in the mirror, motionless.

"You are still very beautiful, Auntie," I hurried on, wanting her to feel good. She looked at me with the gaze that exposed my lies. I looked down to the floor in shame.

"Can you keep a secret for me, Dew?" she said, dreamily.

"Yes, I would do anything for you, Auntie," I responded without thinking.

She reached out for my shirt pocket and removed the pebble. Very swiftly she put it on her tongue and swallowed. She was quick and determined and I was too stunned to react. Then, her eyes dilated while she choked and coughed violently. I screamed out, but the door to Aunt Ginseng's bedroom was tightly closed, and the servants, including Nanny Mai, were all soundly sleeping in their own quarters separated by the interior courtyard. My aunt put one hand over my mouth and the other hand over my throat. For a moment, I could not breathe. She was smothering me. We struggled for a while until she calmed down, letting go of my throat. We collapsed together.

But the pebble was just the size of a peanut, and it had not hurt my aunt, although I knew she would eventually get sick. Lying next to me, the invalid woman began to talk.

"Dew, that's the secret. I just swallowed the secret. You promised you would keep a secret."

"You are ill, Auntie. I need to tell someone. You need to go to the hospital. That pebble—"

"No I won't, I won't go anywhere. I am home, remember? This is where I grew up. I won't be sick anymore. I just swallowed Lady Trieu's armor and it stays with me."

I stared at the tissue around my aunt's crooked lips. The ragged flesh vibrated together with her speech. My aunt was not crazy. Not at the moment. She knew what she was doing.

"To get this secret, Dew, they would have to cut open my stomach, and I won't let them. They already pierced my womb and cut my breasts, Dew."

"Auntie, please." I winced. "Don't talk about it."

"But I have to, Dew, I have to talk. I have to."

I got up and rushed out. I went to my room and locked the door. I left my aunt alone.

—

I heard noises from her quarters all night. Strange, shrieking noises. Furniture being dragged on tiled floor, cloth torn by hand, without the aid of scissors.

I did nothing. Nothing. I just sat by the window and stared out at the magnolia tree under all that silver moonlight. Hours passed and then I saw my aunt limping out to the front yard. Just as I had seen Ma the night of Ginseng's homecoming. The servants were all in their quarters and nothing could stop Ginseng.

"Where is your gold armor, Auntie Ginseng?" I whispered from the window.

My very ill aunt Ginseng had all of a sudden become very strong, and she was dragging and moving chairs to the yard all by herself. She tried to pile them up beneath the magnolia tree.

She struggled. She failed. She fell. She got up again. She limped around until she achieved what she set out to do. She was very skillful and determined. After all, she was the female warrior who had pursued Lady Trieu's dream. She had picked up the golden pebble for me from a stream, and she had kept going until they pierced her womb and cut her breasts. And then she swallowed the secret and made me join her.

So I joined her by watching from my bedroom window. She dragged the lace curtains into the yard with her, and then she climbed on the pile of chairs and reached out for a strong branch. She knew how to pick the strongest of all branches like an expert. No matter what, she had come home.

The lace curtains Ma's seamstresses had sewn for Ginseng's homecoming flew around the disfigured woman who reached out for the magnolia tree. And then she became the falling bloom herself, dangling in the air, forever, until the moonlight caught her and off she flew. I knew it was too late. And I, her beautiful dew, sat by the window and watched. The same way I had watched the earthworms die.

The air was still and cool, as though my aunt had brought back the fog.

I left my aunt fluttering in the night and went to the mirror and took off my shirt. I saw a skinny girl, so pale her skin was almost tinted blue. I was no female warrior and could only hold a shovel. My world was confined to Ma's front yard and the steps of the red-brick schoolhouse called Lycée Dong Khanh.

I imagined myself without nipples and a pair of stabbed breasts and wondered how it felt to have darts of hatred pierce through my womb. When streams of blood flowed, they would permeate the ground and come to life as reddish earthworms. I whispered to Auntie Ginseng that I wanted neither the footsteps of Lady Trieu nor the solitude of Ma, who was always waiting. I whispered that for the rest of my life I would just plant, plant, and plant. I promised Auntie Ginseng that I would give her the best of magnolia trees bearing the smoothest petals so the young cheerful girl could pick them and throw them around like table tennis balls, in ripples of laughter surrounding a peaceful childhood.

I brought my palms together and formed a little pond, in which I could see the wiggling helpless earthworms stabbed to death, their blood smearing all the lace curtains that circled and strangled my aunt. I went to bed while white magnolias danced around my aunt, drops of dew gathering on her damp skin, healing scars and softening rough tissue to make her beautiful like the past. I let her be.

I placed my head onto the pillow and realized I had never asked my aunt why she loved throwing magnolia blooms. Out there, I knew she would find a way to tell me, somehow, sometime, and she would not blame me for sitting and watching. After all, it mattered very little why she did what she did. To me, in the end, she had chosen to return home.

To her magnolia tree.

PART FOUR:

HUE, SAIGON, PARIS, AND MANHATTAN

1. THE CHILD PERFORMER AND HER NIGHTINGALE

(New York City, 1990)

Like most young girls growing up in Vietnam, I learned of the ancient country's golden era through fables and myths. In the beginning of history, before the Hans' arrival on the plateaus of the Red River, Vietnam was a tribal society ruled consecutively by the eighteen Hung kings. This went on for two thousand years, a long time of peace, harmony, and tranquility before border wars erupted and the Hans took over the Viet peninsula, commencing the age-old border conflict between China and Vietnam.

Back then, as early as 4000 BC, the daughters of Hung kings were called Mi Nuong. The word *mi* symbolizes a Vietnamese princess from the peaceful Hung era. Grandma Que took great pains to instill in me the pride that we were descendants of Huyen Phi, the Mystique Concubine of the Nguyen Dynasty. Grandma Que wanted to be sure that in memory of our ancestors, all female descendants would have compound first names beginning with *mi*. My mother was Mi Suong, Beautiful Dew. She married a commoner, so her two daughters bore a last name that was not royal. Yet we both inherited the *mi* in our first name—I was named Mi Uyen, Beautiful Lovebird, and my younger sister Mi Chau, Beautiful Gem.

Grandma Que frequently talked of the kind of inner beauty *mi* signified—the aesthetic of the soul that transcended the physical world. At a minimum, the first name beginning with *mi* would always remind us to conduct ourselves with the kind of decorum worthy of our royal past.

As a young girl, I did not feel the need to learn the *mi* origin of my name. It did not help solidify my sense of aesthetics, decorum, or the business of the soul. I thought, instead, of a note on my piano. *Mi-mi-mi-mi*. I equated the *mi* sound with pure, vibrating sounds that began with the closing and opening of the lips. When the lips were gently brought together and then opened upon a breath, the air brushed slightly outward, and the sound was delivered with the softness of a caress.

From the beginning of my existence, I was a child in love with sounds.

———

In the summer of 1990, my mother called me in Manhattan to wish me happy birthday. I had turned thirty-five, and tiny lines had appeared underneath my eyes, yet my mother still thought of me as the twenty-year-old former beauty queen of Saigon's College of Law, a maiden who once practiced singing.

"You know I won't sing 'Happy Birthday' to you," she said. My mother was tone-deaf. "You, on the other hand, have both Truong Chi's colorful voice and Mi Nuong's face," she added ruefully.

Mi Nuong, the daughter of the eighteenth Hung king, fell in love with the singing voice of Truong Chi, a fisherman whom the princess had never met. He lived by the river across from her palace, and sang every day at sunset. His voice mesmerized the princess, who became lovesick to the point of being bedridden. King Hung summoned the man with the beautiful singing voice to the palace, in hopes of saving his daughter. But Truong Chi was so physically ugly that upon seeing the face that trapped his beautiful voice, the princess quickly recovered.

I thought perhaps Princess Mi Nuong never fully recovered. Disappointment and a death wish must have remained with her. One could never recover from facing the contradiction between life and dream, between ugliness and beauty, between our need to live and our dark desire to perish. The poor man's ugly face must have mirrored certain ugly parts of the princess's soul, and she must have lived on with that discovery. The unfulfilled love story between a Vietnamese princess and her Quasimodo always invoked in me the urge to sing.

—

I thought of the soprano voice as a nightingale flying into a limitless sky, surpassing the stilted confines of a human life.

In childhood, my voice once lingered around the high *do*, the C on the right hand side of my piano keyboard, and then I managed to reach the high E, the *mi* note, spelled like the beginning of my first name. Then, it's beyond the *mi*. At some point, I was prepared to go all the way to the high A, the *la*. The sound traveling like a silk thread reaching the sky—the flight path of the nightingale.

This was how I tried to reach the full soprano range.

Yet, by my thirty-fifth birthday, I knew I would never become an opera singer, a diva, and I would never reach a perfect A, the high *la*. It would always be a struggle to deliver that high note with perfection. In Vietnam, I was once a young girl practicing the scale. In America, I became a lawyer instead. The nightingale I once knew had forever left.

The nightingale came to me quite early in life when I started singing after the radio at five years of age. We were living in Hue at the time. Then, the stretching of the voice seemed so natural and effortless, and I was free to follow my nightingale when its wings lifted the heaviness from my chest and flapped air into my lungs. My mother said I sounded like a clear bell.

Those days, my mother took delight in training me on my stage gestures. She supplied me with the handkerchief, telling me how to hold it with one hand while swaying my little body. I was to raise the other hand in midair, and then to press it against my heart. At times, I would tilt my head to one side and place my cheek on my palm while waving the handkerchief to my mother with my other hand. "Slower, slower," she would tell me. "There you go!"

We made a good team, combining the natural instinct of a five-year-old and the creativity of a young mother. By age five, I was already performing for my mother and her guests from Lycée Dong Khanh, where she taught literature. Everybody at her tea parties told her what a precious child I was.

My mother was not surprised that I sang so early in life. She had always said the gene ran in the family, despite the fact that my mother could not sing. So, where did my voice come from? Everyone took it for granted. A theory was implicitly shared among my relatives and the women of Hue that the fabulous voice would reappear and that someone along the bloodline would be destined to sing. It was just a matter of time before that bell-like voice resonated again, linking the past to the present.

Everybody in Hue knew that my great-grandmother, the legendary Paddle Girl of the River Huong who later became the renowned Mystique Concubine of the Nguyen Dynasty, had sung all her teenage life on the River Huong.

I could not remember exactly how I first acquired the story of my great-grandmother's death. In one version of her life story, the storytellers of Hue maintained that my great-grandmother's fabulous voice attracted the young king of Annam, who came to her boat to hear her sing and to take her to the palace, where she was ordained a royal concubine at fifteen years of age. But the French protectorates exiled the king to Africa, and my great-grandmother—that legendary singing queen of Hue—stayed in Hue and died in loneliness. Since his exile, she was a queen without a throne, a singer who no longer sang, and a beautiful woman without a lover.

The day my great-grandmother died in Hue, I was told, nightingales gathered all around her bedroom window. Her eyes were still cast forlornly toward the violet horizon beyond the window, in hope of her husband's return. It was then that her heart stopped beating. The nightingales all mourned the voice they shared with her. Death forever silenced it.

I was told, too, that on the day her spirit departed, the waves of the Perfume River awakened and sparkled into tingling sounds. Someone even said that the moon dropped tears onto those sparkling waves. The moon's teardrops hit the surface of that Perfume River, creating a vibrating chord. In the symphony of nature, my great-grandmother's spirit went away, but the inhabitants of Hue predicted that her spirit would return. Her voice was destined to come back one day, and one of her descendants would sing in her place.

That descendant was supposed to be me, the wide-eyed child who sat on the steps of a miniature stage in the Tan Tan portrait studio in Hue, serene and self-composed, with a silk bow on her hair. When I turned five, to prepare for my celebrity singer status, my mother took me to Tan Tan, the best photography studio in Hue. She had me sit demurely with my hands together under my chin, or posed me in a dance, with my knees and feet together a certain dainty way so they could form the shape of leaves underneath a rosebud. I learned to stand and sit like a flower.

The inhabitants of Hue claimed that at five years of age, I was already acting like a queen.

—

Tales were told to me throughout my childhood in Hue, and by the time I reached my teens, I had turned into a hopelessly romantic young girl—naïve, of course, and melancholic. When I sang Vietnamese folk tunes, I thought of the moon, the waves, the Perfume River on the best nights and days, and the image of my beautiful great-grandmother lying motionless in death while nightingales gathered around the frame of her half-moon bedroom window.

In 1960, the radio also played the Twist and rock and roll, imported to South Vietnam from America. At five years of age, I already instinctively wanted to sway to the wild music. With the help of my teenage aunt, Y-Van, my father's younger sister who was living with us at the time, I began to perform the Twist for families in the neighborhood. We were living in the only apartment building in Hue, the two-story Phu Cam complex on Nguyen Truong To Street, the main thoroughfare that connected the Phu Cam Church across the Ben Ngu River to Hue University, where my father taught.

I remembered the Phu Cam Church by its stark orange dome and multiple spikes that combined a touch of European gothic with the ancient East Asian architecture. To my eyes in those days, at sunset, the church turned bright orange, its spikes edged against the low sky of sleepy Hue. The brown bridge that swung across the dark green Ben Ngu River resembled a pathway that flowed right into the church, which appeared still and stagnant, like a painting of primitive colors and minimal strokes. The Phu Cam complex housed Hue's middle-class families, including officers in the South Vietnamese army and teachers at various high schools and the university. Everyone at Phu Cam was pretty much up to date on Western culture—primarily French and American, communicated to us in the popular French magazine *Paris Match*. All youths at Phu Cam welcomed the arrival of the Twist. Apart from the Twist, the girls also idolized beautiful Jackie Bouvier Kennedy, with her square jaw, distinctive chin, and deeply set brown eyes that were too far apart, quite often hidden behind those world-famous signature sunglasses. Auntie Y-Van trained me on the Twist, as well as on how to recognize Jackie in *Paris Match*.

My Twist performances started with Aunt Y-Van's network of boyfriends. Sixteen-year-old Y-Van loved to hang around college students and senior high school boys, and there were plenty of them at the Phu Cam complex. Somehow she managed to brag about my talent to their families, who all loved to watch the cutest little girl of the Phu Cam complex wiggling her body. A typical performance consisted of the following steps: first, Aunt Y-Van would bring me into a family's living room, and all of the family members would sit in a circle. Then, someone in the family would put an Elvis Presley record on a turntable, and I would do the Twist. I earned money doing it, at the suggestion of Aunt Y-Van, who collected a piaster from each member of the audience. She acted as my agent, promoter, and manager. My performances were always in the afternoon, after my nursery school. Aunt Y-Van was supposed to baby-sit me until my mother got home from Lycée Dong Khanh.

The pop culture of America reached Vietnam through the radio in the early sixties and helped establish me as a legitimate professional child performer, one who earned money as well as applause. Yet all this time, my mother thought I was only singing popular Vietnamese love ballads and the folk tunes of Hue—a testament to the reincarnation of my great-grandmother's eternal voice.

2. TWIST—LOVE BETWEEN GENERATIONS

I could never forget a Vietnamese Twist song named "Love between Generations" (*Tinh yeu giua hai the he*). The lyrics went like this:

> *When you were twenty years old,*
> *I was just born.*
> *When you turned forty,*
> *I reached my glorious twenties...*

Aunt Y-Van taught me the lyrics for special performances, when my childish voice took over and the turntable was closed, and I sang and danced at the same time, without accompaniment, except for Aunt Y-Van's clapping hands and her boyfriends' whistling and expert finger-snapping to mark the beat for me. For these special performances, my earnings for the song were increased from one piaster per audience member to two. Aunt Y-Van kept the money, promising to deposit all those bills into a clay pig so that when I grew up, I could have money for my first *ao dai*—that silk, fitted bodice Vietnamese tunic worn by young women, slit high on both sides such that the lank flaps seemed to hug the girl's legs. Serious singers, Aunt Y-Van said, wore their silk *ao dai* over white pantaloons when they sang love songs in Saigon's nightclubs, in contrast to Twist and rock-and-roll singers, who wore black miniskirts and stiletto shoes called *escapin* in French, upon which they pressed their pointed toes to the floor to do their Twist.

Needless to say, I never saw the money. Before my sixth birthday, the precocious Aunt Y-Van was sent to a secondary boarding school in Dalat called "Couvent des Oiseaux." It was known in Vietnam that the *couvent* in the Dalat highlands was the most proper place to train Vietnamese debutantes. Aunt Y-Van kissed my cheeks, shed a few tears, gave me my clay pig, and told me not to tell anyone about our Twist performances. I cracked the clay pig one day and found only a few coins inside. I saw none of those green paper piasters I had earned by yelling at the top of my lungs while swaying my hips.

Much later, after we had moved from Hue to Saigon, I once asked Aunt Y-Van what had happened to my clay-pig money from those days in Hue, and she looked baffled, not knowing what I was referring to, although she remembered how cute I was doing the Twist in front of her neighborhood boyfriends and their families. I asked my mother, too, whether she ever discovered I was doing the Twist for money in those days, and she laughed and gave me no direct answer, saying instead that Phu Cam was a close-knit community in sleepy Hue, and people always talked about how cute and talented her daughter was. She also gently reminded me how Aunt Y-Van had been shipped immediately to a boarding school in the highlands in the summer of 1960, so that the Catholic nuns could reform her into a proper *couvent* girl, one who should repent for having spent little niece's clay-pig money on silver fingernail polish. To the best of my knowledge, Aunt Y-Van never reformed. In California, the sixty-year-old Aunt Y-Van still wore silver fingernail polish even when the dotted freckles of old age had appeared on the top of her bony hands.

Later on, in America, at alumni parties, Auntie Y-Van always talked proudly of her brief stint at Dalat's Couvent des Oiseaux, how she played tricks on those devoted, stern-faced French nuns dedicated to the reform of wild, rosy-cheeked Vietnamese girls. For example, Aunt Y-Van once put a *Paris Match* clipping inside the Bible and placed it on the desk of La Mère Superieure. The clipping was of a voluptuous and topless Brigitte Bardot appearing in *Paris Match*, covering her breasts with her crossed arms and puffy hair. "*Et Dieu créa La Femme*" (And God created Woman)—the precocious Vietnamese teenager wrote the name of Bardot's film across the chest of the sensuous French star.

3. THE FRENCH VILLA
ON NAM GIAO SLOPE

After my aunt Y-Van was gone, my father—the bookworm professor of Hue University—decided to divert his attention from his books to his parental role and my education. He enrolled me in a French Catholic school, the Jeanne d'Arc Institute. At Jeanne d'Arc, I was given the name Simone. The nickname "Si" (my parents' way of shortening Simone) came with weekly piano lessons given by an old French nun called Sœur (Sister) Josephine. When I was left alone in a practicing room, my mind often wandered away from the scores of my music book, *La Methode Rose*. My fingers went from songs such as "Au Clair de la Lune" and "La Valse de Venice" to the popular love songs of Vietnam in the sixties, which I heard from the radio and learned to play by ear.

That same year, I turned six, and we moved from the Phu Cam complex to Grandma Que's old villa in Nam Giao, a suburb of Hue.

My earliest memory of Grandma Que was of her dark eyes, her heart-shaped lips painted with deep red lipstick, and the quiet silhouette of a slender woman, with long hair rolled up into a bun. She dressed in black silk and satin and walked around on velvet slippers without making a sound, as though she simply glided among muslin curtains, carved wood pillars, delicate bamboo screens, rosewood chairs and divans, and the bowls of cut lotuses floating in water that graced the top of her shining lacquer tables and cabinets.

The highlight of Grandma Que's altar room was her huge, dark brown cinnamon log, sitting in a porcelain pot and emanating the spicy and pungent scent that characterized, according to her, the forests of central Vietnam. The hunters from the Quynh Anh hamlet, where she had been raised, had given the cinnamon log to her as a gift of longevity, since her given name, Que, meant cinnamon. The hunters had searched out the oldest cinnamon tree in the deep jungle of the Quang Tri province. The tree was supposed to be hundreds of years old, paralleling the development of the region. Grandma Que believed that magic originated in the deepest part of the jungle, where old trees took on holy and powerful spirits.

Nam Giao was a hilly area glutted with green. The villa, located on Princess Huyen Tran Street, had a front yard with beautiful trees, the tallest of which was an old magnolia tree giving off white flowers. The front yard merged with the luscious green grass surrounding the villa. The open green area, studded with flowers and fruit trees, circled the white colonial structure, keeping it in shade. There was a river across the street—not as large as the Perfume River, more like a stream—a body of calming, dark mossy green water that sparkled under the moon and stars at night.

Immediately after we moved into the ancestral house, my mother began to landscape our front and back yards. Grandma Que said my mother had loved gardening ever since she was a child my age; the shovel had always been her best friend. My mother read books on horticulture late at night, and I often hopped onto her lap, peeping at colorful pictures of flowers, leaves, and plants on those glossy pages. On the weekends, I was used to seeing my mother's slender back and her cotton hat rising and moving among those beds of soil she had built with her shovel. She hired an old man to assist her, and he usually followed her as she moved along the soil beds. She wore rubber gloves and stopped whenever she saw earthworms. Those poor creatures wiggled, fighting desperately for life against the remorseless shovel that stabbed them. The old man would stoop between the flower beds to remove them. I often sat by my bedroom window to watch my mother and the old man until my eyes grew tired and then my head would drop on the table. Quite often when I got up and rubbed my eyes, the two of them were still moving around in the garden while the sun slowly died out, its rays turning yellow-brown on my mother's slender back.

It took six months before our front and back yards blossomed with new beds of flowers. By the time the flowers bloomed, I overheard my mother tell the old man that soon the butterflies would come to land. She wanted to plant the violet French pensées and the blue Forget-me-nots, especially for me.

Planting those flowers in Hue would be a difficult task because those species of flowers needed the cooler climate of the highlands, the old man pointed out. The difficult did not deter my mother. "Those tiny flowers will be nice for Si when she grows up," my mother said. "She can put them inside her scrapbook. It's the kind of things girls want to do."

At night, I began to dream of chasing butterflies and picking violet and blue flowers out of my mother's flower beds. I ran wild in Mother's garden, even in the middle of a dream.

—

During weekdays I often took an afternoon nap after school, and when I got up, Grandma Que would feed me an afternoon snack, usually a French flan floating in dark, caramelized syrup, and then I would ride my bike and Grandma Que would walk along to accompany me. Together we traveled slowly down one of those slopes of Nam Giao, on Princess Huyen Tran Street, along the bank of that small, dark green stream. We passed quiet green areas and stately looking villas until Grandma Que signaled it was time to go back. On the way back to the house, we had to go up the slope, so she would push my bike, and I would put my feet up on the bike frame, almost to the steering wheel, no longer pedaling, laughing my six-year-old laugh. The first thing I smelled as we approached the villa was the sweet, overpowering fragrance of the white magnolias. Grandma Que said white magnolias often housed the spirits of beautiful women. The soft white blooms resembled a beautiful woman's face.

During those walks, Grandma Que also spoke to me. All those exotic phrases and concepts sounded so fascinating simply because they came from her heart-shaped lips.

"*Oan chi nhung khach tieu phong, ma xui phan bac nam trong ma dao,*" she said. It is no use to lament, those rose-cheeked, ill-fated women of the East, she explained. That was why the Mystique Concubine was so unhappy with her life as a royal concubine and encouraged her children to join the Revolution to challenge Heaven's mandate. Of her three children, Grandma

Que, as the oldest, had to stay home to take care of what constituted the family's heritage.

"Concubine…what's a concubine? Revolution…what is a revolution?" I kept asking, and she kept telling me to wait until I grew up a little more. Meanwhile, she pushed my bike by the saddle, up the slope, against the wind.

Before we entered the house, we would stand in front of the gate watching the sunset. A gust of cold air caressed my limbs when the reddish color of the late afternoon extinguished over the tiled rooftop, and darkness gradually spread upon the sparkling stream across the street and on top of all those green trees. And in that changing color of the end of day, Grandma Que would tell me stories of the Vietnamese princesses from ancient times. Five hundred years ago, Princess Huyen Tran went south to marry the Champa king so Vietnam could gain two provinces, in which lay the city of Hue. And that was why they named the street of our house after the princess, Huyen Tran Cong Chua. Two thousand years ago, Princess Mi Nuong loved the singing voice of an ugly fisherman and could not marry him. She could not bring herself to love the ugly man, just his voice. He, on the other hand, fell in love with her, the real Mi Nuong, and when he died of lovesickness, his heart crystallized into a piece of jade. The villagers carved it into a teacup and presented it to the princess as a gift. Saddened, she shed her tears into the teacup. At the bottom of the teacup appeared the lonely fisherman, singing his heart to her. The cup then shattered into a thousand pieces, signifying his broken heart.

"Why?" I asked.

Grandma Que explained that the fisherman's heart was broken because he loved so much and received so little in return.

I remembered becoming dazed just watching Grandma Que's serene facial expression. I saw how her eyes had become so remote. She was looking straight into the sun that had turned violet, telling me a day had ended. When the sun died, its reddish color faded, and one could look into the sun without hurting one's eyes, she said. When I pulled on the corner of her blouse, she shrugged slightly, removed her eyes from that violet horizon, and squeezed my hand. She told me Princess Mi Nuong was sad because she had expected perfection—that beautiful singing voice of a man she could never marry. Yet, the man's face did not match the perfection of his voice.

I learned then that perfection could be found in the singing voice.

4. ANDRÉ FOUCAULT
AND HIS BAUDELAIRE

When you were twenty years old,
I was just born.
When you turned forty,
I reached my glorious twenties.

I never thought the Twist song of my childhood could have foretold André's arrival in the summer of 1961 in Hue.

André Foucault materialized for me as the image of an angel. An angel, to me, was the product of wild imagination combined with the bits and pieces I had learned about God and Jesus Christ from Catholic prep school. I learned the contours of an angel the same way I learned the lovely French language—with the paradoxical mixture of fascination and detachment I usually held toward any Western product thrust into my life in Vietnam.

At school, the nuns made it clear that angels came from the sky. I was reminded of a nightingale that flapped her wings every time I sang—an image so pure, so far-reaching, so ethereal, so beautiful it could not exist for very long in mundane life, like that fleeting moment when my voice reached the high *la* note, then cracked or faltered. Angels and André fell under the same category as the nightingale that represented the fleeting possession of beauty in my singing. These precious things came into my life to deposit the silt of memory, and when I blinked my eyes, they were gone for good.

—

The day after my thirty-fifth birthday, I woke up in my Manhattan apartment alone in my bed, the urge to sing straining my lungs to bursting, yet I was unable to make the sound. André and Hue and those childhood performances and singing lessons all seemed so far away. My mind became my own Perfume River. On this bank of the river were America, Manhattan, law, and a jailhouse of memory; on the other bank were Vietnam, Hue, André, and my urge to sing.

I got out of bed that day and celebrated my birthday with the malaise of an aging dame. I tumbled to the bathroom, looked into the mirror, and found nostalgia in a pair of forlorn, ebony eyes. I saw a stranger's mouth that had ceased to laugh and when pulled into a forced smile, had lost any radiance of youth.

I bent my head over the sink, seeing the rich brown eyes of André and hearing the words of Baudelaire. *Ma douleur, donne-moi la main…Et, comme un long linceul traînant à l'Orient, entends, ma chère, entends la Douce Nuit qui marche…*I saw my six-year-old self lying on my back with one arm crossing my forehead, one leg up and my toes wiggling, drawing circles onto the misty air. The circles formed words of Baudelaire: *douleur* for pain; *L'Orient* for my home; *la Douce Nuit* for my Night; *linceul* for my mourning cloth for the angel who had departed. Pain, give me your hand. And, like a mourning cloth training toward the Orient, listen, my dear, listen to the footsteps of Lady Night.

At the dawn of a Manhattan day, I could hear the traffic on Fifth Avenue. In broad New York City daylight, I was listening to my Night, to the quietude that carried its own sound. Oh, my Night. Her sweet scent fell all over me. The Night spread and carried with her the words I had written onto the air with my wiggling toe when I was a child. André's words. Those words blossomed into Baudelaire's flowers of evil, his "Fleurs du Mal." Decades later, I folded and unfolded corners of my soul and filled it with those same words. I had to see you again, my memory. Childhood turned into dreams, with symbols of beauty stuck in a surreal corner of the mind, becoming spots of pain. André and Baudelaire, inseparable in my memory of Vietnam, taught me the meaning of pain. Oh my, my, my. I could stop breathing right at that moment and still hear words.

—

I started to think of myself as a woman who housed in her soul the myths of Indochina. Stories told by elderly women bound to me with blood ties thicker than fate. Up, up the ladder of the blood ties, and their stories told to me all became my own. Mysteries crystallized in my heart and made me into the keeper of memory.

At thirty-five years of age, I had become thousands of years old. As old as all those myths from ancient Vietnam.

Wrapping a woolen shawl over my shoulders, I rode the elevator down to the building lobby and walked the streets, my head flooded with memories of those hot summer nights in Vietnam and images of a beautiful man separated from me, not only by an ocean but also by twenty years of age. A man who had viewed my mother's tropical flowers in Vietnam as his Fleurs du Mal.

I stopped at a coffeehouse, smelling fresh bagels and blueberry muffins. I heard from the radio's classical station Beethoven's "Elegischer Gesang," Opus 118. "*Sanft wie du lebtest hast du vollendet, zu heilig für den Schmerz! Kein Auge wein' ob des himmlischen Geistes Heimkehr. Sanft, sanft wie du lebtest hast du vollendet.*" As gently as you lived, have you ended, too holy for grieving! No eye weeps, while your heavenly spirit returns home. Gently, gently as you lived, have you finished.

The sounds of Beethoven became the mourning for the departure of a noble spirit. I mimed the German lyric but could not sing, although the sound continued in my head. The sound chilled me and made me bend. I held my stomach in pain. Oh, André.

5. BIRTHDAY IN HUE

In the summer of 1961, all my mother's work in the yard was completed in time for my sixth birthday party, thrown for me in her newly landscaped garden. The kids at my French school, together with my former friends from the Phu Cam complex and children of our neighbors on Princess Huyen Tran Street, were all invited. I had never had a party like that before. My mother placed chairs and benches all over the front yard and arranged freshly cut summer flowers on a serving table full of my favorite food: sticky rice, syrup drinks, and all kinds of Vietnamese rice flour cakes and French sweets like *gâteaux au rhum, bonbons, petits-beurres,* and *choux à la crème.*

My father had tied colorful balloons to all the trees. I was busy blowing a balloon. When I looked up, I saw a tall, brown-haired man walking through the front gate toward me. He was one of those Frenchmen from *Paris Match*, walking out of the magazine. He moved underneath the shade of the magnolia tree, his shoulders slightly tilting to one side to avoid the drooping branches. Like Santa Claus, he carried a doll and a big bag. For a moment I thought the French nuns' angel was descending upon my life, bringing with him lots of toys, including French dolls with golden hair, who could sing and speak small French phases in a whisper.

He continued crossing the front yard where the kids were playing, the only European, lost yet standing out, towering amid a bunch of Vietnamese children and adults, a lean, muscular frame and broad shoulders under an ivory cotton shirt. Even with the tan, he was lighter than we were. I noticed those deeply set eyes and the delicate bone structure that defined the high bridge of his nose, bony cheeks, and square jaw. From my corner, I ran up to him, craning my neck to look up at his face. I noticed, too, a dimple in his bluish chin. (I found out much later that such a bluish shade was the trademark of a well-shaved man.)

At that tender age, I knew he was beautiful. Like pictures of men wearing trench coats in Aunt Y-Van's *Paris Match*.

"*Je m'appelle Si*," I said, proudly introducing myself. Cute Si, *poupée* Si, six-year-old coquettish Si, as everyone in my family had described me. Si. Si. Si. Like the French word for a note on the piano.

"*Enchanté, mademoiselle*," he said with a smile and a sparkle in his brown eyes. "*Je m'appelle André*." He had just called me "miss," as though I were an adult.

"You are…so tall," I added, in what I thought was perfect French.

He bent and looked down closely at me, a look of surprise as though he had not expected to see me so close to him. His irises were pure chocolate. They smiled at me under thick lashes.

There was something else in his eyes, I thought. A sense of recognition. Much, much later, in Paris, he told me it was the recognition of a treasure long lost: he saw in me that day the eyes of L'Indochine. My tall angel put down the bag of toys, picked me up, and kissed me on both cheeks. He handed me the doll, telling me there were more in the bag. I touched his face, its cool smoothness reminding me of an orange with the finest of peels, silky to my fingertips. He smelled so nice, like soap, candies, lemon, a slight touch of cough syrup, and something else, too. It was a scent I couldn't identify, so different from the cinnamon scent emanating from the mandarin collar of Grandma Que, so distinctive from the fragrance of white magnolias that permeated the air. Only much later, well into womanhood, did I discover it was the smell of a freshly bathed, well-shaved man.

"*Elle est très jolie,*" he said as he turned to my father. Of course I was beautiful, I thought. Unlike my baby sister Mi Chau, who was almost bald, I was Si, a child with thick, long, black hair like a woman. Grandma Que went to great lengths to make sure my hair was beautiful. She sprinkled cinnamon essence on me. She boiled the *boket* nut and dipped my hair in its broth every day. (She had been using the same shampooing method on her own hair all her life, and at her age, her salt-and-pepper hair was still shining, falling to her kneecaps.) Whatever the broth did to my hair, it grew so long and thick my mother was afraid I would trip over it. Everyone in the family, except Grandma Que, was concerned I would not grow and would remain a midget because my hair had gotten too heavy for my body weight. Every day I had to get up at least one hour ahead of school bus time so Grandma Que could braid my hair and tie it with a bow.

My mother had moved the party to the backyard garden and had put some straw mats down on the grass. André volunteered to be my pony. All of the kids lined up, including my sister Mi Chau, but I got most of the rides. Everybody else was jealous.

There was a moment in the pony game when André, my pony, turned over on his back to take a rest. I was climbing onto him. I sat on his chest, laughing and laughing. I spread my legs, wiggled myself down to his stomach, and laughed some more. The next thing I remembered was a tremendous sense of affection when I was looking down onto his face. His hands were resting on my waist, and he was smiling at me. I could see the rose tip of his tongue and his shiny white row of teeth. Instinctively, I bent down to kiss the curvy corner of his mouth. When I looked up, his moving eyelashes reminded me of the evening butterflies hovering over my mother's flowers in the twilight of sunset. The day butterflies were colorful, but the evening butterflies were usually larger, in a somber brown or black. They gathered in the garden only at sunset or at night.

Trying to catch the butterflies, I touched his lashes, and he closed his eyes.

"Your lashes are curly, unlike mine." I touched my own lashes.

For a moment, André opened his eyes, and the evening butterflies fluttered their wings.

"*Oui, c'est ça, ma chérie. C'est la différence entre l'Est et l'Ouest.*" Where was East and where was West, and why did they have to be different? I toppled down off him and began to arrange my newly acquired dolls on his torso. I put my tiny hand underneath his cotton shirt, feeling the light brown fuzzy hair on his chest, his firm stomach muscle, and warm skin.

And then I remembered my old doll. The old doll looked like a miniature version of André.

Before André arrived with his selection of dolls, I had only one Western doll, given to me by Grandma Que's French physician. I rushed inside the house to fetch this old doll, eager to return for fear André would disappear. It was a boy doll, with short brown hair, dressed in a dark blue shirt and matching shorts. His plastic lashes could not move like André's. He carried a water bottle on a strap, and I often filled it with water, so his shirt was perpetually wet. I had had him for so long.

When I showed him to André, I told him that even though the new dolls were prettier, the boy would always be my favorite.

"*Il te ressemble, c'est un garçon*," I said, pointing at André, who was a boy like my doll, addressing him with the informal pronoun.

"*Oui, moi, je suis un garçon*," he said, acknowledging he was a boy.

"*Et moi, je suis une fille, avec les cheveux longs.*" I pointed at my long hair. Boys, like my old doll, had short hair and wore shorts. Girls, like me, wore dresses or silky pantaloons and had long hair.

"*Et toi, une fille très jolie.*" He stroked my long hair, confirming I was a beautiful girl.

The tender moment evaporated when Grandma Que appeared at the door opening onto the garden holding a fan, her silhouette edged against the bamboo curtain that dangled in the wind. Her arrival meant it was time to blow the candles and cut the cake. I would be singing a solo, "Au Clair de la Lune." In the last rays of the sun before dusk, Grandma Que stood still, staring down at the reclining André, who was trying to curl himself upward as I struggled to hold him down with my hands.

Grandma Que's hair was always rolled into a bun in the back of her neck, held in place with an ivory comb connected to a black silk net. She took the comb off, and her long hair fell to her side, almost touching her knees. When she moved, the stream of hair shook behind her like a holy animal. She wrapped the stream of hair around her palm, rolled it up, and held it back in place with the comb.

I knew her well enough to recognize this manipulation of her hair as a sign of her suppressed anger. When she was mad, she would let her hair down and then roll it up again, tighter than before, as though she was determined to hold her emotions in place.

"*Vous êtes le petit-fils de Monsieur Sylvain Foucault?*" Grandma Que asked.

"*Oui, madame, le plus jeune,*" André replied and finally sprang to his feet, sending dolls cascading from him. To Grandma Que he bowed, nodding, confirming that he was the youngest grandson of one Monsieur Sylvain Foucault.

———

Who was Monsieur Sylvain Foucault? I kept asking after that day.

It was a long, long time, years later, before my mother took me seriously and explained the web between André's family and mine.

André was the youngest grandson of a French colonist, Sylvain Foucault, formerly French *résident supérieur* of Annam, the top French administrator to watch over the Annamese Imperial Court seated in Hue. Monsieur Foucault disliked a young Vietnamese king, His Royal Highness Thuan Thanh, and arranged for the king's exile to the Island of Reunion in Africa.

The unfortunate king of Annam, I was told, was my maternal great-grandfather. One of his royal concubines was that paddle girl whose singing voice echoed over the Perfume River and whose spirit allegedly had become the nightingale that helped my voice soar to the sky when I tried to reach the high notes. When the king was exiled, one of his daughters, a baby girl named after the fragrance of cinnamon in central Vietnam, was barely five years old. The baby girl grew up and grew old, had a daughter named Dew who loved to plant flowers and a granddaughter named Simone who loved to sing, and they all lived happily in a villa in Nam Giao.

I knew who the king's daughter was. The villagers of Quynh Anh who came to our house to offer gifts on New Year's Day knew her as "Princess Cinnamon." I knew her as Grandma Que, the old woman who raised me, and whose sad eyes looked pensively into the dying sun when the day ended.

She was the woman who told me all those Hue anecdotes that became my soul.

—

I grew up learning about André in bits and pieces by listening to adults at lunches, tea parties, and dinners. André and his good looks were the favorite topic of discussion for my mother's friends, the women of Lycée Dong Khanh who congregated in Grandma Que's living room. I remembered the details about André's life even if I didn't fully understand them then.

An international lawyer who arranged the adoption of Vietnamese orphans and represented the European shipping industry, those days in Hue, André taught part-time at Hue University and spent his leisure time researching the ancient capital. He had sought out my father's help at the university. My sixth birthday was the occasion for my father to introduce him to the family. Born and raised in wealth, André had left Paris and the Foucault clan and moved to New York City with his American mother when she decided to divorce his French father. When America began to send troops to Vietnam, André had just graduated from Columbia Law School, and had taken a job with a shipping company controlled by his estranged French father for an opportunity to go to Vietnam.

André was in Hue to understand his paternal family's ties to Indochina, and to make peace with us. To demonstrate his goodwill, he had presented Grandma Que with the Vietnamese antiques acquired by the Foucault family. Grandma Que received those treasures nonchalantly, for she had long made up her mind to dislike anyone whose last name was Foucault.

———

After my birthday was over, when all my friends had gone home, I fell asleep on the straw mat until a cold breeze awoke me. I opened my eyes and found my father and André talking.

"You will find your Indochina," I heard my father say to him over his teacup.

"Where is Indochina?" I asked André, in my sleepy voice.

I felt a strong, warm arm drawing me in, and smelled the familiar scent of candies, soap, and lemon. "Here," André said. "Indochina is here." I looked up and found his brown eyes looking down at my face. "I have found my Indochina."

I, on the other hand, knew I had found my playmate.

———

After my sixth birthday, André came to our house every Sunday to learn Vietnamese from my father. My father, who taught French literature, became André's good friend. After their lesson, they would move to my mother's garden. André, my sister Mi Chau, and I all played pony rides. I, of course, always got most of the rides, and André always made me laugh. When the pony game came to a close, my pony would get up from the ground, brush the grass from his clothes, and join my father at tea. The conversation was often dominated by my father's long-winded speech, full of words I could not understand.

"*La France et L'Indochine*. The love and hate between the cruel, arrogant, exploitive colonial master and his beautiful, complex, intelligent, and resentful slave," my father said with passion. I listened, fascinated, grappling with my father's strings of adjectives. "And America. All those shiny GE refrigerators, Coca Cola tin cans, Salem cigarettes, nicely stocked supermarkets with wrapped fruits and vegetables, long, big cars manufactured in Detroit, and New York skyscrapers—all of those nice things topped with the catchy phrase 'Democracy-for-the-Third-World,' a notion existing only in the naiveté of a well-intentioned nouveau riche."

"What is a supermarket?" I asked my mother.

"A market that is super," she answered. "Food is frozen to last for months." My mother gave her simplistic explanation, ignoring the fact that I was pouting.

As my father continued to preach, André's face would change expression, taking on an air of seriousness that set him apart from me, into a different world much above my head. It was then I realized he was no longer my pony or playmate, but rather my father's counterpart. The two men drank lotus tea and talked for hours while my mother attended to her beds of flowers, and I was forgotten.

I found excuses to hang around, listening to the conversations, quite often in a combination of French, Vietnamese, and English. I guessed at the meaning, not understanding all, yet completely mesmerized by adults' use of words and the sounds of three very different languages. I often jumped onto André's lap and put my little hand underneath his shirt, feeling his chest and stomach muscles and the fuzzy hair on his warm skin. Quite often he caught my hand, either tapped on it or raised it to his mouth, turning it over to kiss my palm. I would laugh. At times I would pull his shirt out of his slacks and attempt to crawl under his shirt, scratching his belly, pulling his buttons apart, rubbing my cheek against his chest. He would pick me up, place me on the table, tickle me, and kiss my stomach, his shirt flying open. My mother would shout across the yard that I needed to be spanked and that André was indulging me too much. All this time, my father was too absorbed in his talk to notice my childish prank.

I never had enough of André. He supplied all of the horseplay that my father, a skinny, bespectacled professor and a stern, aloof Asian daddy, never provided.

All was well and good until André announced to my family that he would soon return to France to get married.

6. DOMINIQUE CLEMENCEAU

Grandma Que once told me that to marry meant to live with some-one, to love and cook for that person. I assumed André would be returning to France to live with and cook for his someone.

André's someone turned out to be a blonde, lying on the beach, wearing a two-piece bathing suit and dark sunglasses. Like the women in *Paris Match*.

It was an afternoon high-tea party, and several friends of my parents had come over to visit. André was showing them her picture, and I took a peep. The picture was in color, very rare in Vietnam those days. André said her name was Dominique Clemenceau. I memorized her name and studied her picture, the way she lay on her side, with one leg bent. I also noticed her red lips.

"*C'est une jeune fille que tu vas épouser*," I said. "*Je suis une jeune fille, aussi.*" André was marrying a girl, like me, except for the golden hair, the legs, and the lips. And she had to be much bigger.

Nobody heard me. The adults were talking and laughing. André was describing something called "*la lune de miel.*" The honeymoon. He kept talking about the vacation at La Côte d'Azur.

I pulled his sleeve. "*Qu'est ce que c'est que la lune de miel?*" What is a honeymoon? Nobody paid attention.

"*Je voudrais aller à la Côte d'Azur avec toi,*" I said with a pout. I wanted to go to La Côte d'Azur with André.

Again, nobody paid attention. The focus was on the woman in the bathing suit.

Thoughts rushed through my head. I loved Grandma Que and wanted to cook for her. And I lived with her. So naturally I would want to marry Grandma Que, except that somehow I understood intuitively one could not marry one's own grandmother the way my mother was married to my father. Further, Grandma Que said she was already married, to my grandfather who wore a green turban and sat in the picture on the family altar, and she would not marry another person.

I would not mind living with André. And I would be willing to cook for him, so long as I stood on a chair to reach the stove. And I loved André as much as I loved Grandma Que. So, perhaps I should marry André.

"I want to marry you, André," I said, about to break out in tears.

Still, nobody paid any attention. I ran into my mother's bedroom and sat alone. I wished either André or Grandma Que would come and comfort me. No one did. I thought of the woman in the picture. André would be living with her in France and would not be returning to Vietnam to play pony rides. He must love her and want to cook for her. If he married her, could I still marry him?

I went to my mother's vanity table and looked at myself. I could look like the French woman. I took off my shirt and my skirt and wore only my dotted panties. I took my mother's red lipstick and applied it on myself. I found her Jackie Kennedy sunglasses and wore them. They kept falling over the bridge of my tiny nose, but I pressed them all the way in and managed.

Something was missing. I went to my mother's armoire and found a brassiere. The thing was far too big, so I had to hold it on. Something was still missing. The golden hair. So I looked for my mother's gold scarf and tied it around my head. I also stood on her escapin high heels. I was complete. I checked myself in the mirror again and I was pleased. I could definitely go to La Côte d'Azur with André like this.

And then I came back to the living room. I stood in the middle of the room, on my mother's heels, holding the loose brassiere around my chest with one hand, and the golden scarf around my head with the other hand. The grown-ups were still looking at the pictures.

"I want to marry André," I said timidly. Still nobody noticed me.

"André, I want to marry you!" I yelled at the top of my lungs.

The room fell silent. I never forgot my mother's face, her dropped jaw, the O shape of her mouth, and her wide eyes. "Oh, good Lord!" she yelled, jumping out toward me, while they started roaring: all of my parents' friends. André was also laughing at my efforts to please him.

—

Like the rest of Southeast Asia, Hue had its monsoon rain season. It was a rainy night when my father took André to the airport. I stayed in my room and cried. André had left for Paris to marry Dominique. André said he would return, soon, to his lawyering job and teaching position in Hue, as well as the mission he had undertaken for the children of Vietnam. With Dominique, of course, he told my parents.

My mother did not believe him. "Vietnam is just a fad for him," she said. "He is young, and he'll stay on in Paris with his wife."

The following days and months were gloomy as the rainy season continued. My father purchased a piano for Mi Chau and me, and I no longer had to go to the practice room at the Jeanne d'Arc Institute for practice.

Instead of pony rides with André, my Sunday afternoons were now reserved for piano practice. "Au Clair de la Lune" and "Carnaval de Venise," oversimplified versions of Schumann's "Mélodie" and Chopin's "Berceuse." I was learning so fast that Sœur Josephine stated I should audition for the national conservatory soon.

The days went by and I kept on working at the keyboard. Every Sunday afternoon I sat by my piano, near the window, looking out at the garden. My boy doll, which looked like André, sat on top of the piano, together with my sheet music. No more pony rides, but I kept hoping.

—

The rainy season had ended and the calendar year was almost over. Christmas was about to arrive, and I was chosen to play a shepherd in *That Winter Night,* a Christmas musical composed and produced by Sœur Josephine. The Catholic nun tested the range of my voice and decided she would write a short aria for the shepherd. So I sang her music, four lines to be exact: an uplifting C Major score, with lofty words celebrating the birth of Jesus Christ.

That was the first time I sang on stage. Sœur Josephine told my parents I should definitely be enrolled in the national conservatory.

The week before Christmas, my parents threw a party for their friends. Grandma Que made her specialty dish: shrimp balls on a kumquat tree. She created little mandarin oranges out of shrimp paste, wrapped them in clear cellophane, and attached them to branches of a real kumquat tree. The guests picked the oranges from the tree and ate them, surprised to find out the oranges were made out of fresh-ground shrimp. It was a royal dish.

All the Western expatriates in Hue were invited to the party. My parents wanted me to play my piano for their guests. Wearing a red velvet dress, I played the simplified version of Schumann's "Romance" perfectly. My mother's almond eyes lit up with joy and pride. The guests shouted out, "*Bis, bis*," the French word for an encore. I stood on the piano bench, beamed, and curtsied as my mother had trained me to do.

From my piano bench, I saw André walking in, beautiful as always, with a woman. I instantly recognized her. She was statuesque, almost as tall as André, and much more imposing than in her picture. Her golden hair was tied up in a ponytail, with a multicolored scarf. She wore a bias-cut, flowery Western dress and red lipstick. Her eyes were pale blue. She did not smile.

I stared at the beautiful couple. My broad grin faded. André approached and picked me up, kissing me.

"*Très bien!*" he said, referring to my "Romance" performance. The adults were embracing, shaking hands. French and English were spoken. I remained in André's arms, yet feeling lost and neglected.

"*Un gros baiser pour Tata Dominique, Simone*," my mother said. She wanted me to give a big welcome kiss for Aunt Dominique.

I reluctantly went from André's arms to the blonde woman's arms. She smelled nice, too, like fresh flowers and cosmetic powder, but still she did not smile. "*Elle est si drôle*," she said, looking at my face curiously.

Drôle? I wasn't pleased. Comic? Quaint? Funny? Like a comedienne? No, I was supposed to be beautiful. Not "*drôle*."

"*Elle est magnifique*," André said defensively. To him, I was magnificent.

"*Vous êtes...comme Sylvie Vartan*," I said to her, carefully using the formal form of address. To me, she was like the blonde French pop singer, Sylvie Vartan, whose record was played in my house, and whose picture I had seen in Aunt Y-Van's *Paris Match*. I could not think of anybody else who was blond.

Auntie Dominique started to smirk. The smirk that finally came was so light it hardly brightened her face. "*Comment? Elle s'appelle Simone?*" She turned to André with a question in her glassy blue eyes, her thin, shapely brows coming together, forming lines between them.

"It's just a cute French name, for school," my mother said, defensively. "Her real name is Mi Uyen. Her sister does not have a French name, because she's not in school yet."

My mother pointed to my sister Mi Chau, who was always dirty from eating too much food too hastily. Mi Chau was standing in the corner, behind the lamp, eating a cream puff—her favorite, *choux à la crème*.

"*Ah oui*," Dominique said coldly. Mi Chau had finished her cream puff and was ready to kiss Aunt Dominique, but Dominique turned away.

"*Il fait très chaud, ici!*" Dominique complained about the heat.

"*Très chaud, mais pas trop cher!*" My mother tried to make a joke, a pun on words, reversing "*très chaud*" into "*trop cher.*" It might be too hot here, but not too expensive! Dominique did not respond. I ran from Dominique to my mother.

"Show Tata Dominique your drawings and poems," my mother said. She wanted Dominique to see proof of my talents.

I stayed where I was, with my face buried in my mother's lap. I did not want to show Tata Dominique anything. This blonde woman in a flowery dress did not like us. I could tell. I longed to be with André, but Dominique was sitting with him all the time, her hand resting on his.

I listened in as all the guests talked. André had been back in Hue for months and had been traveling with his new bride through central Vietnam. The highlands: spectacular green hills, valleys, and waterfalls. The famous Pass of Cloud, Le Col des Nuages, connecting Hue to DaNang, the military base of the Americans, where the famous American entertainer, Bob Hope, would be doing a Christmas show for soldiers. The white beaches of Cam Ranh and Dai Lanh, where American troops disembarked from their fleet.

Anger filled my heart; I fought back tears. André had been back for months and he had not stopped by for our Sunday afternoon pony rides. He had not missed me. He spent all his time with her. He left me waiting.

I ran to Grandma Que. Back to where I belonged.

All during the party, Grandma Que sat quietly on a rosewood chair, casting her eyes away from the guests, who raved about her shrimp balls. She did not speak. Something was about to happen. I just knew. I had learned to read the mood of the dignified woman who helped raise me.

7. FAREWELL TO HUE

Toward the end of the party, my father made an important announcement to all of his friends. This was not just a Christmas party. It was a celebration. Also a farewell party.

My father had accepted a tenured position with the Faculty of Letters, University of Saigon. André, too, would be leaving Hue to return to France to practice law. Dominique could not stand the heat and humidity of Indochina. My mother was right. Vietnam to André was just a fad.

My fate was decided, too. Sœur Josephine had written a letter of recommendation. In Saigon, I would audition for Truong Quoc Gia Am Nhac Kich Nghe, The National Institute of Music and Drama. I would also be taking private singing lessons with a French Italian singer, Madame Misticelli, the only opera teacher in Vietnam, and a personal friend of Sœur Josephine.

It meant we were all moving to Saigon. My father announced his teaching would start in January of the new calendar year. So we would be packing right after Christmas.

People were still talking, congratulating my father on his new teaching appointment. Grandma Que stood up from her rosewood chair. She did her usual thing—letting go of her hair and rolling it up again, in one definite motion. But nobody noticed her. She left the room. I stood alone.

My temples began to hurt. The headache came on as a result of overwhelming emotions. I recognized years later that the painful moment must have been the first time I experienced, as an innocent child, the nostalgia of loss. The entire evening and its events had all been too much for me: the arrival of Dominique, our forthcoming departure from Hue, and my separation from Grandma Que. It had always been understood that Grandma Que would never leave the family altar, the house in Nam Giao, or her City. Even at that tender age, I had accepted so clearly that she had chosen to be the keeper of all that which defined her heritage—everything that bonded her to Hue. She had made clear to me that if Mi Chau and I ever left Hue, she would simply wait for us to return.

I ran after Grandma Que into the garden. Of course, nobody noticed our absence from the party. In the clear, starry night, the moon had come out, and Grandma Que stood looking at its bluish shape.

I heard footsteps and turned around. André had noticed our leaving the party and had followed us.

I reached out for him, and he took me in his arms. I began to cry, relieved to let out all those tears that had been suppressed since Schumann's "Romance."

Holding me, André spoke to Grandma Que in his French-accented Vietnamese: "It is a beautiful moon, isn't it?"

"Yes."

"Reminds me of the Perfume River."

"What do you know about the Perfume River?"

"I used to walk along the banks almost daily. Your mother once paddled a boat across the Perfume River and met her Prince Charming that way. I study the lives of your ancestors."

"You mean, the life of my mother?" Grandma Que's face was lit with rage. "From what I can remember of Mr. Sylvain Foucault, you don't look like him."

"I look like my mother, an Italian American. My grandfather said I had his passion, even though we didn't look alike." André said this slowly, his voice careful and sad. "Madame, I would like to talk to you."

I looked up at his face and, under the moonlight, recognized the serious expression that characterized those moments when he drifted into a different world and ceased to be my playmate. He kept talking with a tone of urgency, despite Grandma Que's apparent irritation. His French accent and choppy Vietnamese made it hard for me to follow him.

"You see, as a child, I spent time with my grandfather in his old age, during his dying days, listening to him talk, at a time when he no longer had any interest in life but to reflect upon his deeds in Indochina."

"How noble of him. And what did you find out, may I ask?"

"You have a twin sister. When your father was exiled, your mother was with child, so you also have a brother, madame."

Grandma Que's twin sister and baby brother? My mother's Auntie Ginseng and Uncle Forest. Grandma Que never talked about them, but she must have loved them, like I loved my sister Mi Chau and my infant brother, Phi Long. I was keenly interested.

I looked toward Grandma Que. Still gazing at the moon, she said, coldly, "I don't need you to tell me what I have, Monsieur Foucault."

"But you must understand why your mother did what she did. About the postcards…"

"Please stop, Monsieur Foucault. You have no right to talk about the postcards."

Postcards? What postcards? I was getting confused. When André had left for France, he had promised to send me a post-card—scenery of the beautiful cafes of Paris, the river Seine, and the garden of Luxembourg. I tapped on André's arm, but he earnestly continued on, ignoring me. I noticed he was unconsciously making a fist.

"Forgive me, but I can't stop, madame. If you didn't know, then I must let you know. Your sister and brother both left home and joined Cach Mang, ultimately Ho Chi Minh's Revolution, the Vietminh, at an early age."

The Revolution? I had heard the big word, *Cach Mang*, from Grandma Que herself. I grabbed André's hand and tried to interrupt him to ask questions, but again he was oblivious to me.

"My grandfather was not just an enemy," he said, "or just a business partner of your mother, madame. Your mother wanted to secure the repatriation of your father and the restoration of the monarchy. She knew that my grandfather, the *résident supérieur* of Annam, could protect your twin sister and younger brother, the young revolutionists jailed in Hoa Lo. My grandfather could set them free.

"And he did just that, madame: he secured their safety as best he could, a very dangerous task, an act of treason against France.

You should know, too, that back in France, he died a lonely and unhappy man, and I hope that after so many years, you can find the compassion in your heart to forgive him."

"At least your grandfather died of old age," Grandma Que said coldly, still looking away from André, toward the silver moon. "He lived his long and comfortable life. I won't tell you how I had to bury my loved ones, Monsieur Foucault. Untimely deaths. Without proper burials, without coffins. I was not even able to procure some of the bodies to bring them home."

"It was a very long war, madame. My grandfather and your parents were all extraordinary individuals. They had to do what they had to do. Can you at least try to understand what your mother had to do when she was alive?"

Grandma Que raised her arms and removed the ivory comb, her hair cascading down her side. "Who are you to tell me? You understand nothing about my mother."

"Perhaps I don't, but, madame, I do understand how you feel. Things must have been very hard for you, and I'm terribly sorry."

Grandma Que was staring at him steadily. I thought I saw the fiery reflection of stars in her eyes. "Why are you, a Foucault, saying sorry? What for? You are not part of my family, and as a Foucault, you are not entitled to feel what I feel."

———

After all the guests had left, my father began discussing the move. Grandma Que sat silently in the rosewood chair all throughout the discussion, until finally she spoke.

"I just want to know one thing, master." Grandma Que always addressed my father formally, *ong giao*, as schoolteacher and master of the house. "Will the girls have a piano?"

"They will share one, yes." My father removed his glasses to clean them, disturbed.

"Will there be a housekeeper?"

"Not on my teaching salary."

"Will the children go to French or Vietnamese school?"

"I will decide that later, Mother," my father replied, his voice rising.

"Will my daughter and grandchildren come back to this ancestral house, one day? Your wife is my only child."

"My job is in Saigon, and I doubt if we will come back to Hue, Mother."

I was scared. No one had spoken to Grandma Que in that tone of voice. My mother, unhappy wife and daughter, looked pleadingly at her unhappy husband and unhappy mother-in-law. I sat in a corner twisting a strand of hair, never having felt this sad before.

Grandma Que got up to leave. "I'll leave so you can discuss your move with your wife." She let go of her hair and rolled it up again. "I would like my cinnamon log to go with Si and Mi Chau," she said, decisively.

"That won't be necessary, Mother," my father protested. "Si and Mi Chau are children. They have no use for your cinnamon log."

"The cinnamon log is meant to protect my granddaughters. They should take it with them wherever they go." Grandma Que sat down again. She was just about to turn her hair loose again from the ivory comb.

"If we need cinnamon for cooking, we'll go to the store," my father said firmly.

"You don't understand, Master, this is a very, very old tree—"

"Then it needs to stay with you all the more," my father said, interrupting her.

I grew sadder and sadder in my little corner.

"The tree belongs to the girls, and they need it," Grandma Que said firmly.

"I'll decide what they need. They are my daughters!"

"And may I remind you, *ong giao*, they are also my granddaughters." Grandma Que stood up. She closed her lips, rerolled her hair, and left the room.

8. SAIGON

In the years to come, I thought of life in Saigon as transient, expecting the day we would all be returning to Hue. My mother shared my feelings, although we never openly discussed our longing.

In 1966, Saigon to me was just a noisy beehive. Having been mesmerized by the tall André and having secretly admired the statuesque Dominique as the epitome of classic beauty found in *Paris Match*, I viewed my dainty Grandma Que and her cinnamon-scented villa as the only Vietnamese aesthetic counterpart of Western exotic grandeur. So, to me, the Saigonese were simply little men slouching in their cotton shirts, little women swaying in their colorful *ao dai tuniques* or cotton print pajamas, and little children twisting their rubber sandals on paved sidewalks, swinging their plastic briefcases containing their violet ink bottles and scrapbooks with preprinted lines. I saw none of the elegant image of French "Cochinchine," that "gem of the

Far East," or "Paris of Asia" as the adults had referred to their capital city.

The only thing impressive about Saigon was its magnificent downtown. It overwhelmed me. My mother explained that the French colonists who built Cochinchine must have attempted to incorporate certain features of central Paris into Saigon. But the hot and humid Asian city, bathed all year round either in dust particles dancing in burning sunshine or unexpected tropical monsoon rain, did not exactly turn out to be a miniature Paris, even though the French touch permeated the ambiance of various districts of Saigon, most notably the Catinat downtown district. A giant clock highlighted the facade of the Ben Thanh market, a two-storied shopping galleria stretching through several blocks of downtown Saigon. The landmark clock watched over the weaving traffic on a multilaned boulevard, bordered by tall trees and rooftop nightclubs bearing fancy French names—from the Rex, the Au Chalet, the Crystal Palace to, most notably, the ice cream parlor Pôle Nord, the North Pole, a favorite hangout of Saigonese youths. Once in a while, either my father or André would bring Mi Chau and me there for ice cream.

A white, French-domed opera house occupied one part of what was known as Rue Catinat under French colonization. The opera house was used by the South Vietnamese government as its parliament house. At the other end of the former Boulevard Charner was Saigon's Hotel de Ville, City Hall, an ornate, canary yellow structure decorated with distinctive white moldings, seahorse and angel motifs, typifying French-built architecture. To the left of the opera house was the more than one-hundred-year-old Continental Hotel—a square, white, elegant structure with its ornate French facade, glass windows, and long marble corridor. The traffic of the former Boulevard Charner, separated by a median on which were situated dozens of souvenir shops and busy little kiosks, reminded the French-speaking Saigonese and nostalgic French colonists of the Champs-Élysées.

But perhaps the colonists and the Saigonese fashion-conscious crowd were all dreaming, since at best Boulevard Charner would only be an Asia substitute. The small scale of the shops, the lack of glitz, not to mention the Asian-styled noise and petty unkemptness, took away from Saigon any illusion of Parisian grandeur or romanticism. Yet, the area bore all of the warmth, coziness, glamour, and endearment that made Saigon lovely and unforgettable to its millions of inhabitants.

Not to me, in 1966, when my heart and soul were still with Hue. I disliked Saigon and secretly blamed it for my separation from Grandma Que and her violet world. In comparison to violet Hue and its green River Huong, Saigon was a crude, polluted gray cloud full of chaotic lines and dust particles.

My glimpse of the supposedly fashionable downtown Saigon was always short-lived. I accompanied my mother on those rare shopping sprees for special occasions such as New Year, or birthday celebration dinners where the children were given filet mignon, French onion soup, buttery gateaux studded with raisins, and crisp apples and pears that were imported and wrapped in soft white tissue paper. Unlike Mi Chau, I did not care much for filet mignon or apples, and would rather have traded them for *com tâm*, crushed white rice sprinkled with fish sauce and garnished with Vietnamese bacon bits.

In the early days of our lives in Saigon, my mother talked incessantly to Mi Chau and me about Grandma Que's villa in Hue and its garden. In Saigon, we lived in a barren townhouse in the back of a small alley. Saigon eroded her dreams, my mother said. It had taken away her only hobby, gardening.

"Why do you like gardening so much, Mother?" I frequently asked her.

Most of the time, she did not answer. Once, only once, she dreamily said, "*Comme les fleurs de lys que j'ai cueillies dans le jardin de mes pensées.*" Her beds of lilies became the gardens of her thoughts.

In those moments, my mother and I became the best of friends, and I would gently place my head onto her arms, listening to her talk. My mother spoke of the checkerboard marble floor of Grandma Que's villa, its high ceilings with molded corners and green French shutters. She talked of the beautiful shapes and colors of roses, daisies, lilies, sunflowers, and other exotic flowers of the Far East. She talked of the chimes that ornamented the front and back porches, dangling in the wind, making their clear, reedy music.

Every night, before bedtime, my mother wrote letters to her woman friends in Hue, the female teachers of Lycée Dong Khanh. She read her letters out loud for me to hear, as though she were delivering a monologue before an audience, describing the beautiful time of her life in Hue and her longing to go home. "I am so afraid I will never see flowers or a garden again in these filthy alleys of Saigon. To escape, I turn to poetry and pretend to garden with words."

When my father entered the room, she would stop the monologue and pretend to read a newspaper.

My mother considered life in Saigon too tough for her leisurely, bourgeois style and complained that the power of the American dollar was uprooting tradition and the identity of the Vietnamese middle class.

I was too young then to understand the political role of the Americans, yet old enough to get a picture of our economic life in

Saigon, painted vividly by my frustrated mother. She constantly stressed the need to be frugal. At lunches and dinners, she complained to my father, and I quietly listened. Our family, as well as other civil servants, schoolteachers, and families of combat soldiers, had to struggle to survive the skyrocketing inflation of Saigon on meager monthly salaries. The cyclo drivers and maids who rushed into the city from war zones occupied the bottom of the wage-earning chart. On the other hand, if one worked for or did business with the Americans, salaries were much higher and, therefore, life was better. Landlords preferred leasing properties to American tenants; taxi drivers preferred picking up American passengers. A new type of moneymaker appeared on the scene of Saigon's commerce: the contractors and auctioneers who transacted with the Americans. Desperate young girls from the countryside poured into nightclubs, bars, and dancing parlors serving American GIs. A new occupation emerged: the GI wives and girlfriends, not highly respected, according to my mother, but pleasantly well fed.

I saw them—the GIs—occasionally, on Saigon streets, in their army uniforms, those black and white men, all too tall to fit the low sky and small alleys of Saigon. Either rosy under the sun or glisteningly dark like the night, the GIs were towering, hairy figures, obviously out of place. Occasionally, I found a soft, dark-featured one who looked a bit like André.

"They are not French," my mother would explain. They are Americans. They are supposed to be our friends.

"As my children, you stay away from the GIs, you hear?" my mother would tell Mi Chau and me, pointing her fingers at the horde of children who followed the GIs. Once I challenged my mother's order. "If the GIs are our friends, why aren't we allowed to follow them like the children of the streets?"

"Those children are the *bui doi*," she said, calling them the dust of life. "They are orphans, shoe shiners, and errand boys. You are not the *bui doi*!" my mother exclaimed.

I watched with envy the *bui doi* roaming in their free-spirited way, even if they looked dusty and dirty. Circling or following the GIs, the children shouted in rhythm, "OK, Salem, Coca Cola, and chewing gum!" Those towering figures in army uniforms would smile broadly, distributing items to the children who fought among themselves for the largest share of the goodies. The *bui doi* got all the things they asked for in their broken English, from cigarettes to milk cartons and, most of the time, Coke cans and fruity chewing gum. We got none because we were children of respected schoolteachers and civil servants.

In addition to his tenured position at Saigon University, my father taught at private night schools—those classes that prepared the young men of South Vietnam for their college entrance examinations, which they had to pass to avoid the draft. My father's moonlighting, I was told, was his effort to earn extra money to pay for my private French school. So, despite the hardship of life in Saigon, I continued having my ears filled with lyrical French, my eyes filled with pictures of French countryside, and my thoughts inundated with details about the daily lives of French boys and girls described in the beautiful prose of the best of French writers, like Alphonse Daudet and Anatole France. The French education did little to change my Vietnamese soul. I still preferred crushed rice and fried tofu dipped in peanut sauce over fancy filet mignon and the "laughing cow" cheese, *la vache qui rit*, which my mother forced me to eat to gain weight.

Mi Chau, on the other hand, suffered a different fate. Citing patriotic reasons, my father withdrew her from the French curriculum and put her in public Vietnamese school instead. Behind his back, my mother would whisper to me that the real reason for Mi Chau's Vietnamese schooling was the lack of money. She taught me to be frugal that way.

To return to sleepy Hue under the protection of Grandma Que was my mother's dream. One day we would all be returning to the old colonial house, where her children would be raised among tropical flowers and accompanied by the musical sound of jingling chimes. She never accepted our departure from Hue as a one-way trip. She had a special suitcase, packed with sweaters and fine clothing; Hue is colder than Saigon, and the suitcase would be for that day when she would finally return to Grandma Que's villa.

Yet, just before the Lunar New Year of 1968, the Year of the Monkey, my father reminded us that we would not return to Hue and that Saigon would be our permanent home. My mother's eyebrows came together over her red, sullen eyes. As usual, she did not protest the decision. The special suitcase, however, was never unpacked. She kept it under my bed. Only I knew where it was.

9. THE TET OFFENSIVE— MADAME CINNAMON AND THE COMMUNIST SPY

Time passed. My mother had not even returned to Hue for a visit when the next catastrophe arrived. As it turned out, my father's decision to leave Hue was a good one. The celebration of the Lunar New Year, Tet Mau Than, in February of 1968, entered history as a tragic event.

The Tet Offensive. The massacre of Hue.

As a thirteen-year-old, I was mature enough to grasp the tragedies of the Tet Offensive as my personal tragedy as well. First, Grandma Que was in Hue with the Vietcong. Growing up in non-Communist South Vietnam, I was conditioned to think of the Vietcong as boogeymen and enemies, a mean and dangerous species like snakes, tigers, or cannibals. On the day the radio announced Hue had been seized by the Vietcong, I wrapped myself in a blanket, thinking of Mey Mai's words from the past—there would be another massacre in the City of Hue, from which I would escape. It was happening. The Spirit of the Perfume River was correct. I thought of Grandma Que living alone in the old colonial house. Would the magnolia tree protect her against flying rockets? Or would she likely die buried under white magnolia blooms?

Second, the Violet City—representing memories of that guardian angel of mine, the Mystique Concubine—became a celebrated battlefield. American marines were helicoptered into battle to help recover the imperial city. TV broadcasts of scenes from Hue were available for Saigon inhabitants to view what had happened to their beloved city of romance. The mourning of Hue citizens filled the evening news. It was reported that before the Vietcong withdrew their troops, thousands of civilians were buried alive or executed.

My mother, Mi Chau, and I prayed to the compassionate Buddha every night while the fighting for the imperial city continued. We all cried together watching television; corpses of soldiers were shipped out of the Citadel surrounding the Violet City: from the skinny Vietcong guerilla fighters in their black pajamas, to the equally skinny South Vietnamese soldiers, in their green army uniforms, to the American marines, the gigantic men of the West.

In the end, the South Vietnamese Army and U.S. Marines declared their victory—the Vietcong were completely ousted from the imperial city. Hue belonged, once more, to the American-backed Republic of Vietnam. The broadcast news said the Violet City was badly damaged. My father sighed one evening at dinner and claimed that vestige of a culture and its past glory were almost wiped out. Excavations were conducted for Hue citizens to search for traces of their loved ones. Bodies of Hue citizens were uncovered in all shapes or forms, parts missing, limbs chained together, arms tied behind their backs. It was also reported that among the dead were Western civilians—Germans, French, Americans, British—who had come to Hue for research, medical, academic, or humanitarian services.

"Lucky André and Dominique," my father said, "leaving just in time."

Finally, we got a telegram from Grandma Que. The ancestral house was damaged, but she was all right, thanks to the mystical cinnamon log sitting in the altar room, she said. Apparently, the log's magic was not powerful enough to keep our surviving relatives in Hue after the Tet Offensive. Several of them left to resettle in Saigon, and told us of what had happened to our ancestral house on Princess Huyen Tran Street. The Vietcong had chosen the villa as a place for political meetings. Hue citizens were summoned to hear propaganda talks on American crimes, and Grandma Que was chosen to preside over these meetings. The Vietcong called her Me Chien Si, Mother of Warriors.

Gathering coals and wood logs, she cooked barrels of rice to feed Vietcong troops with the same calmness as she had prepared gourmet shrimp balls on a kumquat tree for Western expatriates at the Christmas party in 1966. Later, we heard that prior to withdrawal, the Vietcong were about to loot her house and destroy her antiques. Grandma Que, twin sister of the heroine Ginseng, daughter of the Revolution, stood in front of the altar and demanded to see the political commissar.

"Take whatever you want in the house before you go back to the jungle," she told him. "But do not touch these artifacts. They don't belong to me. They belong to the culture of Vietnam. Destroy these, and you would be committing the same crime as the Americans. You would be guilty before the dragon and the fairy that represent the country's roots. Even the French had to give these items back, and I am just the keeper. Uncle Ho would agree with me, I am positive. If your men insist on destroying these, I will write to Uncle Ho and General Vo Nguyen Giap myself. Or you can kill this old woman."

I imagined the slender silhouette of Grandma Que in front of the family altar, dainty like a willow. She repeated her hair-rolling routine as she delivered her stern speech to men wearing cone hats and black pajamas, with their AK-47s pointing at her. The Spirit of the Perfume River must have been lurking behind Grandma Que, circling the altar in the smoke of incense, while the omnipresent cinnamon log emanated its mystical power to protect her.

Finally, the men in black pajamas had to lower their heads and bow, pointing their threatening AK-47s to the ground. Even the commissar had to lower his eyes, and ordered his men to leave the house. The antiques and musical instruments once belonging to the Hue Imperial Court remained intact.

Our Hue relatives added a postscript to the story. The well-known medium of the Inner Citadel, Mey Mai, had disappeared after the Tet Offensive. It was alleged she had joined Vietcong troops in their withdrawal into the jungle, back to the Ho Chi Minh Trail. Mey Mai—the psychic, the prophet, the wise one, the Mystique Concubine's loyal chambermaid, Grandma Que's endeared nanny—had always been a Communist spy. In 1968, she served as colonel in charge of information warfare for Ho Chi Minh's National Liberation Front and its Communist cause. The money and gifts she earned through fortune telling had always gone to the Front. She had always been one of the celebrated daughters of the Revolution, following the footsteps of my great-aunt Ginseng.

—

So, Mey Mai was a Vietcong! And a famous one, with a long revolutionary Communist and intelligence career. But I never thought of her as a bad person. She used to embrace me and hold me in her lap. And she spoke to me the words of the singing paddle girl—that powerful Spirit of the Perfume River.

We learned that when the Tet Offensive was over, Grandma Que had to repair the exterior damage the war had done to the ancestral house. In her letters, she stated what I already knew: that the Spirit of the Perfume River, the magnolia tree, and her mystical cinnamon log had protected our ancestral abode.

But my father had a different story to tell. He said it had to be Mey Mai, the Communist spy, who secured Grandma Que's safety and protected our property. Even a dangerous, deceiving Communist spy had loyalty and a heart. Further, the old villa, isolated underneath rows of tall trees and sitting on the slope of hilly Nam Giao, was not situated on the Vietcong's incoming or exiting route. The location made the villa strategically safe from the war. And no, my father continued, Grandma Que would never have written Uncle Ho or General Giap about the matter of preserving her antiques. If she had, the letters would have been ignored. They could have gotten her into trouble with the South Vietnamese government. Imagine a South Vietnamese writing to Uncle Ho and General Giap in the North?

I did not believe my father. When Grandma Que said she would do something, she meant it. The Spirit of the Perfume River, the magnolia tree, and the cinnamon log would never allow Grandma Que to be harmed in any way.

In the summer of 1968, my mother wrote to Grandma Que, begging her to leave Hue for Saigon, for fear there might be another Tet Offensive. Mey Mai had disappeared and, if another Tet Offensive were to occur, there would be no one to protect

Grandma Que against the Vietcong, who condemned members of the royal family and descendants of the Nguyen Dynasty.

Grandma Que refused. She had decided to live and die as the keeper of memories.

———

That summer, when life got back to normal, we also received a telegram from André in Côte d'Azur: "*Heard of Tet Offensive. Please telegram. Anxiously waiting. André*."

So, André had not forgotten me, in spite of Dominique.

The inhabitants of Vietnam learned to insulate themselves from bad memories. The Tet Offensive was soon forgotten, and the war could seem deceptively far away. In many ways our lives before and after the Tet Offensive remained unaffected.

By the beginning of 1969, I had auditioned for and enrolled at the National Institute of Music and Drama. That same year, I began taking private singing lessons from Madame Misticelli at her villa on Rue Tu Duc, a small, tree-filled street representing the best neighborhood of Saigon, with rows of red-brick French villas and yellow and grey stucco estate houses. For regular academic work, I attended Lycée Marie Curie, an all-girl secondary school in the heart of Saigon.

After the Tet Offensive, my mother stopped talking about returning to her ancestral house in Hue. She still wanted to resume her hobby in tropical horticulture, but the townhouse in District Eight had no spare land. In the beginning, my mother remained quiet and sad. Then she became more and more irritated, until the silence broke and she began complaining to my father incessantly about her need to have flowers around her. My father finally gave in. Since the townhouse had no front or back yard, he had to knock down a bedroom, open the roof, and build a patio for potted plants and flowers.

In the patio, my father had built a small fountain made out of cement, grayish and dull, to catch rainwater. My mother would never again have an old man to assist her and to remove earthworms, nor the green grass of a circling yard, but she eventually made peace with potting plants and arranged her flowerpots and crawling ferns and vines around the ugly cement structure. She also put lawn chairs around it. When she was finished, the gray cement fountain appeared bright and cheerful, and the townhome was no longer barren.

By the time my mother's flowerpots all blossomed, we got another telegram from Paris. André and Dominique were returning to Vietnam to live!

"*Call me crazy,* mon professeur," the telegram said, "*especially after the Tet Offensive, but I just can't stay away from L'Indochine. My bride will have to understand.*"

———

My Sunday afternoon routines with André were resumed that same year, in a different form. André no longer came to our house alone. Dominique drove a Deux Chevaux, dropped him off at our house, came in for the courtesy formality, and then left. She would come back to pick him up a couple of hours later. Every Sunday afternoon, I looked out from the living room window and saw them together in the Deux Chevaux, approaching our house and stopping by the curb. Husband and wife sat quietly and separately from each other, staring ahead. I asked my mother whether they were mad at each other. She said I was too young to inquire into such a thing.

Dominique was a lofty and aloof white lily lost in the tropics, her blue eyes and straight blonde hair cool and sophisticated, her flowery Western dresses, silk scarf, and sling sandals all making a striking fashion statement in the dust of Saigon among the polyester-clad and cone-hatted street vendors. She would kiss me on my cheeks but would never smile. I could hardly feel the contact with her thin lips. I was told she taught French and English at Lycée Marie Curie, and when I was old enough to attend the tenth grade, La Seconde, she would become my English teacher. I dreaded the day.

My world in Saigon those days centered around the smiling and plump voice teacher, Madame Misticelli; the schoolgirls and professors at Lycée Marie Curie; the practice room at the National Institute of Music and Dramatic Arts; our indoor patio where my mother spent her leisure time; occasional outings for ice cream at the Pôle Nord; and my Sunday visits with André. The Sunday meetings continued, but the pony games between us belonged exclusively to my memory of my mother's garden in Hue, those butterflies fluttering their wings over violet petals in the yellow twilight of a dying summer day.

The Vietnamese language lessons André received from my father in Saigon gradually advanced to discussions of Vietnamese literature, which included Vietnamese modern poetry modeled after French literary romanticism of the late nineteenth and early twentieth centuries—the images and sentiments of Verlaine, Rimbaud, Baudelaire, and Apollinaire. I doubted if André's Vietnamese had really improved, because during these literary sessions, my father did most of the talking.

Days rolled by and I became a slender teenager, attached to André still, yet afraid of Dominique. André told my parents he would like to be my play uncle. According to him, Dominique did not object to the concept of becoming my French play aunt.

10. YELLOW ROSES AND BAUDELAIRE

In 1969, I turned fourteen. In a moment of teenage moodiness, I had told my mother I absolutely did not want a birthday party with friends my age. I requested that my siblings, Mi Chau and Pi, be sent away for the day.

It had rained all afternoon, and when the rain stopped, I sat by the window looking onto the cement alley, fresh, clean, and wet from the recent tropical shower. André's Deux Chevaux appeared and parked at the curb. Obviously he was coming for his Vietnamese lessons with my father. This time he was driving the Deux Chevaux himself, and Dominique was not accompanying him. The norm was broken and I rushed out to the door.

André was carrying a bouquet of yellow tea roses in his hand, and he bent over to kiss me on my cheek. "Surprise!"

My mother entered the living room from the kitchen, carrying a cake with thick, white buttercream frosting and fourteen candles on its surface. She announced there would be no Vietnamese lessons that day, as Uncle André would be celebrating my fourteenth birthday with us on the patio.

André produced a vase, announcing solemnly that the best of roses should always be presented in French crystal. He also had a wrapped present with him, claiming it was from Aunt Dominique. I tore off the gold wrapping and glistening matching bow and ran my fingers over the fine silk of a colorful scarf bearing the signature of Christian Dior. I had never had anything that beautiful in my schoolgirl's wardrobe, yet I folded the scarf nonchalantly and placed it back inside the bundle of wrinkled and torn wrapping paper, feeling no real emotion. It looked too much like something Dominique would wear. My attention was on the bouquet of yellow roses.

André said the flowers, twenty-four buds, had been ordered especially from the highlands, the resort city of Dalat, where the fresh and cool air of a milder climate produced better roses. I filled the crystal vase with rainwater from the patio's fountain, and sprinkled it on the rosebuds.

It was a quiet, adultlike birthday party, just as I had wanted it. My mother had honored my wish and sent both Mi Chau and Pi to the beach in Vung Tau. Before sunset, I blew out the fourteen candles on the cream cake, *banh bong lan*, and we sat in lounge chairs, listening to André recite Baudelaire:

> *Mon enfant, ma sœur,*
> *Sa douce langue natale...*
> *Aimer à loisir*
> *Aimer et mourir*
> *Au pays qui te ressemble*

I wanted to sing those words.

My child, my sister,
Your sweet native tongue…
Loving in leisure
Loving and dying
In the country resembling you.

I felt a vague sense of sadness. Why did loving have to go with dying? When I looked at André, he met my eyes. His thick lashes moved, and I saw again the nocturnal butterflies of Hue.

It was then that André began talking about himself. I had never seen him in such an agitated, passionate state. His eyebrows pulled together over those beautiful brown eyes, his cheek muscles tensed, and an expression of pain swept over his face. He told us how he had always been a lover of Baudelaire. He had studied comparative literature at Yale and then Sorbonne and had wanted to become a writer. But the Foucault family objected, and he became a solicitor instead.

He turned to my mother and thanked her for all those beautiful flowers that, throughout the years of his friendship with our family, had provided him with the paradoxical images of Baudelaire's "Fleurs du Mal" in the Far East. My mother smiled and said her flowers were not meant to be the image of pain or the darkness of Baudelaire, nor the tearful songs of Vietnam that represented the inspiration of poets. She was planting them out of necessity, for herself and in memory of her own childhood.

André went on and on about the burden of being a romantic and an idealist in a world full of ugliness. His eyes, slightly reddened, wandered toward me although he had begun to address my father. "*Professeur*, I feel at home in Vietnam. It is terrible, the damage done by war to a land so devastatingly beautiful. You know, I would even turn down the Foucaults' inheritance to remain forever in Indochina if I had to, and even if it meant losing Dominique."

My father cut him off and gave him a schoolteacher's speech. "Whether you give up your inheritance, Vietnam is still poor, and the hundred years of colonialism and a continuing war have already taken place," my father said reproachfully.

I was old enough then to understand every word, yet did not fully grasp the meaning of the complex issues—why André looked so stricken with guilt and why my father appeared so exasperated. When I looked over at André, his eyes were still fixed on me and he continued speaking, almost monotonously. I might not have understood everything, but as usual, I memorized his words.

"My family made a fortune out of Indochina. My grandfather was involved in the torture and beheading of Vietnamese patriots, the oppression of Vietnamese peasants on railroads, in rubber and coffee plantations and dangerous coal mines. I happen to know all about those things from my family's living room and my grandfather's study. But I would not call my feelings guilt or shame. I know I should not hold myself responsible for French exploitation and the oppression of her colony. After all, I wasn't even born then. But, *Professeur*, do you believe in mysticism—the unexplained things that happen to us? Why do I love this land so much? How can one explain why one loves a certain color or shape? I never want to leave here!"

"Then why did you marry Dominique, who doesn't want to live in Vietnam?" my father asked. I immediately perked up.

André turned to face my father but said nothing in response. He mentioned, instead, that I was growing up very fast and that one day, it would be nice to have artistic photographs or portraits made of me, dressed in traditional Vietnamese costumes of the 1920s.

He talked of the collection of black-and-white photographs that his grandfather, Sylvain Foucault, had taken of women in the Violet City. The photograph collection had become part of the Foucault library in a castle outside of Paris. André described how, as a boy growing up in France, he had stared at these photographs displayed in his father's study and had studied them. Old pictures of Indochina and the Violet City had been part of his childhood even before he set foot in Vietnam. He mentioned again and again how, with each day, I was looking more and more like the beauty featured in those old photographs.

"What beauty?" I asked, and he gave no answer.

The afternoon sun was about to die out when André asked, "How is Madame Cinnamon these days, living alone in Hue? She has always been alone, hasn't she?"

"It is my mother's fate," my mother said.

"My fondest wish after so many years is to have Madame Cinnamon's forgiveness so my grandfather's soul can rest in peace. I guess she never forgives. I can't blame her."

"You're forgiven, André, if it means that much to you," my mother said gently. "You have it from me. My mother is very stubborn."

The party ended as quietly as it had started, and André's lips barely touched my cheekbone as he headed for the door. After he was gone, my father sat alone in the patio for a long time.

"Poor André," my father said. "He wanted to write a book—an epic—on France, America, and Indochina. But it's been years and he hasn't completed it."

That night, I stood in front of the mirror and wrapped the Christian Dior silk scarf around my shoulders, letting the silk caress my bare skin. My instinct told me the scarf was André's idea, not Dominique's. I took one of André's roses, smashed it against my chest, and let the crushed rose petals fall down along my side.

I woke up in the middle of the night to the fragrance of André's roses, their yellow petals dancing in my head. I repeated those words of Baudelaire. *Au pays qui te ressemble.* Like a drunk, I got out of bed, swayed my fourteen-year-old body back and forth in an imaginary dance, and drifted in and out of romantic dreams. And then I stood still, watching twenty-three yellow roses bloom in a French crystal vase. The crushed petals of the twenty-fourth rose were still lingering on my skin.

A notion entered my head the day after my fourteenth birthday that I would become an international lawyer, writer, poet, traveler of the world, seeker of beauty, and lover of Baudelaire. Like André. I would do all this and sing at the same time.

If my mother had to plant flowers, I, too, had to sing, no matter what.

11. THE MAIDEN WHO PRACTICED SINGING

The day after my thirty-fifth birthday, I walked into my Fifth Avenue office and, from my glass wall, stared at a bubbling Manhattan below. Somewhere in front of the glass was America and behind it, a blurred Saigon of the seventies, all before the fall of a regime that broke my life as a young woman in half. I could still hear the helicopter sounds on top of the U.S. embassy in central Saigon. I could still see myself, twenty years of age, boarding the helicopter alone. When the machine had lifted itself into the hot air, I was still craning my head to look down at the U.S. Embassy building, at all those panic-stricken faces below.

Fifteen years had passed since then.

I mindlessly arranged the papers on my desk, knowing America had welcomed me with all my ardor and aspiration. The papers on my desk spoke of my successful law career. I had done well for myself.

Yet, in this land of dreams and opportunities, I had let go of my childhood dream. I had not taken up singing as a serious pursuit. I had become a Manhattan lawyer and spent the money I earned on trivial things like Chanel goods. To fool myself with a sense of noblesse oblige, in my days as a young associate in my law firm, I spent nine hundred hours a year on pro bono work, in addition to my normal load of two thousand billable hours a year.

All throughout the late seventies and eighties, boat people rushed out to sea to escape Communist Vietnam. One of these boat people was from the village of Quynh Anh. He brought us the news of Grandma Que's death. No details were given.

So, for a decade, I regularly sent money to friends and relatives in my former Vietnam, fooling myself that I was helping those young women who might be trying to reach their own high note, in memory of Princess Cinnamon.

But that was all I did. There was deliberate, self-constructed amnesia somewhere in my brain to cope with the pain. My years went by like a long sleepwalk.

Sitting among stacks of legal documents, I decided to take up singing again. I would seek the best coaches among the voice teachers and music professors in the vibrant artistic community of New York City. I would repeat the arduous struggle to reach *so, re, me fa, so, la,* and then my ultimate high *la.*

I leaned back in the comfort of my leather chair, yet feeling the pain of knowing that in pushing the limit of my voice, I would give up, start again, and then give up. In between, I would cry into my pillow, for something so beyond my reach—the reclamation of my childhood.

Constance, the high-cheek-boned, black-haired German Italian choir director, had reminded me of the need to imagine someone—anyone—reigning in the round dome of the wood-paneled theater. To this someone, said Constance, I should attempt to deliver the heartbeat of a muse.

During rehearsal, she would shout, "Flat! Flat! I can't stand it!" and automatically I would imagine that special person as my sole audience. And then the notes emanating from my lips would become dark, light, opaque, translucent legato, pulsating with vibrato; and the voice would cut through the space like a shooting star. Nothing stood between the streamlike darting of the voice from my lips to the heart of that special someone.

After dress rehearsal I went home and wrote down in my choir notebook, *Cher André, je veux emprunter ton coeur, encore une fois.* Dear André, it's time to borrow your heart, again.

———

Throughout the choir practice of Haydn's "Salve Regina," I kept with me an orange, velvet-covered hardbound notebook, where occasionally I recorded the beautiful sayings I had read:

"*Et c'est l'heure, Ô poète, de décliner ton nom, ta naissance, et ta race.*" And it's time, Oh, Poet, to decline your name, birth, and race. —Alexis Léger (Saint-John Perse).

"But where is what I started for so long ago? And why is it yet unfound?"—Whitman.

"I am thinking of aurochs and angels, the secret of durable pigments, prophetic sonnets, the refuge of art. And this is the only immortality you and I may share."—Nabokov.

I also wrote down the seven notes, from A to G. Each time my voice reached a note, I blacked out the corresponding letter with a marker, the harsh, black ink permeating the pages and smearing the handwriting that made up my favorite literary quotes. Up half a tone on the chromatic scale. And half a tone more. Breathe out on each word slowly, without the chest frame collapsing. Let the voice soar high. Higher and higher. Hold the note, and the vibrato would linger forever, past the point where the sound itself ripples out, dissolving in space. On to the search for freedom. To where the Statue of Liberty holds out her fingertips. And even higher, to the limitless sky. All the way with the nightingale of my childhood.

All letters became blackened except for the ultimate high A. André's name began with an A, the infinitely crisp and clear stroke. In singing, I felt a pulse within me, and I silently called it my "Art," starting with a capital A like André's name. To reach the high note, my Art had to spill out of me. My body became the container of my Art, and I had to break that confine.

Grandma Que used to talk to me about the silkworm that wanted to shed itself into beautiful fabric until all that was left was the naked body of a helpless insect. She said the Mystique Concubine's spirit had blessed the silkworms of her silk farm, enabling the production of the best silk. The beauty it gave belonged to others. All threads were peeled off to expose the soft, pulsing worm inside. The silkworm struggled against the web of threads, among the fragrant cocoon of green leaves. When the threads were removed, the flesh was displayed, and the silkworm perished. To produce perfection and reach freedom, the silkworm had to die.

———

In 1970 André and Dominique lived in a villa on Rue Tu Duc, a few blocks from Madame Misticelli's house in Saigon. On the way to my private voice lessons, I biked slowly under rows of soaring tall trees bordering the narrow street, singing to myself. Occasionally, I saw André walking alone, wearing glasses, holding a book in his hand. He rarely said anything to me. Instead, he merely nodded to acknowledge my presence as though he deliberately kept a distance or was preoccupied with other things. I would hurry to pass him, conscious that perhaps he wanted to avoid me. I missed seeing his beautiful brown eyes underneath those wire-rimmed glasses. I grew sad, as though the butterflies of Hue had finally flown away, beyond my reach.

But those fluttering butterflies came back to me one day. I was practicing the scale in the living room, next to my piano, attempting to reach the high C note, a *do*, and then working myself up to the high E note, a *mi*. I was pushing my breasts forward, drawing a long, deep breath from beneath my diaphragm muscle, lower and lower, deeper and deeper into my abdomen, in order to support the heightened pitch. Yet I simply could not stretch my voice to reach a comfort zone. Frustrated, I stopped singing and looked out at the window.

I caught his gaze. André was watching me. My cheeks were heated, my body, inflamed. I thought for a moment I had stopped breathing.

Outside the window, the butterfly lashes fluttered. My heart fluttered, too, with them.

It was not a Sunday when he was supposed to come over for his Vietnamese lessons. André had stopped by unexpectedly to let us know Dominique had won the battle: the couple would be going back to Paris, and André's Indochina would soon be a closed chapter in the book he still had to write.

—

That year, 1970, I was about to turn fifteen, still a flat-chested, long-haired melancholy girl who stood five feet tall, weighed eighty-five pounds, and looked barely twelve years old. I had become skinnier. My long hair had lost its luster due to lack of care and the humidity and dust of busy, polluted Saigon. Worst of all, the hardship of life in Saigon had made me into an ill-tempered teenager.

The war had escalated, paralleling the skyrocketing cost of living in Saigon. My mother had to take a teaching job at a secondary school. In overpopulated and commercialized Saigon, my parents' salaries could not afford a nanny for my brother Phi Long, nicknamed Pi, or any kind of domestic help then quite common in middle-class Vietnamese households. Houses rented to Americans generated revenues about five times higher than rentals to locals. Contractors doing work for Americans made millions, while civil servants and schoolteachers—the impoverished middle class—could not afford red meat at daily meals. After the Tet Offensive, it became common knowledge that domestic maids and cyclo drivers could be Vietcong agents or sentries. Poor people joined Vietcong underground operations at Cu Chi or retreated into the jungles or Ho Chi Minh Trails, hoping the Communist Liberation Army would eventually prevail and bring about better lives, closing the gap between the poor and the rich.

Naturally, I became the household help my mother could not otherwise afford. She taught in the afternoon; I attended Lycée Marie Curie in the morning. When my mother was teaching, I took care of Pi. Late in the afternoon, my sister Mi Chau would watch Pi for an hour so that I could cook the evening meal. I did everything else in the house, including washing clothes by hand, hanging them over wires that crisscrossed our patio and destroyed the aesthetic appeal of my mother's potted flowers.

"You have to hold on to Pi," I told Mi Chau one time. "You cannot move or let him go until I return."

When I returned after cooking the evening meal, Pi was crying and struggling, as Mi Chau was holding him down. When I took him from Mi Chau, I realized the bed was stained and that Pi had wet his pants.

"You said not to let him go. I couldn't take him to the bathroom," she cried.

I cried, too, feeling sorry for myself. Like my mother, I fantasized about returning to Hue, to the comfort and luxury of Grandma Que's lifestyle.

I struggled on to keep up with my singing practice. Once a week, I had to go to a piano lesson at the Institute, and then a singing lesson with Madame Misticelli. I put Pi on the front of my bicycle and Mi Chau on the back, and biked to the Institute. When I was taking lessons, Mi Chau would stand outside the classroom with my bike and Pi. One day, she wandered off, after tying Pi to the bike with the bicycle rope. After one hour of practice, I came out of the classroom, catching her untying Pi. The child's wrists were bruised and red. I slapped Mi Chau and she screamed.

I slipped down and squatted onto the floor, exhausted and defeated, my vision blurry because of the shock. I could see the front yard of Grandma Que's villa in Hue, the sweet and peaceful time I had lost. My father and Saigon had failed me. He, with all his education in Paris, and Saigon, with its glamorous downtown, could not provide me the comfort and caring given me by Grandma Que and her city of dreams.

Life went on as a struggle until an accident happened: I was standing on a wooden stool and was just about to light the kerosene

stove to cook rice when the stool gave way under me. I lost my balance and fell. Mi Chau had fallen asleep, and Pi had come into the
kitchen and pulled on the stool. I fell on top of him, together with
the kerosene stove. Luckily, the stove was not lighted. But sister and
brother were bruised, and bathed in kerosene. We had no evening
meal that day. That night, my mother wrote Grandma Que:

> I am sorry to bother you again, Mother, but your grandchil-
> dren need your help in Saigon. We can no longer return to Hue
> because after the Tet Offensive, we do not think that Hue is safe.
> Here in Saigon we are living in substandard conditions because
> my husband's teaching salary and mine are not enough to keep
> up with the cost of living here. Si handles Pi and the household
> while I am at work. Today, the kerosene stove fell on them…

She read me the letter and I began to hope, although it would
take a lot for Grandma Que to leave the ancestral house after my
parents had abandoned her in Hue.

In despair, I thought of André. I had written to Paris, sending André my sketches, poems, watercolor paintings, and the pas-
sages of prose I had written about Hue in Vietnamese and French.
I described how I could not practice singing because of household chores and babysitting responsibilities.

My parents received two letters on the same day. The first was
from Grandma Que. She would be departing for Saigon soon to
help my mother take care of Pi and the household. The ancestral
house would be looked after by a villager from the Quynh Anh
hamlet working for wages.

My parents did not show me the second letter, but I'd seen
that it had been stamped in Paris. After dinner, they locked their
bedroom door and stayed inside for about an hour. I could hear

their voices, rapid and intense, but could not make out what they were saying. When they emerged behind the door, they told me I could finish the rest of the school year in the prestigious neighborhood of St. Germain des Prés, Paris, upon one condition: André wanted to have Grandma Que's approval. He wanted the matter to constitute a gesture of trust from the woman who did not forgive.

——

I never envisioned Grandma Que in that filthy alley of Saigon's District Eight. Yet, as I was carrying Pi in my arms after his afternoon bath, exhausted, ill tempered, with his weight bearing down on my side, I looked up and saw her face. Those black eyes and heart-shaped lips that spelled beauty even in a sixty-year-old woman.

Later I found out she had arrived in Saigon unexpectedly and had taken a cab from Tan Son Nhat Airport. Her hair had thinned out some, the gray more pronounced around her temples. Other than that, she was the same as I remembered her, the royal grandmother who always conducted herself with the dignity of a princess.

She showed no reaction to the congested traffic of Saigon, the barren alley of District Eight, or the modesty of our townhouse. She acted as though she had been there for quite some time. Immediately, she started to reorganize the kitchen, getting rid of the hazardous old kerosene stove.

Pi was dressed every day in crisp linen, and I had time to take a nap after school.

I could tell, however, that she had become older and more pensive. It was the first time she had ever left the ancestral house of Nam Giao. She had brought with her to Saigon only three items from the family altar in Hue: the jade phoenix affixed to a gold plate bearing the seal of the Nguyen dynasty, which the king of Annam had given to his Mystique Concubine before his exile, and the two ivory plaques that identified Grandma Que's father-in-law, the Hong Lo Tu Khanh, and her adoptive father, Admiral Nguyen Tung. The day after her arrival in Saigon, she set up a modest altar table and placed these three items on a small pedestal, behind a glass jar full of incense sticks. It was not the same intricate altar in the Nam Giao villa, but it enabled her to resume the habit of burning incense. For the first time, our home in Saigon had an altar and burning incense, just like the old days in Hue.

About a week later, the fourth item arrived: the lacquer divan given to the Mystique Concubine by the king of Annam. The divan was delivered intact, packed perfectly between layers of foam. Grandma Que had had it transported from Hue to our townhome. The shipping had cost her a fortune.

For the rest of my time with her in Saigon until I saw her last, Grandma Que slept on this divan.

It was obvious to me that when she decided to leave the ancestral house, she had also decided that she could not part from the four symbols of her heritage: the jade phoenix, the two ivory plaques, and the lacquer divan. In Saigon, she resumed the habit of polishing them every day.

It also meant that she had decided to stay with us for a long time.

But Saigon forced her to change, as it had changed my mother and me. It was not long before Grandma Que integrated herself into the urban life of the small alleys of Saigon. She no longer wore silk pajamas or brocade *ao dai* or an ivory comb on her hair. Instead, she dressed in polyester blouses and black pantaloons like the rest of the old women of the neighborhood. In many ways she managed to fit in perfectly. She was a natural at haggling over the price of fresh fish and crawling blue crabs at the wet market or at walking home with her plastic basket full of spinach and green herbs in one hand, her other hand holding the folds of her black trousers as she hopped over little ponds of sewage water in the alley. No one in the neighborhood could distinguish her from the old women of urban Saigon whose full-time job was to do household chores and take care of small children. For social activities, they squatted and congregated on the narrow front porches of townhomes and duplexes, and occasionally, Grandma Que would join them.

The Annamese princess in her had given way to the nanny she had become. No one could imagine that not too long before, she had been an old, dainty woman dressed in silk pajamas or brocade *ao dai*, wearing dark red lipstick, the heavy gold bracelets carved with dragon shapes dangling on her two wrists. Not too long before, she had been a stern woman who lived alone in a marble-floored villa with her parrot, white rabbits, and a cinnamon log emanating its spicy scent all over her antiques, even onto an array of photographs on a family altar perpetually covered with the smoke of incense.

———

"You want to go to Paris to be with André Foucault and his wife, don't you?" Grandma Que asked me soon after her arrival in Saigon.

I told her, "Yes, yes, yes." Silently, with my eyes, I pleaded: *Grandma, please approve.*

"You think this French couple would be kind to you?"

I told her, "Yes, yes, yes." With my eyes, I silently told her: *It doesn't matter; please, understand, I want to go.*

"You should go, then. There, the Westerners can teach you how to sing like a diva of the Italian stage. When Huyen Phi was still alive, she once traveled to Europe to sell silk, and she often told me about the Italian stage. How grand it was. Not like here. Ours is a poor country, and performing artists, those Vietnamese leading stars of the southern opera, *dao cai luong*, are not well educated or well respected. It isn't the place for a true first-class lady," she said, as though talking to herself.

With my eyes, I told her again, yes, I agreed with her every word.

"The more I think about it, the more I feel you must go," she said. "But if you are not happy there, rush home." Grandma Que sighed, nodded her head, and went on to prepare for Pi's bath. She did not act overjoyed, but the nod meant the matter of my departure for Paris had had her blessing.

12. MY SECRET AND PARIS

The decision was made. I would be sent to France, entrusted to the care of André and Dominique at least until I finished high school, and perhaps even beyond that point to include my college years if I could attend the Sorbonne. Paris and exposure to the Francophone culture had great educational value; no one in my family would argue with that.

To me, going to Paris meant having the life in *Paris Match* with Tonton André, who resembled the romantic French actor Alain Delon and had the personality of Santa Claus. I frowned at the thought of having Tata Dominique around all the time, but overcame the unpleasantness with the image of a smiling and attentive André. I could not think of any woman or child who would not like being around Tonton André, with all of his dolls and toys and piano music books ordered from Paris. At night, I saw myself appearing in *Paris Match*, no longer as a skinny little girl in cotton Vietnamese pajamas or a plain pleated skirt, but a fashionable young woman, wearing dark glasses, dancing on platform heels in a gray wool coat with a fur lapel.

My excitement about the forthcoming trip was tempered only by the thought that I would be away from Grandma Que, so soon after she had just arrived in Saigon. At one point, I solemnly claimed I couldn't eat French food, things such as beefsteak and *fromage*—the variety of cheeses that makes France famous—so I would like Grandma Que to come along and cook for me; otherwise, I might starve in Paris. Of course, my request was quickly disregarded. My mother, in particular, was very much annoyed. It was impious for a granddaughter to make such a suggestion. She reminded me that Grandma Que was one of the thirty-six children of a Nguyen king, even if he had abdicated and was exiled. If there hadn't been a war, and if history had been different, Grandma Que would have visited Paris on state affairs, accompanied by her own staff of interpreters and domestic help—never as a cook. And, of course, Grandma would never go at the invitation of a Foucault, I should have known.

———

I arrived in Paris in time to see the change of seasons. Paris greeted me with the beauty of a gray sky stooping over rows of quaint, old, red-brick townhomes, narrow paved streets, and sleek branches bursting with red and yellow leaves in the cool air. André and Dominique lived in the fashionable neighborhood of St. Germain des Prés, in the heart of the Left Bank. Paris also held images of a cold and misty River Seine and pairs of adults strolling hand in hand.

In all my excitement and desire, I never once expected that there could be another side to Paris—how awful the City of Light could make me feel.

The first problem manifested itself during school enrollment. "She can't be more than twelve years old, this little girl," the French nun exclaimed when I was presented for enrollment. They reluctantly admitted me upon examining the certified translation of my Vietnamese school record, which authenticated my real age. I was indeed fifteen!

The French nun's sentiment was confirmed by almost every Parisian I met thereafter. The disappointment I felt inside was greater than I could show. I had wanted to go to Paris as a young woman, not as a child. Yet every Parisian I met thought of me as a child. Naturally they could not see my old soul.

The second problem was even more severe than the first. Contrary to my expectation, André was routinely away in Marseille for his shipping business. Quite often, I was surrounded by *les enfants terribles* of St. Germain des Prés: those awful French teenagers who looked and talked so differently, they couldn't be my friends. To avoid them, I had to spend time with Tata Dominique, who was cold and aloof and not at all suited to befriend a melancholy Vietnamese teenager.

Joy did not come so naturally, and I had to train myself to be happy. I learned restraint and solitude in living with Dominique, giving her embraces without feeling the warmth, eating her *petits-beurre* out of politeness without tasting the sweet, speaking a foreign language while afraid of being made fun of.

Life got better only when André was back in Paris in between his business trips to the coastal cities. André opened for me a life full of wonders, giving little thought to what was appropriate or inappropriate for a young teenager to absorb. We went south to the coast to find sunshine when Paris got cold. There, Antibe and its museums left me with images of peach and yellow villas facing cobblestoned, winding alleys bordered with flowering bushes.

I stared at Picasso paintings, fascinated by his lines and shapes, ignorant of the paintings' meanings. Aix en Provence offered me not only its tranquil beauty, but also the Far-Eastern center where André showed me black-and-white pictures of a Nguyen king and his Annamese entourage when they visited Paris. Vestiges of my maternal extended family, he claimed.

Finally, La Cité. We strolled the city, took *l'autobus*, ate ice cream at the famous house of Berthillon in Île St. Louis, climbed the steps of Sacré-Coeur, walked through the narrow streets of Montmartre, and toured the outskirts of Paris in his Citroën. In the boutiques of glamorous Champs-Élysées, André bought me a Dior hat, an extravagance for a teenager accustomed to wearing cotton pajamas to run around the alleys of Saigon. I proudly wore my Dior hat even in the evening hours to accompany him, thinking of myself as his companion and not just a child. My fifteen years of life lit up when the night sparkled and the stream of traffic passing L'Arc de Triomphe became diamond necklaces that graced the City of Light with sparks.

—

It was in Roma, not Paris, that I truly viewed myself as the young girl who practiced singing. In Roma I first heard Haydn's "Salve Regina" sung in a church, where André arranged for an Italian singer who had appeared at La Scala to test the range of my voice.

"*Salve Regina, mater misericordiae; vita dulcedo, et spes nostra, salve.*" Hail, O Queen, Mother of Mercy, our life, our sweetness, and our hope. Hail!

The music was so beautiful it made me cry. Crying because of beautiful music was as easy as crying for love, André murmured to himself. I, as usual, attempted to memorize his words. I memorized, too, the sacred Latin of "Salve Regina." I needed neither understanding nor translation, just the sheer beauty of sound.

"*Ad te suspiramus, gementes et flentes, in hac lacrimarum valle.*" To thee we send up our sighs, weeping in the valley of tears.

The image of the Virgin Mary, pure and good, reminded me of Quan Yin, the female Buddha in her white robe, standing on a lotus blossom floating over the South China Sea. When I told André of my comparison, he nodded but went on to tell me that the tortuous lines of "Salve Regina" reminded him of his soul, yet its lofty sound resembled my noble face, and I blushed in joy.

"*Eja ergo, Advocata nostra...O clemens, O pia, O dulcis Virgo Maria.*" Hasten theretofore, our advocate...O merciful, O pious, sweet Virgin Mary.

So André adored my face, the way he adored the face of a grown-up beauty, although the Italian voice coach, like the Parisians, thought I was a twelve-year-old child!

But the happiness of Roma was short-lived. Back to Paris, to the Gare de Lyon, with its bright yellow lights on snowy nights. Back to the St. Germain des Prés townhouse, where he kissed Dominique on the doorstep and I rushed off to my schoolgirl bedroom, wishing we had never come back.

———

The sweet moments of my stay in Europe were overshadowed and tarnished by episodes of intense arguments between André and Dominique. I walked the neighborhood aimlessly for hours or isolated myself in the living room or the attic, away from the bedroom where harsh and rapid French was spoken. I could not understand all.

And then he was gone again.

Fall and winter in Paris passed so slowly. There was no picture of me appearing in *Paris Match*. I learned to eat *fromage*, including Camembert, and actually liked it. I frequently cut classes and wandered along the streets of Quartier Latin with its abundance of used bookstores and record shops. I hopped on city buses, down to the banks of La Seine, back to St. Germain des Prés with its cafés and *magasins,* where I peeped at expensive boutiques and looked up at barren trees.

Somewhere along the sidewalks, I would hear the sounds of Chopin. Chopin became my best friend. I followed his sound from one draped window to another, along rows of brownstones, until I reached home. Dominique's home. Every day was a wandering journey. Off I went every morning in my little short coat and patent leather shoes, but I seldom went to school. Once it occurred to me that I could just go elsewhere, I freed myself from all that—the pain of being the only Vietnamese among all the French boys and girls in class and being questioned by the French nuns about the contents of all those French books. When asked about school by Dominique, I learned to make up a bunch of lies. It was all so easy.

No one in Saigon was supposed to know my sorrow, fear, and homesickness. In letters sent home, I only spoke of the melancholic beauty of Chopin's music; the townhouse intricately decorated with oil paintings and velvet curtains; Dominique's buttery biscuits, *petits-beurres*, and *soupe à l'oignon*; the svelte mannequins of Galerie LaFayette where Dominique bought me a wool Scottish dress; and the tree-filled neighborhood of St. Germain des Prés—trees that towered over rooftops and chimneys, drawing smoke out of the Parisians' mouths and nostrils when they walked the streets. "*Ça va, ça va bien*," the men in trench coats and hats and the women in miniskirts and high boots stopped momentarily to greet each other in their Parisian French, underneath those trees.

No one was supposed to know the bitter lessons Paris had taught me—that reality could never match the beauty of a dream. I was too proud to tell anyone, especially Grandma Que, about the haunting solitude of a young girl removed from her home. For months, I cried every night, badly wanting to return to the filthy alleys of Saigon's District Eight.

Naturally, my school record turned out to be a disaster, but André and Dominque tolerated this awful result. In fact, they argued among themselves and candidly admitted that my school failure might have been their fault. They discussed what they should tell my parents, and I prayed to myself, hopelessly, that they would never be able to relay the bad news. To my parents, I was supposed to be perfect!

However, my French got much better and I did learn new things—improved piano fingering techniques, operatic singing, oil painting, and a bunch of other impractical niceties that did not require much language proficiency, including an undying taste for French baguettes, butter, escargots, bouillabaisse, and *la haute couture*—the allure of high fashion.

The only consistently nice thing about those days in Paris was the fact that I was always free to practice singing.

———

No one knew Paris also housed my secret.

"*Non, non, nous ne sommes pas amoureux, c'est impossible, c'est formidable.*" He had broken down in tears.

Something happened, something broke, and I did not stay in Paris the full year. The reason given by the Foucaults to my parents was my disastrous French school record. I was to return to Saigon before springtime. So Paris to me meant summer, fall, and winter. Just a little radiant sunshine and then long months of falling red leaves, white snow, and skeletal branches.

Nineteen seventy-one. How happy I was to be hit with the heat and humidity and the dirt of Saigon as the door of the Air France plane opened at Tan Son Nhat Airport, and I knew at once I was home. Back to Grandma Que. The load of hidden sorrow that persisted through my time in Paris was lifted from me, like a leaf twirling off an autumn branch.

I stepped out of the plane and looked back for the last time. The Air France stewardess smiled at me and said, "*Au revoir*." In her clear chestnut eyes, I recalled the scenery of Paris circling around André, who knelt, his hands pressing upon his stomach, his chest heaving.

"Oh, Lord, what have I done to the little girl I once held in my arms?" His hands clutched his anguished face. I tried to catch his arm, and he avoided my touch. "But what difference does it make, Lord, even if I kneel down before you and put upon you the weight of my sins, while indeed for years I already consumed her with my eyes?"

I resented Paris for making me remember André this way. "Stop crying, André," I told him, but he kept shaking his head.

"No, no, no, Fleurs du Mal, the flowers of evil. You will never understand the pain and sins of Baudelaire."

Of course I understood. Only André did not understand. There was nothing he could have done to me that I would not have wanted him to do.

———

In the summer of 1971, according to Grandma Que, I was already on the verge of developing into a young woman. So she began to have dozens of classic *ao dai* made for me, with darts around the bustline, nipped at the waistline—the formfitting style designed only for young women.

All the good food, leisurely lifestyle, and the constant walking around the streets of Paris had done me wonders. I had sprung up wonderfully to five feet five, impressively tall for a Vietnamese girl of my generation. Paris had changed me from a skinny young girl to a beautiful lady, everyone in the District Eight neighborhood of Saigon commented. Paris had also confirmed me as a hopeless romantic, with my newly acquired repertoire of French poems, classical music, and European stars like Brigitte Bardot, Catherine Deneuve, Alain Delon, Claudia Cardinale, Gina Lolobrigida, and Jean Paul Belmondo.

I kept writing André and he kept writing back, but only to my parents, always referring to me as the niece or daughter he would like to have.

I finished high school at Lycée Marie Curie, passed the Tu Tai College Entrance Examination, and was dying to return to Paris to see André and attend the Sorbonne. But my father talked to André separately and preferred for me to attend graduate school in America. To prepare for that course of life, I enrolled at the Faculty of Law in Saigon, while waiting for the right graduate scholarship to the United States.

Sadly and bitterly, I blamed André for not wanting me to return to Paris. How else could my father get the crazy idea that I was better off at an American college?

———

Constance gave a hand signal, and the music began.

"*Lacrimosa son io, perduto ho l'idol mio.* I am melancholy." I have lost my idol.

Six months after my thirty-fifth birthday, boxed in a severe, long, black velvet dress and standing in the first row of a 140-member choir, I sang the gorgeous sound of Wolfgang Amadeus Mozart. Somewhere in the program, a lyric soprano would be singing Schumann's "Träumerei."

In moments of Träumerei, I saw the past. The sound took me back to Rome. I saw again the black-haired, skinny young girl resting her head on André's shoulder. In Paris and Rome, she was supposed to be twelve years old, since she was not big enough for her fifteen years of life.

"My feet are too sore for me to walk," she had complained, so he carried her on his back, one early autumn day, down the foggy street of Rome to her first singing lesson, in the country where the great art of bel canto singing originated. He had promised to show her how the human voice could become the instrument in competition with an orchestra. The voice could stand alone in its own time and space, with all its nuances, colors, and texture.

They went inside a grandiose old church, and he put her down and asked her to walk through a set of tall, mahogany double doors. At the other end of a corridor, a real Italian opera singer would soon confirm the girl was a lyric soprano, a real honor for a sullen Vietnamese girl who loved to sing.

The young girl would be singing Schumann's "Träumerei."

—

The vibrato on the last note of Mozart's "Lacrimosa" quivered and extinguished. Constance gave another hand gesture to prepare the choir for Haydn's "Salve Regina" in G.

"*Ad te suspiramus, Exsules filii Evae. Ad te suspiramus, gementes et flentes, in hac lacrimarum valle.*" To thee do we cry, poor banished children of Eve. To thee do we send up our sighs, groaning and weeping in this valley of tears.

From the corner of my eyes, I thought I saw fog. He emerged from all that fog, a surreal figure, at the end of the music hall. His gorgeous self, in a trench coat, exactly like that day in Rome. I kept on singing and he leaned against the set of closed doors, beautiful and youthful as ever. No one saw him except me. For a moment, time seemed to hold still, until he started to speak.

"*Bonjour, c'est magnifique tout ce que tu as fait. Je t'adore, éternellement,*" he said, one hand in his coat's pocket. "Put your mind at rest. You made the right decision not to return to Paris with me in 1975. You have found your place in America, on your own, singing," he said.

We were having our private conversation across the music hall, above the heads of a bunch of New Yorkers sitting stiff and still, staring at the stage. In my mind, they froze, leaving the world to him and me alone. We silently conversed in the middle of Haydn's choral music.

"*Ad te suspiramus,*" I sang my solo line. More eyes were on me, yet my eyes were on him. No more tears. He stood so beautifully and cheerfully at the end of the corridor.

Could you have saved me from my Fleurs du Mal? No, no, no, he shook his head.

I stayed with the high *la*. Forever on the A note, which spelled his name. There was no gap between him and me on that high A. The audience was clapping, and he clapped, too.

Brava, brava, he said, disappearing gradually, together with the fog.

Bravo for a man, *brava* for a woman, he had told me that day in Rome.

In what was left of the vibrato on my perfect high A, I closed my eyes and saw, again, scenes of Paris.

13. REQUIEM IN THE GARDEN OF LUXEMBOURG

It must have been in the tree-filled neighborhood of St. Germain des Prés and the Garden of Luxembourg in Paris that I first recognized, at the tender age of fifteen, the difference between Southeast Asia and Europe manifested in the colors and shapes of leaves in my two worlds.

In Southeast Asia, tall trees produced thick, dark green leaves that shone as though waxed. Those wide leaves created rich, dark shade. Day upon day, the wide, luscious surfaces of tropical leaves drank the early morning dew and then bathed in sunshine. The trees' huge trunks challenged the arms of children.

I could still see the little girl running around the front yard of Grandma Que's villa until she collapsed to rest in the enormous, cool shadow of a tall magnolia tree, or she simply circled the tree, at times stopping to throw her little arms wide in a vain attempt to embrace it. Grandma Que said the tropical climate did wonders for vegetation. In the wealth of sunshine, a tree had no other way to grow but tall and big, and leaves had no other way but to turn into wide, flat surfaces of luscious green.

The same slender young girl was standing beneath a row of trees—not the thick and tall trees of the tropics, but slender trees with thin branches shedding red leaves that crumbled under a grayish low sky. Here in Parisian autumn, there was no need for leafy shade to protect the girl against a burning sun. Instead, leaves turned red and fell, covering the ground, and then they dried up and broke under human footsteps.

The girl moved on beds of red leaves toward the sound of the piano. She called out, "Tata Dominique," and the door was flung open, and the sound of Chopin pouring out in fuller force. There she was met by a tall, blond woman wearing an apron, leaning against the mahogany door, saying in a husky, melodious voice, "*Berceuse, berceuse!* That's my favorite Chopin, and yours, too, Simone."

Inside, with the cover of the record in one hand, the blonde woman extended her other hand to turn a key and lock the door after the girl had slipped in. The girl made her way awkwardly among dark wood furniture and tiptoed upon those dark Persian rugs. Impressionistic oil canvases matched perfectly with their carved, matted gold frames hung solemnly around the wood-burning fireplace, where fresh logs melted off their sap. The rest of the wall space was jammed with photographs of strangers—men wearing tails and round spectacles slipping down the bridges of their hawked noses, almost down to their spiral whiskers, and women with perfectly coifed golden or chestnut hair, their hands folding grimly over long, bouffant skirts. The room smelled of cream, butter, beaten eggs, and burned sugar.

"I am sorry, Tata Dominique; I skipped school," the girl stammered in her timid voice.

"It's all right for now. You can learn Chopin instead. Appreciate Chopin with me. Chopin is your uncle's favorite," the blonde woman said.

"And I just baked madeleines," the woman added, speaking of her sugary cookies, the kind that invoked Marcel Proust's lost paradise. "You should one day learn Marcel Proust, even if you are going home back to Vietnam. You should learn about the time lost, revived by a sense, a taste, or a feel. That, too, is your uncle's favorite."

Oh, of course, the girl would love to learn anything, anything that is her uncle's favorite. Chopin and Proust.

"Thank you, Tata Dominique, for telling me," the girl said, dreamily. She thought proudly to herself, *I am his favorite. Not just you, Tata, but me, my little self.*

Outside on those Parisian streets, people hurried their steps, carrying newspapers under their arms, shapeless in their heavy coats, their breath escaping them like smoke. Inside, the girl tapped her shoe on the red rug, the braids of black hair and ebony eyes contrasting against her white chemise. When she turned around, the street sign across from the misty set of French windows met her swollen eyes, accustomed already to weeping alone at night.

The sign said *St. Germain des Prés.*

The townhouse belonged to him and Dominique, but in Paris, the little girl also had what she considered to be her own place with him. Number thirteen, Rue St. Baptiste de la Salle. *Walk toward that place reserved for love!* Innocent love, innocent like the young girl who strolled the streets of Paris.

On one of those lonely walks, she heard the voice of someone who sounded so familiar speaking to her so endearingly. In a séance. From the pink and mauve lotuses that filled up the horizon in a city that was all violet. In all those shades of sub-dued and tender colors, the matriarch of Hue opened her restful eyes, as well as her bright red cloak that spelled fire, to show the girl a radiant jade phoenix. The fierce green of jade against the luscious red fabric became the focal point among all that pastel shades of lotuses and mosses.

"I, too, fell in love at the tender age of fifteen, with some-one older who did not share my race. He's Vietnamese, and I am Cham. I was just a child, but he was also the State of Annam." The matriarch spoke of her sorrow, a tear lurking underneath her beautiful lashes.

"What do you hope to find on those streets of a faraway place called Paris?" The matriarch smiled to the child, raising her per-fectly shaped brows. The lurking tear had turned into the sap-phire blue of the Perfume River behind the silver-ebony curtain of her eyelashes.

"Independence, liberty, and the pursuit of happiness, all made possible by love," perhaps the girl might have replied sol-emnly. All those clichés. "After all, this is Paris, the city that has received and housed all the misfits. It's the city of dreams," the girl explained.

"Oh, yes, all of those beautiful concepts worthy of the best of dreams." The matriarch sighed and closed her eyes, shutting off the blue of her Perfume River with her sparkling eyelashes. "But, my dear, if misplaced, the pursuit of independence, liberty, and happiness, no matter how beautiful, can be just as deadly as infan-tile love—the kind of love that bears no responsibility because it is just a notion of perfection in a dream, never to be materialized fully in the real world!" Her final words blurred away.

—

Fall had begun, and sunbathing Parisians had all headed home from their vacations on the southern coast. Toward November Paris was chilly and gray. Somewhere near the St. Germain townhouse that was not hers, outside that white-shuttered window from which Chopin was heard, perhaps the church of St. Germain was tolling its Sunday bell. On the other side of town, on Rue St. Baptiste, she was awakened to an apartment full of the pleasant scent of freshly baked baguettes and brewing coffee. She could happily call this place her own.

A pair of dark brown eyes behind wire-rimmed glasses was looking down into her sleepy eyes. "Get up, *ma petite chérie.*"

This was her own world with him. No sign of Tata Dominique or her sugary madeleines.

The girl's eyes followed the mass of dark, curly hair and the bluish-gray sweater that shaped the torso of the man. Her very own André. He had moved toward the window and was pensively looking out, the porcelain coffee cup going back and forth between the table and his tight lips. She did not like seeing him like that. Tense and sad, with those lips so tight, as though they were holding in complex emotions she never quite understood.

Those days, the girl had become used to life in Paris, and her eyes were no longer weepy at night. *Le Monde* was in the man's other hand, and he was about to swing it across the room to the sofa. She whispered to him, "*Je t'aime.*" Of course, he acted as though he did not hear her words.

She tumbled from the bed over to the table, reached for the jar of honey, and dipped one finger into the sticky golden liquid. She wrote "*Je t'aime*" across the table with her honeyed finger. He could not have read her words since he was looking outside the window, but she rejoiced in writing the words anyway. It made her feel like an adult in love. What else could it be to explain the powerful and intense affection she felt for him?

He turned around from the window, frowned, and for a moment she could see the blackness of his coffee almost spilling, as though his hand were trembling. His unhappiness did not concern her too much, for she had made up her mind to hold on to him, having been amused by the secret they shared. She was glad the *tata* had left for the coast, and thought of all the places she wanted to go with him: the castles of Loire, the forests of Fontainebleau, the vineyards of Beaune, all those fishermen's villages between Marseille and Cassis. She imagined all those wild rabbits running across potato fields and grape leaves stretching to the horizon. The Parisians regarded her slender frame as that of a twelve-year-old, and she might as well benefit from that misleading notion. She could remain a playful child. She rubbed her honeyed finger onto her front teeth, and he caught her wrist, complaining about her lack of manners. She smeared honey onto his lips, ignoring his frown as he awkwardly turned away. She grabbed his chin and forced him to face her.

Je t'aime. Tant. Tant. Tant. I love you, far, far too much!

Just a few days before, the Catholic sisters at the conservatory of St. Germain des Prés had all been all shocked when she'd locked herself in the water closet. The nuns called upon Madame Foucault, who had left for the coast. So Monsieur Foucault rushed to school in his trench coat, kneeling down before the locked door and talked in a language the nuns could not understand to the young girl curling up on the other side of the door. She felt so sorry for herself. She told him for the first time how bad it had been for her in Paris. The Foucault couple had fought all the time, books and plates flying across the room, leaving the young Vietnamese girl tiptoeing alone around the living room packed with French

Renaissance paintings and eighteenth-century antiques. She missed the dusty alley of District Eight in Saigon and did not want to go back to the luxurious townhouse in St. Germain des Prés.

Monsieur Foucault wrapped his trench coat around the girl and took her home, a different home, an art studio converted into an apartment on Rue St. Jean Baptiste de la Salle, where he had lived before he got married. There, away from his wife, he had his books, manuscripts, typewriter, records, even the philosophy papers from Sorbonne and pictures of old girlfriends, together with all artifacts he had brought home from his various trips to Vietnam. The apartment was his hideout away from his troubled marital life. Outside the apartment's window, one could see the tip of the Eiffel Tower.

At Rue St. Jean Baptiste de la Salle, the girl calmed down. He prepared her bath, and she sat in the tub for a long time, lonely and upset.

The apartment had two bedrooms, and the girl stayed in the guest room, on a carved Chinese poster bed the man had brought back from the Orient, among piles of ornately embroidered pillows and blankets—traces of her Orient. In the middle of the night, the girl got up, crying, and crawled into the man's bed, where the mattress was plush and warm. She hung on to his side, placed one leg over his belly, and cried onto his chest. She spread her legs and climbed on top of him and pressed her face onto his heart. She was terribly lonely. In a trance, she wanted to repeat the pony ride of childhood. She took his arms and wrapped them around her like a security blanket.

And then she was frightened. She felt the tense muscle, and he moaned and shook, and as the Parisian moon from the window hit his face, she saw him grimace in pain, and he was grabbing her rib cage. She thought she had hurt him irreparably. She could see nothing in the dark.

He lay still, panting, and then broke out crying. She felt the man's face, and it was soaked with tears.

"Sorry, sorry," she said, panicked. "I was a bad girl to make you cry!"

He rolled over to cover his tearful eyes. "God knows in my heart I must have known this was no accident, and I must have wanted it this way," he anguished between sobs.

For the first time he spoke to her of death. This did not scare her. She was excited about other things.

She knew they had shared a secret. She knew, too, that she now had a hold on him. She had turned fifteen, and the game was far too exciting. She was more than ready to discover adulthood. Yet he kept crying for days and said he wanted to die for betraying her family's trust and spoiling her innocence such that she should be sent home. Her real home, much earlier than he had planned.

He wanted to flee from her, heading down south to join his wife, leaving her with the housekeeper who prepared for her to cross the ocean.

Before his departure, he took her back to the St. Germain des Prés townhouse and then to Le Jardin de Luxembourg. There, she found so many chestnut trees that shed their brown nuts onto the damp ground. They shared the same color with his eyes and hair.

No more pony rides. They strolled the garden, sat on a bench among the pigeons and falling leaves and statues whose names she could hardly remember from French history books. He recited contemporary poems by Jacques Prevert.

> *Les feuilles mortes se ramassent à la pelle…*
> *Toi, qui m'aimais…*
> *Moi, qui t'aimais…*

The poem spoke of love. She stood barely below his chest, light like a bird. At the Luxembourg garden, inside the black and gold iron gate that separated nature from the bubbling streets of fashionable Paris, she began to understand the fate of falling leaves, just like those who left their home. Leaves descending from treetops, only to reach uncertainty and then to be crushed by the callous steps of humans. She told him falling autumn leaves in Paris meant tragic beauty.

"What does a young girl know about tragic beauty?" he asked, with raised brows. "What happened between us, *ma chérie*, is tragic beauty," he said mournfully.

He said loving poetry meant she was about to become a young woman, bidding farewell to childhood, like young leaves maturing for fall. If growing up means good-bye, *adieu*, and good morning sadness—*bonjour tristesse*—then let me be a child forever, she said.

He had not understood her words, no matter how simple they were. *Je t'aime. Tant. Tant. Tant.*

She kicked off her shoes and tiptoed over the bed of leaves, imagining them crying under each step. Looking back, she caught his eyes gazing at her naked heels.

"*Tes pas d'enfant...mon silence...T'en souviens-tu de mes pieds nus?*" Remember your childlike steps? My silence...Oh those naked heels...

Why do I have to move from here to there, she wondered, only to destroy the fragility underneath my feet? She thought of the trip back home. Her parents had written about the national literature contest, the debate team, even a teenage beauty pageant, and national scholarships, including the choices of the Sorbonne, Australia, Japan, England, or the United States. All would be far better than the bad grades earned by a teenager who frequently skipped school in St. Germain des Prés. A plane would depart from Charles De Gaulle toward all of these splendid things awaiting her in Vietnam. And it would be just a beginning for a future so bright any young girl would have been envious.

—

"*O clemens; O pia; O dulcis Virgo Maria.*" Oh, sweet Virgin Mary, have mercy, have pity on us. Our weakness, our vulnerability and fragility in the wretchedness of our life. Your sacredness, your beauty, your purity, in the holiness of your light.

The music died down. The applause began and then extinguished. The black-clad men and women of the choir turned a certain way and left the stage section by section, and Constance beamed with satisfaction from the conductor stand.

Never rush off stage. In singing, never rush anywhere, he had said.

Rush. I've turned thirty-five safely in America, yet all I want to do is rush so that nothing good can be taken away from me again. Someone handed me a rose backstage, and a few choir members were talking about late-night tea in Greenwich Village or Soho.

I said yes, yes, desperately wanting to rush, hearing again in my mind the sound of a helicopter roaring on top of a building in central Saigon decades ago.

I heard, too, the French manager of the Continental Hotel in Saigon yelling, "*Putain!*" to those young Vietnamese women wearing miniskirts and platform shoes, with their mascara running down their blotted cheeks in the heat of April 1975.

On that day, I had gone to the Continental Hotel by myself to meet a man and beg for his help. Later, I thought by starting a new American life with Christopher Sanders, I could accept and forget.

14. REFUGEES IN DIAMONDALE—NOVEMBER 1975

The summer of 1975 was a long, drugged sleep. I woke up one day and Vietnam had been miraculously replaced with America. I had boarded, by myself, from atop the U.S. embassy, one of the last flights out. Months later, I reunited with my family in Fort Chaffee, Arkansas, one of the resettlement camps. We settled in Diamondale, a small town in Southern Illinois.

Diamondale was no diamond, its rural sleepiness perked up only with the college football and basketball games or weekend sales at the KMart™ on Main Street. Commerce included a Steak and Ale and a Holiday Inn near the tiny airport that provided the only airway to the major metropolitan area of Chicago, and just enough shops and restaurants to serve some thirty thousand inhabitants, about twenty-five thousand of whom were college students at Southern Illinois State University.

In the beginning, while my parents were looking for jobs, the sponsoring Lutheran Church let us live in an old house in a mixed neighborhood, on a street full of big, old pecan trees. An old colleague of my father on the political science faculty gave him an interest-free loan to buy a used car. The house, provided rent-free, was old enough to suffer all kinds of heat and air-conditioning problems. Parents and children were crammed into the little old house, but we were just thankful for a roof over our heads until we could afford our own place.

I thought then that I had survived.

Yet in Diamondale, I kept recalling scenes of the Continental Hotel in downtown Saigon, the hairy arms and legs of a man I hardly knew, and the infirmaries in Guam, together with the faces of Red Cross workers, military nurses and doctors, and church volunteers. Finally, I recalled the scene of myself lying alone on the beach of Guam Island on a starry night, listening to the waves of the sea, crying to myself and blaming God. Those days I was not sure whether my family had safely fled Saigon, so I kept strolling the beaches of Guam by myself until my feet turned sore and my eyes blanked out. Only then would I lie on the hot sand and stare into the sky.

One night in Guam, after strolling the beach in despair, I stabbed the lower part of me with a mess hall fork. My memory of what happened thereafter became spotty.

In Diamondale, I withdrew into my own world, stopped talking to my parents and siblings, and took a waitressing job at the town's only Chinese restaurant, where greasy chow mein and ready-made sweet-and-sour pork were considered the house's gourmet specialties. I postponed all plans to go to college until my parents could find more permanent employment and we could save enough money for a better life.

—

We had not had any snow in late November, but the roads of Diamondale were icy, and the trees had lost all their leaves, bringing back sad memories of Paris. I got home around eleven from my waitressing job that night.

My sister, Mi Chau, opened the door, her cat eyes lit up. "Guess who's here! Tonton André!"

So he had come to find me, but perhaps it was all too late. Perhaps he was thinner. Perhaps he had aged some. Perhaps his thick, wavy brown hair had thinned out, making his forehead higher. Perhaps more lines had appeared around his beautiful brown eyes. My palpitating state of mind rejected all details. I saw him as I had seen him those days in Paris.

"Oh, Si," André said, "you have…grown so much." He kept his arms pinned to his sides as though they longed to reach out. His eyes sparkled with unspoken messages and the surreptitiousness of an accomplice. It was the first time since the incident in Paris that he faced me in the company of my parents.

It was an awkward moment. I spoke very little, fearful that my parents would detect my uneasiness.

He came up to me and wanted to embrace—the French way. The verb *embrasser* meant a kiss as well as a hug. So I hugged him and kissed him on his cheeks. Since the time in Paris, my breasts had fully developed, and I blushed when his arms slightly brushed upon them.

I turned away from him, coldly told my parents I was very tired from my job, and would like to go to my room. My brother Pi was dancing around André. "Tonton André, would you play pony with me?" Pi cried, beaming at him. "Would you take me to Paris?"

I went to my room and changed into a nightshirt. I heard the door moving and pretended to bury my face into the pillow.

"What's wrong, Si?" My mother sat down by the bed.

"Nothing."

My mother's eyes were sad. They had been sad since our departure from Vietnam. She and I avoided talking about Grandma Que, who stayed behind.

"André and Dominique are getting a divorce," my mother sighed, pausing to test my reaction. "Dominique is talking to publishers now. She wants to write a book on Indochina. How ridiculous, the woman was barely there. Now that South Vietnam has fallen, everybody wants to write a book about us."

She stroked my hair. "André has talked to us. If you want a Christmas vacation in Paris, you can go with him."

"No," I said feebly.

"I have always known," my mother said gravely. "Only your father is blind. Back then, I took a chance sending you to Paris because I knew how badly you wanted to go."

I leaned against the headboard, puzzled.

"You are grown now, and he is about to be free. Go with him if you want. He is a good man, though he is twice your age."

I sat still. What exactly did my mother know?

There was one thing she could not have known: the Continental Hotel. The man there was more than twice my age.

15. THAT DAY IN APRIL

Five days before the fall of Saigon, I stood hours in the sun before I entered the Continental Hotel. For a moment I couldn't read the room number, 210, engraved on the door. The room of an American journalist, Christopher Sanders, a friend of my father's. When I entered, he was in his bathrobe, dictating into a tape recorder.

The man looked up from the desk and asked, "Room service?"

I said no, I had come on my own.

He asked if I was sent by the embassy. I said no.

Irritated and impatient, he asked who I was.

I stood on *escapin* high heels, in my best *ao dai*, made for ceremonial occasions, with its dignified high collar, and embroidered golden dragons on black satin. My father was at home sleeping, exhausted. For days he had been running around town looking for a way out. From the defense attaché's office to various embassies. He had gone home defeated. Finally my mother said to him, "Sleep, my dear. Take a nap." She got him a hot towel. Made him a lemon soda. I watched them. I saw despair and panic written on their faces. So I said, "Let me try; leave everything to me. After all, I am the oldest daughter and speak fluent English."

I introduced myself to the man in the bathrobe. Mr. Sanders. I was Hope's oldest daughter, I told him. Hope, the nickname this man had given to my father, the American equivalent of L'Espoir, the pen name my father had taken during his college days at Sorbonne. My father, the college professor at the Faculty of Letters, University of Saigon, had become a stringer for the Associated Press—the stringer who had helped build this man's reporting career in the country.

The man's face softened only slightly at the mention of my father's nickname. "I know now," he said. "You want a way out of Vietnam. There's nothing I can do."

"Mr. Sanders," I said, "I am begging you. Those people from the North who will be coming out of the Cu Chi tunnel— they don't like us. French-educated professor. Informer for the Americans. Bourgeois. Annamese aristocrat. We stand for what the people from the North have been trying to destroy. I won't watch my father sent to a Communist jail. I have young siblings who need a future elsewhere. My mother is a fragile woman who loves to plant flowers and faints in times of crisis!"

He pointed to the high window looking out at Saigon harbor. His pale face seemed worn from watching the devastation mount around him. He suggested that I try the sea merchants who were selling spaces on their boats, at ten gold taels or so per head. He must have known we didn't have that kind of money.

I offered him the two ivory plaques, made out of elephant tusks thousands of years old. One had belonged to *nhat pham trieu dinh, hong lo tu khanh,* a mandarin of the first rank of the royal court, and the other one to an admiral of the royal fleet that once watched over the Port of Thuan An. I offered him the luscious green jade phoenix, once held by a royal concubine of the Nguyen Dynasty.

Grandma Que had removed these items from the altar and given them to me when I told her I had to go seek a way out of Vietnam, before the Communists came in. "Go, child," she said, "Westerners like antiques." For her to part with these items meant we were facing a matter of life and death.

The man refused the gifts, embarrassed, as I had expected he would. Christopher Sanders told me to go home and wait with my father. Or—he pointed again to the high window from which we could see the ships afar, where transactions for a way out were also taking place—an alternative escape route that he should have known my family could not afford. He was just trying anything, anything to get me to leave him alone. So I followed his hand gesture and walked past him to approach the window just to buy some time to think. I looked out at Saigon's waterfront, on one side, and the giant clock over the Ben Thanh market, on the other. Everything outside that window was the same—the same dock, the same clock—yet it was not the same city.

So I made up my mind. There was only one thing I could afford to do.

I had heard the hotel manager screaming at the throngs of desperate bar girls waiting in the lobby for their American boyfriends to get them seats on the last airlifts. They were all in bell-bottoms and miniskirts and platform shoes, with their fake eyelashes, foam enhancers inside their bras, and all that heavy makeup and broken English. "*Putain!*" the manager had screamed, losing his cool, waving his arms and pushing them back from the stairs.

"At any moment," said Mr. Sanders, "with a signal from Washington, Voice of America will play 'White Christmas,' and all U.S. personnel are to report immediately to the embassy. I'm supposed to be here twenty-four hours a day, around the clock, waiting for the tune of 'White Christmas' over the radio. I am to cover the end of the war. My nerves are raw..."

"All you need to do is to put us on the plane," I said, cutting him off. "Tell your boss in America I am your wife. Tell them anything, anything. Take us to America and I'll be your maid. I'll sweep your floor. I'll do anything. Either I stay here with you, or I go into another room. Any room. I'll find myself another American man and make my offer to him. A GI, perhaps."

Mr. Sanders looked down at the floor. "No please, don't do that," he said quietly.

The floor was gray marble, cold even in the April heat. His eyes traveled back up to my face, lingering along the curves of the gold dragons around my waist.

Numbly, I took off my *escapin* shoes, held them in my hands, and walked barefoot over the marble to where he was sitting, behind his desk. The cold spread up my legs through the tendons in my ankles. I knelt in front of him and put my shoes down on the marble floor. I began to unbutton my *ao dai*.

"You make it very difficult for me, mademoiselle," he said. "You are exquisite."

16. WINTER IN DIAMONDALE— NOVEMBER 1975

I lay down for at least half an hour in the bedroom I shared with Mi Chau, trying to sort out my confused head. I could hear Mi Chau trying to practice French with Uncle André outside. In emotional exhaustion, I dozed off.

I could not have gone to sleep for too long, because when I woke up, it was still dark outside, and I still heard my father's voice from the living room. Finally, I had to come out. The old house had no separate dining room, and we used an old, chipped dining set as living room furniture. André and my father were sitting at the table. I stood behind the door to the den and listened. André's voice was like a taut wire.

"Keep this check, for Si's college education."

"My daughters are smart," my father said. "They can get scholarships."

"What's wrong with getting a little more?"

"I work, and my wife works. We are not used to charity."

"It isn't charity. It's my responsibility."

"Your responsibility? If you meant the Foucault–Thuan Thanh saga and family feud, it's stale."

"Then take it from a friend. Or a former student. You were once my tutor."

"Maybe your money should go to my in-laws in Vietnam. My mother-in-law, Ms. Que."

"I can have a separate sum set up for that. But the money can't get to them now. My contacts said they can't find Ms. Que, either in Hue or Saigon."

"I fully intend for Si to go to college, no matter what," my father continued. "She'll graduate, on fast track, hopefully to get a job and help us."

"I think she ought to sing," André said.

"Don't be a bad influence, André. Don't talk to her about singing. It's all over now. The country fell. What she must have is a college education that leads to a job."

"What if I take her to France? She'll go to the Sorbonne or do whatever she wants to do, whether marketable or not. You won't have to worry about her for the rest of her life. I'll take care of everything."

I looked around the door into the dining area. My father was sipping a cup of tea, that same habit from the garden of the old days. André was staring nervously at his own hands.

"Si is no longer a child, André," my father said. "She is a young woman now, resourceful, courageous, and she can take care of herself. She brought us out of Vietnam."

"What?" The frown on André's face deepened.

"While we were still trying to contact you in Paris for help to leave Saigon, she went out and secured a list from the American defense attaché's office from some friend of hers at the College of Law. She refused to tell us who. The list had the names of our whole immediate family and secured our access to Tan Son Nhat airport. A grandmother was not considered part of the imme-diate family, so the list did not include my mother-in-law. So Si stayed on in Saigon to get her grandmother. But Ms. Que refused to leave, and Si left on one of the last helicopters."

"*C'est...extraordinaire,*" André said, twisting his fingers together.

"Stop talking about me! There's nothing extraordinary about what I did!" I yelled, jumped out of my hiding space, and ran outside.

"Si, stop!" André ran after me.

I heard my mother's voice. "André, here is a coat for her."

My father yelled, "Ignore her; she's out of line!"

I leaned against one of the tall pecan trees that bordered the street. It was freezing cold, and I was wearing only a nightshirt and socks.

A pair of arms took me in, put a coat over me. André turned me around and I found the same shoulders and chest, smelled the same familiar musky smell from the man I had long desired.

"I wish you would go away," I stammered.

"I know you are upset, *bébé*. It was hard. But many others are in worse position than you."

"That's not it." I managed to push him away in quiet resigna-tion.

"I know you lost your scholarship, your plans, going to the university of your choice."

"You don't understand! I am not Dominique, but everyone in Saigon said I was beautiful. I had nothing else to go by."

He held my hands together. "For all these years since you left Paris," he said, "I haven't been able to sleep well. My marriage is over."

"That's not what I meant. Don't worry, my parents don't know what happened in Paris. No one blamed you."

"But I'm ready to tell your parents. Si, all this happened for a reason. We can be together, even get married."

White flakes had begun to fall from the sky. *All I see here is snow, white like death,* I told myself. "I want to be left alone," I stuttered in the wind, my teeth clapping together. "I can't marry you, André. You abandoned me in the final days. You were in Paris with Dominique."

He let go of me. Silence ensued. The flakes were falling over my hair. I did not have shoes on, so my feet were trembling. So he picked me up and walked, as on that day on the streets of Roma. He stopped at a streetlight next to a tall pecan tree. He sat down, leaning against the light pole, and I was in his lap. Snowflakes were all over his brown hair and pale face.

"You've grown up, and you don't like me anymore, Si?"

Oh, how could I not like him? All the time in the Continental Hotel I kept thinking of him. America and Gerald Ford had saved some 150,000 South Vietnamese by airlift. I was among those lucky ones, but somehow they had not saved me.

"*D'accord.* You don't have to like me," he said. "We won't get married then. But come with me to France. For a better future. Here, you are in the middle of nowhere. It's the rural Midwest. People don't understand your culture here. Your father doesn't have a real job. His fellowship at the university hardly pays enough and it will expire soon. Your fragile mother works in a factory."

"I can't go with you," I said, exhausted.

"In Paris, you can have your own friends. I won't touch you. You'll meet some boy your age. You can sing."

"There won't be any boys. André, *il y a quelque chose que je dois te raconter. Avril 1975…*"

The nausea that once struck me down on the beach of Guam returned to me temporarily, and I heard again the voice of the kindhearted Red Cross nurse who had found me and brought me to the infirmary. "You've hurt yourself, miss," she said. "You stabbed yourself with a mess hall fork, and that could hurt your baby. You can't be self-destructive, miss. Remember, you are pregnant, miss. Where is the father of your baby? Is he still in Saigon, miss?

Too many questions asked of Miss. After all the things Miss had done to get her family out of the country, Miss was by herself, knowing not whether her family had safely escaped. Her grandmother had refused to leave, and the father of the unwanted baby stayed on to cover the end of the war. Miss was to board the last helicopter alone. Then the nausea came, and Miss wanted to die. Why couldn't you leave her alone to die, Madame Red Cross? So I told the nurse I had no husband and wanted no baby.

My stomach must have been dancing with the snow of Diamondale when I bent over André's arm, like a piece of silk over a wire. In all that snow I kept hearing the words of the Red Cross nurse about the baby I had lost.

The kind Red Cross nurse must have stayed with me all throughout my nightmare. "You will have more babies later," she said, "later, when you are ready." She had stroked my hair. Despite her soothing voice, her green eyes remained blank, with no real sign of empathy, and I went on with my monologue. "I'm a Buddhist who went to a French Catholic school, dear Madame

Red Cross Nurse. For me, a Buddhist girl, life begins at conception and sins begin with thoughts, not action."

I wiped the snow off my face and blurted out to André strings of words, without breaths in between. I went on and on. But his face was blank, like that Red Cross nurse's. He had not understood a word. I spoke in a marathon. Completely in Vietnamese.

"Slow down, *bébé*. Tell me, in English, in French, please; my Vietnamese isn't good enough anymore."

He picked me up and walked toward the house. It was snowing heavily and we would have died together in the cold if I had continued telling him my secret. He was carrying me like a small child, just like the old days in Rome. When I looked up, I could see the black sky and thousands of whirling flakes.

I closed my eyes. All of a sudden, I realized I was in a different place.

I wanted to start all over again in this land of wonders. The past could vanish with the name of a republic that had lost a war. I opened my eyes to look at him, deep into the brown eyes I had come to love.

"André," I said in English, "there has been someone else in my life. Even my parents don't know. Five days before the fall of Saigon, I was married to an American journalist. He got most of my family out. I am indebted to him. I tried to pick up my grandmother on the way to the Embassy, but she locked herself inside the house and refused to leave, fearing she would jeopardize my chance of leaving, since she wasn't on the list. It's just a matter of time before I have to go to him. He's waiting for me in New York City."

—

In the morning, my father was to give André a ride to the airport. My mother was frying eggs in the kitchen for breakfast, and my father was reading the *St. Louis Post Dispatch*. I had stayed in the bathroom for a long time, putting on eyeshadow to cover up my puffy eyes. Instead of my routine outfit of jeans and sweater, I put on a pullover and a long skirt. Part of me still wanted to be pretty for him.

"What's that stuff on your eyes?" my mother said when I came out. "You don't need makeup. You see what America has done to her already, André?"

"I don't know when I will see *mes amis* again," he replied, looking at me.

"Oh, don't be sentimental, André," my father said, putting his newspaper down. "We just lost a country, but we are still living."

André looked haggard, with dark circles under his eyes and disheveled hair. "I stayed up writing a poem. I'll leave it with Si," he said, handing me an envelope. "It's meant to be her birthday present."

"Cool," Mi Chau said, chewing on a piece of toast.

"It's a temporary present, Si. The real one for your next birthday will be coming soon. What about an apartment in Paris, overlooking Champs-Élysées? It will be yours whenever you want to visit."

"Thank you, but I'm very busy here." I tried to be nonchalant.

Soon, it was time for André to go to the airport. My father had gone outside to wipe off snow from the car. André and I were alone, together, for a fleeting moment.

"Will you practice singing again, Si?"

I tried to smile.

"Please, think about what I've said. *Au revoir, mon Indochine*." And then he was gone.

17. HIS BLACK ROSE

I sat at the dining table with André's envelope in my hand. I opened it. The poem fell out, together with a cashier's check for twenty thousand dollars.

I looked at the poem. It was written in French, in free verse, abstract and vague. It described a maiden who sang, hoping to achieve a mythical voice. One day in singing, she turned into a black rose.

The black rose. Those three words struck a core of familiarity in my confused head, reviving images of the art studio on the eighth floor of number thirteen, Rue St. Jean Baptiste de la Salle. I saw the young girl sitting in a bathtub, crying. I saw André leaning against the doorframe, turning his head away. *My black rose*, he called her, in order to soothe the young girl's black mood. When she calmed down, he explained that it was a type of flower that existed only in one's imagination. There was no such thing as a black rose.

My reverie stopped and I was brought back to Diamondale by the sound of my mother's voice. She wanted to know if I was all right. I pretended to sip on my coffee. I skipped blocks of stanzas in André's poem and shifted my eyes to the last line before the piece of paper fell onto the carpeted floor. I had just caught sight of the Latin phrase.

Nec amor, nec tussis celatur. Love is like a cough. Cannot be hidden.

—

I stayed up that night and scrutinized myself in the mirror. My body had filled out in the right places. The curves had matured, and there was no more trace of the slender teenager who wandered the streets of St. Germain des Prés and asked to be carried in Rome.

When I finally dozed off, I dreamed of André. I felt his hot breath on my skin, and then we were both swimming in a warm ocean. I was wide open and engulfed the ocean and André in me.

When I woke up, I could still taste the saltiness of the ocean. The images and sensations of Paris in 1970 revived. His touch, his feel, the contours of his body, the fuzzy hair on his skin. My mind drifted to the fresh air of the South of France, the greenery of French country roads, and the vibrating sounds emanating from the grand churches of Roma. Finally, my wandering mind stopped upon the panoramic view of Paris with its Tour Eiffel piercing the sky, towering over the balcony of *numero treize*, Rue St. Jean Baptiste de la Salle. Night had fallen over the balcony of the art studio. It all first happened in Paris.

I read André's poem about the black rose, word by word.

Toward the end of the poem, the black rose was destined to wilt. So before the moment of wilting, the black rose asked the poet—the narrator—to peel off all petals and preserve them inside his poetry collection. The poet agreed and began peeling. Fragrance emanated and sensations heightened at the tips of his fingers, upon his touch. Finally, the black rose disappeared. What remained of her were dried petals, nestled between pages of his poetry.

I did not just read, I consumed and savored André's poem. Feeling feverish alongside my inner thighs. I tossed and turned on the floor of the tiny bathroom as though a pair of brown eyes were focusing on me. I felt as though layers of my body and soul were being peeled off. Every petal of his black rose corresponded with every part of me. My hands touched and felt as the pair of eyes dictated. I reached a dimension too secretive, too private, a newness of self I had never experienced. I became the silkworm my great-grandmother had become, weaving the most beautiful fabric for Annam. I lay bare, like that silkworm hopelessly reaching for perfection while being ruthlessly removed from all those silk threads. The silkworm was the product of its own creation, acknowledging the naked truth about itself.

I realized then that since those days in Paris, my mind had become that of a maiden. That was how I had saved a sacred place for André. That night in Diamondale, crawling on the bathroom floor, I let André's poem dissolve the maiden's mind-set. With André's poem in my hands, I lay drowned in remembrance. I became drunk on the memory of the obsessive brown eyes fixed upon me outside the window in Saigon's District Eight, when I was trying to reach high A note. I relived the moment of a once-in-a-lifetime passing, so consumed I had to lose myself. Unable to refuse. Or resist.

But the passion of André's words soon fell apart. The chill returned to me when memories of April 1975 crept back into my head. In the Continental Hotel, I had kept my eyes to the room's gray marble floor all the time, feeling the icy cold of loneliness. Likewise, in the U.S military infirmary on Guam Island, I had grabbed the cold headboard of the narrow iron bed because there was no one dear to hold my hand, and even the kind Red Cross nurse would soon leave.

—

In the morning, I got out of bed at around five and began to pack. Life decisions made in crisis could happen in a split second. I took out the business card bearing the emblem of the Associated Press, on which the man in the Continental Hotel had written down his address in New York City. I had carried the business card with me all through the exodus. Quietly, I planned my life. In the scheme of leaving Saigon and what happened afterward, Christopher had shared my secret. In Guam, when I rid myself of his baby, I had sinned. I hardly knew him, yet he bore my shame. He was the only witness to the use of my body in exchange for a ticket to America. I thought that somehow, now, by facing my shame head on, I could regain my peace. I thought also of the jade phoenix and the ivory plaques that belonged to Grandma Que's ancestral altar—the essence of her life. I had turned them over to Christopher that day in April. On the deathbed of a city.

My sister Mi Chau and I shared a bedroom, and I tiptoed around carefully so I would not wake her up. I wrote a long letter to my parents explaining everything that had happened in Saigon and in Guam, and the future I planned for myself in New York City. I put the letter inside an envelope, together with André's cashier check, and sealed it. I went through my pockets and wallet and got all the cash together for a one-way bus ride to New York City.

Later on, career success defined the course of my life. The achievement of my American dream. The illusion of satisfaction. Beneath that success were the seeds of resentment. But whom could I resent? Myself, Christopher, or the wheel of history turned by those war- and peacemakers whom I did not know?

18. THE PERFECT WIDOW

That next morning, in the winter of 1975, I took a bus ride from Diamondale, Illinois, to New York City and reunited with Christopher Sanders, much to his surprise. He had not expected to see me show up on his doorstep.

During the first year of our cohabitation, I kept seeing myself standing before the Vietnamese judge in Saigon. The judge had looked at me with pleading eyes, telling me again and again that if he signed the marriage certificate without questioning, somehow he would want me to procure a way for him and his family to go to America, too. Being a judge in the South Vietnamese government, he would surely be persecuted by the Communists. The taxi driver who took Christopher and me to the precinct for the hasty marriage ceremony waited for us outside, and he, too, had pleaded for me to help him leave the country. That day in Saigon, I got sick during the ceremony, and Christopher had to hold me up when we exited the judge's office. I covered my face until I entered the taxi, citing the harsh sunshine as an excuse. In fact, I thought that seeing me with Christopher that day in April outside the precinct, all Saigonese must have known what went on in the Continental Hotel—what I had to do to secure the ticket out of the country.

In New York, as Mrs. Sanders, I never had to take another a waitress job. A strange, unexplained bond developed between us, despite my deliberate avoidance of communication. In so many ways, Christopher became my accomplice, my security blanket, my husband of convenience, and the bridge to my American dream. As Mrs. Sanders, I escaped my Vietnamese identity, in which the haunting memory of my childhood and André always existed.

Despite my denial, part of me always wanted to follow André's footsteps, so I made my best efforts to be admitted to Columbia University. I succeeded, and did not stop there. After graduating from Columbia with a business degree, I went on law school. I passed the New York Bar and became the first Vietnamese refugee hired by a Wall Street law firm, specializing in mergers and acquisitions. I remained Christopher's wife until he succumbed to cancer in 1985, in the middle of our contemplation of divorce. So I moved back into our condominium to care for him. When Christopher's cancer put us permanently in separate bedrooms, part of me had silently celebrated. Yet I nursed him through long days in the hospital with the dedication of a devoted wife, frequently bringing my work to the hospital to read, watching nurses sedate him with morphine, and staying with him at the hospices during the final hours. My dedication won me the approval of his family members, who, prior to his death, had never accepted me as Christopher's Vietnamese "mail-order bride."

Christopher died at age fifty-five. I was then only thirty years of age, bearing the clammed heart of a young widow unaffected by the loss of her husband, because she was not in love. That "mail order bride" attended her husband's funeral with a tearless and stoic countenance. After the funeral, I did not eat for days, consumed with guilt for not having loved him, yet part of me felt free.

Despite the sense of freedom, Christopher's death added little to the emotional void that already existed in my heart. In the first year after his death, I made it a habit to bring flowers to his grave and talk to him. In one of these gravesite monologues, I finally told Christopher about our baby whom I had killed, and asked both father and child for forgiveness. At some point during the following year, the flower habit and visits stopped altogether. My late thirties became the debut for a new, superficial life. I dated business acquaintances and other lawyers, all good-looking, healthy, cheerful, and successful men. Many were Christopher's age. A few were younger than I. No one looked like André or reminded me of him. One by one, they came and went. I went to dinners with them, lay down with them, took off my clothes, smelled toothpaste or coffee or cognac on their lustful breath, and let them push themselves onto me. I gave them the language of ardor but never of love, passion, or romance, always conscious of the division between my heart and my flesh, painfully realizing that for years I had been holding on to the same maiden's mindset. My mind and heart were always locked away with memory of André, no matter how many casual relationships I had had. Those years in New York City, I just gave that same maiden's mindset a different kind of manifestation. I called this new manifestation the perfect Americanization of a woman without a soul.

In addition to casual dating, I also let America brainwash me with its pop culture, the yuppie lifestyle of the eighties, New York

City's fashion, business hype, and fast-paced materialism. To insulate myself from the memory of my years with Christopher and his illness, I purchased a suburban house in New Jersey in addition to keeping a Manhattan apartment for work.

There were also purchases of a new luxury car for the commute, as well as antique furniture, artwork, crystal, and china for the new house. There were all kinds of trips to make for business and pleasure, although I always consciously stayed away from Paris. There were also Thanksgiving, Christmas, Fourth of July, and other American holidays. Superficial friendships and business networking. Power lunches and breakfasts and shopping sprees at Saks, Bloomingdale's, and Bergdorf. The corporate ladder to climb, the partnership track to grab, clients to please, and money to be made in the practice.

And of course, more and more casual dating to camouflage the maiden's mind-set.

19. RENDEZVOUS IN NEW YORK CITY

At the beginning of 1990, the year of my thirty-fifth birthday, I heard from André for the first time since that snowy night in November of 1975. Seeing his handwriting after years of despair and longing, my heart raced as though I were about to faint. Disappointingly, his letter was short, and no contact information was given, except for a return address with a postal box in Paris:

Si, for years I have never stopped thinking about you. Kept in touch with your mother occasionally, enough to know about your graduation from Columbia Law. If you are unattached, please consider going back to Vietnam for a visit with me, now that the government has opened doors to the West. André.

Despite my overwhelming emotions, I knew that, realistically, I could not make the trip. I was at the peak of my law practice, which filled up my days, hours, and minutes. So I wrote him back, despondent and full of regret, asking him if he could delay the trip.

I kept writing to the postal box in Paris. There was never a reply.

———

I heard from André again that same year, this time by phone, about two months before my thirty-fifth birthday in November. The phone call was made from Vietnam. He had made the trip without me.

The phone line was frequently interrupted with static, and obviously our conversation was monitored by the operator. I could hear clicking noises and even heard the operator's voice cutting in occasionally.

"It's probably the government," André said.

He sounded like a stranger, his voice feeble and nervous. Occasionally he lost his train of thought as though it were hard for him to concentrate. Words got caught in my throat and I, too, had difficulty expressing myself. Still calling me "*bébé*," he asked whether I was involved with anyone. No, no, no. No one, I said.

He asked to spend time with me upon his return from Vietnam, assuring me that there were good reasons why he had never replied to any of my letters. My hope was full and high when he mentioned that on the way from Vietnam back to Paris, he would stop by New York. There would be so much to tell, and share.

So we made a date to meet in New York City. We blocked out a week as a start. He said he could call at the beginning of that week, once he got to New York City. We could spend that whole week together, and perhaps more, I thought.

In the following days, I relived the sensations of my life in Vietnam and my teenage days in Paris. I went to my safe-deposit box and retrieved André's poem about the black rose and cherished every single word. I recalled the moment of languor when I spread myself on the tiny bathroom floor reading it. I dreamed of my hands resting in his hands, his breath on my nipples, our legs intertwined, and my long black hair falling all over his shoulder blades—all those things I had dreamed of giving to André but never had the chance to bring to life.

In anticipation of our reunion, I looked for my copy of Baudelaire's *Les Fleurs du Mal* and read "Recueillement" until I fell asleep. I looked forward to André's arrival with the naïve and bubbling heart of a young girl falling in love for the first time, expecting to see his brown eyes, dashing smile and lean frame. I expected my angel to descend on my life again—this time, no longer with French dolls, but instead a suitcase of memories from the garden of my childhood. Days passed in anticipation and nervousness. I dialed wrong phone numbers, made typos on documents, and forgot my keys. I even put my contacts into the wrong eyes and mismatched stockings. I caught myself staring at the empty space, smiling vaguely as I filled my head with thoughts about André. My heart palpitated from all the André longing that could not be diffused or controlled with my daily routines. Sitting in a restaurant or walking through Saks Fifth Avenue or Central Park, I would perk up every time I saw a slender, virile-looking male with Mediterranean good looks and dark brown hair.

I existed in that high-strung state until the week our rendezvous finally arrived, but André's phone call never came during the first part of the week, contrary to his promise.

For the entire week, I checked with my secretary and the building concierge constantly, leaving instructions on my whereabouts, inquiring about any unexpected visitors. At night, I listened to my answering machine over and over, hoping to hear his French accent and husky voice.

Finally by Thursday of that week, the wait wore out, and disappointment sank in. Then vibrant New York City became dead and dull, like my law practice. On Thursday night, I plunged into a depression and had difficulty getting out of bed Friday morning. In sorrow, I concluded that he had decided to do without me. To make up for the void, on Friday morning I started making phone calls to round up a date for the weekend, hoping to recommence the fill-in-the-blank dating ritual with some superficial man about whom I did not care.

By the end of business Friday, when all hopes had vanished, I gathered my strength to resume my routines. I was leaving my office, down the hallway, hoping to head to the gym, when I heard my name being paged by the law firm's main receptionist.

"Ms. Sanders, please call your secretary. There is an emergency call for you," the pager said.

I almost twisted my ankle on my high heels as I whirled around and headed back to my office. Too anxious to finish the walk, I stopped at a secretary's station and picked up the line.

"Simone," my secretary said, "I am glad I caught you in time. There is a man on the line who speaks both French and English. He sounds urgent and upset. He said you were supposed to meet him, and pleaded for me to find you. I think this must be the friend that you are anticipating."

"Will you put him through right away?" I said in one breath. "And please, don't cut him off."

A moment passed, seemingly an eternity, and then I heard André's voice, too far away, too soft, too hesitant, and too fragile to be real. "Hello, Simone? Simone, Simone, Simone," he repeated my name several times as though to assure himself that I existed at the other end of the line. "Are you there, are you there at all?"

"Of course, I am here, André. I've been waiting all week," I said, reproachfully. "Oh, André. I can't describe what it meant to wait for you."

I heard myself sounding sullen and resentful, just like the old days, when I was still a little girl and could not get my way with him. The past reeled through my head, our pony rides, the recitation of poetry, all such sweet times in my mother's blossoming garden of Hue and her patio in Saigon's District Eight. My hand trembled and I wanted to cry.

"Where have you been, and when did you arrive in New York, André? Why didn't you call me sooner? I almost gave up!" I pouted like a little girl.

He told me, barely coherently, that he had been in New York all week, but had not felt well. So he had stayed in a small hotel, avoiding sunlight, and did not have the courage to call me. "Please forgive me, Simone. Just forgive. May I see you now? I am leaving for Paris in the morning."

Something had clearly gone wrong for him. I did not know whether I should be joyous or sad. He had been here all week, and all the time we could have together was Friday night?

I tried to hide my disappointment and stay calm. "Where are you now and where can we meet, André?"

"I've been wandering around Manhattan all day thinking about what to do, Simone. About whether to see you, to tell you, all about, well, things…" He sounded broken on the end of the line. "I am somewhere near Orchard and Delancy, right outside of Chinatown."

—

It was getting dark when I emerged from the subway station. My feet ached from all the running and walking in a rush. I dashed my eyes around to look for André. He was nowhere to be found. I stood by the subway entrance, on high heels, in a heavy cashmere coat. Another wait, another eternity. I decided to walk around the block looking for him. Just before I started to move, a skinny old man approached me.

The man was gray and feeble, almost staggering in the cold evening hours of New York. I saw disheveled salt-and-pepper hair, and dark circles under bloodshot eyes that stared without looking, and looked without seeing. I instinctively moved away from the old man when he leaned forward, almost falling onto me with one skinny arm extending in an effort to touch. He lost the momentum and raised his eyes to meet mine. At first glance, I did not recognize him, until I backed away again and looked, from a distance, with a frown. He was holding a book in one hand.

André stood before me, but gone were the lean muscles of a young man. Hollow chest. Hollow cheeks. Hollow eye sockets. The skin on his face tauter. Wrinkled eyes, saddened by the fact that I had backed away.

It took a moment for me to get over the shock. I approached him and took his hand. It felt dry, trembling, and cold.

It was a time of awkward reacquaintance. I felt alien toward him. But gradually the bond of childhood somehow thickened and filled the space between us. In an instant, I realized how time could be too slow and too fast. In Hue and Saigon, I had longed in frustration to grow inches taller so the top of my head could reach André's chest, and time was hatefully slow then. In adulthood, all of a sudden, while I failed to notice, the velocity of time swept away all youth, beauty, and vitality. Like Princess Mi Nuong of the Vietnamese folklore, who had to see the man's ugly face that trapped the beautiful voice she loved, I had to see how time had damaged the beautiful image of a man.

"André," I babbled, "in 1975, I made a mistake. I should have gone with you to Paris."

He shook his head and put his hand over my mouth.

We spoke very little after that, just small sentences, but I could tell he was very depressed and agitated, as though a threshold had been reached and he was desperately holding on to me as an anchor. He said he had come to my building and spoken to the concierge, who told him I was at work. Like a madman, he had wandered around Manhattan for hours before he had he courage to call my office.

It was the irrational, desperate act of a dying fish gasping for air, a man wandering around Manhattan in the early evening rush hour.

I asked him if he would want something to drink or eat, but he only wanted to walk. So we walked in the cold of a New York winter night. As we passed a row of brownstones, he stopped and held my face with his hands. People were passing by and he stood there, the lifeless eyes affixed to my face, his two hands awkwardly framing my cheekbones. He told me I was a beautiful woman, as he had always predicted I would be, and that I would remain beautiful for a long time after he was gone.

And then he started talking as though he were reciting Baudelaire again, with such intensity it was hard to follow. He talked of those days in Paris, when, between bouts of drinking, he had shut himself off from the world and a vibrant City of Light. In those moments, America, France, and Indochina all rejected him and let him down. He talked about how his law practice had crumbled, how he had tried to get Dominique back, how manuscripts had been rejected and the motivation to work was reduced to zero, how difficult the struggle had been, how the world and his friends had all turned against him.

The book he wanted to write was never finished. He talked of how the Foucault brothers and sisters had bitterly fought over the division of property and estate, and how the Foucault empire had tumbled down, its connection to Indochina reduced to the past glory of a colonial industry.

He talked of his recent return to Vietnam, now an alien world run by the new comrades and foreign investors. The new government had suspected and followed him. Vietnam was no longer a place of romantic tranquility where, despite a devastating war in the jungles, deltas, and villages, he could sit in a garden and recite Baudelaire to a young Vietnamese girl who looked at him with adoring eyes.

He talked of how buildings were going up with Hong Kong style and semi-American luxury and comfort, and how the French architecture and charm that had persisted for a hundred years were gradually disappearing. How the greedy and poverty-stricken young women of Indochina who looked just like me had tried to get his money, how the new prostitutes of Vietnam had approached him—they were as young as I the day I descended from the Air France aircraft to rush into his arms in 1970.

He talked, too, of the Asian prostitutes of Pigalle with eyes that resembled the shape of a boat lying upside down on the white sand of a deserted beach, amber skin that smelled like the tropical rain over coconut palm leaves, and pointed breasts small enough to fit in his palm, smooth and taut like a sweet green mango. He talked of the rapid deterioration of his health and good looks and spirits, so devastating that he no longer had the confidence to respond to my letters.

He talked of how he had composed his Black Rose in the longing for the smell and feel of my skin. How he had often relived the experience of number thirteen, Rue St. Jean Baptiste de la Salle, with the same surreal intensity, remembering always how it felt when I spread my legs and climbed onto him in the dark. How he had smoked and drunk and wilted away, all the time dreaming of the darkness of my eyes and hair as though the image of me was but a hallucinated vision in opium smoke. He talked, too, of all of the longing for a time when I became a woman and could be his, with all the alluring darkness of the hot and humid summer nights in Indochina, where the blondness and coolness of his wife's hair and brows seemed so out of place.

"*Aimer et mourir. Au pays qui te ressemble.* Loving and dying. In a country resembling you."

He talked of the unfulfilled poet, of creativity and failure. How the emptiness was so immense and the destructiveness so terrifying they killed off the will to create. And then he kissed me, his hands lingering on my cashmere coat. I could feel he was shaking. It was first a small kiss on my cheek, and then he brought his mouth to mine, his lips nervously opened and grabbed on to mine. I could not breathe, and then his darting tongue was parting my lips. It was as if he were trying to penetrate through, grasping what was left of life. The desperate neediness of someone who was close to death.

I yielded to his wish.

The moment seemed to last forever, yet I was too confused, fearful and overwhelmed by the course of events to feel anything real. The night was so cold and I was all covered up in the heavy coat, tired from walking on high heels, after the long day of hard work in the law office.

When he let go, he looked deep into my eyes. Terror rose in me, because as I looked into his lifeless eyes, I could no longer find images of the nocturnal butterflies of my mother's garden in Hue.

He stumbled a little, waved to a cab and then disappeared inside it, leaving me with my own sadness of knowing the brown butterflies of my childhood, once hovering over my mother's tropical flower beds, were to be buried with the still image of an angel.

In kissing me, he had dropped his book, and I picked it up after his taxi had rolled on. It was a volume of Baudelaire's *Les Fleurs du Mal.*

"*Je t'aime, toujours,*" I said under my breath. "*Attend,*" my heart cried out to him. "*Ne me quitte pas. Avons nous une dernière chance?* Wait. Don't just leave me, André. Do we still have our last chance?"

But he could no longer hear me. Only I could hear the cry of my heart: *I love you, always, André, no matter what.*

That was the last time I saw André.

———

Again, I plunged into work and a superficial social life to make up for the loss. The nostalgia for André came back to me once, one early evening at the Metropolitan Museum of Art on Fifth Avenue and Eighty-second Street. I was strolling in the museum to relax after a major corporate acquisition closing, a long, drawn-out project that had kept me sleepless many a night.

I caught the eyes of a young man, looking at me.

For a moment, I stopped, tottered, and almost lost my balance, as though I were seeing, again, twenty-six-year-old André walking under the magnolia tree of my childhood—dark hair, dark eyes, and an elegant, virile frame. But the young man's face did not have the romantic, melancholy touch of André's. Mouth too full. Nose too long. The facial skin too coarse. The young man's countenance carried the earnest, mischievous look of a hungry animal looking to start a pursuit.

His brown eyes, however, were obsessive. He was eyeing me, the curve of his mouth ready to pull into a flirtatious smile. He started a conversation, full of trite lines used a thousand times by his gender to lure a woman into a casual relationship. "My name is James. Have I met you somewhere?

"I like art, don't you?" he continued.

"No," I told him. "I prefer dinosaurs to art," I said, imagining stuffed dinosaurs on display among medieval paintings.

In an era of animal rights protection and activism, I was wearing a mink coat, vestige of my life as the companion of the late Christopher Sanders, part of New York City's old money. I leaned against a railing, the coat fell open, and I displayed a glimpse of my naked thigh. I wore a short skirt and black stockings that stopped at mid-thigh. I looked twenty-eight. The young man was staring. He wanted to buy me a cup of coffee.

At the sidewalk cafe, I discovered he would prefer reading reviews of books, rather than the books themselves. He would rather see action movies and thrillers than off-Broadway plays. He told me he wanted to write a sci-fi novel, a fantasy, or a mystery. He claimed he could produce a novel in a month by fully utilizing his engineering background. Given twelve months of unemployment, he could produce twelve novels with no sweat.

He was everything André was not, but that day, I saw young André's face cutting against posters of Parisian scenes—the cafe-sitters of Rive Gauche. I looked into the brown eyes of a young man named James, someone I hardly knew, and found a sense of déjà vu.

After we finished the coffee, I went home with him, some studio apartment in some building on the west side of town. Young

James was elated and proud when I lay down on his blue-striped bed sheet, the mink coat flung open. It had been too easy, he said sincerely, asking me again and again whether I would change my mind.

He did not know me, so we talked for a while about him, his hand travelling up my stockings. He tried but could not undo the snap of the garter belt, his fingers nervously and greedily moving away from it, up to the dark triangle above. I told him there was no hurry, and we kept on talking. He was half Italian, and had never known a real Asian girl. He bragged about how he had traveled to Europe with a camera. Priding himself as an engineer, he was also a fitness freak, always working on his muscles, always watching out for his diet of vegetables and energy drinks, believing he would find himself, his fortune, and beautiful girls that way.

I did not contradict him and began to undress. He wanted to watch. I took off my silk blouse and skirt, garter belt, and stockings, and he asked that I leave the matching black lace bikini set on underneath the mink coat. It was an erotic fantasy of his, he said, predictably. His hand fumbled underneath the black lace and I felt cold. So cold that I grabbed his wrist and told him to stop. I threw on my clothes, grabbed my purse, and ran.

I could not get the brown eyes and lashes and the Mediterranean features of this man named James out of my mind, so I called him and returned to his West Side apartment the following day, upon his promise that he would first show me his new computer system—state of the art—one of his hobbies. This time, I had on a long, full skirt and a turtleneck sweater. When we got through with the computer, James stretched and casually lay down on his couch. I looked over and found André's eyes.

Beyond all control, I longed for the pony ride of childhood. I moved my leg alongside James's rib cage, although there was no desire in my heart. It was an aggressive invitation, because I was a woman and no longer a child. James grabbed the front of my turtleneck sweater with his clumsy and greedy fingers. His eyes lit up, and he flashed a beautiful smile at me. A look of surprise, followed by a smile of misplaced confidence, reflecting the knowledge that sooner or later he would be my lover.

I looked to James's square face and bluish chin, and found again the pair of beautiful, clear brown eyes under thick, curly lashes, which gave me peace. It was the same pair of cheerful eyes that had looked up at me when, in the tropical garden of Hue, I spread my legs and sat on a beautiful Western male—a man with a complex conscience and the spirit of a melancholy poet, a man who bore almost a hundred years of my history and a collective guilt upon his shoulders from the black-and-white photographs he had seen of Indochina, such that as a grown man, he had to become attached to a little Vietnamese girl. I had bent down and kissed him in the garden, before pain and anguish crept in. In that pair of eyes, I found myself—the clear, happy, compartmentalized innocence that dangerously approached ignorance, the selfishness of tender youth that could easily and unintentionally destroy the peaceful sanctity of childhood.

—

I kept going back to James's West Side apartment and making love to him only because he looked like André, in a short-term relationship described at best as repeated one-night stands. Like most women, I closed my eyes during the act. Occasionally in the middle of lovemaking or the restful state of the aftermath, I would be struck with the terror of abandonment. So I opened my eyes to make sure André had not disappeared, and found, next to my face, those beautiful, thick, curly lashes, closed in contentment under languorous lids. I was peaceful again. But soon I realized the lashes were James's. Sorrow swept through my limbs when I realized I had offered my body to a stranger who did not care why I did what I did.

And as I closed my eyes again, I painfully realized that with my consent, this stranger, a user of my body, was entitled to love me this way, a way I had never been able to offer to André.

19. THE PHONE CALL

About a year after my thirty-fifth birthday, sometime in November of 1991, I was in my Manhattan office when I received my mother's letter telling me that my family had heard from Dominique. Dominique would like to talk to me about André.

Holding my mother's letter in my hand, I looked out at Manhattan's sky from my office window. Something inside me signaled the warning that perhaps disaster had hit. Instinctively, I dreaded the moment I would have to call Dominique in Paris, yet I could not understand the source of my anxiety. All of a sudden, I remembered Grandma Que's story about the Mystique Concubine's haunting anxiety. It was all about the Face of Brutality awaiting her outside her half-moon window of the ancient Violet City: the threatening power of uncontrollable fate.

In the days to come, could there also be the same Face of Brutality awaiting me in the daylight of New York City? My own sense of fate?

Constance had announced the rehearsal schedule for the next concert series, with Haydn's "PauckenMasse" and Mozart's "Misericordias Domini," K. 222. I had used the rehearsal schedule as an excuse to delay the phone call I would have to make to Paris. One Sunday night, I decided to stay in my Manhattan apartment, skip rehearsal, and order a pizza, knowing I could not go on avoiding the inevitable.

I moved the telephone from the nightstand to the floor. The telephone sat on the hardwood floor, and I stared at it, twisting the cord around my wrist.

I got up to put a load of laundry in the washing machine.

My heart raced and I could not concentrate. I kept sorting and resorting my dirty clothes. Folding, unfolding, and refolding bed sheets. Turning the dryer on and off. I tripped over the laundry basket. I spilled detergent on the hardwood floor. Finally, I dumped all of my clothes, dirty as well as clean ones, dry ones and wet ones, into the washer and closed the lid.

I went to my bedroom and dialed the Paris number my mother had forwarded in her letter.

"*Allo, allo, qui est là?*"

She sounded the same—the elegant Parisian accent and husky resonance.

"*Parlez, s'il vous plait. Qui est là?*"

I couldn't make a sound.

"*Ecoute toi, salaud.*"

She was getting impatient and vulgar, calling me an SOB. Typical Dominique. Cool, aloof, and elegant at times. Temperamental and crude at times.

"Tata Dominique," I finally uttered tiny sounds. "*C'est moi, Simone.*" I stuttered in rusty French, small courtesy sentences, carefully constructed.

A moment of silence ensued at the other end of the phone line, and then the Parisian accent sharpened. "Simone, I knew you would call. It took longer than I thought."

I stared at the wandering patterns in the ceiling stucco.

"Aren't you going to ask, Simone? About the papers, Simone?"

She said *les papiers*. Some personal papers? If she meant the newspapers, she would have said *les journaux*.

"All those pictures of Indochina, Simone. The things he kept."

The ceiling was about to drop. I swallowed several times to keep it in place. "Tata Dominique, I don't know what papers you're talking about."

"I want to give you those papers. That's all."

Twenty-one years ago, at times her Parisian accent could sound so sweet, when she was baking *petits-beurres* or stirring her *soupe à l'oignon*, forcing me to eat so I could quickly grow tall. All I ever wished then was to have a Parisian voice like hers.

"He did it, Simone!" she yelled. "Get it into your head. About a year ago, in November. And mind you, he was Catholic."

My head became the pillar holding the ceiling in place. It would collapse on me, soon. Oh, Simone, *poupée* Si, cutie Si, coquettish Si. Back to your laundry, Si. And then perhaps life would be normal again. My thoughts went back to my birthday last year. November of last year. My birth month; the year of my thirty-fifth birthday. Where was I? What was I doing? Did I feel a stab in my gut? Did I feel anything at all? Life could have been hatefully normal over a year ago, on such a day, or a night.

Dominique was calling me a *poseur*. The ceiling moved and became dozens of faces, hanging over my head and nodding in agreement.

"Ask, Simone. Ask how he did it. I am ready."

I felt the lump in my throat. I could not make a sound.

"Let me ask you then," she said, slowing down. "He went to America to see you, didn't he?"

"He was here," I said.

"I knew it. What did you do to him?"

"Nothing," I said.

"Liar! You fucked up his mind, again. You did a lot, Simone, even when you were still a child. He told me everything. What happened at number thirteen, St. Jean Baptiste? I've known for so many years. Remember, I was his wife and his friend. I saw your eyes the first time in Hue. You were a child with eyes of a woman."

She was speaking all in English. I wished she would revert back to French, as I did not want to understand.

———

"The balcony, Tata Dominique?" I asked.

"No, Simone. There was no more balcony at Rue St. Jean Baptiste. Get it into your head. Come to Paris and check it out yourself. They renovated the building. And chopped off the Roman pillars."

She kept speaking, and I saw you, André, standing on the eighth-floor balcony of number thirteen, Rue St. Jean Baptiste de la Salle, twenty-one years ago. The morning after our fated night, you were climbing over the Roman pillars. You were walking on the limestone railing, your arms stretching wide to help you keep your balance, like an airplane. You were not looking down, although Paris must have spread herself below you, in the transparent white, gleaming sunlight. You were about to fly.

"Please don't jump, André!" I had screamed that day in Paris. "I promise to be a good girl!" I had cried out.

291

The "Dalida" record was playing inside. *"Les yeux battus la main triste et les joues blêmes. Tu ne dors plus tu n'es que l'ombre de toi-même."* Those beaten eyes, the sad hand, and the ghastly cheeks. You don't sleep anymore. You are just the shadow of your-self.

I kept yelling, but you couldn't hear me. You kept on walking, tiptoeing, balancing on the limestone railing. Away from me. The top of the Eiffel Tower was not too far away. Perhaps you were trying to catch it.

"Oh, please don't jump, André, please, nothing can that bad. I can't be that bad." I could still hear my own voice shrieking.

———

I did not really want to know. But Dominique kept on speaking.

"Oh, *mon Dieu*, it's not the balcony, Simone!"

"The bathroom, Tata Dominique, the bathroom." I spoke of memory, where he first showed me image of a black rose.

"Oh, God, not the bathroom. It's the bedroom at St. Baptiste. Isn't that what you want to know? Why didn't you just ask, pervert? You are insane, Simone. When you came into my house," she continued, "you touched things that weren't yours. And he let you. With eyes of a woman and poisonous hands, the child touched and everything turned black."

Black, black, black—the word duplicated itself, like a broken record.

The black rose!

On the other end of the phone line, she went on to supply me with all of the details I did not wish to hear.

20. REQUIEM IN NEW YORK CITY

In my Manhattan apartment, I went to the washer and opened the lid. I looked inside the washer. Dry clothes. Wet clothes. Dirty clothes. Clean clothes. Socks and bed sheets. I kept putting more things in. Filling up the washer. My life was in it. I closed the lid. The familiar noise of the washing cycle numbed my eardrums.

I sat there, for hours. Perhaps Sunday night had passed. Slowly.

—

I saw it, André. I saw what happened.

You stood by the glass door. You were looking out at the stars and the moon. Perhaps it even snowed slightly. The lights of Paris filled the horizon, and the Eiffel Tower pierced the blackened sky. City of Love. City of Lights. You were watching, André. Simply watching the city of memory. You stood motionless. In a robe.

It was the same robe. Inside it was dark like this, André. Dark like my Manhattan room at this moment. There was no more balcony, she said. So you could not step outside to walk on the railings of the balcony. You were turning, André, toward the dark space inside. Leaving Paris to the thousand lights outside that glass door. I let you walk through that dark space. Alone.

Toward the bathroom. You kept on moving toward the bathroom.

That was where I had gone, André, at number thirteen, Rue St. Jean Baptiste. I turned on the bath and I was cold. You went to the kitchen to boil water. You returned to fill the tub with warm water and scented soap.

Under the bubbles, I kept crying. I wanted to prove to you how ridiculous it was for the Parisians of St. Germain des Prés and the nuns at the music conservatory to mistake me for a twelve-year-old child. But you turned and walked away.

I stayed under the bubbles for hours.

Finally, you came in and gave me a towel and told me there was nothing to fuss about. All it meant was the process of growing up. I threw the towel back at you. You looked away and left the bathroom in a hurry. When I cried again, you stood behind the door and told me I would have to wrap the towel around my bubbled body and stop being a child. I promised to be good, and you reappeared and gave me a rose, telling me it was to celebrate my coming of age. I stopped crying. I was safe. I dipped the rose in the bathtub where the water seemed to turn pink to my eyes. I asked you what would happen to the rose. You said it would dry up. And the rose would turn black.

In that bathroom, I held the rose he'd given me. I had something no one else had. I had a black rose.

—

You were inside the same bathroom.

Hold on to life, André, hold on and wait. For me.

I began to run. I ran toward you, André. To Rue St. Jean Baptiste de la Salle. I bumped into the concierge of my building.

I could hear him calling my name behind me. Ms. Simone? Ms. Simone!

Monday morning. Manhattan was awakening. It was no longer dark outside. The night lights were all extinguished, replaced by a gleaming sun. Thousands of New Yorkers were out on the street, beginning their hectic day all over the city. In and out of subway entrances. With their newspapers. Hot dogs. And bagels. They moved on. With life, André. Moving on. I kept running, in between them. I kept bumping into them. Some of them cursed. Others stared. Others did not notice.

It was dark, André, where you were. It was light and sunny, André, in Manhattan. But both places were cold. I was here and you were there. You were still rummaging in the dark.

Stop, my gorgeous André. Stop wrinkling. Stop aging. Stop going in there and rummaging. What were you looking for? All those black-and-white pictures of the faraway past, of a L'Indochine that obsessed the melancholy young boy of Paris? L'Indochine was gone and you were still looking.

I kept running.

I passed Bergdorf Goodman. Saks Fifth. Henry and Bendel. Sixty-eighth Street. The Ritz Carlton. I passed all the vibrant spots of Manhattan.

I screamed and held out my hands. I aggravated pedestrians. I antagonized busy New Yorkers. Still I could not get where I wanted to be. I couldn't reach you.

Wait, André, wait.

The blade.

In the bathroom, you found the blade.

You took it and went from the bathroom into the bedroom.

—

Back in the bedroom.

You lay still, panting, weeping, and I was still on top of you.

In confusion, I smiled my innocent yet deadly smile. I wanted to stand up, naked, hairless skin and raised nipples.

Precious André, why are you weeping?

I rolled and put a white pillow between my legs. And I looked sideways at you, from the corner of my eyes. My eyes beamed. I rolled my childlike naked body over your weeping self. I was just a lonely child yearning for affection, wanting to repeat the game of childhood. So, I kept moving and rolling until the slippery wetness and your cry made me frown…

Oh, André, precious André, perfectionist André, for all that happened that one night, there was nothing else. Nothing deliberate, nothing willful on your part. Then why did you suffer so much, torture yourself so much, for so long? Let your guilt be mine. Why did you have to take it all and condemn yourself with it? And then I turned away from you, to leave you alone with your pain…

Hearing your agonizing sobs, even in sweet innocence and all the excitement, even then, for a moment I was terrified to face what I had done.

But then, it was all too late!

—

You stood in that same bedroom, staring at the bed. Was it the same bed?

In the dark, you were raising the blade.

I was still running. In Manhattan. Breathless. Blurred eyes. Dry mouth and empty stomach. My breath turned into smoke, André. It was cold here. And it was cold there.

No, André, No.

———

I stopped at the traffic light. Hurrying, impatient New Yorkers had to stop with me.

You hit the hardwood floor. You bent and curled up into a fetal position. Embracing your own wounds.

I bent, André, embracing my own wounds. It hurt where you hurt, André. I bent, but it was not over for me. Somebody picked me up. The green light was on. And people around me moved.

Blood flowed and flowed, André. It flowed forever, until it could flow no more. And then blood turned black. And froze. Into the color and shape of the black rose.

There was a black rose, André, in the dark space where you lay.

Someone was dragging me on. A few people gathered around me. A few more. And then a circle was formed. Curious faces bent over me, separating me from Manhattan's sky. Curious faces, but not concerned faces. Whoever dragged me to the sidewalk must have passed by a New York hot dog stand. Or perhaps it was fresh pretzel and mustard. Smoke must have come out of the hot dog grill, or was it my breath, my sign of life? Life was all around me, and I smelled death.

Call an ambulance, someone said. Over my head.

Wait, André. Why couldn't you wait?

21. POSTCARDS

The package from Dominique arrived from Paris about a month later. That night, I emptied the contents onto the bed. Old black-and-white photographs and postcards, yellowed and curled at the edges and corners, cascaded down from the brown envelope. The first was the picture of a costume-clad Vietnamese teenager, perhaps fourteen years of age. The emperor boy. His brocade gown was embroidered with shapes of dragons, clouds, moons, suns, and stars. A metal belt pulled the cloth together around his waist. His boots were studded with gems. He wore a fitted crown, curved up on both sides of his head, marked in the center with a large gemstone. Swallowed in the grandeur of his clothes, the teenage boy stared uncomfortably at the camera, restricted in his armchair, lost and dazed in his environment. His gaze was defiant and stubborn, his lips, tight and pouting. He did not smile.

The caption under the postcard said,
Coronation, His Royal Highness Thuan Thanh, King of Annam.

The small legend at the bottom of the postcard showed a credit line attributing the picture to the collection of Foucault Gallery, 53 Rue Jules-Ferry, Hanoi.

I reached for the largest postcard with gold trim, inside an intricate cover made out of silky fabric, the gathered layers of which were sewn together with red and gold thread. The ensemble of postcard and cover seemed so fragile and old as though they could immediately crumble under human touch. I raised the oversized postcard to my eyes. Surprisingly, from the feel underneath my fingers, I realized both the folded cover and the picture inside had been laminated with plastic. Someone in France who had taken care of the collection must have wanted to protect and preserve the special image.

The postcard consisted of two pictures of the same lovely woman. In the first picture, the woman sat sensuously in the middle of a carved lacquer divan, looking over her shoulder, her naked back turning toward the camera, her hair woven into a chignon that hung low at the back of her neck. The strings of her camisole dropped down her hourglass back, accenting the smallness of her waist, which curved into the roundness of her hips like the silhouette of a cello. She turned halfway toward the camera, the corner of her eye glancing amorously at the photographer's lens. The pear shape of her perked breasts was displayed alluringly underneath the soft camisole. A dozen diminutive young men and women gathered around the divan, either kneeling or sitting on the floor. The men were dressed in traditional Vietnamese costumes at the turn of the century, the sheer organza fabric of their loose-fitting *ao dai* draping over their crisp, wide-legged pantaloons. The women, all petite and childlike, wore identical satin silk Vietnamese *ao dai*, trousers, and gold pendants. Their hair was parted in the middle, sleekly combed, and tied back in a bun. Their hands rested docilely in their laps, and they looked sideways, demure, shy, and self-conscious before the camera. The beautiful and stately woman who sat among her entourage had her naked feet dangling down the divan, her dainty toes almost touching the edge of an oval-shaped blue-and-white ceramic sink. Her hands, bejeweled with numerous carved bracelets, gripped the divan's edge.

In the second picture that occupied the remaining half of the oversized postcard, a closer view of the woman showed her upper body, her arms wrapping around her shoulders, covering up the shape of her breasts. Again, the strings of her camisole dangled down her naked back. As in the first photograph, she turned sideways, displaying the distinctive jawlines and elegant profile of her face.

The caption under the postcard said,

Un coup d'oeil, La Concubine Mystique du Roi Thuan Thanh.

A side glance, The Mystic Concubine of King Thuan Thanh.

I hurriedly went through the rest of the black-and-white photographs. The same woman in the postcard was featured again and again in various poses, both in long shot and in close-up. She stretched on the divan, either alone or among the group of costumed men and women who gathered docilely around her.

The next group of photographs showed scenes of various French chateaux, with their steep slate roofs and harmonious facades of pale stonework, their round corners underneath the spikes, reflecting over sparkling tranquil lakes and ponds and nestling among little poplars and willows, specimens of fine oaks, fertile meadows, and striking green hills. Against those landscapes of castles, bushy trees, and vast gleaming lakes, the same woman, dressed in Western attire, stood next to a stocky, whiskered Frenchman. In some of the pictures, they were holding hands. In other pictures of Paris cafes, the same woman, fashionably dressed in flapper style of the thirties, sat forlornly in an iron chair underneath cafe awnings. The same whiskered Frenchman stood behind her, either holding an umbrella or resting his hand on his thick waist.

I turned the scenes of France upside down and moved my shell-shocked eyes to the set of the immense lotus ponds and dainty curved roofs of the Violet City, savoring memories of my beloved Hue. Among these photographs, I found a portrait of the same woman.

I could see her face more clearly. In the portrait, the woman looked about forty years old, the trace of maturity and life experience undeniably reflected in her stately gaze at the camera. Her dark hair was sleekly pulled back into a tight chignon behind the strong, square jaw, which contrasted distinctly against the soft oval chin. The dainty neckline of her *ao dai*'s mandarin collar slightly opened in the middle. What was seen of her dress, around the delicate shoulder blades and over the roundness of her breasts, suggested a very fine, silky fabric. Her face had become more mature and fuller, her eyes serene and sad. Gone was the amorous flirting with the camera. I scrutinized those widely opened eyes, limpid and probing, too big and too deeply set to typify the slanting shapes of northern or eastern Asian eyes commonly found in the Koreans, Japanese, or Chinese.

I recognized my own eyes in those photographs. It was also the face. The woman had the same face as mine, as though I were in the portrait, only dressed a different way. I turned the picture over and read the handwriting in dark, blue ink on the back of the photograph, already smeared in several places:

Mon amour, ma reine, ma tendresse, ma douleur, torture de mon âme, crie de ma conscience, chagrin de mon coeur. SF.

My love, my queen, my tenderness, my pain, torture of my soul, cry of my conscience, chagrin of my heart, SF.

The handwriting was strong and fierce, the ascending strokes connecting together with grace and definitude, the descending strokes refusing to end, culminating in ink dots, already smeared and blurred with time.

I could not deny the reality that existed before I was born, the secrets I did not wish to know.

I pulled my strength together to overcome the shock, and browsed through the rest of the photographs. In a number of them, the same woman was seen with two identical little girls.

I picked up other photographs of the two little girls and tried to study their faces. In one picture, the girls leaned cheerfully on both sides of the whiskered Frenchman, who was dressed in shorts and a khaki shirt as though he had just come back from a safari. The three of them stood in a Vietnamese garden full of tropical trees and landscaped bushes.

In another photograph, the girls wore traditional Vietnamese silk pajamas, posing demurely in a studio setting, their braided hair falling on both sides of their face, their almond eyes staring at the camera. There, I could see their facial features more clearly.

I saw, again, my own face on the two little girls. They looked just like the young me, the serene little girl who sat on the stairs in Tan Tan's photography studio in Hue.

My fingers trembled as I turned the picture over to look at the handwriting on the back:

Cong Chua An Nam: Huong Sam va Huong Que.

Ginseng and Cinnamon, the princesses of Annam.

I fumbled next across a portrait photograph of a teenager, sweet and innocent, smiling with both her almond eyes and her heart-shaped lips, her long hair falling lusciously to her shoulder blade, the lapel of her pajama top accented with a strand of pearls. The back of the picture stated,

Nam Tran Cong Chua, Cong Tang Ton Nu Huong Que, 1921.

The Princess of South Sea Pearl, Cinnamon Fragrance, 1921.

It was a picture of Grandma Que, taken when she was fifteen.

But the face was mine, that sullen fourteen-year-old teenager who listened to André reciting Baudelaire in my mother's patio in Saigon.

Shivering, I turned off the light. For the rest of the night, I drifted in and out of the scenes and images from four generations, hearing in my head the choral music of Beethoven's "Elegischer Gesang."

My lips silently mimed the German lyric. "*Sanft wie du lebtest hast du vollendet...*" "Finally, your heavenly spirit will return home. You lived gently, the same way you finished." I spoke to those loved ones who had lain down under the mosses and ruins of the past.

I mourned in silence for all those gentle, departing souls that had made up my history.

PART FIVE:
THE NEW VIETNAM

SIMONE

Ombra mai fu di vegetabile
cara ed amabile, soave piu…

(There never was a plant's shade
more dear, amiable, and mild…)

—G. F. Handel

1. HOUSE AND TREES, MOTHER AND DAUGHTER

(New Jersey, 1994)

Nineteen ninety-four. It was time to leave the United States.

It was a spring day in early April when I stepped to the balcony of my house in New Jersey and looked down at my front yard below with a different eye. My pink saucer magnolia tree had blossomed. The redbud tree, too, had lost its pale green leaves and had turned violet pink with its clusters of tiny flowers burdening those brown, flower-laden branches.

I no longer saw America. The journey into the past would have to be made.

I left the balcony, went back inside, gathered white bed-sheets, and headed downstairs to the living room. Soon, the bed-sheets would cover up my piano, velvet armchairs, and collection of porcelain dolls. All the books in my study would be placed in carton boxes; all art frames and mirrors crated, rugs rolled up, and china wrapped in foam. I had sold my house, and this was my moving day.

I had my mother with me that day. She was sitting in the living room looking up at me. She had moved into the house in New Jersey to help me plan my move from the East Coast. That meant cooking for me and helping me with household chores while I buried myself in folding up my Manhattan law practice.

She was sitting near the fireplace in my contemporary Italian loveseat, looking small and lost. I could see her clearly as the sun-shine darted from the mini-blinds to her sallow skin and painted parallel lines onto her face. She had on a pair of Vietnamese black pantaloons. In such traditional Vietnamese attire, she belonged somewhere else, in an ancient Confucian house with rosewood pillars and embroidered satin scrolls. If she had been in Hue that day, she would have rolled her hair inside a velvet turban, or worn it in a bun behind her neck. But she was in America, and her hair was cut short, style-less and chin-length, like a young girl's hairdo framing the face of an old Asian woman. Her teeth slightly protruded underneath her wrinkled lips, and her nostrils flared.

My mother rose slowly from the loveseat, her small stature edging against the Andy Warhol poster hanging on the wall, and I recognized once more how out of place she was. She walked with small steps to the front door and out to the front yard, and I followed her. For the first time, I noticed how slow her move-ments were and that her back was slightly stooped.

For months, she had cooked my meals in the kitchen, moving around in the smoke and mist that emanated from steamy, boiling water and sizzling oil and broth, chopping *kai lan* and scallions and stirring brown sauces over the stove. In those moments, she perked up, lively and animated, and in the beginning of her stay with me, I had assumed she would always be that way. Later on, I discovered that she was only comfortable in the kitchen cooking Vietnamese food, where she came alive in the smoke and smell of Oriental spices and vegetables. The rest of the time she sat or tiptoed around the big house like a shadow, quite often escaping my notice, although occasionally I saw her small stature pass by my study. She was too careful, moving from room to room, as though fearing my furniture and afraid of disturbing me by making noises with her heels. So, she either sat still in her room or passed from room to room like a ghost. I noticed, too, that in the morning it took her hours to make her bed. Yet when I casually looked into her room, I saw that the comforter was not tugged underneath the pillows. Instead, she had folded the comforter and placed it at one end of the bed, the Vietnamese way. Perhaps conscious that she was not making the bed the right way, she preferred keeping her door locked. So I stopped looking in.

—

We stood in the front yard of my New Jersey house, mother and daughter, and when I looked over, I could see the thinning top of her salt-and-pepper hair. She had turned to look up at me, and I no longer saw the pair of eyes that reminded me of Grandma Que. I had assumed our eyes would remain black forever. But that day, I noticed for the first time that the irises of my mother's eyes had faded into a grayish color, like the irises of very old people, and the corners of her tired eyes looked watery.

The pink magnolias that smiled radiantly in my front yard no longer spoke to me of America, but rather, reminded me of my mother's life as a young woman in Vietnam. Back then, she loved a different type of magnolia. Big, white flowers that grew on very tall trees in the tropical climate, giving sweet-smelling, silky white petals that curled at the edge.

"Do you miss your white magnolias, Mother?" I had to probe for a way to find out my mother's wishes when I had a chance to return to our ancestors' house.

I knew what those white magnolias meant to my mother. The story she told me of her Aunt Ginseng, the night after the séance in 1965, was still as fresh as yesterday.

But there was no answer, as if she were avoiding an answer that would simply acknowledge the obvious—the permanent place that white magnolias held in my mother's own childhood. Slowly she was walking away from me, toward the row of spiky rose stems in my front yard. She stopped to examine and caress each bloom as though gently looking for defects. Among those long-stemmed roses, I saw my mother as who she really was: the quiet gardener, creating life and growth, even in transient places. I knew why my mother had chosen to become her family's gardener, and her sadness when the fall of Saigon took that role away.

When she first moved in with me to New Jersey, she had insisted on planting rows of roses in all colors along my living room windows. Since then, the roses she planted had bloomed. Initially, I tried to stop her, painfully aware of my need for a life change and the possibility that soon I would sell the house, and then all her gardening efforts would be wasted. She knew this. She knew, too, that her stay with me was temporary, and whenever the house was sold, she would be leaving, back to Texas, where the rest of my family had settled for the warmer climate. Yet quietly she called a charity working with senior citizens, and the social worker came over to take her shopping at the nursery.

The roses came in white, yellow, deep red, and pink, among which one rose stood tall, displaying the unusual lavender touch to the edges of its petals. If Grandma Que had been around that day in New Jersey, she would have said that the beautiful lavender rose represented the spirit of the Mystique Concubine in exile.

On the day of my move, among those bright colors, my mother walked my garden silently as though saying good-bye to the roses. She was mumbling something.

"Roses are so impermanent. They wilt so quickly." She had turned and raised her voice to tell me this. She said that when I settled down again in another house, I should plant a strong, tall tree that gave my life some sense of permanence and some comforting shade. "Although nothing is permanent these days, including tall trees," she added.

I wondered if she meant that there could never be anything permanent for an old immigrant living in exile like her, including the bond between mother and daughter, houses and trees.

In America I had never owned the shade of a strong, tall tree.

—

I rushed toward my mother and almost scratched myself against a tall, thorny rose stem in order to reach out and hold her hands. Her shoulders automatically jerked back, and she looked at me in confusion and amazement, her eyes dazed under their drooping, epicanthic folds. My years of living away from her, my lack of time to talk to her, and the orderly coldness of my house must have caused her to feel alien toward me. Such a house and my schedule as a practicing corporate lawyer were a far cry from the disorderly comfort of my childhood in District Eight, Saigon.

"*Maman*." I addressed her by the French word for mother, like in childhood. "I am not coming with you to Texas. The Americans are officially returning to Vietnam for business. I have volunteered to return to Vietnam to help open my law firm's office there. I'm leaving next week."

We stood for a long time in the front yard feeling the morning breeze of springtime and inhaling the scent of blooming roses. I held her hands all this time. Faintly, I felt her trembling.

"In Vietnam," she began, quietly, "will you do something for me and go find—" She stopped in the middle of the question.

I was expecting her to tell me to go find Grandma Que's tomb.

But she said nothing about her mother. We had never known where Grandma Que was buried. Perhaps the bond there was too sacred, and the separation at the fall of Saigon and Grandma Que's death were all too painful to be articulated or mentioned in words.

Instead, my mother repeated and finally finished her question as though she were speaking to herself.

"Will you go back to Hue and try to find the villa and the magnolia tree? That was your grandmother's world. Just find it and let me know if it's still there."

2. HO CHI MINH CITY, 1994

I arrived in Ho Chi Minh City, my former Saigon, on a hot and humid summer day. But neither the tropical heat and humidity nor the familiar clipping sounds of the tonal, monosyllabic Vietnamese language spelled any welcome-home message. Instead, exiting the plane, I found myself squinting at the blazing sun in disbelief. Gone were the bright lights and glass windows of the passenger lounge overlooking the airport runway. Gone was the elegant, canary yellow compound that connected the passenger lounge to the row of office buildings that once housed American military headquarters. Bare ground and unkempt hangars had taken their place.

I was shocked by the primitive austerity of the new scenery.

The alarm in my mind started to buzz as I observed customs officials in their mustard green uniforms, with their blank faces, flat cheekbones, greenish skin, and yellow teeth. The Vietcong, the enemy, the wicked and brutal—the buzzwords and irrational fears of childhood fed by widespread propaganda—quickly revived in my head. I feigned nonchalance by adjusting my sunglasses and smoothing my linen pantsuit, although my heart pounded. I had to apply the one Asian trait that had helped me make it through life—the ability to stay emotionless and bury my feelings deep inside.

Wait and wait patiently, even if it means eternity, went the saying from my childhood.

So I waited patiently in a long line of nervous Vietnamese expatriates returning home, all looking exhausted and restless, yet still arguing about baggage that contained gifts for relatives, representing the excess and comfort of America. A fellow traveler, a middle-aged, jovial Vietnamese woman, put her mouth to my ear. "Put a ten-dollar bill inside your passport, my dear, and you'll make it through the line quicker."

I thanked her for the tip, but bribing my way down the path homeward was something the lawyer in me would not do. When it was my turn to present my American passport and the entry form bearing the heading "Socialist Republic of Vietnam—Independence, Liberty, Happiness," I decided to address the young immigration official in his mustard green uniform, who was staring at my passport picture, by the familiar pronoun "*anh*," and referred to myself as "*em*." For that moment, the young man had become my respected older brother and I was his little sister, a feeble female looking up to his fraternal power. (In informal conversations, the Vietnamese address each other by familial relationships, even if they are not related.) Nineteen years ago, this customs official would have been my enemy, the Vietcong. The young man flashed a smile.

"Born in Hue?"

"Yes," I said.

"A lawyer?"

"Yes."

"Make lots of money in America?"

"Not really."

"Any gift for fellow countrymen?"

"No, I'm on a commercial, business mission, not allowed to carry gifts."

He stamped the entry form and returned my passport, and I headed toward the exit.

A horde of haggard people gathered behind the metal fence separating the airport from street peddlers, taxi and cyclo drivers. For a fleeting moment, I saw the crowd outside the airport gate as the same group of anxious and despairing people I had seen climbing over barricades outside the U.S. embassy that day in April of 1975. After two decades, these same people just looked poorer. Their hollow faces, shallow skin, sunken torsos, and chopstick arms and pant legs all spelled the hard life of the developing world. They leaned against thin ropes and the metal fence that separated common life from the privileges of a plane taking off, away from the plague of poverty, to a better life elsewhere.

The crowd had signs with names of the foreign guests to be picked up. I, too, was welcomed with one such sign. It said, *Ms. Simone Sanders.* Not a Vietnamese name. I walked toward the sign, passing two woman selling oranges and grapefruit at a wooden stand. I caught their stares, lingering upon my linen suits and leather purse.

"*Tay hay Ta?*" one of them said to the other, wondering whether I was "foreign" or "domestic."

"*Tay,*" the other woman said definitively. She considered me foreign. I was glad to hide behind my dark sunglasses.

My driver holding up the sign for me was a typical middle-aged Vietnamese man with squinting eyes and balding hairline. An old polyester shirt hung loosely over his diminutive torso. Those eyes occasionally cast scrupulous glances toward me, as though a straightforward meeting of my eyes would show equality and hence disrespect. He was eager to please, wanting to take over the carrying of all of my luggage. He flashed broad smiles, showing his bad teeth, and crammed my luggage into the trunk of an old Toyota. The car rolled on through the crowded streets of Saigon, weaving through crisscrossing seams of cyclos and mopeds. Thousands of mopeds rushed around us from what seemed to be thousands of directions, as though at any moment a collision could have taken place, springing these cyclists into the air. The residential streets of Saigon were framed with food carts and street vendors. The display of culinary delights ranged from dried cuttlefish to boiled peanuts wrapped in newspaper, and beef noodles served in chipped bowls glazed with a thin film of yellowish oil.

Despite all that animation, the city appeared dreary. A few rare spots of green trees diversified the urban chaos, yet were unable to brighten it or sweep away the dust. The smoky sky of Saigon became a huge movie screen. I was the only spectator and an actress, watching and reentering that surreal movie, back into a place I'd once called home.

3. LOOKING FOR
THE MARBLE FLOOR

By 1994, the Socialist Republic of Vietnam had made the historic Continental Hotel of Saigon into a state-owned joint venture project. The hotel had become an investment of non-French investors in partnership with the government. The French owners were long gone, together with the elegance and luxury of a colonial past, although French architectural features remained in the structure's cheery white facade. Inside the lobby, the French touch remained only in the intricate wood beams and dark wood paneling.

Earlier, I had asked the reservation clerk specifically for room 210, overlooking Rue Catinat, now called Dong Khoi, or Uprising Street. As soon as I opened the door, I looked down to the floor.

There was no gray marble underneath my feet.

Although the French owners were gone, the new management still placed French instruction booklets, greetings, and menus on the *table de nuit*, which was no longer a copy of a Louis XIV antique but, rather, a Hong Kong–made nightstand. The cheap nightstand did not go well with the grandiose opera curtains covering an entire wall—the only real vestige of old French Indochina left in that drab room. I had no recollection of the curtains, either, although I remembered distinctly the moment when Christopher asked me to approach the window. There, nineteen years ago, I stood with Christopher behind me, looking out at Saigon skyline, harbor and downtown district. Apparently, those heavy and stately curtains were opened and drawn up back then. Perhaps I was too confused and self-absorbed then to notice the details of the room.

It was 1994 and I stood in the middle of the room, seeing vividly the twenty-year-old girl who walked away from the tall French windows that had allowed her one last look at the city, before she was determined to leave it behind for good. Quietly, she unbuttoned her *ao dai*. The gold-embroidered dragon danced its last dance when the black satin fabric dropped to the floor. The first cold breeze of conditioned air hit her belly like a sharp blow when the black silk pantaloons finally rolled off.

In my business suit, I knelt on the carpeted floor, crawled toward a corner, dug my fingers under the baseboard, and peeled off the carpet.

I recognized the cold gray marble floor underneath.

———

I drew up the deep red velvet opera curtains and stood pensively at the window overlooking Dong Khoi, as I had done that day in April. Farther, on my right, toward the other end of the downtown district, the round clock on top of the gate to the Ben Thanh market still defied the passage of time.

I could see it. It was the same clock.

I craned my neck to look to my left, back at the white Opera House, a Saigon landmark. The white dome and the French colonial facade had endured. In front of it, what was once known as Saigon's miniature Champs-Élysées had lost the glamour, yet was busy still, with pedestrians, cyclo drivers, and its four-lane traffic separated by paved medians that housed bazaar-style kiosks and souvenir shops. The city, though deteriorating and impoverished, was still intact, except for one thing. At one end of the shopping square, the statue of a paternal Uncle Ho, grinning among a group of children at one end of Dong Khoi Street, had replaced the bronze statue of a South Vietnamese soldier of pre-liberation days.

I left the Continental Hotel and walked down the street. A little girl selling postcards followed me all the way, her large, black eyes pleading. I took a one-dollar bill out of my purse, and dozens of other large, black eyes immediately appeared from nowhere, quickly forming a circle around me. Beggars—women and children with their rugged brown faces and toothpick limbs—tugged at the hem of my skirt, uttering small, pleading phrases that sounded like refrains of a mourning tune.

It took me almost an hour to escape from the singing beggars of the new Saigon.

Back on the balcony of room 210, I watched the night fall, peering into the darkness that bestowed its threatening presence upon the city. There were no streetlights. Suddenly, I understood why my great-grandmother, the Mystique Concubine of the Violet City, had analogized the night to the image of a villain whom she called the Face of Brutality. Somewhere, in all that darkness shared with such a villain, floating in the blackened sky, André's dreamy Indochina smiled her amorous smile, exactly the way she was portrayed in the Foucault collection, sluggish and languorous and mystical in her undying romance, awaiting a revolution or the last conquest.

She faded away, André's L'Indochine, leaving me alone with memories that did not die. I understood the place of memories. For those who quickly forgot, memories did not exist. For others, they got tucked away somewhere waiting to be uncovered.

4. THE LACQUER DIVAN

I went back to the town house in the back alley of District Eight; paid a healthy lump sum to the present owner, a government cadre named Minh; and asked to spend one night in his living room. He was hostile at first, obviously concerned that I might be attempting to reclaim the house. "The government deeded the house to us!" he declared.

By the time I had doubled the size of the initial offer and placed the cash in his hand, he pretended to smooth the corners of the dollar bills I had given him, tapping one foot lightly while dancing his eyes around to avoid my gaze. He placed the money inside his trouser pocket, a signal that he had graciously acceded to my request. "Please feel at ease and look around," he said.

The house had been chopped into three quarters, occupied by three cadre families as the government's reward for their contributions to the People's Revolution. Cadre Minh, my host, occupied the largest quarter, a three-meter-wide claustrophobic room filled with old furniture and spider webs in all corners.

The old tile floor, now heavily stained, used to be the part of our living room where my piano sat. There, I had practiced my scales while André looked on from the window. The tiles had moved beyond merely yellowing; a brownish shade had overtaken what used to be a translucent white, each piece of tile blackened at all four corners with accumulated dirt.

My eyes drifted from the broken chair to the chipped table before I caught sight of some sparkling thing in the corner, underneath a torn, flowery cotton curtain. I stooped to look and saw the carved glistening phoenix wings made out of mother-of-pearl inlaid onto lacquer, underneath a layer of dust.

I raised the curtain and gasped.

Under a torn mosquito net, the old lacquer divan, too flashy and stoic for the meager surroundings, occupied a dark corner, as though it had been waiting for my return all this time. Despite the abundant scratches and chipping of the mother-of-pearl inlay, the enduring woodwork shone stubbornly, mocking and challenging its filthy surroundings.

———

For another exorbitant amount, I persuaded Cadre Minh to let me spend my night on the divan. In the beginning, he wanted to bargain for a better price, bragging to me that because the divan looked so antique and beautiful, for years, despite extreme poverty, he had been reluctant to sell or dispose of it. He knew it was an antique. I let him go on with his bragging until he detected my impatience. Only then did he voluntarily stop his song-and-dance with a wide yawn.

Nothing would have prepared me, however, for his next reaction. When I quietly told him that I was the great-granddaughter of the original owner, his face turned white as a sheet.

"My children, my wife, and I, even our relatives and guests, have tried to sleep on this beautiful thing. None of us could stay the whole night," he said. "We all had terrible nightmares about being drowned in a river or caught in a fire. At times we felt someone was pulling on our legs or pushing our backs so that we would fall off. The truth is, by the time word got around, no one would want to buy this divan, even if we had wanted to sell. I thought of chopping it up, but every time I raised an ax, something stopped me and I just couldn't destroy this beautiful thing."

I stared at him, speechless. Was he telling me the truth, or was he simply playing with my emotions, knowing of my background and reasons for returning to the house for a visit? How did he know to use the images of a river or a fire, if the story he told was not true? I tried to rationalize. The country, after all, was deceptively complex, and the city, despite its growing population, still functioned like a small town, especially when the Ministry of Interior and the neighborhood police, the Cong An, actively controlled the flow of information, tourists and visitors, as well as the lives of its citizens.

Whatever the possibilities, Cadre Minh and I stared at each other from opposite sides of the divan for a long time. A chill traveled down my spine as I peered down at the luscious mother-of-pearl dragons and phoenixes dancing around the divan's four legs. I wanted to ask Minh more questions, but he had conveniently left the room.

———

Minh came back to give me a thin blanket that smelled of mildew. The extra service cost me a dollar, or ten thousand Vietnamese *piasters*. The amenities did not include pillows, so I had to put my overnight bag under my head.

I spent the night on that familiar lacquer divan.

My back ached as it came into contact with the hard wood. Unable to sleep, I focused my eyes intensely on the flickering light coming from a kerosene lamp. Electrical blackouts had become routine for the inhabitants of modern Saigon. A humid odor—a combination of mildew, sewage, damp soil, and kerosene—filled my nostrils.

I felt the cool and smooth wood surface underneath my back and limbs. I could still hear Grandma Que speaking to me on that same divan while tears fell down her face. It was indeed very rare that she cried.

I went back to the past and needed no sleep to relive the nightmare. It was Grandma Que's nightmare, related to me in 1972, after I had returned home from Paris.

5. THE COFFINS OF CINNAMON

My father's townhome in District Eight of Saigon had no extra bedroom for Grandma Que, and while I was in Paris, Grandma Que had slept in my bedroom. Upon my return from France, she insisted that I was grown enough to have a private bedroom all to myself and that she would be sleeping on the divan, which had been placed next to the family altar table, adjacent to the dining area. So, my father set up a rattan screen that separated the lacquer divan from the dining area and the altar. What was behind the screen became Grandma Que's modest quarters. She adjusted to the small space quietly, never once mentioning the luxurious spaciousness of her villa in Hue.

Those days, I hid my broken heart about André by studying hard for the final two years of high school before the college entrance examination. Quite frequently, I stayed up very late to prepare outlines for classes. I studied at the dining table, where I could spread my papers and homework.

It was a late, quiet night in the summer of 1972. The air was stuffed with humidity, as air-conditioning was not part of the lifestyle of the average Saigon household. I had dozed off from studying, my head falling to the table, when I was suddenly awakened by sobs from behind the rattan screen.

It took me a few moments to adjust my vision. I had forgotten to blow out the kerosene lamp, which flickered on, casting shadows of the furniture onto the tiled floor. In the still night, the sobbing sounded eerie and tragic. I listened carefully. Grandma Que was crying in her sleep.

Until then, I had never heard or seen her cry.

Terrified, I went behind the screen and found her quivering. She was awake, her eyes wide open, her trembling fingers clutching to the edge of the pillowcase in the flickering yellow light of the kerosene lamp. Tears filled her distorted face and dropped onto her salt-and-pepper hair, spread on the pillow.

I took her slender frame into my arms, not knowing exactly what to do. I did not realize how much I had grown until I felt her trembling against me, delicate as a child, and I was able to embrace her fully. I, the spoiled and weepy Simone, was comforting my strong-willed grandmother, a woman in her sixties, my protector, my guardian who always made things right for me.

In tears and sobs, she told me of her nightmare. In the dream, Grandma Que had been sitting alone by a riverbank, facing a tranquil river, the cooling stream of water flowing downward, its movement obvious and distinct, yet eerily silent. The silence was absolute, and although the river was moving, time had frozen in place. There were objects flowing downstream in harmony with the flowing water. They, too, floated in silence.

"Coffins," she whispered, "floating coffins—so many of them, I couldn't even count. It was my job to catch them, but there was no use. I could not reach out."

Listening to her and holding her in my arms, I could feel the stuffy air over the flowing river, and see the image she painted with her words: eerie coffins, all floating downward, passing by me, in utmost silence.

I told her what seemed natural to me—the lacquer divan was causing her nightmare. It wasn't the most comfortable bed to sleep in. Despite its huge size, it had no modern mattress, and one had to rely on plenty of pillows, cushions, blankets, and wrappings for true comfort. Further, the origin of the divan was mystical enough. Grandma Que herself believed that the wood had come from the deep jungles of Vietnam, where trees became the sanctuary of wandering spirits. I assured her that when I finished college and started working, I would buy a luxurious new house in Saigon, with plenty of bedrooms, to replace the villa in Hue, and we would donate the divan to the national museum, where it should be.

It was a solemn promise, I told her.

"Oh, Si, you are such a child." She held on to my arms. "It could not be the divan. It was something else. That Face of Brutality haunted my mother for so long. It must have followed me, too. I wish my mother would come and let me see her face."

"What do you mean, Grandma, seeing the Mystique Concubine's face?"

I, too, had heard of her great beauty. Yet I had never seen any picture of her.

"Oh, Si, she was destroyed. My beautiful mother. Why does everything beautiful have to be destroyed? I was never able to hold on to what was mine. All those beautiful things."

She was hanging on to me, palpitating as though in shock.

"What do you mean, Grandma?"

"The way she died, Si."

"With nightingales singing outside her window, around her bed, the symphony of music, and those stars and the moon. Crystal teardrops falling into the water—" I dreamily described the same old details of the romantic fairy tale that had been told to me a thousand times as I grew up.

"No, no, Si, it was a lie. I lied. I couldn't change what I saw that day, when the fire broke out. Lying was the only way I knew how to…"

"What fire?"

"It was a summer day, the year after the Communist farmers' uprising, the Soviet Nghe Tinh movement, of 1930. My sister Ginseng and my brother Forest had both left home to join the Cach Mang. My mother was still very beautiful then. There were fighting and gunshots in the villages between French legionnaires and the Cach Mang, so all inhabitants had to leave the hamlet to avoid the rain of bullets, just to stay alive. A river behind the silk farm flowed through the hamlet of Quynh Anh and provided transport to the adjacent villages. So my mother sent Son La, Mey Mai, and me off on a boat, up the river to the next village where we could take refuge, while she stayed on with the silk farm and the ancestral house in Quynh Anh, waiting to meet the Cach Mang troops. She was hoping she could be reunited with my sister and brother or at least send news to them. When I turned around the last time, from the boat, I could still see her face behind the window frame. She was looking out at us, the same way she had been looking out of her window frame at night before bedtime, her eyes sad and pensive."

My heart raced together with Grandma Que's panicky words. She had stopped for a moment to breathe, and I wiped off her tears. She opened her mouth for air, and I held her head up.

"We got to the next village safely. That night, I couldn't sleep. I sensed that something bad had happened to my mother. I felt pained in my rib cage, and my entire body was burning hot. Oh, Si, I felt like I was set on fire."

"I felt like that once," I said, breaking in, recalling the séance in Hue. "I had just turned ten, and you had taken me to see Mey Mai inside the Citadel. At the end of the séance, I felt the heat around me, burning me. My soul must have flown high above the flame, since I felt that I was looking down at my own body on a burning bed of straw."

I held her up and wiped away her tears, but Grandma Que kept crying into my palm. She went on,

"I couldn't bear the anxiety, so before sunrise, as soon as the gunshots subsided, I was determined to board the boat. I was ready to paddle home. I knew I had to come back to my mother, alive or dead. Mey Mai and Son La tried to stop me. Useless! So they got on the boat with me. We traveled down the river, back to the silk farm. Oh, Si, how can I ever forget what I saw during that boat trip? Green bamboo trees once bordered the riverbanks. Yet, when our boat approached the village of Quynh Anh, toward the silk farm, the bamboo trees were all gone. It was as though the whole bamboo forest had burnt down. We began to smell that awful smell of dry heat and fire. You see, either the French or the Cach Mang had set fire to our property. The fire had spread around hamlet.

"I don't know who did this. You see, there were people who hated her. She was involved with the French, some say she was sleeping with the enemy, and she was also financing the Vietminh, the Cach Mang, at the same time. And yet no one protected her. All she had was me. Son La and Mai were loyal, but they were old and powerless.

"There was nothing left when I got back home. The ancestral house in the village of Quynh Anh she built had been burned to the ground. The silk farm was severely damaged. I walked through the ruins and smelled the awful smell of burning flesh. I followed the smell and found her corpse by the dirt road leading to the riverbank. She lay there, blackened and stiff like an ill-smelling coal log. She must have run from the fire toward the river, the flames burning on her back and engulfing her as she made the last effort at life—trying to jump into the water."

I stroked Grandma Que's salt-and-pepper hair to calm her down. Yet I felt rotten inside. I had to shake my head continuously to control my own emotions. I was about to cry for those nightingales singing outside Huyen Phi's bedroom window, and for the image of Huyen Phi, beautiful in her death. The fairy tale had dominated my childhood. Yet those images were forever gone. No teardrops disturbed the surface of the Perfume River so the sparkling waves could harmonize with the twittering birds. No beautiful woman lay peacefully on the lacquer divan in her royal costumes while nightingales sang in harmony with nature and music came from a thousand directions. I silently mourned the loss of the fairy tale. The twitching muscles on Grandma Que's face spoke of the excruciating pain she bore inside.

"My mother's face was gone. All that luscious, beautiful hair was gone. All the soft and pink flesh on her limbs was gone. I picked her up and wrapped her in my smock, that awful smell of burning flesh sticking to my skin. I held and rocked her as though she were my child. I inhaled into my lungs and heart that awful smell. Hysterically, I started digging a hole in the ground with my hands to bury her, but Son La and Mey Mai ripped her away from me and pushed me forward. There was no time. The fighting was still going on, and we had to move on to stay alive. We had to run along the river under gunshots. So I closed my smock around her and left her there, among all those ruins. Oh, Si, I had left my mother burned to death in that awful fire, her corpse unburied and rotten."

———

The fire did not wipe out all of Huyen Phi's silk empire, which was scattered all over Hue and Annam, not just concentrated in the battered village of Quynh Anh. In tears, Grandma Que told me how the fighting subsided when the Cach Mang rebels withdrew back into the jungles, and French legionnaires ceased shooting into the villages. A few days later, Grandma Que and the two trusted servants returned to the village of Quynh Anh to gather the remains of her mother for cremation.

"My mother had decomposed, you see. I saw tiny white worms, maggots, and beetles crawling out of her—or what was left of my beautiful mother. Mey Mai, Son La, and I cremated her in the back garden, and I saw those worms wiggle under all that fire. Her ashes were spread over the Perfume River, and I began concocting the tale about my mother's death. I made Son La and Mey Mai promise they would go along with my story. Later I gave out five hundred *piasters* to any villager who could repeat my beautiful tale with accuracy. I paid handsome rewards to have the tale drilled into people's heads. So the story continued to spread, acknowledged by even those who knew about the fire or who had helped me collect the remains of Huyen Phi. I wanted her to remain the beautiful mystery she was meant to be."

Grandma Que buried her face into my palm, and sighed.

"To start all over, I moved away from the village to the resort villa in Nam Giao, built by my mother at the suggestion of foreign merchants who were her trading partners. We were able to keep the lacquer divan and altar items intact, since they were kept at the Nam Giao villa. There, I set out to re-create what I had lost. I repurchased antiques and replaced those items lost in the fire. I rebuilt the silk farm and made it operational again. I was determined to produce the most beautiful silk in memory of my mother. A year after the fire, I commissioned a portrait artist to create a painting of the Mystique Concubine. But the man did not have anything to go by, so he painted onto silk a stereotypical image of an ancient Asian maiden."

That same year, Grandma Que went on to tell me, she began caring for the young magnolia tree her mother had planted, in the front yard of the villa at Nam Giao.

———

"Oh, Si, my child, I had successfully re-created everything possible, except for the beauty of her face. All I could do was to commission a silly silk painting. Even my memory was no longer intact after that fire, and all I could remember about my mother was that blackened, ill-smelling, blistered, and puss-oozing corpse. And all those little white worms that crawled through her burned and rotten flesh."

She was leaning against me, her mouth gasping for air in between words.

"And when my sister was released from Hoa Lo, I thought I could have that notion of beauty again. Perhaps I could recall my mother's beautiful face in my beautiful sister. But my sister came home an invalid, an imbecile."

She calmed down and let go of my hands.

"For years, I prayed every night that God would allow me to see again my mother's beautiful face or to hear my sister's laughter again in a dream, but never once could I dream of either one. Instead, I began having this recurring nightmare: those floating coffins. Floating at their own pace, like they have a life force of their own, in all that silent, hot air and on that sparkling water."

"But the face isn't gone, Grandma," I told her ardently, trying to convince both of us. "Look at me, Grandma, I am here, with you. You've told me all my life that the spirit of Huyen Phi has come back in me. It has, Grandma, I know that for sure now, because that day when you took me to the séance at Mey Mai's house, the spirit spoke to me. That day, I knew nothing about the fire. No one had told me. Yet at the séance I saw fire, all over me. I was floating in and out of all that heat. I saw so many women, all strangers, dressed as the dancers of Champa, I guess, from the ancient temples and towers of some lost kingdom. The dancers came and gathered around me, revering and protecting me, lifting me up above that fire.

"No, Grandma, you have not been lying at all. The images just came to you and became the story you had to tell. There were indeed nightingales, Grandma—in my voice, when I sang. I saw them. Felt them. Heard them. And petals of magnolias, too, danced around me, before I finally flew to the top of the magnolia tree you had planted. And later on, after the séance, I once dreamed of a floating coffin made out of the red brocade of her cloak. It opened like a red flower, and I saw a beautiful woman lying in it. That had to be the Mystique Concubine. Oh, Grandma, I saw everything you saw, and I felt everything you felt!"

I talked nonstop, drunk on the images I created and remembered from my own dreams, afraid that if I slowed down, I would stop believing, and then I could no longer convince myself.

"Feel my face." I took her bony fingers and placed them on my cheeks. "You see? It is still here, with you all the time. No fire can ever, ever take away the face."

———

"What's in the floating coffins, Grandma?" I asked her after a long pause.

She turned away, obviously not wanting to share with me the rest of her nightmare. She started crying again, softly. "I couldn't catch the coffins. I could not keep and protect what I love. And I am afraid of dying alone."

"No, that's not true, Grandma. You have always protected me and made things right for me. And I will never let you die alone."

"If I die," she said, "bury me in silk, a nice coffin, sealed and stuffed with fragrant cinnamon. Like your mother, I am afraid of earthworms. Put my jewelry inside my mouth and ears to keep those earthworms from crawling in." Her bony body shivered in my arms.

I heard a noise at the door. I turned around and Mi Chau was standing there, sobbing. She crawled onto the divan, nuzzled her head against Grandma Que. "Oh, Grandma, I love you!" Mi Chau cried. "I love you even more than Simone can ever love you. She left you to go to France. I will never do that. I'll take care of you always. I hate coffins. I don't like earthworms. Please don't die!"

After I blew out the kerosene lamp, both Mi Chau and I crawled onto the divan with Grandma Que. I dozed off into my own dream.

I was standing by the river with her, watching floating coffins. "*I promise, I promise*," I yelled across the river to the beautiful old woman who sat demurely with her head cocked to one side, her stream of salt-and-pepper hair sparkling against the afternoon sun. I glided on that gleaming body of water, approached the coffins, and kicked one of them open. I looked inside, but it was dark. I could not see what was inside.

I woke up from the darkness inside the coffin I had kicked open, to be greeted by the morning sun spreading its gleam across the room. The day had begun. Mi Chau and I were alone on the divan, inside the white mosquito net. I heard Grandma Que in the kitchen and then out on the porch, chatting with the neighborhood women about the wet market, in the same calm voice that commanded respect. I got up and watched with amazement as she continued the routine of her day. She prepared my breakfast, never once mentioning what had happened the previous night.

—

I had just spent the whole night on that same divan after a nineteen-year absence. I had dozed off intermittently, and when I woke, an unbearable sorrow nibbled at me as I realized that, for all my years in America, I had never been able to dream of Grandma Que.

That morning, I offered Cafre Minh another healthy sum to purchase the divan, pleading to him that I needed to hold on to what was left of my family history. He readily accepted the idea, yet continued to haggle over the price. He called it "fair negotiation," citing the years he had spent taking care of it. He kept raising the figure.

I finally gave up. "Best of luck with a divan that invokes bad dreams for whoever lies on it!"

I pretended to walk away. I badly wanted the divan but did not know how to get it within my means. I was on the verge of tears when Minh called out to me, announcing that, out of kindness, he would be ready to return the precious divan to the descendant of its owner. We reached an agreement and finalized the details. He talked constantly about emotional values while counting the dollar bills.

There was the problem of shipping the divan out of Vietnam, since Vietnamese law prohibited the export of antiques. Minh emphatically reminded me: my problem alone, not his.

I decided to go see Mai Anh.

6. MAI ANH

My childhood buddy at Lycée Marie Curie of the former Saigon, a beautiful girl named Mai Anh, daughter of a former South Vietnamese colonel, had transformed herself into a carefully made-up woman in her late thirties. She was still a sensual beauty with her almond-shaped eyes, swollen lips, and delicate arms and legs. Yet her coarse, uneven skin, yellow teeth, and those dark circles under eyes bordered thickly with what looked like blue crayon belied a former beauty queen who had stayed up too many nights, smoked too many cigarettes, drunk too much hard liquor, and made love to too many wrong men. Her complexion, once fair and pale, showed the creases of early wrinkles and too much oil from bad makeup. Her fingernails and toenails were painted orange. She bragged to me that all her makeup, skin care, clothes, and shoes were imported.

She greeted me with the warmth and ardor of a long-lost best friend, holding and squeezing my hand the whole time we spoke.

Unlike the typical poor Saigonese receiving his or her relatives or friends from America, she expected no financial help, accepting only the Lancôme makeup kit I had purchased for her at the Changi Airport in Singapore. She didn't complain about her life in Saigon or the hardships she had had to endure in its dark days, right after the Russian tanks rolled in and the comrades of the north began to nationalize property and industries. She told me, however, that many families associated with the former regime were moved to economic zones near the jungles, mountainous areas, or on undeveloped deltas.

All for the good of the reconstruction of the country, she said. I could not tell whether it was an ironic statement.

She revealed that her father had died in a concentration camp and that her mother had died, too, at sea when they tried to escape in 1977. Mai Anh survived the shipwreck but was arrested and jailed. She emerged from jail as a new woman, she said. From that point on, she set out to master the ropes of the new regime.

Mai Anh hired a car and a chauffeur and treated me to an outing at sea and a fresh seafood feast at the port town of Vung Tau, the former Cap St. Jacques of colonial days. When we got back to Saigon after the day trip, she took me to a karaoke bar and showed me how the young girls of Saigon interacted with wealthy Asian businessmen while Hong Kong music played in the dark. She told me of extravagant banquets held in exclusive restaurants in Saigon, where potent Chinese dishes like shark fins, bird's nest soups, and tiger bone marrows were served, and young and beautiful Vietnamese hostesses spoon-fed foreign businessmen all throughout the meal. Mai Anh was determined to show me a glimpse of what her life was like and what my life could have been had I not entered the Continental Hotel that day in April. The message she gave was clear: in the poverty-stricken, transitional

Vietnam of the early nineties, Mai Anh had become a rich and savvy woman who knew the trade of femininity.

She kept an air-conditioned apartment in District Three, paid for by one of her Taiwanese clients. God knows how many wives and girlfriends the man had had in Vietnam, but the arrangement kept Mai Anh well fed, she readily admitted. She told me the Taiwanese, who ran a new hotel in central Saigon, was about to go home. He had made arrangements to pass her on to his friend, a Korean petroleum engineer representing South Korean oil interests in Vietnam. The engineer was in Vietnam for a one-year contract of offshore drilling work. That mythical sea dragon of the Vietnamese culture, Lac Long Quân, the forefather who stretched himself along some 2500 kilometers of narrow and winding coast, must have blessed the country with rich mineral resources deep in the blue sapphire waters. Conveniently, the mystical blue dragon also blessed Mai Anh with her next meal ticket and luxurious lifestyle by giving those foreign petroleum project engineers and managers a reason to be in the developing Vietnam. All for the good of the country, Mai Anh retorted.

"But what happens when the engineer's one-year contract expires?" I asked.

Quite often, Mai Anh explained, local women in servitude concocted a fantasy—that somehow the cohabitation would lead to a marriage and a ticket out of the country. In some cases, the fantasy came true, providing the majority of the girls with more impetus to dream on of a way out.

"Out of the country's poverty and backwardness," Mai Anh added emotionlessly, explaining to me that her deep pockets were always filled by middle-aged Asian men. "White men, who often stink and are far too hairy," she declared, "can be quite stingy and expect to get it for free after a meal and a night of slow dancing."

She showed no shame, talked bluntly, almost defiantly, and considered herself lucky compared to other women. Some walked the streets. Others rode their mopeds alongside foreign shoppers who were carousing to make their Far East experience worthwhile. These butterfly-like silhouettes in their charming *ao dai* could propose and negotiate just as skillfully and boldly as the pimps, who could either be teenage boys or white-haired old men.

Her crude comments made me flinch. No typical Vietnamese girl, demure, indirect, and non-communicative, could be that blunt. But Mai Anh was not a typical Vietnamese girl. She was the Lycée Marie Curie girl who had survived jail and the tragic deaths of both parents during the dark days of Saigon.

I told Mai Anh of my desire to export the old divan, considered an antique by the authorities, and thus, by law, prohibited from being taken from the country.

"Have you heard of the law of the jungle, my friend?" she asked me mockingly.

I told her I understood.

"Welcome to the Socialist Republic of Vietnam," she said.

She advised me to give up the official application procedures through customs. She knew a kept woman in Hanoi, mistress of a powerful cadre at the Ministry of the Interior, who could help. She said given sufficient time, she could get to almost everyone of power in Vietnam who had a mistress. She said she had found her place in the new Vietnam but was concentrating on leaving the country, even if she had to leech onto one of her wealthy foreign hosts, just like the native girls she disdained.

I spent the night with Mai Anh in her air-conditioned apartment and listened to her tape of Vietnamese music in the seventies, banned at one time by the Communist government.

The music brought us back to our old days at Marie Curie. For a split second or so, I thought she might have shed a tear.

In the morning I left Mai Anh and headed for a meeting at the Century Hotel, where my English and Australian law partners talked of how the government was attempting to curtail the practice of law by foreign firms in order to protect the new law graduates of Vietnam. Those few privileged lawyers of the new Vietnam were eager and needy to enter the international commercial world.

It was the era immediately following President Clinton's lifting of the U.S. embargo against Vietnam. My law partners warned me that the office phone line could still be tapped and that documents generated from the office could still be secretly screened by the Local People's Committee or the Ministry of the Interior through the network of local employees that the government furnished to foreign enterprises. The discussion at the meeting centered on the various ways international law firms could legalize their presence in Vietnam and bypass local regulations prohibiting foreign lawyers from practicing Vietnamese law. The suggestions included teaming up with the so-called friends of the government as co-counsel, even if the "friends" had no legal training, and disguising time sheets showing the international lawyers were practicing Vietnamese law, or international law on Vietnamese soil, despite the prohibition of the Socialist Republic.

"So, we complain about the country's lawlessness," I blurted out, "yet we find ways to evade or break their laws, in order to make a profit."

All the lawyers sitting around the breakfast table stared at me as though I were a monster, incomprehensible, out of place. I felt sick to my stomach and left the meeting early.

Mai Anh's hired chauffeur took me onto bumpy Highway 1 stretching between Saigon and Hanoi. The endless, winding road was waiting for World Bank's infrastructure development loans to fill the bumps. I passed through the greenery of Vietnam, the breathtaking Col des Nuages, or Pass of Clouds, nestling against the whiteness of flying clouds, hovering over perpendicular cliffs that soared from the sapphire sea below. I passed white sand beaches and green forests, square rice paddies with sluggish, skinny water buffalos dipping themselves in muddy water. I passed quaint bamboo tree entrances to villages that have endured for centuries, with their old low-roofed, yellow schoolhouses. In the front yards of those schoolhouses, shoeless children wandered toward the side of the dirt road, their necks craning out, their inflated bellies protruding over bony kneecaps.

I arrived in Hanoi just in time for its nostalgic fall season, its cool breeze welcoming new foliage and buds of plum flowers, stirring tiny and peaceful waves on Hanoi's tranquil lakes. I walked through government offices in buildings that seemed a hundred years old. Their classic French architecture and facades contrasted with the neglected interiors, the chipped coats of paint and baseboards, and the old Oriental furniture sitting over stained tile floors. I came in and out of these buildings, frustrated with red tape and the inert bureaucracy, saddened by the Hanoians' poverty, yet bewildered and awed by the city's overwhelming air of history.

I followed the steps Mai Anh had carefully outlined for me, meeting with her contacts, one person after another, mostly in the famous fish restaurant La Vong located in the old commercial neighborhood of Hanoi, the *ba sau pho phuong*. There, grilled fish was served in a clay pot of sizzling oil over a tiny coal stove, next to a clay plate full of fresh dill, lettuce, and mint leaves. I followed someone into a house near the West Lake in the outskirts of Hanoi, where I was told to drop off an envelope full of U.S. currency.

I never met the mysterious mistress of the Ministry of the Interior official, but when all had been said and done, the woman sent one of her runners out, promising me that my divan would be delivered at the dock of Singapore's World Trade Center within a month. The runner said part of his job, at the instruction of the madame, was to entertain me on a night out in Hanoi. A taxi picked me up and took me to the Metropole Hotel for dinner, and then to a dance club in the outskirts of Hanoi. The darkness of the place, together with the silhouettes of slender, red-lipped women wearing black dresses, wasn't far from the feel of the second-class discotheques and mini-nightclubs of New York City. Under the dim light, the women all reminded me of Mai Anh.

Just when I was leaving the dance hall, I caught a glimpse of a familiar face at the door. I recognized the English partner at my law firm, his thin hair and clean-shaven chin lighting up over his necktie as the neon sign outside the dance hall beamed across his balding forehead. He was getting into a cyclo with a petite Vietnamese girl who looked half his size and his age. Crowding into the narrow sedan seat of the cyclo, she sat in his lap, resting her childlike frame upon his potbelly. I knew the man's Christian wife and his three children, all living in Singapore while he set up business in Hanoi and made trips back to Singapore during the weekend. I felt nauseous. Off I fled, leaving the neon sign of the new Hanoi.

7. O-LAN

In the following days, I managed to take a trip to Hue and looked for the old places. It was in the late afternoon when I strolled by the French villa at Nam Giao. An earlier visit to the People's Committee of Hue confirmed what I had expected to hear—the villa had been nationalized into a guesthouse for government workers. Plans were underway to evict the residents and convert the villa into a bed-and-breakfast hotel to meet the needs of foreign tourists attracted to Hue's royal tombs, vast open land, and dreamy scenery.

I walked around the villa several times. Peeping inside the stone wall encircling it, I saw again scenes of my sixth birthday. I walked to the front gate and met a man in his early thirties, who introduced himself to me as the house manager.

"I saw you circling the property," he said. "What do you need, miss?"

"Nothing," I said. "I just want to look. It's not a crime to look, is it?"

He looked at me strangely, perhaps noticing the dampness in my eyes. "You are from abroad, aren't you? I'll let you look, but only for a few minutes."

He opened the gate. Part of the front yard had been blocked off, and a narrow cement walkway had been built, leading to the front door. I recognized the high ceiling and cool, checkerboard marble floor, but the entire open living room had been chopped up into smaller rooms. The villa had been divided into small, filthy apartments, all facing a dark hallway. Tiny doors and windows opened to rusty iron balconies, painted in gaudy orange, where trash was not contained in bags, and dripping wet clothes were clipped to old, unused electrical wires.

I stood dazed in the dark and humid hallway. The wretched poverty of modern Vietnam had taken away all the romanticism of memory.

———

"Someone must have lived here once," I said to the house manager on my way out to the gate, "before liberation, before the nationalization of private assets. The house once belonged to someone."

He looked at me defensively. "This house belongs to the people of Vietnam," he claimed.

I observed his obstinate face. He could not have been more than thirty-five years old, speaking with the coastal accent of North Vietnam instead of the musical accent of Hue. I moved to the front yard, and he followed me.

There was no magnolia tree. I saw instead piles of dirt, lumber, rusty sinks, clay containers, and metal bars. Like a construction site.

I went to the spot where the magnolia tree had once been. It was difficult to make my way through the piles of dirt and metals. I finally located the spot, convinced it was the right location.

"This is the commune's patio," the man went on. "Residents come here to work, cook, and the children play after school. The water does not drain properly in this patio, so they are undertaking renovation. They are doing all this work themselves."

I was bending over to look for traces of the tree, among piles of metal bars. "Where is the tree?" I asked. "You've cut down the tree!"

"Excuse me?"

"Where is the tree?" Tears stained every word I spoke.

He lowered his head, and his voice softened almost to a whisper. "You used to live here, didn't you?" he asked, already knowing the answer. "I moved here from the North. I don't know the history of this house." He avoided my eyes.

"Someone died here. By hanging herself fifty years ago."

"A woman?" he asked.

"My mother saw her die."

"I am not surprised, miss. You must have heard the rumor. The residents kept talking about some ghost. I told them there is no ghost. Even if someone did die here, it was too long ago. Enough time has passed for all ghosts to be reincarnated. They must have started their new life already. Besides, in this country, so many people have died through the years. Good cause. Bad cause. We don't have enough room for the living, let alone ghosts."

—

"Wait, miss," he called after me.

I had been standing on Princess Huyen Tran Street, watching the sunset. Somewhere I could feel the unobtrusive silhouette of Grandma Que in her black silk pantaloons, standing still, looking into a dying sun. Next to her was the little girl in her ponytail, holding her bike.

In front of me now, the same sun was dying. The stream across the street was still there, but it was muddy and full of trash. The body of water no longer had the cool, calming color of imperial jade. Trash accumulated on both banks, and the green grass had turned dry and yellow.

I turned to face the comrade as he walked toward me.

"I heard about the princess and her silk farm," he said. "She died after liberation. She had no family."

"She died," I could only repeat. "Tell me how she died." I forced a smile.

"There was a housekeeper here once," the man continued, his eyes glancing downward, his hand hanging in the air in a gesture of guilt and embarrassment, perhaps, as though he were too proud to apologize for his earlier lies. "I know who you are, miss. You've come back to find what was once yours."

His fluttering hand seemed to tell me: *I am not responsible for your loss.*

"The housekeeper, they call her O-Lan," the man said slowly, pausing to wait for my reaction. "She used to live here to take care of the altar when the princess was away in Saigon. All before liberation. I heard from the people around here."

"Where can I find her? This O-Lan? In the village of Quynh Anh?"

"Do you have relatives there in the village?"

"No, I have no one," I said. "The person I cared for so much in Vietnam is dead. And I have never met this O-Lan."

"I would not go to the village if I were you. Let me find O-Lan for you."

I opened my purse and took out all of the cash I had with me. I expected him to grab the green U.S. dollars, but he pushed my hand away.

"No, no, please don't do this," he said.

"Why are you being so nice?"

"You have something to do with this place, and I saw tears in your eyes. You're very sad. You are out of place here. I like you and don't want you to wander out to the villages. That would make you even sadder."

"Why?"

"It's now 1994, the last decade of the twentieth century. Yet there is nothing in the village but sheer poverty and deterioration. Central Vietnam is the poorest part of a very poor country."

I thought of the shoeless children in half-abandoned school-houses I had seen during my voyage through Vietnam. It was almost the end of the twentieth century, and shoes for schoolchildren in the countryside were a luxury. Unaware of my thoughts, the cadre went on, describing the same scenes I had seen of Vietnam.

"The villagers are very poor. For example, children have no shoes, and they smell. Further, the village is not sanitary like your hotel. You may get sick drinking and eating there. Those villages just recently got electricity, and there isn't enough of that. The villagers expect you to give them cash and gifts—you, as one of the lucky and wealthy Vietnamese who live overseas and return home to visit. Those poor souls will follow you and expect things from you. Are you rich enough in America to feed an entire village, and many more, for the rest of their lives?"

I shook my head.

He stopped talking and looked down at his feet.

"Why do you care?" I asked.

I sought his eyes and he looked away. For a while, his eyes were riveted to the spot where the magnolia tree once stood, as though he were trying to find ways to tell me more. His eyes shifted toward the river across the street, and he began talking again, this time nonstop, as though he were hurrying through to hide his emotions.

"When I went south after the war, I, too, found a different world. I may be from the North, but my family is originally from Hue. The people from overseas come back home and spread their money around. Or the people here ask for money. Coming home becomes a money transaction. Done for love, family, pride, duty, whatever, it is still a money transaction. This takes place everywhere in Vietnam nowadays.

"But I want to say Hue is different. There are Hue citizens who will do something for the sake of doing it and who are not for hire. Also, we from the North got the bad reputation: mean, stupid, unreasonable, argumentative, greedy Commies who blinded themselves in Ho Chi Minh thoughts, took out their hatred and jealousy on the people of the South, and got rich because they robbed the South of its property. But there are exceptions, too. You don't have to pay me to help you, miss."

I was speechless. A sudden gust of wind plucked the cluster of green dollar bills from my hand and sent them flying.

"You should hold on to your money, miss!" he yelled at me in his Northern accent, agitated to see the cash fly away, his hungry eyes following the dancing bills.

Together, we chased down the green dollar bills scattering down the street. One bill flew toward the stream. He ran after it, crossing the street, and returned with it, breathing heavily.

"We almost lost it to the river. That's a lot of money, miss. A U.S. twenty-dollar bill. It's more than what I make in a month as a government cadre."

He went on to promise me again he would try to find O-Lan in the village of Quynh Anh. And then he would send her to my hotel. All free of charge.

———

My room at the Huong Giang Hotel overlooked the Perfume River. Once used as housing for the Regents of Hue University in the sixties, the formerly colonial structure had been transformed into a three-story complex that resembled a schoolhouse, rather than a first-class hotel. Yet, the hotel was still a proud display of the Socialist Republic's economic joint venture process, where foreign capital joined forces with the state in hopes of transforming the old structure into a commercial enterprise, supposedly to the international three- or four-star standards of the hotel industry.

The hotel sat solemnly by the riverbank, grave yet modest in its washed-out peachy color: a thin shade of diluted limestone solution, brushed hurriedly upon the stucco walls by a careless artisan. The peachy structure looked vague, as though it had no real identity in the vast, picturesque scenery that surrounded it: the Perfume River sparkled underneath the grey Truong Tien bridge that imprinted itself upon the lavender sky, dreamy like a Monet landscape, tugged in a corner of this sleepy, sluggish, ancient town.

Earlier in the evening, at the front desk, I had encountered a young woman in her flowing polyester pink *ao dai*. She asked me whether I was a Vietkieu, the term used for a Vietnamese expatriate returning home. She glanced surreptitiously at my U.S. passport with my name printed in all caps, SIMONE M. U. SANDERS. I told her that M. U. stood for Mi Uyen, a metaphoric name that was sufficiently Hue-like in style and spirit for her to guess at my native connection to Hue. Sure enough, she immediately told me that the name Mi Uyen could not suggest the simple background of a village girl.

I pretended not to hear her. Instead, I asked her whether she was a *canbo*, one of those privileged Communist cadres, the ruling class of the country. She readily said no, as though she were hurrying to deny something sinful. Her coral lipstick, coquettish smile, and gentle Hue accent were all too bourgeois to fit the revolutionaries who had walked into Hue from the jungles or coastal regions of Vietnam. I had always imagined those *canbos* to have high cheekbones, flat faces, brown teeth, and the unique high-pitched accent that typified the rural area of North Vietnam or the coastal regions of the Gulf of Tonkin, where all *r*'s are pronounced as *l*'s, and all *l*'s are pronounced as *n*'s.

I watched her meticulously write my name down in the hotel registry. If she was not a *canbo*, I thought, then she must be the relative of one of those guerrilla war participants, undercover agents, or symphathizers who had made their contributions to the revolutionary cause—a contribution substantial and well remembered enough to have earned her this post.

I am on your side—her eyes sparked the unspoken message as she responded to my gaze with the knowing smile of an accomplice. She complimented me on my white T-shirt and black jeans and silver-buckled belt, and told me it must be really nice to live in America. Her gentle Hue accent and sweet manner lessened the harshness of stereotypical, class-conscious terminologies such as Vietkieu and *canbo*, which so far had marked my return to the ancient city of my birth.

The calm water of the Perfume River made me feel immediately at home. The hotel had kept the riverbanks well cared for; no trash accumulated there, and the water maintained its distinct shade of deep, dark bluish green, the color of sapphire mixed with imperial jade.

Only in Hue did the night have its own fragrance.

On the balcony of my hotel room, I inhaled the smell of freshwater shrimp and snails mixed with the ripeness of yellow bananas and fermented coconut milk, the richness of boiled peanuts and peanut oil, and even the musky scent of bloodlike betel juice and homegrown tobacco, which dyed and cracked the lips of those old, toothless country women who came to visit Grandma Que from the hamlet of Quynh Anh. All the scents and scenes of my childhood.

What was lacking, I whispered to the night, were the sad folk songs on the pentatonic scale of the East, vibrating through the small waves of this calming, mysterious river—the sound of that Nam Binh song, which typified the spirit of Hue: "*Nuoc non ngan dam ra di, cai tinh chi, muon mau son phan, den no O Ly, xot thay vi, duong do xuan thi.* Thousands of miles an exodus from home, a heart full of sorrow, O pity her, paying her debts with her spring days."

The telephone rang inside and pulled me out of my reverie. The receptionist in the pink *ao dai* was on the line. "Ms. Mi Uyen," she addressed me by my Vietnamese name, "there is someone here to see you."

———

My visitor was standing next to the elevator bank, a plump, old country woman, carrying a straw bag, dressed in black pantaloons and a polyester shirt, her gray hair pulled back, hidden under a Vietnamese cone hat.

"Mey Mai!" I cried out in shock as I recognized the old, gray-haired woman who had once danced in an incense-filled room, pivoting on one foot, her head swirling underneath a satin silk cloth. Many, many years ago, she had told me the tale of the Spirit of the Perfume River.

In a country filled with undernourished citizens, she was rather plump. In a city full of sad inhabitants perhaps still mourning the massacres of the past, she was rather cheerful, her animated eyes dashing around from the hotel cashier's counter and the magazine stand, onto the elevator banks, where her eyes focused on the open-shut movement of the elevator door.

She stood quite a distance from me, still not recognizing me even as her eyes lingered upon my face, probing for some familiarity, and then moving on, back to the movement of the elevator door. The curiosity in her eyes revealed her fascination and awe at the luxury of the hotel.

Turn, Mey Mai! I cried to myself. *Speak to me again, in the language of the Paddle Girl of the Perfume River. I am home, at last!*

"Mey Mai," I called to her again.

This time, she turned toward me and her eyes fixed upon my face, for a long time. And then she smiled broadly as she moved closer toward me, her face brightened with apparently the sign of recognition.

"Oh Heaven Buddha," she said, "you look just like the young Madame Cinnamon, dressed in Western clothes. You are Madame Cinnamon's granddaughter, aren't you?" She laughed wholeheartedly.

"Oh, no, I am not Mey Mai," she went on. "I couldn't be that old and still living. I am O-Lan. My mother, Mey Mai, would have been over one hundred years old this year, if she was still living."

———

From that point on, she acted as though I were a long-lost relative. I invited her to my room so we could talk, and she became very excited.

"I have never ridden an elevator before! Will I get caught between those metal doors?" She approached the elevator on timid steps, leaning onto my arm with obvious apprehension.

I reassured her, and we slipped inside the elevator.

"All you need to do to stop the door is to touch it slightly," I told her, illustrating my point by standing in the path of the elevator door. But the closing door did not bump lightly against me and reopen as I had expected. Instead, it closed forcefully upon me, knocking me off-balance. I struggled to push myself against it. The scene of my struggling must have looked ghastly to her, because the old peasant woman started to scream.

I was not crushed, but in the moment of embarrassment, I cursed myself, concerned that she would never trust me again. I had failed my demonstration. I had forgotten that the Huong Giang hotel was once an old schoolhouse, renovated in haste. Technology had reached Vietnam, but not in the most reliable way.

The old woman had turned pale, still screaming her heart out. A couple of young men from the hotel's front desk rushed over to help. The old woman stood riveted inside the elevator as though she were glued to the metal wall, with the straw bag in between her black trousered legs. She refused to get out. I had to ask the two young men to block the metal door while I took her hand, pulled her through the narrow space, and led her toward the stairway. Outside the elevator, she held the straw bag against her chest, sighing with relief, telling me she would never again enter an elevator.

There was a tea tray in my hotel room, with a kettle of hot water. I poured a cup of tea for the old woman, who kept feeling the edge of my bed and commenting on the thickness of the foam mattress, informing me that in the village of Quynh Anh, she slept on a bamboo bed covered with a straw mat that squeaked at night.

"Your grandmother called me O-Lan; Miss Lan, that's what O-Lan means in the Hue style."

Comrade Chuyen, the house manager at the villa, had sent his men out looking for her. As usual, O-Lan, a food peddler, was busy that day selling glass noodle soup from the coal-burned pot that she put in a basket. The other basket contained bowls and chopsticks, and she carried both baskets with a pole that rested on her right shoulder. She was going from door to door, village to village, the two baskets rhythmically bounding with her footsteps, when Comrade Chuyen's errand men passed on the news to her that I had returned.

She had been waiting all these years for my return, she claimed, so when she heard the news, she immediately carried her baskets to the Huong Giang Hotel. She had left the baskets outside the entrance with the cyclo drivers who congregated in front of the hotel, leisurely waiting for the next tourist to emerge from the hotel lobby—and then the fierce competition would begin. The tourist was up for grabs by the luckiest and most persistent cyclo driver, who would follow his prospect, pouring out his pleading words, refusing to leave, until the potential client felt guilty or exasperated enough to step on the cyclo's sedan chair.

—

"Comrade Chuyen is a nice man," she said. "Too nice to be a comrade."

"I never knew Mey Mai had a daughter," I said.

"A bastard." She gulped down her tea, slipping from the edge of the bed to the floor, where she comfortably squatted. A faint smell of cut onion emanated from the flap of her blouse. She had at last overcome her shock about the elevator and appeared to feel at ease to talk, "My mother had me when she was already in her forties. A shameful thing for an old maid. It was because of me that your grandmother sent my mother away. To give birth somewhere else, away from the community gossip, and to look for my father. I was born in the foothills of the Truong Son range, which later became the Ho Chi Minh trail."

O-Lan talked about her life emotionlessly, as though she were describing someone else's life, from an opera, or a book, having nothing to do with her.

"I've lived in the village all my life. Used to take care of the silk farm. I raised the worms and took care of the threads. The farm continued to generate silk until the cadres from the North took over in 1975 and ran it to the ground. Now it is a deserted place—just the four walls, and no life.

"All these years before liberation, your grandmother helped support me. I was hidden away, since it wasn't a good thing for people to know that my mother, a virginal medium, had an illegitimate child. After the Tet Offensive, my mother disappeared, and your grandmother brought me to her villa. I lived in your house, taking care of the altar, making trips back and forth to the Quynh Anh village to attend to the silk farm. But you know, after the Tet Offensive, business was no longer good. From Saigon, your grandmother still sent me money every month, and the farm was still running moderately. After liberation, the cadres took over the silk farm, kicked me out of the house in Nam Giao, and I returned to the village."

"So it wasn't the 1945 famine or the Japanese occupation that caused Nanny Mai's departure," I said. "My grandmother never mentioned you to us, O-Lan. There were too many things hidden in my grandmother's heart. For example, my mother never knew her father. All she knew was a black-and-white photograph of an Annamese mandarin wearing an *ao dai* imprinted with embroidered Chinese characters."

I was talking more to myself than to her at this point.

"Ms. Que's husband supposedly passed away young during the Indochinese War. At least your mother had a photograph of her father. I have none. I might as well believe I've fallen out of the sky," O-Lan said, and finished her tea.

"What happened to Mey Mai?" I asked.

"I assumed my mother died on her retreat into the jungle, when she went with the withdrawing troops of the Vietcong after the Tet Offensive." She mentioned the death of her mother with the same nonchalant attitude she exhibited when recounting her life story.

"Why are you, daughter of a famous revolutionary, selling noodles on the street?" I asked ruefully. "Where is the government's reward for Mey Mai's contribution to the revolution?"

"Oh, miss, where have you been?" She had raised her voice, exhibiting an outward expression of emotion for the first time. I could not decipher whether it was sarcasm, irony, anger, or disappointment. "I don't know what my mother was—revolutionary or medium. But I know she was not from the North. And the revolution, how the hell do I know what it was supposed to do? I just got poorer and poorer. Even the cadres from the north got on a boat and fled to America after liberation. North or South, winner or loser, the whole country had nothing to eat.

"And your grandmother—my supporter, owner of that silk farm and that beautiful villa—starved herself to death. All during her illness, I fed her spoons of *bobo*—the grains they fed to horses, given to us by the Russians, so I heard. We had no rice to eat, the healthy and the sick alike. So she died, miss, without a coffin to be buried in."

8. HUE RECITAVO

My face felt hot. *I promised you a nice coffin. Satin inside. Cinnamon scented. Properly sealed so no insect could invade and disturb you in your journey to the other world. I would make sure all your antique jewelry and artifacts would be placed in the coffin with you. Those things you guarded all those years—including what had been returned to you by the Foucault family and presented to you by young André—would accompany you on that journey. But I have failed you.*

"No, no coffin," O-Lan went on. "We were all too poor. I was too poor to buy a coffin for your grandmother. We did not have a bed to sleep on, let alone a coffin to bury her in. So, I wrapped her in a straw mat and buried her in the wet rice paddy."

"What happened to all those antiques and jewelry?" I despaired.

"I don't know anything about antiques or jewelry. Don't suspect me of taking them! If I had, I would not have been a peddler selling noodles for all these years. Perhaps you should ask the government. Comrade Chuyen and his men.

"I was with your grandmother till the last minute, about a year after liberation. That was the hardest year. I am getting old and can't remember anymore." O-Lan frowned in an effort to remember details, her fingers fumbling with the hard edge of the straw bag.

"Your grandmother wanted to save this for her granddaughter to remember her by." She put her hand inside the bag. "I knew you would be coming back."

O-Lan pulled out from the straw bag a long salt-and-pepper wig. The stream of hair swept against O-Lan's hand, cascading down, defiantly alive, like an animal. I saw Grandma Que standing, removing her ivory comb and the velvety net that held the stream of hair in place. Set free, the stream of hair danced its way down her flank.

"I cut off your grandmother's hair and made it into a wig and saved it for you, as she wanted me to." She placed the wig in my hand.

—

That night, in her monotonous voice, O-Lan told me what happened to Grandma Que after my family had left for Tan Son Nhat airport.

Communist North Vietnam celebrated its victory by tightening its iron hand on the South, cutting off the country's ties to the West, sending South Vietnamese to "reeducation camps" and newly created economic zones. The winner of the war nationalized the assets of private citizens, especially those who had fled the country. Grandma Que joined the rest of South Vietnamese in that fate. The neighborhood sentries called the *ba muoi*—a nickname for these temporary rulers of Saigon, meaning "Products of the 30th Day [of April]"—and kicked her out of the townhome in District Eight. Grandma Que packed a couple of suitcases and bought a one-way bus ticket back to Hue, only to learn her French villa and what was left of her silk farm had been nationalized. So she returned to the village of Quynh Anh. Poverty plagued Vietnam and changed victory and liberation into a joke. Two decades of warfare resulted in a starved country.

Back in the village of Quynh Anh, Grandma Que and O-Lan moved into a hut and sold off Grandma Que's belongings to survive. One day Grandma Que did not feel well and went to the infirmary in the outskirts of Hue. The health care cadres told her something very bad had happened to her internal organs, but there was no firm diagnosis by any trained doctors, nor was any medicine available. O-Lan thought Grandma Que's internal organs had become rotten from too much sorrow. Maybe a bad seed had grown into a tumor and caused her pain. "*Rau thui ruot*," she said—too much sorrow and suffering could rot the gut of a warrior, let alone a fragile woman like Grandma Que.

The health cadres at the infirmary told her she might need an operation to remove the rotten part from her gut. The infirmary had no anesthesia. If she wanted to have an operation, she would have to travel to the big cities, perhaps back to Saigon, and even then there was no guarantee. She said she already knew what was wrong with her gut. "*Rau thui ruot*," she told O-Lan. She needed no medical diagnosis.

She no longer wished to live.

So she went home to the hut in the village of Quynh Anh and lay down on the straw mat. She never got up again. O-Lan fed her *bobo*, the foodstuff for horses, holding her nose, forcing her to swallow to keep up her strength. Grandma Que persisted for months and then stopped eating altogether, the bobo grains foaming around her blistered lips. All during those months, she never mourned. Never spoke. Never cried. She just wilted away. When the last moment was near, O-Lan turned her over to wash her and found her back full of puss-oozing open wounds and nasty broken blisters, developed from lying too much, too long, under unsanitary conditions.

—

O-Lan was still talking about the village, the country, the revolution, her mother, my grandmother, and all the things that made up the decades to which I was not privy. I no longer had the capacity to listen. As she spoke, I fell into a trance.

I am inside the villa again, on Nam Giao slope. I am tiptoeing barefoot on the cool marble floor, and the checkerboard design dances under my feet. I am reentering the ancestral house, my naked heels pressing onto the checkerboard marble that cools off the heat outside. I stop, concentrating on my heels while feeling in the pores of my skin the silence that embraces me in its enormous presence. The silence becomes a cold wind that sweeps through me. In perfect rhythmic synchronization, I move along with that cold wind.

I crawl inside the mosquito net that waves like a layer of mist, and find her lying still with her eyes closed so I can't see the soulful black longan seeds underneath her thin, smooth eyelids, with their tiny wrinkles that hold the secrets of her life. Her mass of long hair, salt-and-pepper, spreads to one side of her body. I lie down next to her and talk. There is so much to tell. I have in my mind images of barren trees, skeleton branches, and red leaves that fill up the damp ground of St. Germain des Prés, Paris, or the suburbs of New York

City. She has never seen red leaves. Nor has she seen the kind of scentless magnolias grown in the West.

I find myself falling down a cliff, the space below me so blackened I cannot see the bottom. It is an excruciatingly slow fall. Slowly, slowly, tumbling like those leaves departing the trees of St. Germain des Prés, reminding me of the fate of the exiled. I am falling down the course of Exile. In my descent, I hear every word of her whisper. She says, "What good does it do to go on living when all your loved ones are gone and you never know when you will be able to see them again?"

And then she says the last thing that sticks to my mind, following me until I hit the bottom of the cliff. The fall makes no sound. I land and the heaviness of silence will not let go of me. But in that silence I hear her. She reminds me of all my promises unfulfilled. Put her on the lacquer divan in the old French villa at Nam Giao. Let her hang on to her jade and diamond earrings and gold bracelets—memory of a royal concubine, artifacts already blessed with the holy water from the bottle of the compassionate Quan Yin. Place the rings inside her mouth to keep insects away, the bracelets on her chest to protect her heart, earrings tucked inside her ears, blocking the ear canals from the beastly sounds of darkness.

My very strong grandmother wants to be safe. She once talked about the baskets of violet orchids hanging all around her French villa. She said that when my grandfather—the man she loved—was still alive, the only flower he liked was a mauve orchid. Orchids prefer shade and only occasional sunshine. Gentlemen grow orchids for the women they love a lifetime, and for the cause they pursue. In death, let her be with the gentle fragrance and violet shades of the flower that signifies the dignity of her womanhood and symbolizes the color of the horizon of her beloved city.

———

I held Grandma Que's hair in my arms. I caressed the hair that had waited years for my touch and embrace. The presence embraced me as much as I embraced it. I felt her and saw her in her last moment on earth.

I held on to the salt-and-pepper wig and thought of all the losses. No more magnolia tree in front of an old villa to welcome me home with those hanging baskets of violet orchids and a chime-filled porch. No more dainty white mosquito nets hanging over a mother-of-pearl inlaid lacquer bed. She had wanted all those physical things within her upkeep to welcome me home, once I turned old and gray and tired of life in exile.

I was not yet old and gray, and I had returned home.

Grandma Que and her world were gone.

I raised the wig and pressed it to my heart. The pain revived and cut me in half, sharp like a sword piercing through. I bent along its gradual and precise path into numbness.

9. LAST GIFTS

I had offered O-Lan money. Just like Comrade Chuyen, she refused my gift. She did not come to see me for money, she said.

"Is there anything you want or need, O-Lan?"

She hesitated for a while and then spoke, almost too eloquently, as though she had planned the speech. "I have grown children, and many granddaughters. They are all healthy and good. I would be pleased if you could take one of my grandchildren to America. You can just pick one among them. Any particular one you like. A little girl, perhaps?"

I had not thought of this before. A crawling baby girl under my care, even if there was no *longan* tree in America to provide a shade over her, the way I was once shielded?

"*Chung toi ngheo qua, co oi!*" O Lan drawled. "You see, miss, we are poor, too poor. The parents would be grateful to give the child away to an adoptive parent like you, and no one will create any problem for you. It would be the greatest deed you could do for me."

When she detected no overt sign of enthusiasm from me, she deflated like a flat tire.

"O-Lan, I will consider it seriously," I assured her, watching her mouth open again with hope. "I will just have to let you know. But I can't just pick up a child on this trip."

"Perhaps the next trip, then?"

I could not give her any more assurance, so I opened my suitcase and took out my mid-length wool coat. "It gets cold in Hue," I said, "so please keep this from me." I put the coat inside her straw bag.

"If I accept this," she said, "you will still consider adopting one of my grandchildren, then, or will this be all? You wouldn't think you have paid your debt to me for burying your grandmother by giving me this coat, would you, miss?"

"No, no, no," I said. "I'll do all I can."

She jumped up to squeeze my hand. "One more thing," she continued with her excitement. "The silk farm."

"What about the silk farm?"

"Deserted and abandoned by the government. Without silk, the village of Quynh Anh is dead. For years, I have been selling noodles instead. Nowadays, fabric is smuggled from China. But Vietnamese silk is good—darn good! So delicate, so fine, and I know all about silkworms. All my children and grandchildren and in-laws can work. The village can revitalize. Maybe you can get your friends in America to be interested in rebuilding that silk farm. That would make your grandmother's soul very happy."

She sounded sophisticated and solemn, as though she were delivering another practiced speech. My eyes searched for O-Lan's, and she met me there. I found, again, the pair of animated eyes in an animated old woman, like that day at the séance, in all that incense smoke. Through these eyes, I had met the Spirit of the Perfume River. I found in that pair of eyes the sincerity that gave meaning to my homecoming. I had to believe in the rare signs of goodness in this ravaged land. I had traveled in that land like a stranger, not knowing for sure whether it was indeed dear to me. I had to hold on to my own conviction that it loved me, honestly loved me, like Grandma Que had loved me, and that I could do some good to the place.

—

Another item, old and fragile, tugged at the bottom of O-Lan's straw bag. O-Lan said it was a handwritten notebook prepared and kept by the eunuch Son La until his death in 1935. Grandma Que had kept it on the altar, hidden behind the photographs, and had managed to retrieve it from there before the North Vietnamese closed the door to her villa at Nam Giao. After she died, O-Lan became its custodian. Son La's notebook, the eunuch's recording of my great-grandmother's life in the Violet City, was meant to be with me. So O-Lan turned it over, together with the wig.

I saw O-Lan to the door and bought the rest of her chewy tapioca noodles—the *banh canh*—so she would not have to worry about her income for the day. I gave the basket to the hotel's restaurant staff.

"Everyone in town knows O-Lan," one of the waiters said. "She wanders around talking to tourists and concocting stories all the time to win sympathy. What were you doing with the *banh canh* peddler, miss? Be careful, and don't believe everything she said! That old, shrewd woman must be up to something."

10. RIVER, COFFINS, AND MEMORY

In the aromatic air, the Perfume River sparkled under the bluish moonlight. A lamp hanging from the balcony shone onto the eunuch's notebook that I held in my hands.

I began to read Son La's handwritten notes, describing the making of a royal concubine—the transformation of the poor paddle girl of the Perfume River into the legendary Mystique Concubine of the Violet City. The loyal old servant had recorded the tale in the new Vietnamese, *Chu Quoc Ngu,* using the Roman alphabet. He had devoted to the new alphabet the same intricate attention as to his Chinese calligraphy. The handwriting shone in perfect penmanship, meticulously leaning toward the right. The even strokes, blurred and stained on old notebook paper, resembled scripture from rolls of an ancient Egyptian text.

Son La's notes stopped with the Mystique Concubine's departure from the Violet City for the hamlet of Quynh Anh. Those who had knowledge of what happened thereafter were all dead. All I had to go by, as the returning child of Hue, was the notebook of the old eunuch confirming what I had heard at a séance performed by an old medium, a former royal maid and professional guerrilla spy accustomed to deceit.

My thoughts drifted back to those old photographs and postcards that arrived in New York City from Paris, all bearing the trademark of the Foucault gallery and containing secrets I might not wish to know.

Where was the truth?

I became the wandering soul looking for roots buried under ruin, denied forever the certainty of full knowledge.

—

I closed Son La's notebook and stared down at the Perfume River, hoping to find, amid those sparkling ripples, a familiar image. I was looking into depth and darkness that never ended.

I began to see a film of fog. Amid all that fog, a slender almond shape of a paddleboat began to appear. It moved slowly and silently in the tropical air of a hot autumn night. A slender silhouette of a long-haired woman was paddling. The small boat took more vivid form before it blurred again. It kept flickering. And then at the blink of my eyes it was gone for good.

I heard the eerie sound—*Mee-Ey! Mee-Ey!*—that noblewoman of ancient Champa. Fear not death. Fear not exile. Let her soul rest on those sparkling waves. She has become part of her river and her earth. The chorus became the promise of her eternity.

I looked to the riverbank. The hot air filled my nostrils, burdened my chest, and rushed my breathing. I blinked again and saw Grandma Que, as I had remembered her for all my life in America. Moonlight shone directly on her, and the stream of hair—salt-and-pepper, like lacquer marked with snowflakes—flowed alongside her fragile frame.

She was looking forlornly at the River Huong. Coffins. Coffins. And coffins. Catching sparks of the moonlight beam above them. Coffins were floating slowly and silently, on that cool stream of water, in that hot air.

The silence seemed to last forever, until she turned to face me, with those same sad and serene eyes.

I saw her face. So clearly. The wrinkles could not take away the beauty of the fine bone structure. But the face was changing, transforming into the face of a young girl. The identical twins in André's picture and postcard collection. The five-year-old Simone who sat on the stairway of the photography studio of Tan Tan.

The girl grew slowly older and older, gradually turning into the fifteen-year-old princess of the South Sea Pearl photographed by the Foucault gallery. The face of Cinnamon. The same face appeared on the fifteen-year-old misplaced Simone who strolled the streets of Paris and sang the scale in a church in Rome. The face got older and older again, until it became the forty-year-old, solemn-looking woman in the portrait that bore the stamp of the Foucault gallery.

It was my face all along.

The face continued to age, older and older, until wrinkles filled it and the eyes became almost hidden behind the drooping folds. She returned to being my Grandma Que. The face I had remembered all my life but could never see in a dream.

I was facing her, again. Just her and me, with the silent river behind us.

She smiled assuringly, and the sad *longan* eyes beamed. *Mi Uyen, my beautiful lovebird, you are the princess of Annam; Si, poupée Si, coquettish Si, Si of the Jeanne D'Arc Institute, Si of Lycée Marie Curie, Mi Uyen of Saigon's College of Law, welcome home, my child!*

11. HOPE, LOVE, AND EXILE

I returned to Saigon the following week and stood in front of the villa that had once been occupied by André and Dominique. The name of the street, Rue Tu Duc, had been changed to some contemporary revolutionary's name. The villa had been converted into a French Vietnamese restaurant catering to European patrons.

I entered the restaurant and ordered a meal for my thirty-ninth birthday celebration. I ate alone.

The knowledge that in this place a long, long time ago, André and Dominique had lived their married life sank my mind into the mud of nostalgia. As the waiter placed my favorite French flan before me, I closed my eyes and imagined André and Dominique, young and serious, loving once, laughing once.

When I left the restaurant, the sun's yellow rays at the end of day were still lingering on Saigon's sidewalks.

I traveled the streets between my former house in District Eight and what used to be the National Institute of Music and

Drama, where, as a young girl, I had biked and sung under the shade of those tall tropical trees.

I took a cyclo to Saigon's Notre Dame Cathedral, a miniature of Notre Dame de Paris, nestled in the heart of Saigon, amid rows of green trees—one of the few spots in Saigon that remained unchanged. It was the late afternoon hours when I got off the cyclo and walked toward the cathedral. For a moment, I thought I saw André in between rows of trees, young and energetic, swift and extraordinarily handsome, yet reflective and wistful still. Holding a copy of *Les Fleurs du Mal*, wearing his wire-rimmed glasses, he was walking toward me, nodding to acknowledge my presence, and when I passed him, his beautiful brown eyes obsessively followed my footsteps.

Nec amor, nec tussis celatur. Love is like a cough. Cannot be hidden.

In agitation, I closed my eyes. Sorrow sank in, as I realized perhaps in my life I had fallen in love too early. At fourteen years of age, when somebody gave me yellow tea roses and read Baudelaire to me in my former Saigon.

Nec amor, nec tussis celatur.

When I opened my eyes, I thought I saw Christopher's reproachful gaze as on the date of our wedding in Las Vegas. "You are the bride who wants no wedding or honeymoon," he had said. "Why did you come to me in New York City? You owed me no obligation. Once you landed safely in America, why not stay with your family and look for the one you truly love?"

"Because," I whispered, "I wanted to know with certainty that I had boarded the plane."

Somewhere I still heard the angry roar of the last helicopter atop the U.S. embassy.

"You did board the plane," my husband seemed to say. "But you never left the place. It is always in your heart, Simone. I can never blame your heart."

My late husband, symbolic of America's largesse, had never blamed my heart. In fact, the largesse was so great that he never asked to occupy my heart, knowing that I had left it behind. "*Allow me to say I'm sorry,*" I said to Christopher before he faded away.

Standing in the heart of the new Saigon, I began to rediscover my feelings for André, persistent and haunting since childhood, in a completely different light. He was the only one outside the culture who understood the bond between my soul and those of all the women in my bloodline. My love for him became the genderless, asexual love that persisted through time and space. The young boy of Paris had grown up into the young man of America, and had traveled so far to find in me images of Indochina that no longer existed. We stood at different corners of the world. To start that far from each other, loving was an impossibility, a taboo, a forbidden fruit. But we did meet in a war-torn place, bound together by the same melancholy and mysticism that housed our respective remembrances of childhood, and then off we went again, far from each other, locked in separate places, swept away by our own weaknesses and circumstances.

When the last bit of sunlight died out over the Notre Dame Cathedral of the new Saigon, I thought I saw once more André's soulful eyes and fluttering lashes. Those eyes told me they understood the coffins of Cinnamon. His fate was tied to mine, in ways too mystical to be expressed in words. André shared in the perfect world that I had lost with the fall of Saigon. Once I realized our bond, my love for him became the love I had for my own humanity, my birthplace, and generations of political immigrants—those nostalgic people, homeless in their sphere, stateless in their world. I loved him anew, beyond all manifestations. Beyond this transient existence.

The realization shook me, and all of a sudden I wanted so badly to sing, to reach those high notes on the right-hand side of my piano keyboard. Into the skyline of the new Saigon. Until night fell and darkness subsided so the evening butterflies of his eyelashes would gather and follow me into my nocturnal tune, where finally, as the young woman who practiced singing, I would reach a perfect *la*.

I closed my eyes again, knowing my childhood was gone and both Christopher and André had departed from this world. From the points of their departures, all my fear and sorrow were mine alone to bear. Part of me had become the lonely paddle girl who appeared in the fog, and part of me had become Grandma Que sitting by the bank of the River Huong watching and mourning the deaths of her loved ones.

In the hot and humid air of tropical Vietnam, I heard again the choral music of Beethoven's "Elegischer Gesang," sung for the departure of a gentle and noble spirit. The symphonic chorale filled up Saigon's sky, rising to a crescendo that lifted me to the top of the cathedral.

Silence ensued after Beethoven ended.

And then, in all that utmost silence, across the River Huong where coffins floated, I heard again the clear voice of a young woman, singing the phrase I once knew so well, in the wailing sadness of the Nam Binh pentatonic tune:

"Nuoc non ngan dam ra di...
"In the one-thousand-mile exodus,
"Wait, and wait patiently..."

———

375

"Wait patiently, still, Simone, Mi Uyen of the past," I said to myself.

Alone in the country of my birth, I reminisced over all the old dreams and disappointments that seemed to have ebbed softly away, like the last note of the choral symphony before silenced rushed into the hall.

In that silence, I found in me the seed for a new longing. From the muddled stream of lives crossing and recrossing, O-Lan's exclamation leaped clearly to my mind: *a silk farm and a baby girl would make Grandma Que's soul very happy!* The words shone on me and became a broad spray of light for the future. Somewhere in the village of Quynh Anh, there was an abandoned silk farm, almost a century old, waiting to be rebuilt. There was a baby girl, waiting for the tender arms of a lonely woman who had loved and who had lost. I longed to touch silk wrapped around the feathery warmth of a child.

The day had ended, and I looked up to Saigon's sky, hearing my voice lingering on my high note, my question echoing in the air:

In this life, will I let go of Cinnamon's floating coffins and the garden of a place that is no more?

THE END

APPENDICES

Historical facts that supplied the background for *Daughters of the River Huong, Mimi and Her Mirror,* and *Postcards from Nam,* the trilogy written by Uyen Nicole Duong

I. Chronicle of Vietnam as a Nation

Prior to 257 BC: Kingdom of Van Lang, ruled by Hung kings—the Hung or Lac era.

257–207 BC: Kingdom of Au Lac, the Thuc era.

207–11 BC: Kingdom of Nam Viet, the Trieu era.

3 BC–203 AD: The district of Giao Chi, under occupation and domination by the Han Dynasty [first part].

40–43 AD: The reign of Trung Vuong (the Trung Sisters) independent from China (the Han Dynasty).

203–544: The district of Giao Chau, under occupation and domination by the Han Dynasty [second part of the Han Dynasty, including the Tuys and the Ngos (Wus)].

225–248: Resistance and uprising led by Trieu Thi Trinh (Lady Trieu) against the Wus.

544–603: Kingdom of Van Xuan, under Ly Nam De.

603–939: The district of An Nam, under occupation and domination by the Tang Dynasty.

968–1054: Kingdom of Dai Co Viet, the Dinh Dynasty.

1054–1400: Kingdom of Dai Viet, consecutively ruled under the (first) Le, Ly, and Tran dynasties. During the Tran Dynasty, General Tran Hung Dao defeated and blocked the aggression of Khan's army on Bach Dang River.

1400–1407: Kingdom of Dai Ngu, under Ho Quy Ly.

1407–1427: Occupation and domination by the Ming Dynasty.

1427–1802: Kingdom of Dai Viet, under the (second) Le Dynasty, including the period of civil war between the Trinh Lord (north) and the Nguyen Lord (south). This period of time included the reign of the Tay Son Dynasty (founded by Emperor Quang Trung, who defeated the Manchu army in aid of King Le, in what is now known as Hanoi).

1802: The Empire of Viet Nam, declared by a descendant of Lord Nguyen and founder of the Nguyen Dynasty, Emperor Gia Long, who began to build the royal palaces (Cung Thanh, the Citadel, a miniature of Bejing's Forbidden City). Cung Thanh was later named the Violet City (Tu Cam Thanh) by Gia Long's successor, Emperor Minh Mang.

1884: The Treaty of Hue or Protectorate Treaty was concluded (June 6, 1884) between France and Vietnam. The treaty, which formed the basis for French colonial rule in Vietnam for the following seven decades, was negotiated by Jules Patenôtre, France's minister to China, and hence is often known as the Patenôtre Treaty.

July 1885: The Mandarins' Revolt in Hue, under the leadership of twelve-year-old King Ham Nghi and his two regents. Armed resistance at the Mang Ca Post led to the massacre of Hue. The French stormed the royal palaces. King Hàm Nghi and part of the royal family left Hue for Quang Tri. The guerrilla resistance movement of Can Vuong ("Mandarins in Aid of the Emperor") began.

1933: The execution of Nguyen Thai Hoc, a college student and founder of the Vietnamese Nationalist Party, and his twelve compatriots at Yen Bai, for having led a military coup against French colonial authorities.

April 1945: Ho Chi Minh declared independence. The last monarch of Vietnam, King Bao Dai, abdicated.

1945–1954: The Indochina War between France and the Vietminh (joined by several nationalist parties).

1954: The battle of Dien Bien Phu. French troops surrendered; an accord under the Geneva Convention was signed, dividing Vietnam into two states, North and South, awaiting a general election.

1954–1975: Era of the Vietnam War and the United States' involvement—armed conflict between South Vietnam (backed by the United States) and North Vietnam (the Vietcong) (backed by the Soviet Union and China).

February 1968: The Tet Offensive by the Vietcong, the Lunar New Year of the Monkey. The Vietcong took over the City of Hue and rocketed Saigon. U.S. Marines and the South Vietnamese Amy reclaimed the city and uncovered thousands of bodies of Hue citizens (the massacre of Hue, attributed to acts of the Vietcong), and successfully removed the Vietcong from Saigon.

1972: The Paris peace treaty officializing the withdrawal of U.S. troops from South Vietnam.

April 1975: The fall of Saigon and the end of the evacuation of South Vietnamese refugees by the United States (South Vietnam became a defunct state. Subsequently, approximately 150,000 airlifted Vietnamese refugees were settled in America. South Vietnamese associated with the former Saigon regime who stayed behind were sent to labor camps by the new government.) Thereafter, Saigon was renamed Ho Chi Minh City.

1976: Reunification of Vietnam into the Socialist Republic of Vietnam.

1978-79: The new Vietnam was again at war with Cambodia (the Khmer Rouge) and China.

1975–1990: Period of Boat People escaping Vietnam at sea and the implementation of family reunification/humanitarian immigration policies by the United States.

1985: The Socialist Republic of Vietnam first opened itself to the West under a "Renovation" policy.

April 1994: Lifting of the U.S.'s trade embargo against Vietnam. The first waves of commercial contracts between Vietnam and U.S.-based multinationals were signed.

1995: Normalization of diplomatic relations between the United States and Vietnam.

II. History of the Extinct Kingdom Champa and the Southward Expansion of Vietnam

982: Vietnam force led by General Ly Thuong Kiet attacked and pushed Champa's border to south of Hoanh Son (the province of Thanh Hoa in what is known today as central Vietnam).

1069: King Ly Thanh Tong of Vietnam invaded Champa.

1307: Vietnamese princess Huyen Tran married King Jaya Sinhavarman III of Champa (Che Man), in exchange for the two provinces, Ô and Ly' (encompassing the City of Hue today).

1402: Vietnam again invaded Champa. Vietnamese ruler Ho Quy Ly forced Cham King Campadhiraya to concede Indrapura (today's Quang Nam, south of Hue) and the territory of Amaravati (north of Champa) to Vietnam.

1471: Vietnamese army led by King Le Thanh Tong captured and destroyed Vijaya. Vietnam annexed the new land as provinces of Thang Hoa, Tu Nghi, and Hoai Nhon.

1578: Lord Nguyen Hoang annexed the Cham region of Phu Yen.

1653: Lord Nguyen Phuc Tan invaded the Cham region of Kauthara and pushed Vietnam's southern border to what is known as Port Cam Ranh today.

1692: Lord Nguyen Phuc Chu annexed the remaining Champa territory as the new prefecture of Tran Thuan Thanh. The Kingdom of Champa ceased to exist. It became what is now known as central Vietnam, including the ancient capital city of Hue.

ABOUT THE AUTHOR

Vietnam-born Uyen Nicole Duong arrived in the United States at the age of sixteen, a political refugee from a country torn apart by war. She received a Bachelor of Science in Communication and Journalism from Southern Illinois University, a law degree from the University of Houston, and the advanced LLM degree from Harvard. She was also trained at the American Academy of Dramatic Arts in Pasadena. She has been a journalist, public education administrator, attorney, law professor, and a self-taught painter whose work focuses on l'Art Brut. The author resides in Houston, Texas.